The Masque of the Red Dress

"Byerrum makes the scenery come alive not just with descriptions of gorgeous couture of multiple eras, but with the unique personalities populating the struggling-to-survive newsroom. A welcome return to an enthralling and always entertaining mystery series." (Cynthia Chow, *KRL News & Reviews*)

Sherlocktopus Holmes, Eight Arms of the Law

"The rhymes are so happy, some will make you laugh out loud. If you read it aloud to others you can all enjoy the wordplay. And each verse will help you discover clues to your case." (Wendy Kendall, *MLT News, MyEdmondsNews.com*)

"Great rhymes! Wonderful clues! A first detective novel for young readers. The illustrations are marvelous." (Beth Schmelzer, *BestBooksByBeth.wordpress.com*)

"This clever children's book combines rhymes, education and entertainment, in a charming story that's a tale of mystery accompanied by colorful illustrations." (Nancy J. Cohen, author of the Bad Hair Day Mysteries)

The Woman in the Dollhouse

"An ingeniously crafted psychological thriller that bewitches on page one and continues to mesmerize until its shocking conclusion. We can't imagine a better read. Byerrum has deftly structured a compelling narrative that never lets go. You won't either, by the way. This is one book you're practically guaranteed to finish in record time." (*Best Thrillers.com*)

"Reminiscent of the best of gothic suspense fiction, readers will be thoroughly entertained by Tennyson. Her strong will and even sharper wit ensure that readers will be cheering for Tennyson to break free and discover the truth. That the book starts with such a vulnerable beginning only makes the crafty conclusion all the more satisfying." (*Kings River Life Magazine*)

By Ellen Byerrum

The Crime of Fashion Mysteries
Killer Hair
Designer Knockoff
Hostile Makeover
Raiders of the Lost Corset
Grave Apparel
Armed and Glamorous
Shot Through Velvet
Death on Heels
Veiled Revenge
Lethal Black Dress
The Masque of the Red Dress
The Brief Luminous Flight of the Firefly

Thrillers
The Woman in the Dollhouse

The Cassidy James Stories
The Last Goodbye of Harris Turner
The End of Summer

Books for younger readers
The Children Didn't See Anything
Sherlocktopus Holmes, Eight Arms of the Law

Plays, writing as Eliot Byerrum
Boom Town Blues
Interviewing Techniques for the Self-Conscious
Red She Said
Ghost Dance
A Christmas Cactus
Gumshoe Rendezvous
Father Jeremy's Christmas Jubilee
The Angel of Death Rises Early

The 1940s Prequel to
THE CRIME OF FASHION MYSTERIES

The Brief Luminous
Flight of the
Firefly

ELLEN BYERRUM

Lethal Black Dress Press

Published by Lethal Black Dress Press

All contents copyright © Ellen Byerrum 2021
All rights reserved
Cover art and book design by Robert Williams
ISBN 978-1-949582-06-2

DEDICATION

THIS BOOK IS dedicated to the late Marge Muzillo, who was a young woman marine during World War II and who helped me understand what daily life was like during the war, and the late Claire Marie Byerrum, my distant cousin, who also was a young woman during WWII and who wanted to know how my series ends.

This book is not the end, but it is certainly the next step in the series' evolution. Whatever heavenly clouds Marge and Claire occupy now, I'm sure they'll be following the action.

ONE

SOMETHING FELT OFF tonight. Maybe it was the heat, or the change in the atmosphere, or the headache that squeezed her temples. Or maybe it was the uninvited servicemen at the dance, who seemed less polite than usual and somehow menacing. And Tilly wasn't there. Tilly was always part of the crowd when they went dancing.

But not tonight.

"Come to the dance at Chinquapin tonight," Mimi had said. "Just to be out, in company."

"You mean well, I know, but I'm too tragic," Tilly said. "I'd infect people with it, and I couldn't do that to one of those boys. And God in Heaven, Mimi, I couldn't risk losing another man."

Tilly trudged miles up and down the Potomac River every day, after her factory shift. One foot after another, over and over, contemplating the dark water. Mimi prayed this wouldn't be the night.

In these uncertain days, with everyone consumed with news of death and battles won or lost, all Mary Margaret Smith, known to everyone as Mimi, wanted to do was to savor the small perfect moments. She sought refuge outside in the dark—and yet *not* the dark.

Half-remembered lines from *Romeo and Juliet* lingered in her mind. *Some consequence yet hanging in the stars / Shall bitterly begin his fearful date / With this night's revels.*

But the lights Mimi saw weren't stars. They were fireflies. Drawn to the tree line, she was dazzled by the defiant flickering insects, hundreds, thousands—no, hundreds of thousands of flashing lights in the trees. She thought they were the prettiest things she'd ever seen.

Not even the wartime blackout drills could order the fireflies to dim their lights. Delighted that nature had superseded regulations, Mimi supposed the bugs couldn't be seen from the skies, even as they illuminated the forest below. *Maybe they have an exemption.*

The fireflies loved it hot and humid, feverishly signaling each other in their mating game. It was less comfortable for humans. There was no breeze to be had in Alexandria, Virginia, on this steamy June evening in 1943, only her second June in the Washington, D.C., area.

Mimi lifted the heavy curtain of her dark auburn hair from her neck. It was no use, it didn't cool her at all. She let her thick wavy hair fall back over her shoulders and continued gazing at the flickering lights, some long, some short, some at ground level, others all the way up at the top of the trees.

What did it feel like to have your body light up the skies? She wondered, as sweat trickled down her back.

"Mimi, come on," Rosalyn complained in her dulcet Southern tones. "I thought you were right behind me! Franny's already here, and they're just bugs! The dance is hopping, it's full of *men*, and Mimi Smith wants to stand around and stare at lightning bugs!"

"You don't understand. Fireflies don't exist where I come from. They're *magic*, Roz."

"No, they're *bugs*," Roz declared.

Every time the door to the Chinquapin Village recreation hall opened, Mimi caught faint strains of "Comin' In on a Wing and a Prayer."

The hall was plain and painted white, but it had perky red linoleum floors, full of dancers. The buildings weren't much to look at, new and hastily built, and the landscaping was only a wish. The village sheltered families of workers at the U.S. Naval Torpedo Station, the torpedo factory.

The housing was purely utilitarian, but it was perched on top of a hill and ringed by the trees and stream of Cameron Run and those magnificent flickering fireflies. The rec hall was a handy outlet for the families and their friends and kept them close to home, as gasoline and tire rationing created hardships in traveling.

"It can't be any cooler in there," Mimi said, "not with all those bodies jumping and jiving."

"Course not, sugar, but they have fans blowing the hot air around." Rosalyn tapped her heel on the ground to little effect and pointed out her own thick dark curls. "My hair is exploding. And if that's going to happen, I'd rather have it happen because of a hot foxtrot. And a red-blooded man."

A dance, with the promise of able-bodied men, had drawn Mimi Smith and her friends there tonight. Even though this was a dance for the torpedo factory workers and their friends, some soldiers and maybe a sailor or two were sure to be there. And even though a mere record player provided the tunes, not a live band, there was a saying about beggars and choosers. No one could afford to be choosy these days, whether they were single women or the families who lived at Chinquapin.

"My neck is soaked," Mimi complained. She could hardly believe it was only June.

"Just remember, honey, Southern ladies never sweat. Unlike Yankee women, we glow."

"You're not sweating?"

"Glowing to beat the band." Rosalyn Chambers, known as Roz, wiped her forehead with a delicate handkerchief. "You're lucky you're not really a Yankee."

Somehow because Mimi was from the West, she had escaped being labeled a Yankee by Roz, who had her own rules about things. To Roz from Richmond, Mimi was as exotic as if she had come from Mars, and Roz always wanted to know about *cowboys*.

"Do you know any cowboys?" she had asked Mimi when they first met. "Do you ride a horse?"

"We live in the city, Roz. Not on a ranch."

"But the men, Mimi, what are the men like?"

"Like everywhere else. Good men are scarce," she had said. "And so are cowboys! You've seen too many John Wayne movies."

"Are you telling me that Denver is just the same as Alexandria?" Roz persisted. "I don't believe that."

"Not at all. Alexandria is greener. More trees, more water, more rain. It's softer on the eyes. I prefer it. And did I mention the fireflies?"

"You and your fireflies! I'd like to find myself a cowboy."

"Be my guest. Life on a ranch is no round of cocktail parties."

"A ranch! That would be so exciting. Do you know any cowboys who own ranches?"

Trying to catch a breeze outside was impossible. The hot air was so thick her breath came out in puffs of steam. But she'd rather breathe hot steam in the Virginia summer than be back in Colorado. After all, she came to Washington to do her part for the war effort. They all had.

Washington was the epicenter of the war effort. The Roosevelts were in the White House and the city was a giant hive of workers with one goal—to win the war.

Excitement, grief, anticipation, and tension lingered over everyone's head. The tension that silently gripped every muscle and wouldn't let go, except in the odd hours. Boys Mimi and her friends met one week might be dead in a field in Europe the next.

There had to be an outlet for that pent-up energy, and for Mimi and her friends it was dancing.

They danced to beat back the fear. They danced after hearing someone else they knew had died in a foreign land or was reported missing in action. They danced to be so exhausted they could sleep. They danced to shut off the voices, the questions, the uncertainty.

And sometimes, they simply danced. Mimi could lose herself in swing and jitterbug and Lindy Hop until she was spent, and the tension momentarily lifted.

"Get a move on, little doggie," Roz urged again, wiping her face and décolletage with a lace-edged handkerchief. "Let's get inside before I melt!"

Mimi found her own hankie and carefully dabbed around her eyes. She didn't want her precious and carefully applied mascara smudged under her baby blues. Raccoon peepers weren't her best look. She'd also have to make sure the carefully drawn lines down the back of her legs to approximate stocking seams had not smeared in the steamy night. She could feel the slickness of sweat trickle down her legs.

"Bye-bye, firefly."

Mimi decided she'd take a walk down the river tomorrow night, when no one would interrupt her contemplation of their wondrous displays. Maybe fireflies would make great dance partners. Or maybe she'd go with Tilly.

Mimi and Rosalyn forged their way into the noisy crowded hall.

TWO

"HEY BEAUTIFUL! WANT to dance?" An eager GI grabbed Mimi's arm the moment she walked through the entrance. He didn't wait for an answer.

"You're too fresh, soldier boy." Mimi shook him off after the first spin.

"But baby, I've been waiting for you all night."

"You'll have to wait a little longer."

She headed for the punch bowl. She looked back and saw her friend Franny Long being wooed by the same soldier. He swept her onto the packed dance floor. Roz appeared at her side.

"That wolf is dancing with Franny."

"It won't last." Mimi glanced back at her long, tall friend. "That man is a grabber."

"He'll find out she can handle herself and ten torpedoes," Roz agreed. Franny had a reputation.

Like Rosie the Riveter, Franny and Roz worked at the torpedo factory during the day, along with their friend Tilly. Wearing coveralls and bandanas to protect their hair and keep it from being tangled up in machinery, they also kept a red lipstick near at hand. They became entirely different and exotic females after work. At twenty-one, Mimi was the youngest of the four friends by a year or two.

Roz was delicate-looking, in her pink cotton dress with short lace sleeves. Yet it would be a mistake to fall for the candy-colored packaging. She had developed impressive muscles since starting work at the factory and she wasn't afraid to use them. But once a belle, always a belle. She could simper and bat her eyes with the best of them.

Franny was no less impressive. Tall, athletic, and strong, her plain face was attractive in motion, lively and animated. Her large eyes were green, and her light brown hair neatly curled under at the shoulder. She was not one to dress fancy, except under orders. Even her yellow-and-brown cotton plaid dress looked practical. Franny was outspoken, shockingly blue words could pour out of her mouth, and she was always surprised when others objected. After all, they were just words.

Franny waved to her friends mid-twirl, signaling she would join them soon.

"By the by, that's a cute dress, Mimi," Roz said.

It was more than a cute dress, Mimi reflected. It was a Gloria Adams original design.

Mimi's polished cotton emerald-green sleeveless dress was new, and this was the first time she'd worn it. It came with a wide black-and-green ivy patterned cummerbund that emphasized her small waist.

Pretty clothes were a comfort to Mimi. They provided the hugs she wasn't getting elsewhere. The design and the pattern were courtesy of her friend Gloria, a dress designer who hadn't quite been discovered yet. She was working her way up in a clothing factory in New York's garment district, high on her dream. Gloria Adams provided the dress pattern and Mimi herself had stitched the outfit.

Unfortunately, Mimi was a slow seamstress and never seemed to catch up to the pile of fabrics and patterns she kept in an old steamer trunk.

There were many women here tonight, but Mimi had no worries about competition. There were twice as many men. She was willing to share the servicemen who had found their way to the dance, even without an invitation.

She noticed five or six soldiers hanging together toward the back, swilling their punch (no doubt spiked with liquor from a flask), and staring at the women, weighing their chances. They flattered whoever was in their arms. They spread around words like *baby*, *beautiful*, and *gorgeous*.

Smart women like Mimi told themselves to have fun, but never to trust a wolf pack of GIs.

Mimi Smith was pretty without being perfect. She had straight white teeth, sparkling blue eyes, and luxurious wavy auburn hair that behaved *most* of the time. She also had freckles, a sprinkling of them across her nose and cheeks. She hated being called "freckle face" and she did what she could to cover them up.

But those rebellious freckles would peek through and apparently wink at every man who walked by. She particularly disliked men who flattered the freckles on her nose. They were not cute, in her opinion, they were not adorable, and they were not "friendly," no matter what others said.

Still, Mimi knew she stood out. She secretly admitted there was an attractiveness about her, but she would never say it out loud. As part of her Catholic school training, she tried not to compare herself with others. "Life is not a competition, except with yourself," Sister Harriette Jane used to say.

Rosalyn of the dark curls, blue-veined white skin, and delicate features was more attractive, Mimi believed. Every detail of her friend's appearance was carefully planned, from her ruby red lips to her matching fingernail polish, to the pink rouge on her cheeks, and her matching pink frock and pink cloth wedge shoes. She looked like Snow White singing to the birds in the woods, and everyone looked her way. Oddly, Mimi had heard more than one man say Roz Chambers was just "too much work."

Franny, on the other hand, seemed like a guy's best pal. Someone he could spin on the dance floor at night and take fishing the next morning. She never suffered a lack of male companionship. Franny was from further out West than Mimi, from Big Sky Country in Montana.

Like Mimi, she often declared she would never go back.

"Back to Hick Town and all those cows? After Washington? I don't think so. I like it here."

"But there are cowboys in Montana, aren't there?" Roz always asked.

"You deserve a cowboy," Franny would say. "With a mouth full of chewing tobacco! Birthing cows in the middle of the night!"

Mimi helped herself to the watered-down punch and surveyed the crowd. Franny Long, finished with her dance, sidled up next to Mimi and Roz and scooped up some of the thin Kool-Aid. The ice ring that cooled it was nearly gone.

"Damn, it's hot. This dancing is thirsty business," Franny said, lifting her cup. "What flavor is this supposed to be, anyway?"

"Wet, I'd say," Roz remarked. "It's just colored water."

"It'll do," Mimi said.

"And Franny, ladies don't say 'damn,' at least not in public," Roz chided.

"This lady does," Franny said. "Where's Tilly?" She craned her neck.

"Not coming," Mimi said. "I talked to her earlier."

As if the music gods had heard their conversation, the next tune on the record player was "Don't Get Around Much Anymore." It reminded Mimi of all their friends, like the absent Tilly, who didn't get around much—because they were grieving for dead men.

"She's got to get back out there," Roz said. "Time waits for no woman."

"I imagine it's pretty difficult," Mimi said. "They were engaged. For a little while, anyway."

"It hasn't been that long, Roz," Franny interjected. "Give her time. But of course, she's got to get back out there. Still, it's a damn shame."

Neither Franny nor Roz had yet experienced that kind of heartbreak.

"I agree," Roz said. "Nothing's going to bring her Dave back, but that's no reason for her to crawl into the grave with him."

"She would if she could—if she could see Dave again," Mimi said. "Crawl into that grave, I mean."

Her conversation with Tilly replayed in her head.

"I think about it all the time," Tilly said to Mimi earlier that day. "Whether I should throw myself in the river and be done with it."

"Don't say that, Tilly. It's a terrible thought. Life is precious." It didn't always feel precious. Mimi knew that.

"Maybe, maybe not. Maybe for you."

Tilly was a slight woman with an elfin face. Her lank brown hair refused to curl, but her hazel eyes used to gleam when she was with Dave. Since the news of his death, she'd lost so much weight that her friends were alarmed. Her skin was so taut, her bones threatened to break through. Mimi tried tempting her with some of her landlady's honey cakes, but after a bite or two, Tilly would be overcome with sadness. She made it through her days at the torpedo factory and at home with her family on Lee Street, but the Tilly everyone knew wasn't home anymore. A new and somber model had replaced her.

Mimi knew something of what Tilly was going through, but Tilly's grief was fresher, and perhaps deeper than her own. She had grown up with Dave and put all her eggs in his basket. Now it was empty.

"I'll check on her tonight." Franny was reading Mimi's faraway thoughts.

"We both will," Roz added.

Mimi would never consider suicide. It wasn't merely because her religion forbade it. She had a lust for life, painful and searing as it was. Even so, there was a scar inside Mimi. A scar labeled Eddie Falcone.

He was never coming back to her. He had flown too high, like Icarus. Though he was gone, Eddie came to her in the odd hours. In her dreams. His ghost, her imagination. She told him to go away, to go back to where the dead dwelled.

But now he was telling her to take a chance. One little dance can't hurt.

THREE

"HELLO, SWEET PEA, you want to trip the light fantastic?" Another soldier stretched his hand out to Mimi, interrupting the three women's huddle. The "sweet pea" line, that was different. The rest of this soldier looked the same as the last one.

"Okay, flyboy, I'll take a chance." Mimi took the soldier's hand.

"I'm no flyboy," he said with a grin, "but I'm your man."

At least he didn't mention her freckles. After that dance, Mimi grabbed another cup of pale Kool-Aid punch before she was twirled off again to the red-speckled dance floor, this time by a sailor. He asked her politely, and he chattered politely all through their dance. She closed her eyes as if she were a good listener. As if she were actually concentrating on "In the Mood," which clearly she was not. She followed the dance steps by rote.

Mimi smiled and next let a marine trample on her feet in an attempted fox trot. After all, she thought, he might be bleeding in a foxhole the following week. As she dodged the soldier's knobby knees knocking against her own, she was glad she didn't have a special sweetheart. Not anymore. It would hurt too much to lose someone again. Even this terrible dancer.

She opened her eyes in time to avoid falling over the GI's legs. On the edge of the dancefloor, she saw a young woman surrounded by a group of servicemen. That wasn't uncommon, but a strain in the atmosphere told her something was wrong. Mimi turned for a clearer view.

"Here, Kitty, Kitty," one of the men was saying to the woman.

"Kitty Cat, come back, come back," another chimed in.

"Kitty, Kitty, come lick my face," a third one said.

A fourth one meowed at her and the woman looked stricken. "Kitty, Kitty, Kitty."

It wasn't her cheap red rayon dress that matched the color of the floor, too tight and too shiny, or her badly applied makeup which marked her as out of place. Or even her gaudy rhinestone jewelry, as if her outfit wasn't eye-catching enough. The woman's pale blond hair was most unusual, almost platinum, with long silvery strands escaping the three attempted victory rolls on top of her head. Yet her hair color looked natural, not something out of a bottle.

No, there was something about this taunted woman. Despite her garish attire, she had a sweet face and a lightness to her. Why was she the target of their catcalls? No woman deserved that.

"What on earth?" Mimi said to no one in particular. She abruptly broke away from the sailor she was dancing with, and another woman stepped right in to take her place.

Mimi watched the clean-cut servicemen surrounding the blonde. They were even of feature and tan of skin, with trim physiques. They could have been wicked fraternity boys and just as slyly mean. In their uniforms, they were practically indistinguishable, but one wore "butter bars" on his uniform, marking him as a second lieutenant, slightly higher in rank than the others.

Butter Bar was clearly their ringleader. He had a dark buzz cut and his eyes leered at their victim. He was medium height and wiry and he seemed tightly wound.

"Kitty, Kitty, here, Kitty, Kitty," went Butter Bar's singsong catcall. The others joined in.

"What do you have for us, Kitty, Kitty? Where's Hattie? Hallelujah, Hattie's got something for Shaw."

"And what happened to Polly? Polly's the dolly who fell on the tracks," Butter Bar crooned. "Polly's the dolly who's not coming back."

"Who is she?" Mimi whispered to Roz. "And who the heck are Polly and Hattie?"

"Not a clue," Roz whispered back. "But that one? Strictly Tobacco Road, if you know what I mean."

"She's very pretty," Mimi protested. "She simply doesn't know how to present herself. Her hair. And the makeup is a bit overdone."

"A bit! Honey, look at that dress. Don't be so naïve, Mimi. Mark my word, that girl is selling it."

"Selling it?" Surely, Roz couldn't mean— "No, no, I've seen her before. Somewhere. She simply has no sense of—of fashion. That dress is too shiny, too tight."

Roz wasn't listening, she'd waltzed off with another interchangeable GI. The blonde broke away from the circle of men and ran to the ladies' room. Butter Bar kept up his catcalls as she ran. Mimi walked right up to him.

"Back off, lieutenant. Just what do you think you're doing?"

"Me? Just being friendly. What is that tart doing here at a respectable dance, anyway? You a friend of Kitty's?"

Kitty. It clicked into place where Mimi had first seen her. Yet this tormented creature was a far cry from the young woman she remembered, in overalls, kerchief, and beekeeper's bonnet. Mimi had worked with her last fall at her landlady's beehives, during the honey harvest.

"She's got as much right to be here as you," Mimi said. "More, because you servicemen weren't even invited. You always cause trouble."

Butter Bar leaned close to Mimi, his dark eyes menacing. "I'd be careful if I were you, sweetheart."

From his accent she figured he was from New Jersey or New York. A tough guy.

"Well, you aren't me. Sweetheart." Mimi balled up her fists, put them together, and let him have it, right in the solar plexus. She heard an "oof" come out of his mouth. "Don't ever call me sweetheart again, you jerk."

He grabbed his gut and doubled over as his buddies mocked him. "Hey, Lieutenant Shaw, that little lady slugged you good. Where'd you learn that, Slugger?"

"That wasn't very ladylike," Lt. Shaw wheezed to Mimi, trying to catch his breath.

"Is that right? I learned it from my grandmother, and don't you dare say my grandmother's not a lady."

She left him wheezing, and his buddies laughing, and followed Kitty into the ladies' room. The only place he wouldn't dare follow.

Kitty. Katharine "Kitty" Hawkins. That's right, the honey harvest.

The pale blonde may have looked fragile, but Mimi remembered she was good with the bees, fast and unafraid. She came from a farm in—Somewhereville, West Virginia, the next state over.

Mimi's landlady, Addie Richardson, ran a thriving side business as a beekeeper. An enterprise that was remarkably successful, with a product highly sought after, in these times of sugar rationing. Kitty Hawkins was one of Addie's helpers, the ones who harvested the honey. Mimi had taken turns with Kitty working the centrifugal extractor, separating the honey from the beeswax.

Like Mimi's landlady, Kitty's family kept beehives when she grew up. The bees provided food for the hives, sweetener for her family, and enough left over to sell at a stand on the road. But this was a strikingly different Kitty. How did she get from there to here?

Mimi squeezed herself into the cramped lavatory. The woman in the wrinkled red rayon dress was trying to rescue her victory rolls, without much luck. Tears ran down her face. She looked very young and heartbroken.

"It's not that bad," Mimi said. "Let me help. Kitty, right?"

"Right." Kitty threw her comb in the sink. She squared her shoulders and faced Mimi, an invisible chip firmly in place. "And yes, it is that bad."

Her words had a raw Southern twang.

"Those guys are idiots."

"Worse than idiots." She turned back to the mirror. She was finished with the conversation, but Mimi was not.

"Why were those men mocking you, Kitty?" *Could Roz possibly be right?*

"You look smart. You figure it out."

Mimi wet a towel and handed it to her. "Wipe your face, your makeup is running."

The blonde did as she was told. She sighed and stared at Mimi. "Look at you, your dress is exactly right. Mine is all wrong."

Mimi knew her emerald dress accentuated her blue eyes and auburn hair. It seemed so simple to her.

"Do you mind if I help?" With an eye for attractive clothes, Mimi took pleasure in what she wore, and she read *Mademoiselle* and *Vogue* religiously. Kitty simply had no experience with fashion, she decided; that much was obvious.

Kitty rubbed her eyes and sniffled. She peered at Mimi. "I've seen you."

"We met during the honey harvest."

"The honey?" The light went on. "Oh, over to Addie's hives. I remember you now. Molly?"

"Mimi."

"Mimi Smith," Kitty said. "We spun the honey together."

"We did. Why don't you just wear your hair down? It's easier. And prettier. Especially with hair this color. You have such beautiful hair."

Kitty turned and stared as if Mimi had two heads. "But this is supposed to be more sophisticated. All the magazines say so."

The victory rolls hairstyle was more suited to the factory floor, Mimi thought, to keep a woman's hair out of the torpedo parts, than as a sophisticated style. "But it's not what the movie stars wear. Not usually. Well, except for Betty Grable."

"Why do you care?"

"Why shouldn't I?" Mimi pulled out a comb. She took out Kitty's hairpins and released her platinum tresses, too fine and silky to hold that complicated style. Mimi smoothed the hair out into gentle waves that turned under and brushed her shoulders. "See? Now, you're Veronica Lake."

Kitty regarded her reflection in the small mirror. "It's kind of plain."

"But elegant," Mimi insisted. "Pretty. More refined."

"I am probably the least refined person you ever met, Mimi Smith."

"Doesn't mean you can't *look* refined. Now let's clean up your face."

"I suppose you don't like my dress either." Kitty splashed water over her face and took a towel to wipe off the rest of her makeup.

"It's very—bright."

"Yeah. I can see it looks cheap. Now I can. I didn't think so at first, but then I come here and there are so many pretty dresses. I just wanted to feel different for a night. Like I fit in. Somewhere." She sighed deeply, again on the verge of tears.

"It's the material. Rayon looks fine until you wash it. Then it really falls apart. Wrinkle, crinkle, stretch. But now people will be admiring your hair and your face, not your dress."

"Where did you get a thing like that, like you're wearing?" Kitty asked. "I've never seen anything like it."

"My friend designed the pattern for me. She's going to be a famous designer someday."

"A designer? My goodness. Where I come from everyone makes their own clothes. Course I got this one in a store. Paid good money for it too." Her shoulders drooped.

Mimi started repairing Kitty's makeup and smoothing the dress to take some of the wrinkles out. "My friend Gloria has to start somewhere. She's working in a shirt factory in New York, getting to know the big shots there."

"Why do you care about me?"

"I guess I hate mean people. Mean men."

The Veronica Lake lookalike laughed. "You must hate a lot of people."

"Yeah, I do. Nazis. And various other mean people."

Roz stuck her head in the door and stared at Mimi and Kitty. "Mimi, what's going on? Did you die in here or what?"

"Keep your shirt on." Mimi put her hand on the door to signal Roz to leave. She turned back to Kitty. "You look nice this way, Kitty. Really."

The blonde gazed at her reflection in the mirror. She knew she drew the stares of men, whether she looked uptown or down.

"What they say about me—those men. It's true. It's not pretty, but it's what I am."

"Nonsense."

"Don't you get it, Mimi? I'm trash. I just didn't think everyone would know it here. I should have known they would. My mama always said you could tell a tarnished nickel."

"You're not a nickel. You're not tarnished. You're a shiny silver dollar." Mimi pulled out some powder foundation, lipstick, and lotion. "Rub some of this lotion on your face, Kitty. Tears do terrible things to the skin. The salt will sting."

"Sounds like you've shed a fair amount yourself."

"Haven't we all? There's a war on, you know."

Kitty did as she was told. Mimi put her skills to work, redrawing Kitty's eyebrows with a lighter brow pencil in a more natural line. Black brows were too harsh for her, she cautioned her, with such pale blond hair. After a few more tricks, Mimi pulled out a rosy red lipstick and applied it to Kitty's lips.

"See, your whole look is softer now."

Kitty was beautiful to begin with, but now she had a glow that would have flattered a debutante. The dress was still too bright, too tight, and the wrong color, but most people would see the woman and not the dress.

"I don't look like myself."

"That's good, right? Just for a change?" Mimi had done what she could, she thought. She put her hand on the door. "I'll see you around, Kitty."

"Probably not." She hesitated. "Thanks, Mimi Smith. For talking to me and—and everything."

Mimi ran into a soldier lingering outside the door. He put out a hand to stop her, but he didn't dare touch her. She pushed him away and he jumped back.

"Where's Kitty?" he said. "Tell her Tom Cat is waiting."

"Well, Tom Cat, you better leave now. Soldiers are welcome here when they behave. Not when alley cats bring the alley inside with them."

Bert Styers, one of the self-appointed chaperones from Chinquapin Village, appeared at their side. "Everything all right back here?"

"Depends on these gate-crashers." Mimi indicated Tom Cat.

"Huh. This is a respectable place, young man. No rough stuff." He gave the soldier the eye. "We don't allow anyone to molest our young ladies."

"No problem," the GI insisted. "No harm meant, mister."

"Not the way I see it. I want all y'all out of here. Now. You and your buddies. Or I call the MPs."

Out of the corner of her eye, Mimi saw the ladies' room door open. Kitty, looking dry-eyed and much improved, slipped out through the front door, followed by a flyboy who blocked another man from leaving.

Four

MIMI STEPPED OUTSIDE to see where Kitty had gone, but the woman and the airman had disappeared.

"Hey, missy," Lt. Butter Bar called out to her. "Who died and made you Eleanor Roosevelt?"

Mimi glanced up to see an ugly sneer on his face. "What did you say?"

"We were just having some fun with the little tramp."

"Fun? It wasn't funny, and you don't know she's that kind." Mimi wasn't sure she was right about that.

"Oh, yes I do." He said it with assurance.

"Your name is Shaw, isn't it, lieutenant?"

He lurched toward her with a menacing leer, but at that moment Franny and Roz stepped out of the shadows, followed by Bert. The soldier stopped cold. Bert wasn't normally an intimidating man, medium height with a slight build and thinning pale brown hair, in his mid-forties. But Bert hefting a baseball bat like he knew how to use it was a different guy altogether.

Lt. Butter Bar put up his hands. "No harm meant." He backed up.

"I don't care what you meant, soldier," Bert snarled at the man like the Army captain he once was. "What's your name?"

"Shaw, sir. Second Lieutenant Howard Shaw."

"If you don't want a lot more trouble, Shaw, you leave and take your buddies with you. Don't come back."

"No problem, sir. But what about Slugger here?" He jerked his shoulder toward Mimi.

Bert glanced at Mimi. "Slugger gets to stay. I'll even let her borrow my bat."

Shaw's eyes went wide. He backed away and whistled for his buddies.

"Hell, Bert, we didn't know you had it in you," Franny said.

Bert was some kind of foreman at the Naval Torpedo Station. He had served in the first World War. Now he had a wife, a couple of teenage kids, a barebones duplex at Chinquapin Village, and a quiet life. He wanted to keep it that way.

"All we want here is a nice quiet dance." Bert started to walk back into the hall. "You ladies be careful. These men? Well, they can get out of hand, especially if they think— If they get the wrong idea about a woman."

"Thanks, Bert. You're a stand-up guy," Franny said. "Thanks for standing up for us tonight." She stood half a head taller than Bert. "Don't worry, we're not going to give anyone that idea."

"Especially not Eleanor Roosevelt here."

Roz poked Mimi in the ribs. She glared at Roz. Mimi respected the first lady greatly, but she didn't care to be compared to her.

"I like to call her Slugger," Franny said.

"I've had enough," Mimi said. "I'm going to call it a night."

"Personally, I thought that Lieutenant Shaw was kind of cute." Roz winked at Lt. "Butter Bar" Shaw as he departed with his buddies in a Jeep. "Even if he is a Yankee."

"I'm good to go too, Mimi," Franny said. "Those boys were getting all kinds of handsy. I didn't want to have to drop one."

"You would have too," Roz said with some regret. "I saw one of them pouring something from a flask into the Kool-Aid."

The three decided to walk back to downtown Alexandria, a little over three miles. There was no caravan heading back that way yet. It wasn't a hard walk, and it was a quiet night. Instead of taking the road, where they could be accosted by soldiers drunk on flask whiskey and Kool-Aid, they took the tree-lined trails at Cameron Run as far as they could before diverting onto King Street.

Though Franny and Roz worked at the torpedo factory, they didn't reside at Chinquapin. They were single, and the village was strictly for families. They boarded together in the top floor of an old house on Lee Street, near Tilly, renting their digs from a widow who was glad for the money and their ration tickets. Mimi lived on St. Asaph Street in a similar attic room, although she was the lucky only renter. She had the room to herself.

The women changed out of their heels into walking sandals, stashed in their purses just in case. The fireflies were still illuminating the woods, so Mimi didn't need her flashlight—but she kept it in her hand. It was large and heavy, and she had used it before to ward off an overly amorous beau or two.

"You and your flashlight. You are bound to get a reputation," Roz said. "Nobody likes a prude."

"Did you ever notice that the men who call you a prude are the ones you wouldn't want to touch you anyway?" Mimi said.

"You got a point there."

"Beats being mistaken for a Tobacco Road kind of woman," Franny added.

They all knew who she was talking about. Mimi wondered about Kitty Hawkins. How could someone go from looking like Tobacco Road to a movie star with just the right touch of makeup? And how could that fresh-faced Kitty that Mimi had met at the honey harvest say she was exactly the kind of woman everyone took her for? Did Kitty even know what she looked like?

"She must be a magpie, that's all," Mimi said. "Likes to pick up bits of sparkle."

"Bits? I'd say she grabbed the whole crate." Roz flicked her curls out of the way.

Roz could say cutting things about people like Kitty, even though she was overly sensitive to what people said about her. Still, Roz could be fun company. She was pretty and vivacious, though at times she proved unbearably "delicate," which most people blamed on her being *oh-so-Southern*. Mimi knew she wasn't her best self around Rosalyn Chambers, and she could give in to cheap gossip. Roz had lived a mostly charmed life, Mimi decided, and would never understand about the Kitty Hawkinses of the world.

"What do you really think of her, Mimi?" Roz broke into her thoughts. "You were with her for *hours* in the ladies' room."

"Fifteen minutes. And unless they're wearing a uniform, I think it's pretty easy to get the wrong impression from someone's clothes."

"Not if you shop at the right stores," Roz said.

"You are such a snob, Roz," Franny said.

"That is not the worst thing in the world."

There was no proof that Kitty was involved in prostitution, Mimi told herself. People were just judging the woman on her clothes, and her Jean Harlow-blond hair.

And did it matter what Kitty said? Too many women were too willing to think the worst about themselves—and each other.

Mimi's grandmother, Eileen Finerty, would surely understand. If it were true about Kitty, Grandma Eileen would just call the woman a "magdalen," as in Mary Magdalene. Her grandmother thought it a nicer name than "prostitute" or "whore," when she wasn't tagging such women as "poor unfortunates" or "soiled doves."

Mimi concentrated on the fireflies, who certainly weren't ashamed of what they were up to that night. The temperature dropped a bit downtown. Near the Potomac River, it was always a little cooler in the summer and warmer in the winter. She breathed a sigh of relief as she headed down St. Asaph to the Richardsons' house where she boarded.

"You want us to walk you the rest of the way?" Franny asked.

"We could," Roz said. "But we were going to go see Tilly."

"Go ahead. Say hi to Tilly for me. It's only a couple of blocks. I'll be fine." Mimi waved them off and headed home.

"You're sure?" Franny asked.

"I'm well-armed." Mimi saluted them with her flashlight.

 os

It was halfway through 1943 and it seemed the war had already been going on forever. Would it ever end?

Everyone Mimi knew wanted to do their part for the war effort, yet too many made decisions based on the war. Cataclysmic decisions. They raced against the Grim Reaper, who daily swung his scythe and forever separated families from their sons, brothers, and lovers. Newly minted husbands and wives were strangers who had met at dances or in cafés and on the streets. They too-often paired off, wedded and bedded, or the other way around, after a few short days of passion. The ever-present tension released its hold for a moment, then gripped them tighter.

Those left behind fought the fear that they would never know love, never even share a bed. And that fear brought many unwise choices, not to mention unexpected children. The men were off to war again, to fight the Nazis or the Japanese. The women, sometimes pregnant, were often widowed. Sons and daughters would never know their fathers.

There was no guarantee Johnny would come back whole. He might be destroyed by the bloody sights he had seen. He might be violent, he might be a drunk, he might never talk of the war that fractured his soul. While a lucky lady would be happy to hear her soldier boy, sailor, or marine was alive, she might also dread the day the stranger she married would come marching home again.

Mimi remembered Eddie Falcone. His memory walked her home. Black hair, long lashes over unexpectedly green eyes, beautiful olive skin, and a smile that made her quiver, these were things Mimi remembered about Eddie. He was not brawny, but brainy. Their romance the summer before had been brief, a matter of weeks, yet intense enough that he and Mimi talked about marrying when the war ended.

His Italian background and his tales of his rowdy and passionate Catholic family fascinated her. His people were nothing like her reserved "lace curtain" Irish and English family, but they were everything she thought she wanted, warm, expressive. Eddie and Mimi's backgrounds were different, but their religion was the same. They were sure their love would win out, with blessings all around.

Fate had other plans. Eddie Falcone was a paratrooper, one whose parachute failed to open. They called them "streamers." Mimi received the news belatedly in February, but she'd felt it months earlier. Somewhere in her soul, a light had gone out. He died on a classified mission, jumping from a B-24 bomber, the Liberator, the plane that "couldn't be shot down." Last month's *Esquire* had raved about how the Liberator gave and took a lot of punishment. Their photograph showed a bomber shot through with holes like Swiss cheese, but still flying. Mimi could not finish reading the article.

She had received the news about Eddie as her girlfriends were talking about the bridesmaid dresses they would wear to a friend's nuptials. At first her grief was like a knife. She failed to understand how she could go on breathing when Eddie would never breathe again. She hated Hitler, she blamed Hitler. She also blamed God.

All she had left of Eddie Falcone was a photo of him in his uniform and a few precious letters. She had no ring and almost no proof they had loved each other. Her reaction had been tears for a week, then something else took over—a hard-headed practicality that life would go on, no matter how empty. She thought of the years to come after the war and briefly regretted they hadn't married.

But time gave her insight. How much worse to be an unexpected widow at twenty-one!

And her memories of Eddie were fading. There were times Mimi wondered if she'd known Eddie at all. When people dated, they were on their best behavior. They had no chance to see each other at their worst, or to see how they handled the everyday moments, the good and the bad.

What if Eddie had hated her mother? What if he became domineering and controlling? Would he cramp her style, her ambition, her curiosity? What if they both came to resent the very things they found attractive about each other in the first place?

Mimi would never know.

In recent months, she decided their romance had been too quick, too hot, too sudden. She hadn't had the chance to get to know him. In normal times they would have had a real courtship, slower and steadier. Still, there was always the question: Would there even be a world left after this war?

Tears wouldn't bring Eddie back. His bright toothy smile that made her heart skip would never grace her again. Letting his memory fade felt like a sin. Yet it was something she couldn't quite control. Now she had to look at his dashing picture simply to remember his face.

She never wrote her family about him, neither about their romance nor his death. Mimi had wrapped her grief around the scar called Eddie Falcone and let it harden. Mary Margaret Smith vowed she wouldn't marry during this war. She wouldn't give in to a brief treacherous passion, resulting in a brief heartbreaking marriage. She wouldn't be a widow left holding the bag—and the baby.

This war was also grim for the women who were engaged but destined never to wear that white wedding gown. Women like Tilly Parker, whom she had met through Franny. Tilly worked with Franny and Roz. Now she could barely get through the days, and the evenings were so terrible she contemplated the river's embrace every night.

Mimi was with Tilly when she received the telegram from the War Department. Tilly didn't make it beyond the words, "I regret to inform you..." before the screams started. She changed overnight, as if a phantom had taken up residence in her body. The life drained out of her, leaving only a shell of Matilda behind. Now her friends worried about whether the Potomac would cough up her corpse one day. And no one knew when, or if, David's body was coming home.

Women were everywhere, in the factories, driving cabs, and playing baseball. Young men on the hoof were scarce. It was no wonder every female Mimi knew was boy crazy. Almost all the healthy able-bodied men were gone from the cities, making for a lopsided life.

However, Washington was different. In D.C., military men cycled in and out with regularity. The brand-new Pentagon in Arlington, Virginia, was filling up with servicemen. Uniforms from all the service branches could be seen all over the region.

But those men in Washington shipped in, received their orders, and shipped out. Most of the ones who stayed permanently were either boys or old men, or married, or otherwise off limits. Some were 4-F, unfit for service. Some had finished their fighting and come home with an empty sleeve, or a pinned-up pants leg and a crutch.

But what about women like Kitty? Mimi wondered. Was she doing her part for the war? She ordered herself to stop thinking about the woman, but she couldn't. In Mimi's mind Kitty would always be associated with the honey harvest.

And now with drunken soldiers in a circle, laughing and whistling and catcalling.

"Here, Kitty, Kitty, Kitty."

FIVE

"**Y**OU'RE BACK EARLY for a Friday night." The voice had a slight West Virginia accent. It was Mimi's landlady, Addie Richardson, well-informed, well-intentioned, and well padded. And, Mimi suspected, the honey queen of northern Virginia. Her dark curls were pinned on top of her head, and she wore a roomy blue house dress.

"A little earlier than normal," Mimi acknowledged.

Her landlady sat on a bench under a rose-covered arbor on the side of the imposing house, sipping a tall iced tea, no doubt liberally laced with honey. Tea was hard to come by, but Addie had a store of it in reserve, and she stretched it with herbs and juices.

Addie's house had an unusual side garden. Most of the older homes in Alexandria's downtown area were built side by side, without so much as a narrow walkway between them. Addie's "English garden" was one of her pride and joys, of which she had several. Her victory garden full of vegetables was behind the house, but the side garden was filled with flowers.

Mimi was glad to be home. Addie's garden was most pleasant after dark, after the heat of the day, when the scent of roses and honeysuckle filled the air, as well as a few fireflies, though not as many as on the wooded path to Chinquapin.

"Care for some sweet tea?" Addie hardly needed to ask.

"Love some."

Addie poured Mimi her special blend from a glass carafe into a bright purple aluminum tumbler. The sweet tea went down easier than the watered-down Kool-Aid at the dance. The price of the refreshment, Mimi knew, was information. Addie enjoyed knowing what was going on. Mimi inquired after Addie's husband.

"Derry retired early. Too much law work this week. Too many wills."

"It keeps him busy."

"He's a good man," Addie said.

Derry Richardson was a local attorney, from a family of attorneys. He was quiet and reserved and sometimes seemed bemused by his live wire of a wife. Mimi liked Derry. He never seemed to lose his temper, he had a good sense of humor, he loved Addie's cooking, and he was a patient father to his son Richie, who adored him.

"I take it Chinquapin Village is not exactly the Ritz?" Addie inquired.

"Not exactly. I saw Kitty Hawkins there."

Addie's glass lowered. "Kitty! My goodness. Haven't seen her for a while."

"I barely recognized her." Mimi took another sip. "I only met her that once, during your honey harvest. She looked different."

"I don't imagine she was wearing a beekeeper's bonnet."

"A shiny red dress. Very red, very shiny."

"Funny how many blondes like red, whether it suits them or not. Just so you know, her hair doesn't come from a dye bottle. Kitty always had that white-blond hair. Even when she was a little girl."

"Didn't think so," Mimi said. "Looks too healthy to be dyed."

"But menfolk, they're always drawn to blondes, don't it seem?"

"Even when they aren't nearly as pretty as Kitty."

"It was inevitable she'd have problems with men."

Addie seemed to know a lot about Kitty that she wasn't saying.

"Problems?"

"Men were always coming around to see her when she was working, always wanting—something. Maybe that's why she found comfort in a beekeeper's hat and overalls."

Mimi reflected that Kitty seemed pretty comfortable in that revealing scarlet frock.

"There were soldiers, Addie. These soldiers— They were taunting her, saying ugly things. Maybe it was more the way they were saying them. Her makeup and hair were— Well, 'tarted up,' as my mother would say."

"I'd heard a few rumors around 'bout how Kitty was paying her rent, but rumors aren't facts. Course where there's smoke—"

"These men, they were bullies. They kept saying, Here, Kitty, Kitty. Come to Tom Cat."

"I suppose they could have said worse." Addie sipped her iced tea. "And what did you do? Did our fiery redhead just stand by and watch?"

Addie had some funny ideas about redheads being volatile. And Mimi never thought of herself as a redhead. Her hair was auburn, she would say, not *red*. She let the comment go, this time.

"Before I found her in the ladies' and made her wash her face?"

"That's a start."

"I may have punched one of them in the stomach. A second lieutenant. He was horrible and smug. He reminded me of all the bullies my brother used to bring around. And well, my hands just might have clenched together in a big fist. Like this."

Mimi demonstrated her move, then calmly sipped her tea. Addie chuckled.

"Sounds like he deserved it! But you know, Mimi, that could've backfired."

"Not with everyone there watching. Either 'Butter Bar' backed down, or we were going to have a riot."

"Leave it to Mimi Smith to pick on an officer and not a lowly private."

"Privates can be princes compared to that guy. Shaw was the name. Good thing I'm not in the Army, I'd be in the brig. He just made me so mad! Besides, none of the uniforms were invited to the dance, but they always find out somehow. I guess they're tired of the USO. Bert, one of the chaperones, played hero. He showed up with a baseball bat and ordered them all out."

"Good for him. And Kitty?"

"She slipped out the door with a flyboy. She didn't say goodbye."

"I wouldn't be too hard on her. Kitty comes from dirt-poor folk, a dirt-poor town. A place that ought to be forgotten. I reckon that's why they call it Forgotten Creek."

"Isn't that where you're from too?"

"*From* is the most important word there," Addie drawled. She plucked a dead rose off a vine. "I saw my chance and I took it. Not a lot of ways to make a living in Forgotten Creek. General store, farm, work for the electric company. None of those appealed to me. Or to a girl like Kitty, I imagine."

"And running moonshine?" Mimi prompted. "I've heard tales from my friend Marge. Course she's in the Marines now, down in South Carolina. She didn't run moonshine. She just drank it a time or two. Said it was mighty potent."

"It certainly is." Addie paused. "So I've heard. And that's dangerous work. My family stayed far away from all that. Don't think Kitty Hawkins would be suited to it."

"I told Roz and Franny that Kitty simply doesn't know how to dress or wear makeup. She sends the wrong message."

Addie sent Mimi a look. "She's probably pretty confident about what message she's sending. Kitty doesn't come from a fine family, like you and the Smithsonians, but she knows the score."

An ambitious ancestor named Smith had given Mimi's family the highfalutin name of Smithsonian, borrowing it from the museum upon his arrival on these shores from the UK. Mimi always felt like an impostor wearing that name. Inspired by the hit film of 1939, *Mr. Smith Goes to Washington*, and the freedom of living far from home, Mimi had legally changed her name back to the original Smith. Smith was simpler to live with, she decided, required fewer explanations, and made it easier to blend in with the crowd.

Her mother and father took this as a personal insult. They were still upset.

Mimi wasn't sure about how "fine" the Smithsonian family was, though their home always had books and music and lively discussion. In fact, they argued constantly, over everything from weather to politics. But the Smithsonians didn't have a home as fine as Addie's on St. Asaph Street. They lived in a modest bungalow on the west side of Denver, Colorado, along with the other Irish and the Italians and the Mexicans, all Catholic.

Mimi was a trial to her family, except for her mother's mother, Grandma Eileen Finerty, who adored Mimi and encouraged her high-spirited ways. She was the only one who supported Mimi's decision to move to Washington to work for the war effort. Her parents had absolutely forbidden it—as if that would stop Mimi. Her grandmother even slipped her the money for the taxi that took her to Denver's Union Station and beyond, one night while her parents were out to dinner with friends.

"Kitty's not a college girl like you." Addie broke into her thoughts.

"I haven't finished school yet." Mimi put returning to college on hold for after the war. On hold, like so many other things. But she already had plans to transfer to a school in Washington, D.C. She was never going back to Denver.

"You will. Kitty finished high school, but no one cares about that back in Forgotten Creek. All you're supposed to do there is get married and work like a serf your whole life."

"Why would she sell herself to those men?" Mimi asked. "I mean, if she was."

"Troubled times breed desperation. I wouldn't hold it against her. Course I've known her since she was a little girl. Sweet skinny little thing."

"Kitty said her mother called her a tarnished nickel."

"Oh my. Sounds like Netty Hawkins. That woman—" Addie closed her mouth tightly, as if biting off her words.

"That's a terrible thing to say about a person. I believe there's something about Kitty, something sweet and naïve, despite it all." Addie finished her tea.

Kitty's tears in the ladies' room were the tears of a heartbroken child, a hurt little girl. Not a hardened harlot. Maybe she'd never had someone to stand up for her. Mimi was grateful she grew up with at least one champion. Grandma Eileen had *backbone.*

"I know what you mean," Mimi said.

"She's not like your sassy friend, that high-hat Rosalyn Chambers."

"Not at all like Roz, or Franny, or Tilly, or anyone I know."

"But Kitty's not simple. Appearances can be deceiving, Mimi Smith. Don't go falling for some act, even from Kitty, with her angel hair. Her halo might be a bit tarnished, but she's more gold than nickel."

SIX

*E*VEN THE FIREFLIES seemed sleepy. Mimi wished her landlady good night and retired to her third-floor room. On her way up the stairs, she heard a fiddle rendition of "Goodnight, Ladies."

"Young man, you better be getting to sleep!" Mimi heard Addie holler to her son from outside. His open window was right above the side garden.

"I am asleep, Ma," a voice answered. "It's my fiddle had to say good night to Mimi."

"Good night, Richie," Mimi called out to the invisible fiddle. "Pleasant dreams."

A swirl of grace notes followed up and wished her a final good night as she entered her room. Mimi suppressed her urge to laugh. She was lucky. She knew that.

While Roz and Franny were living practically on top of each other, Mimi had a room to herself and the ultimate luxury, a small bathroom of her own. Cross ventilation and a ceiling fan made it comfortable, or at least bearable, most of the time. The rooms on the third floor were probably at some time in the past occupied by servants. Mimi didn't mind. She was sleeping in an antique four-poster bed under a lace canopy.

Like other cities around Washington, Alexandria was bursting at the seams. Residents were asked to open their homes, if not their hearts, and rent extra rooms to the thousands of workers who needed a place to stay for the duration of the war.

Even though she had volunteered to let out her spare room, Addie Richardson had been reluctant. It would be unpatriotic not to offer, yet no one who rang her bell in hopes of landing a room in her house had quite suited Mrs. Richardson. Mimi was warned by the local agency handling the referrals that "it probably wouldn't work out." Addie was at the top of their list of impossible-to-please landlords.

Mimi was weary and wilting from the heat when she knocked on Adeline Richardson's door the previous summer. The imposing federal style three-story home on St. Asaph Street was nothing like the compact Denver bungalow where Mimi grew up. It was so imposing, so grand, so beautiful. Even the front hall, with its black-and-white marble checkerboard floor and graceful staircase, seemed like something out of a storybook.

Her first view of Addie was of a plump matron in a cocoa-colored rayon dress printed with yellow fans and yellow buttons. Her hair was swept up on top of her head in a froth of bouncy brown curls. Small yellow fan earrings festooned her ears. The outfit was on the flirty side, but her light brown eyes were intelligent, and they assessed the seeker of the room.

Mimi had come straight from work in an indigo dress that matched her blue eyes, but it had rumpled in the heat, her auburn waves were more out of control than usual, and she was sure her freckles were glowing on her shiny nose. She hoped she didn't look as disheveled as she felt.

"I'm here about the room."

Addie barely hid a sigh as she looked her up and down.

"You best come in before you melt. You a government worker?"

"I work for the Office of Price Administration. I know lots of people don't care for that agency, but it's a job and it's necessary."

Mimi figured she might as well get it over with. So many people hated the OPA. Everyone wanted the other guy's prices controlled and rents regulated and black marketeering reined in—but not their own. No one thought they were part of the black-market economy. That was something *other* people did.

Addie shrugged and opened the door a little wider for Mimi to enter. "We all got our crosses to bear."

She instructed Mimi to take a seat in the front parlor before one of Addie's large electric fans. Somewhere in the house, music began to play, the sweet notes of a baroque melody. It came from a violin whose strings seemed to weep and then explode with joy.

"Is that the radio?" Mimi smiled and cocked her head. She closed her eyes for a moment to concentrate.

"No, that's my son, Richie." Addie looked at Mimi and seemed to be waiting for something.

"It's gorgeous. He's exceptionally talented."

"He plays his heart. What he's feeling." The notes soared higher.

"Does he play in an orchestra?"

Addie shook her head and the curls followed. "No, you see my Richie's got a gift for music. He can play any stringed instrument, any tune, and make his own music, but his mind, no, his *attention*— Well, he'll always be a bit of a little boy. He's not what you'd call practical. We've mostly taught him at home. School can be cruel. And other children—"

"I see," Mimi said, although she wasn't quite sure what Addie meant.

The music stopped and a dark head dodged quickly in and out of the room.

"It's all right, Richie," Addie said. "You can come in now."

Tall and thin, the boy kept his head down, glancing at Mimi with huge dark brown eyes, then looking away. She guessed he was in his teens, maybe sixteen. He carried his violin in one hand.

"Hello, I'm Mimi Smith." Mimi extended her hand to shake. "Short for Mary Margaret."

He wiped his face. Then he wiped his free hand on his pants before putting it in hers.

"I'm Richie. Short for Derry Richard Richardson, the Third."

"You play music with wonderful feeling."

"It's a gift," he replied, matter of factly. "That's what everyone says. I just like to play."

"They're right. You do have a gift. I like to sing, but I'm not as good as you."

"Really? I could play for you! And you could sing!"

"We'll talk about that later, Richie," his mother said. "Why don't you go get yourself a snack?"

"Can I get one for Mimi Smith too?"

Addie nodded. "You see what I'm saying? He's such a sweet boy." Richie went off without further ado. "Just not—an ordinary boy, who plays baseball."

"Does that matter when he's playing music from the angels?" Mimi mused aloud. "As if they touched him with their grace notes. Richie is far more rare than some grubby boy playing baseball in a sandlot. To make beautiful music every day, that really is a gift. At home we had an old radio with so much static, you practically had to stand it on its head to get any music out of it. And we played an old upright piano, usually out of tune. But Richie is wonderful! Does he ever play requests? Like 'Claire de Lune'? Oh. I'm sorry, Mrs. Richardson, I'm running on. I didn't mean to."

She could feel herself blush to the roots of her auburn hair. Richie must have overheard. The opening notes of "Clair de Lune" emerged from the kitchen. Addie looked at Mimi for a long moment.

"Would you care for some sweet tea, Mimi dear, and a piece of honey cake?"

Mrs. Richardson bustled into the kitchen without waiting for a response. She returned in short order with sweet tea and a generous slice of cake for each of them.

The first bite was heavenly, with just the right amount of sweetness. Mimi detected a bit of cinnamon and a touch of nutmeg. She closed her eyes and savored the cake as it melted on her tongue.

She remembered herself and said, "Oh, I'm sorry, Mrs. Richardson. I have a bit of a sweet tooth."

Mrs. Richardson's smile grew brighter. "Isn't that nice. You may call me Addie."

Out of sight, the violin soared again. "I recognize that tune," Mimi said. "*Afternoon of a Faun*. More Debussy."

"That means he's happy. Richie likes you."

"I like him too."

The room-renting matter was soon settled, over sweet tea and honey cake. Addie listed her house rules and the few chores Mimi would be expected to perform. It fell in line with what other renters found all over town. Mimi was expected to turn over her ration coupons for food, sugar, and coffee, as Addie would be supplying many of her meals.

Mimi's only reservation was that she might gain a few pounds at Addie's table. At a time when sugar lovers were severely restricted by war rationing, Mimi had landed in a pot of honey. Luckily, she found Addie's sweets and home cooking were countered by all the walking she did, not owning a car. But people with cars had their own challenges: Gasoline was strictly rationed, as well as such essentials as tires.

This evening, with her mind a jumble and sleep far away, Mimi turned to her most prized possession—her old steamer trunk, a gift from her grandmother.

"Everyone deserves a trunk full of dreams, Mimi," Grandma Eileen had told her, when she was planning her escape from the Smithsonians' bungalow. "And this one has made many a fine journey already. It's yours now."

"I can't take it," Mimi protested. She knew it was her grandmother's one tangible treasure.

"It has served me well. Now it will serve you when you travel to Washington, D.C. Giving it to you will make me happy, Mimi. Besides, your mother thinks it's just another old-fashioned bit of nonsense."

Mimi knew her mother would rather have something shiny and new, even if it wasn't as fine.

"Everyone's against me going."

"I wouldn't say *everyone* now." Grandma Eileen had no Irish accent, yet the way she talked and phrased things seemed to come from her ancestors.

Mimi hugged her grandmother, who seemed to be getting smaller with every year, more delicate. Except for her warrior's heart. "I don't know why they even want me here. I only annoy them. There has to be something else for me out there, beyond the prairie to the east and the mountains to the west."

"You simply weren't meant for this town, Mary Margaret, and if your parents had any imagination, they would know it. I expect they'll come around eventually. You might try telling them you want to be an *actress*."

They both laughed. Mimi's parents thought a life on the stage or screen was tantamount to abandoning all morality. Her grandmother recounted the well-worn tale of her two sisters, Mimi's great-aunts. They left home to work as schoolteachers, but when they wrote home and said they were going to be actresses instead, Old Man Finerty dragged them back and made them get married.

"It's a shame! They would have made fine actresses too, my sisters, so dramatic they were. They were long on ambition, yet sadly a little short on backbone."

"You didn't want to be an actress?" Mimi asked. She knew she did.

"Maybe once or twice. All thoughts of the stage fled when I laid eyes on your grandfather. Such a passion consumed me, and burned for all of his life, so that I couldn't imagine being with anyone else."

Her grandmother always refused to discuss her late husband beyond that.

Mimi stroked the trunk fondly. "It's had many lives."

"Aye. It came from Ireland, County Meath, during the famine and arrived here with your great-great—I don't know how many greats—grandmother. Maura McEntagart and her trunk, and her daughter, and her favorite horse, arrived in Kingston, New York, in 1849. Her daughter Anna inherited the trunk and traveled across this great country to Pennsylvania, and so forth with her daughter, traveling to points West, until it arrived in this high-and-dry desert. With me."

"It looks like a pirate's chest."

"Maura McEntagart had a good bit of the piratical in her. I think anyone who made it here had to have a lot of gumption, Mary Margaret. Optimism. Life was hard in the old country and so many died of the hunger. And the English. The pessimists stayed behind, so wedded to their misery they were."

"How did your family make it here?"

"Maura's husband died. And granted, they had more than many poor souls did. She sold everything she could lay her hands on, except her prize horse."

"She really took her horse?"

"Brian Boru, named for the chieftain."

"And the song, 'Brian Boru's March'?"

"Exactly. Those McEntagarts had a small horse farm. You know the Irish, they love their horses. It was amazing they had that much, being Catholics. Well, I won't get into the Protestant question, because of my blood pressure. At any rate, Maura gathered her belongings, her family, and carrying her rosary the whole way, made it to this country."

"With this trunk."

"This trunk. She spent a good bit of money on it. She was quality, you know. Lace-curtain Irish, they called them."

The impressive leather-clad steamer trunk had seen better days. The fastening straps were frayed and torn. The once-handsome black leather was scarred and faded. Yet it had scads of room inside, enough for so many dreams in all of its pockets and drawers.

Mimi drove the trunk in her family's aging Model A Ford to a saddle and tack shop where the black leather covering was reconditioned, the frayed straps replaced, and the buckles polished. It now held pride of place in her room and in her life.

She filled it with memories and fabrics, dress patterns and fashion magazines. She also saved letters from home and friends in one of the drawers.

The trunk held so many materials for clothes, she was afraid of being accused of hoarding, but most of it she had acquired before the war and the government's fabric restrictions. She liked to run her fingers over the silk velvets, the bright taffetas, the wool crepes, and the sturdy cottons.

She tried to stay away from rayon. Though rayon was lauded as the miracle synthetic fabric that replaced silk and satin, Mimi didn't like the feel of it. It required a lot of care, and she thought most of it looked cheap. Like Kitty's unfortunate scarlet dress.

Rayon pulled, wrinkled, sagged, and pilled. Of course, Mimi was reduced to owning rayon stockings, a poor replacement for nylons. They felt funny on the legs and they required a lot of diligent care, and they had to be washed immediately after wearing.

Rayon made her think of Kitty Hawkins. Kitty clearly loved that red rayon dress, too tight, too short, too shiny, like a child who hadn't developed her own style yet. Mimi hoped she hadn't ruined the dress for Kitty. On the other hand, if any dress deserved to be ruined, she thought, it was that one.

Compared to Kitty, Mimi was living the life of Riley and her challenges paled in comparison. If Kitty's cheap red dress was any indication, the woman's lodgings would be equally cheap. Kitty might be sharing digs with two or three other women, or more.

Everyone was squeezed for space in Washington and Alexandria, even the women in the WAVES. If rumors were true, Navy women were triple bunking in shifts at the Lloyd House on Washington Street, a beautiful historic home now bursting at its historic seams. Out of twenty-four hours in a day, the women were allowed eight hours in a bed before being kicked out for the next WAVE to take her shift.

But where did Kitty live? Would people even rent a room to a 'magdalen,' if they knew? What kind of place would that be? Would Kitty's landlord or landlady be charging her the regulated rent? Or was extra money changing hands under the table, a silent form of blackmail? An illegal raise in the rent, in exchange for not quibbling over her profession?

That question interested Mimi. Her agency, the OPA, in addition to their other black-market enforcement activities, investigated rents. All rental rates had to follow the established apartment and rooming-house guidelines and rent ceilings. Finding out the truth, however, was sometimes another thing entirely.

Unfortunately, Mimi was not an investigator. Not yet, but someday, she hoped. She had a bad habit of getting ahead of herself.

Mimi tried to shake these thoughts from her brain, or she would never sleep.

When she finally nodded off, she dreamed of bees fighting for space in a crowded honeycomb.

SEVEN

"**S**HE'S A MAGICIAN," Mimi remarked once.

"Nope, my mom is just a smart lady," replied Richie, who was fast becoming Mimi's musical shadow.

Addie Richardson's "magical" honey business was not a small endeavor, a housewife's little kitchen-table hobby. It was a bustling cottage industry and guarded carefully. Honey was becoming more and more valuable, as sugar was the first commodity to be rationed and the first to suffer shortages. There were times when there was no sugar to be had, even if people had ready money and ration coupons to purchase it. Honey was a critical alternative sweetener.

The first time Addie showed Mimi her inventory in the basement, Mimi felt as if she had stepped into a fairytale world. Hundreds upon hundreds of freshly filled jars of saffron-colored liquid lined the cellar walls. Every size of mason jar of the sweet nectar was interspersed with squares of honeycomb and a few other special honey-filled concoctions, created by Addie. She explained that the delicate flavors of the honey came from various local fields of flowers, including clover, honeysuckle, and wild roses.

She tended several hundred hives with a friend on property down the Potomac River near Fort Hunt. They harvested at least twice a year, sometimes three times, but the big harvest would come in September.

Altogether, the glass jars created an amber glow that suffused the below-ground rooms. The golden light sifting through the cellar windows made Mimi think of caves full of long-lost treasure, a quiet underground cathedral where shades of bees' nectar replaced stained glass.

Most of the jars were spoken for and labeled with names, promised to friends and neighbors who were hungry for sweets. For a price, of course. Customers brought back their empty jars and waited for the next harvest. Addie always kept an accurate tally. Still other containers were set aside for Addie's domestic use, the occasional gift, and something to sweeten a tough negotiation.

Addie understood the value of her product.

While sugar was rationed, honey was not—if it could be found. When it was available, it vanished rapidly from grocery shelves. Enter Addie Richardson, the local neighborhood beekeeper, who was increasingly popular among her neighbors. She might have been considered a little odd in the past—her lawyer husband, their big house, their talented but unusual son—but now everyone appreciated her skills.

Restricting sugar and sweets made people hungry and resentful. They didn't want the government telling them what they could and couldn't eat. Sure, it was for the war effort, but in these tough times they longed for the comfort of pies and cakes and cookies. They wanted sugar in their coffee and tea—when they could get coffee or tea. They went to movies so they could watch actors eat the foods they could not. They pooled their government-issued coupons for "ration parties" so they could make special treats.

Addie Richardson wasn't one of them. She could figure out how to adjust any recipe to be made with honey instead of sugar. Her kitchen was regularly filled with neighbors and friends taking impromptu lessons in adjustments and measurements. These were the women who bought her honey and stored their labeled mason jars in her basement.

Addie was familiar with their needs; she even kept a calendar noting her neighbors' big events, the occasions women would want to mark with a special dessert, like Mrs. Walker's anniversary or little Tommy Benson's birthday. And Addie wasn't above holding back a few jars of honey for those days.

Like Kitty Hawkins, Addie's family had always kept bees. Her family wasn't wealthy, though much more prosperous than the Hawkins' family. When Addie married and moved from Forgotten Creek, West Virginia, to Alexandria, she took her beekeeping skills with her. In return, the hives always supplied her with her own small income and a sense of power. Before the war, Addie occasionally sold her honey at the Alexandria Farmers' Market at City Hall. But as soon as the government started talking about rationing, Addie was swamped with business. She expanded her operations.

In addition to the three good-sized basement rooms full of honey, there was also a room secured with two sets of locks that contained multiple bags of precious white sugar, which fed the bees over the winter. Beekeepers were allowed more sugar than the average person, and the more hives, the more sugar. Mimi had caught a glimpse of the sugar room stacked high with fifty-pound bags of the sweet stuff. It was jarring to see that much in one place. No wonder Addie kept it locked up tight.

Addie herself was a bit of a mystery. Although she played the part of an everyday housewife with a "little" beekeeping business, Mimi suspected Mrs. Richardson was a ruthless businesswoman with a mind like a ticker tape, a gambler who knew every angle to play. She was as sharp as any chief executive officer of a big company, but she preferred to keep things manageable. And of course, she had to watch over her son Richie.

In the meantime, Addie's hives were producing, and she developed a few related side businesses. She made delicately scented beeswax candles, useful for mandated blackouts and to save electricity. She cleverly incorporated royal jelly into luxurious homemade face creams. Her own lovely skin, with nary a wrinkle on her pleasantly plump face, was her best advertisement. And even though she told people she wasn't *really* in the business of fine face creams, women came to her door regularly with their empty jars. Sometimes they offered cash, other times eggs from their backyard chickens, or a pound or two of flour.

What could she do? Addie was a Southern lady and unfailingly polite. Mostly. "Here. Try this," she would say, offering Mimi some new concoction.

"What is it?"

"Something terrific for your face, courtesy of my bees."

Mimi knew better than to say no. Addie's creams were perfumed with the most delicate honey fragrances, and it felt even better on the skin. Her complexion glowed—although it did nothing to hide her freckles.

Addie had a way with people, and she was tenacious and determined. Months before, Addie had gone toe-to-toe with a hard-nosed, tightfisted gent at the ration board, one Mr. Deacon. He was refusing all the beekeepers' requests for extra sugar for overwintering the bees. Mimi was grateful she had nothing to do with OPA's local boards. Some had a reputation for being petty tyrants.

"That ignorant fool simply knows nothing about bees," Addie told everyone at the dinner table.

"What are you going to do about it, my dear?" her husband Derry inquired, passing the potatoes.

"I shall educate Mr. Deacon, of course. That is the kindest thing to do."

Derry Richardson nodded mildly. He knew Addie had an angle. Neither her bees nor her customers would suffer from some government drone.

She showed up at the ration board the next day with two extra mason jars of honey in her shopping bag. She pulled them out and sat them on Mr. Deacon's desk, just out of his reach. She explained that of course there was always a little honey left in the hives for the bees, but in the lean days of winter, they simply needed extra nourishment. She recounted how thrifty she was, but with so many hives, a lot of bees would need extra sugar. It would be inhumane to let them starve, and who would want that? She also noted that the government used beeswax to coat planes and other equipment, and to waterproof other items. Beeswax prevented rust. It was indispensable.

Addie didn't tell him she supplied none of her honey products to the government, and he failed to ask. Deacon couldn't take his eyes off those jars of honey.

"I could see the longing for that honey in his eyes," Addie later told Mimi, Derry, and Richie. "I informed him that honey helps all the poor housekeepers, keeping up their spirits and uniting them in a home-front cause. All it takes is a little extra sugar. He eventually saw it my way."

"And the two jars of honey?" Mimi asked. "Where are they?"

"Sweetening him up, I imagine. In the meantime, my bees will not go hungry."

This blatant, though minor, bribing of a ration board official did not escape Mimi. But it would be useless to argue the fine points of legalities with her landlady. Besides, to Addie, that honey was not a bribe, it was *educational*. A public service. Addie tiptoed around the laws and regulations, but she did not break them. Not technically, anyway. She knew people needed their small games, their feeling of winning once in a while. Her jars of honey kept society moving.

Who knew what would happen if Addie Richardson were unleashed on the world, instead of only her neighborhood in Alexandria, Virginia? The thought made Mimi laugh. One irony of the war was that even as more and more women filled jobs in factories and businesses, as they drove taxis and pumped gas, some men would never see them as the intelligent, resilient creatures they were.

ରେ

Mimi reserved Saturday mornings for her chores, including sweeping the basement and making sure the honey jars were clean. She liked to ponder the puzzle of Addie as she dusted the shelves. Weekends were also the time Addie let Mimi do her laundry. Mimi used the ringer washing machine and hung her laundry to dry outside, taking great care with her delicates, nightgowns and slips and underwear. During bad weather she draped her wet things over clotheslines in the basement. Richie's music helped the time pass.

Richie wasn't allowed in the cellar by himself. Addie feared he would break things, being a boy after all, and he was also instructed to stay out of the way when Mimi was down there.

"Mimi is working and she doesn't need your distraction," Addie said.

"I could help her," Richie had insisted.

"No, you couldn't."

As a compromise, Richie was allowed to sit at the top of the basement stairs and play his violin, though sometimes he chose the banjo instead. This morning he played her Irish jigs, "because they help a person work. I know, 'Honey in the Jar'!"

It was actually "Whiskey in the Jar," but Mimi thought his version was more appropriate. She sang along in her pleasant mezzo-soprano.

಩

Mimi's first experience with the honey harvest starred Addie Richardson as the maestro, running around in her canvas coat and veiled beekeeper's hat. Mimi was required to work, just like the rest of the family. It wasn't as if Addie gave her renter a choice; it was a given that the big September harvest was an all-hands-on-deck effort.

Besides, Mimi could never refuse a landlady who provided such tasty meals and sated her sweet tooth with every variation of honeyed delicacy, whether liquid or baked.

Addie provided Mimi an old beekeeper's overalls and veiled hat and set her to spinning the centrifuge, which extracted the honey. It was hot and messy work.

Even Richie was put to work, although he occasionally took a break to play his music on an older fiddle. "The Flight of the Bumblebee" seemed to be a favorite.

"Our queenie bee is fond of this tune," he told anyone who was willing to listen.

Some of the other women Addie had wrangled to help out were not nearly as fond of the tune as the queen bee, but he played it over and over. Addie paid a pittance, but her workers really came for the honey. She would give them a small allotment of jars, depending on the work they performed.

Mimi was stationed in a screened-in shed far from the hives, for which she was grateful. Despite the intense heat, there were no bees in there trying to protect their honey. Mimi wasn't afraid of the bees, but she didn't love them either. The shed was where she first encountered Kitty Hawkins, also covered from head to toe in canvas overalls and veiled bonnet. Kitty was experienced in honey-making, and she was endlessly patient with Mimi's questions and Richie's chattering.

"She is a fairy princess," Richie told Mimi. "She comes here for the harvest, but then she flies away. She doesn't let us see her very often, but she is like Rapunzel."

Kitty laughed. "My hair is not that long."

"Maybe not, but it is that beautiful."

Mimi didn't get a good look at their visiting "princess" until lunch break, when she took off the hat and unzipped the overalls to get some air and eat one of Addie's sandwiches. Small and delicate, and without makeup, with her hair in a braid, Kitty did look to Mimi like a fairy-tale creature, perhaps an elf.

"Why did you come for the harvest?" Mimi asked her.

"Not for the money, that's for sure." Kitty was small, but she could eat. She wolfed down a second sandwich. "But Addie's good people and I'm making good honey."

That September the harvest had been abundant, and it took days. Mimi started Friday after work and worked right through the weekend, with only a break for church on Sunday. She was never so glad to see Monday morning, and to work at a non-sticky desk, while Addie and the rest of her crew were still harvesting honey.

It was funny how people's lives crossed, Mimi reflected. She might have forgotten all about Kitty Hawkins, if the woman hadn't shown again up at the Chinquapin dance. She hadn't learned much about Kitty. She didn't even know where the woman worked or lived.

Now the cellar floor was swept, her laundry was drying, and the honey jars gleamed, reminding her of that harvest. Nothing about that experience had prepared her for the Kitty she'd met the previous evening. Mimi tried to put the whole episode out of her mind, but the taunts of those beastly men kept running through her mind.

Here, Kitty, Kitty.

EIGHT

"**D**RESSING UP" WAS unpatriotic, according to some people. Mimi suspected many of them were simply not up to the task. In her opinion, dressing up *was* patriotic and kept spirits up as well. Mimi sacrificed style on Saturdays, but not completely; standards had to be maintained.

Today she wore her jeans rolled up to her knees. Her crisply ironed plaid shirt was knotted at the waist, and she rolled up the sleeves. Her tooled-leather sandals from Mexico were old but comfortable, and she twisted her wild auburn waves up in a kerchief, leaving a few curls loose to frame her face. She wore Victory Red lipstick from a new tube.

A dollar and a key to her room occupied one pocket. In her other pocket were an older lipstick and a small comb. She also carried a small canteen of water on a leather shoulder strap; it was a hot day. Mimi might be mistaken for a torpedo factory worker, or Rosie the Riveter. Good enough for a stroll, she decided, and she didn't anticipate running into anyone she knew.

After a lunch of a fried Spam sandwich and canned cinnamon apples, with musical accompaniment from Richie, she headed out for a walk. Alexandria was endlessly fascinating to Mimi, a real East Coast city, with real history. And a real river. She strolled down the old Manassas Gap railroad line toward the Potomac. It was near St. Mary's graveyard, a prime firefly habitat, and she made a mental note to check it out at dusk.

Someday soon she planned to walk all the way to the river and try to visit the old lighthouse on Jones Point. It had been taken over by the Army Signal Corps, and according to the locals, the Army was working on classified communications there. Some type of war industry occupied most of the area, from Jones Point and the old Ford plant, now a Navy munitions factory, to the U.S. Naval Torpedo Station farther up the waterfront.

Down the river, off the George Washington Memorial Parkway at Fort Hunt, other war activities were ongoing, but no one was quite sure what they were. There were whispers of high-ranking German officers being held there. Perhaps the product of someone's imagination, but Mimi saw no reason it couldn't be true. "Loose Lips Sink Ships," the ubiquitous posters said, but the rumors persisted.

Roz, always quick with a tantalizing tidbit, had mentioned that bobbing up and down on the Potomac were several floating bordellos plying the world's oldest trade—servicing the servicemen. Business, Roz said, was booming. Kitty Hawkins might know something about these boats of ill repute. Mimi wondered whether she'd ever have the chance to ask her.

Mimi never tired of walking up and down Alexandria's pretty streets with their quaint architecture. Some of the homes were grand brick edifices, like the Richardsons' house. There were also tiny "spite houses," one a mere seven feet wide, built by the original owners in the side alleys next to their homes to stop foot traffic and carriages from pouring through.

Even a tiny spite house was valuable now, no matter how small. People were grateful for any place to lay their heads. The population boom affected all the towns surrounding the Nation's Capital. Washington itself, with a prewar population of half a million, had doubled in size. It was almost unimaginable to Mimi. She wondered again where Kitty Hawkins resided. For that matter, where did she work? Where was her cat house?

As if she had conjured Kitty up, Mimi saw the woman herself, emerging from a small brown brick pharmacy on Washington Street. Kitty gave no sign of recognition. She was wearing another cheap rayon frock, this one purple, with shiny worn patches on the seat, and ankle socks with peep toe wedge sandals. A blue kerchief was wound round her head like a factory worker. Mimi suspected it hid pin curls—or maybe she wanted to hide the platinum blond hair that drew men to her like moths to a flame.

Kitty sauntered all the way to Wythe Street, where she turned left. Mimi followed her. She didn't quite know why. Maybe it was what Roz had said about "cheap goods" and "Tobacco Road," and Kitty crying in the ladies' room, telling Mimi she wouldn't understand. Well, she wanted to understand. Her Grandma Eileen would want to know.

Kitty walked on for six blocks, then she turned right on West Street, to an unassuming brick bungalow next to an alley. She walked into the yard, but instead of going up to the door she detoured around to the back. The house wasn't far from the train tracks. On the right side of the tracks or the wrong side? Mimi had no idea.

Mimi passed the house, went around the corner, and turned into the alley, where she could see the yard behind the bungalow. No sign of Kitty. All she saw was a blocky concrete structure, its back wall flush with the alley. A gate in a low fence led from the alley into the yard. Mimi wouldn't quite call the structure a house, but it wasn't exactly a shed either. It was a squatty concrete block with four doors and four windows, a sagging electrical cord strung from the main house. Each section was barely large enough to hold a bed and a chair. The whole structure was painted a cheerful pale pink, but it still looked depressing.

Perhaps they were small living quarters, she thought, a sort of annex, and the main house was a rooming house? But even with a war going on and housing at a premium, these didn't look like rooms to let.

"Why, that looks like cribs," Mimi said to herself. "Crummy little cribs." Four cribs, like the ones Denver's notorious "soiled doves" had used when they plied their trade. Mimi wasn't as naïve as Roz thought. She'd been raised on her grandmother's tales, among them stories of Denver's once-notorious red-light district. The old bordellos with their tiny cribs as numerous as honeycombs were still there, now turned into offices or warehouses.

Mimi wasn't sure whether Grandma Eileen thought these stories were cautionary tales, or merely sensational, or simply an illustration that there were many kinds of people in this world—but she only told them out of earshot of Mimi's parents.

Grandma Eileen told her she had met more than a few soiled doves in the course of her church work. Why, she even knew Madam Mattie Silks, the most notorious Denver madam of them all. Just in passing, of course. Grandma Eileen always said Madam Silks couldn't be all that bad, because she provided a home for her aging "fallen flowers." Sort of an "old whores' home," her grandmother called it. Mattie Silks had also introduced Denver to jazz, hiring black piano players from New Orleans to play in her parlor. Grandma Eileen was very fond of jazz, as well as traditional Irish tunes. She was a constant scandal to Mimi's mother. But Mimi loved her raucous tales.

A prostitute in the Old West, Mimi had learned, worked and lived in a crib, a tiny room with a bed, a chair, and a trunk that held all her earthly possessions. There were probably more sad endings than happy. But there were few women on the early frontier, so a goodly number of Madam Silks' soiled doves succeeded in leaving that life, marrying, and having families.

These hardy magdalens were among the first white women on the frontier. They had a much larger hand in civilizing the men and the towns of the Old West than they were given credit for. Because they were the ones who had the babies, they were the ones who brought the churches and the schools for their children.

"And don't you know, when the miners were dying of smallpox and cholera, it was the magdalens who traveled into the mountains on donkeys. They nursed those sick men with not a thought to themselves," her grandmother said.

Mimi pondered this as she walked back to West Street, past the little bungalow. This strange setup behind the house told her that Kitty Hawkins was indeed "selling it," as Roz said. Mimi hated Roz being right. But why Kitty?

"You, girlie girl," she heard a man say to someone she couldn't see.

Mimi ducked into the yard next door, between the large azaleas and the boxwood hedges. Through a gap in the bushes she could see the four doors and windows of the cribs, but no one could see her. She hoped. A soldier popped out of one of the doors with a smile on his face. He rapped on the next door over.

"Hey, hurry it up, Dogface. We're due back at the base."

Mimi could see the four doorsteps and the shoes and feet that came and went. A sailor arrived and knocked loudly at another door. It opened and a woman's voice welcomed him in. She heard soft laughter. In a few minutes the sailor hurried out, adjusting his uniform trousers.

"So long, Kitty. See you next time."

Mimi couldn't see the woman, but she heard Kitty's voice.

"There won't be a next time, Lou. I'm clearing out. I won't be here when you get back."

"Well, I'll miss you, kid. Good luck." With that, Lou marched away.

Mimi caught sight of Kitty's feet in gold lamé mules, her toenails painted bright red. The feet didn't turn back to her crib. They walked straight toward the hedge.

"Get up, you," Kitty said. "What are you doing in there?"

"Hiding."

Mimi got to her feet and stepped out of the bushes, feeling idiotic. Kitty looked annoyed beneath her garish makeup. Her hair spilled over her shoulders in a froth of platinum curls. She was wearing a thin wrapper belted at the waist, apparently with nothing underneath.

"Doing a pretty poor job of it, I'd say, Mimi Smith."

"I haven't had enough practice, I guess."

"You plan on sneaking around on people for a living now?"

There was a new hardness to Kitty, but she seemed amused too.

"I don't have a very good answer."

Kitty laughed. "I guess you wouldn't."

"I saw you walking this way."

"And you decided to follow me, like a private eye out of a cheap detective magazine? I know that's what they do, because that's what I was reading last night. Till business picked up."

Mimi pulled her lipstick from her pocket as a peace offering. "I wanted to give you this. It's a better shade for you, a rosy tone that would look wonderful on you, dramatic but softer. Not garish. I usually have to wear a true red, because of my hair and skin."

Kitty rolled her eyes in exasperation, but she took the lipstick. She tried it on her wrist.

"You might be right. Thanks."

Mimi wrinkled her nose. "I smell like boxwood."

Kitty sniffed. "You do. It's just like cat pee. Serves you right. Why were you following me?"

"I'm sorry for following you. I just saw you on the street. I didn't believe you were a—"

"A whore?"

"A magdalen, my grandmother would say."

"Call it what you like."

"I never met anyone like you before. Not personally," Mimi said.

"I can safely say I've never met anyone like you either." Kitty tucked the lipstick in the pocket of her wrapper. "You better get out of here before someone thinks you're a working girl. Like me." Mimi felt her eyes grow big and round. "You never know. Some of these men haven't seen a woman in a long time. They'd give you a try, even if you looked like you could rivet their bomber together."

They were distracted by crib door number three suddenly opening. Another uniformed boy left with a smile on his face, followed by a woman rubbing her back. She spotted Kitty and frowned.

She couldn't have been more than twenty, but she had a tough look that had nothing to do with her unnatural brassy red hair and too-dark lipstick. She was small but muscular, and one of her arms sported an impressive scar from wrist to shoulder.

"She's a real street fighter, that one," Kitty said to Mimi. "Gretel. It's German or something. We all think she should change it, so she doesn't sound like some Kraut. GIs hate Krauts."

Freckles showed through the powder on Gretel's face, far more than on Mimi's. Her dark eyebrows were overly drawn, but her eyes were pale green, cold and calculating. The woman's dingy green wrap dress was unbuttoned almost to the waist. She wasn't wearing underwear either. Gretel was covered in sweat.

"It must be hot in there," Mimi commented.

"A little like Hell," Kitty agreed. "We got fans, but they don't help much. Everyone calls it the Chicken Shack."

"Better than the Cat House, I guess."

"Don't get me wrong. I don't think Gretel's bad all the way through, but I wouldn't turn my back on her. She swiped my best lipstick, so thanks for this one," Kitty said.

"She looks a little hard." Kitty, even with her tarted-up face on, could never look that scary.

"Those claws of hers can do real damage. We got into it one day. She thought I took her dough. It wasn't me. I mean, I've got principles. It was Polly and me set her straight. But there's no love between me and Gretel."

"And Polly, where's she?"

"Dead."

Mimi stopped still, her heart beating fast. She recalled the odd singsong rhyme she'd heard Lt. "Butter Bar" croon at the dance: *Polly's the dolly who fell on the tracks, Polly's the dolly who's not coming back.*

"What happened to her? When?"

"A month back. No one really knows whether she walked on the train tracks or was pushed."

"She was hit by a train?"

"That was the end result, yeah. They had to pick her up in pieces."

"Did she have a last name?"

"The one she went by was Brown. Not her own, but an easy name."

"How did it happen?"

"Far as I know, cops said it was an accident. Or suicide."

"Do you think someone pushed her?"

"You have an odd turn of mind, Mimi Smith." Kitty cocked one eyebrow at her. "I got to get out of this business."

"That's what you told the soldier. What was his name? Lou?"

"Yeah, Lou's a regular, at least until he's assigned out. He's a good guy. Efficient, quick. Takes the time to say hello and goodbye. Leaves a tip." Mimi hadn't expected this much detail. Her surprise must have shown. "Hey, it was never my plan to wind up like this," Kitty said.

"I'm sure it wasn't. I never thought—"

"I just wanted you to know that." Kitty lifted her head and listened. "Someone's coming. You better get out of the yard. I was kidding before. You look like a torpedo factory gal, you'll be fine once you're out on the sidewalk." She pointed the way.

Mimi turned to go. "I'm sorry, I didn't mean to spy on you at—at work—"

"Listen, you want to come visit me? Come to my boarding house, not here. Course I don't know why you would, but it's slightly more respectable. On Henry Street." She told Mimi the address. "I bunk with some of the other girls. At least it's got a couple of windows to catch a breeze." Kitty grinned. "And you could bring me some honey."

NINE

WHAT HAD GOTTEN into her? Mimi felt ashamed and embarrassed and in need of a bath with some strong soap, to eradicate the cat-pee scent of boxwood. She made it to King Street in a quick trot.

"Mimi, where are you going like a house on fire? What have you been up to?"

Mimi stopped to behold Franny, long limbed and lanky in her Saturday overalls, looking like she could rope a steer. Her strength and size no doubt came in handy at the torpedo factory. Franny was always friendly, like her Big Sky Country. Mimi stopped, short of breath.

"No place in particular. I've got things on my mind."

"And on your trousers."

Mimi stared at the mud and grass stains on her pants. "They were clean this morning."

"Looks like you've been having fun."

"Not really." She rubbed at her jeans.

"Spill, Smith. What's up?"

She didn't know what Franny would think. "Oh hell, Franny, what I am thinking is not fit for polite society."

"All the more reason to tell me. I'm no East Coast snob. Brighten my day. The more scandalous, the better."

"I just ran into Kitty Hawkins. I was following her, like some cheap detective in a pulp magazine."

"Kitty? The red dress at the dance last night? The one that got Roz so worked up?"

"That's the one."

"This sounds promising. You got a future as a detective?"

"The jury is out on that one."

"Why'd you follow her, Mimi?"

"Haven't a clue. I've never known anyone like her up close before."

Franny nodded. "I'm heading to the dime store. Want to get coffee and doughnuts at the counter?"

"I'm a mess," Mimi said.

"Think anyone cares? Look at me. You could be coming off a shift, like I am."

"You sure?"

"I could add a bit of grease on your cheek for authenticity, but you'll do."

"Very funny."

"Mimi, it's the dime store, not the Ritz."

The doughnuts were small and plain, and the coffee-chicory blend was watered down. Mimi was trying to make hers last. She fingered the heavy green Jadeite cup. There was something comforting about a cup of coffee, even bad coffee.

"You're saying she's a hooker?" Franny was asking. "Damn! That pretty girl in the cheap red dress? I mean, I know that's what Roz said, but Roz says a lot of things."

"Shh, keep it down." No one was looking at them. "Let's just call her a *magdalen*."

Mimi described the cheap concrete block shed where the women worked. The Chicken Shack.

"Makes sense it would be near the train tracks. Know why they call it a red-light district? Cause the train men would leave their red lamps hanging in the windows while they did their business."

"Franny, how you talk. And I already knew that. You're not shocked by all this?"

"I'm not bored either." Franny signaled for another cup of coffee. The dime store had no more doughnuts, so she settled for a piece of cherry pie. "We can split it. What on earth made you follow this woman?"

"Who knows? Maybe because she seemed so sad. So hurt. And those clothes! I thought maybe I could give her some, you know, fashion advice."

Franny laughed out loud. "I'm pretty sure she likes those trashy dresses, Mimi. But I might take your fashion advice sometime. Let you dress me up all elegant."

"You might regret that."

"I might. Might not."

Mimi smiled. Her friend was tall and lean and would look good in anything. "What about Tilly? You talked with her?"

"She heard Dave's brother is coming home. Dennis. He's got a leg wound. At least he's alive."

"Maybe they can share their misery."

"As long as misery *really* loves company. Roz told her to think about him having to deal with her death as well as Dave's, especially if she threw herself in the Potomac. At any rate, Tilly didn't walk the river last night, she was busy baking cookies for Dennis."

"Sometimes Roz can be so blunt, it can shake you up." The waitress set the pie between them with two forks. "Maybe it's a good sign."

"That's what I thought," Franny said after a bite. "Good pie too."

It wasn't as good as Addie's, Mimi thought, but it was good enough. Mimi was relieved that Tilly was thinking of someone else and not her own loss, but the whole episode with Kitty made her melancholy. She couldn't fix anything for Kitty, she knew that. The memory of that pink concrete sweatbox with no room to breathe refused to go away.

Later that day, from her third-floor perch in the Richardsons' house, Mimi watched the neighboring rooftops and a slice of the Potomac River. It was always milder by the river. She thought about poor Kitty, stuck in a horrible concrete cell. And Gretel, the "working girl" in the crib next door, was not to be trusted. What a place. And imagining two people on a tiny bed— Mimi tried to shake that thought out of her head. She reminded herself that the crib's bed was not for sleeping.

But had Kitty chosen this life? Or had she been driven to it by desperation? Mimi had chosen hers, so far. When she left home she had practically made her own emancipation proclamation.

"The war is on, I have to do my part, and I'm going to Washington, D.C.! There are plenty of jobs for women there."

"There are jobs for women in Denver," her father blustered. "First you have to go to college, now you drop out to do *this*? You ever gonna finish that degree?"

"After the war is over," Mimi said. "I will finish my degree."

Of course her mother said that wasn't *really* necessary, as long as she planned on getting married. She had already benefited from college's "finishing" effects. But Mimi's grandmother was all for it.

"You'll never know where your fortune lies, Mary Margaret, if you don't go out and look for it."

Her mother rolled her eyes. Mimi's parents didn't so much relent as throw their hands up in defeat. Mimi came from a long line of Irish women who had followed their own sense of right and wrong. Now it was her turn.

She had toyed with the idea of joining the women's military service, the Navy's WAVES, or maybe the women pilots. But two things stopped her. One was *rules*. Following all the rules and living with so many other women? Mimi preferred skirting the rules, especially when they made no sense to her. And the uniforms stopped her cold. She didn't think she could wear the same thing every day for years on end, no matter how smart they looked now.

Being a cog in the government's huge machine in the Office of Price Administration wasn't the most glamorous or noteworthy job, but there Mimi could serve her country in her own way. It was hard sometimes, working for an agency that made strict rules and restricted commodities for her fellow Americans, but she told herself it was for the good of the country. When friends held illicit ration parties, pooling their coupons for sugar and eggs to bake a cake for a birthday, Mimi just closed her eyes.

Did Kitty Hawkins tell herself she was serving her country?

No, Mimi decided, serving your country and servicing your men were two different things. Kitty must have had choices. Perhaps she made the wrong one.

To clear her head, Mimi opened her steamer trunk and pulled out her latest sewing project. It would be a dream of a dress—someday. It was going to be a glorious formal gown in the most heavenly shade of violet, not too blue, not too pink. It was a vibrant shade, but not a shout of a color. The jersey fabric was a dickens of a material and she struggled with it. Mimi had to use twice as many pins to keep it from sliding around while she was cutting the pattern.

Time to pin it on the dress dummy, to see it come together. She took her box of materials downstairs and gathered the sewing equipment she needed. She had doubts that the color would really look that good on her.

I'll know soon, Mimi thought.

Once just fabric and multiple pattern pieces stitched together, it was always a bit of a magic trick to see a dress take shape on the mannequin, coming together as if it had a life of its own. When Mimi was transforming the material into the gown, it felt as if her friend Gloria Adams, the future famous designer, was in the room with some fanciful pronouncement. She compared it to a cloud at sunset. Some violets were white and some violets were blue, Gloria had declared, but this color was stronger than pink and truer than blue.

Nevertheless, there was something elusive about this violet creation—and Mimi promised herself she would discover its secret.

TEN

*J*UMBLED THOUGHTS CROWDED her brain all night, making sleep elusive. The June heat didn't help, and Mimi kept tossing and turning. She told herself she might as well have headed to the USO and danced away her demons, but after the night before, she wasn't as eager as she might have been. She didn't need any more tragic women crossing her path.

Though she usually attended an earlier Mass on Sunday mornings, she barely made it to the last service at St. Mary's and slid into a pew in the back. She was still yawning when she caught sight of Kitty Hawkins in one of the front transepts. Mimi had a one-sided mental conversation with her Grandmother Eileen, who reminded her that Kitty had as much right as anyone to sit in the front row on the right side of the altar.

Kitty wore a brown dress, not flattering, almost frumpy, but perhaps that was deliberate. She had covered most of her braided blond hair and a short veil obscured half her face. Camouflage must be a useful skill for anyone in Kitty's profession, Mimi decided, and she seemed to have mastered it. Mimi recited the prayers by heart while pondering other things, from fashion to wondering whether Kitty had Sundays off. When they emerged from the church, Kitty fell in step with her. Mimi was gratified to see Kitty wearing the lipstick she had given her. She was right about the color, that rosy red was much prettier.

"Aren't you the fashion plate," Kitty commented.

Mimi wore a deep rose sleeveless polished cotton dress with a white eyelet jacket, trimmed in the rose material. Her straw picture hat sported a pink band that she could switch out to give it different looks. She and Kitty both wore short cotton gloves and carried compact purses.

"Thanks. It's summery."

"Another one of your friend's designs?"

"Gloria recommended the pattern and the material. I sewed it. And yours?"

"Believe it or not, this was my best dress back home," Kitty said ruefully. "Now it's my don't-you-dare-look-at-me dress. Perfect for church."

Mimi took off her hat and shook out her hair. This didn't cool her off, and she put it back on. Kitty's hat with the veil stayed in place. The heat wasn't bothering her.

"I didn't realize you were Catholic," Mimi said.

"I don't claim to be a good Catholic. But you go where you know, you know? I like the Latin and the hymns here at St. Mary's. Besides, I don't like all the whooping and hollering at some of these crazy churches. The only one around here who would really recognize me is Addie, and they go to some Baptist church."

"Do you sing?"

"A little. I thought about joining the choir at St. Mary's, but what if someone found out about me? I couldn't chance it."

"Hey, you want to get a soda or something?" Mimi asked. "I know the Majestic on King Street is open."

Mimi had skipped breakfast. And at a diner you could almost always count on doughnuts.

"You're living kind of dangerously, Mimi Smith, being seen with the likes of me."

"I'll plead ignorance. You think anyone would recognize you?"

"No one who would admit it." Kitty giggled. "And coffee sounds good. I got plenty of ration coupons too, if you want some breakfast. Some waitresses like to take them as tips. They're worth more than a dime."

"You have extra ration coupons?" Nobody Mimi knew had *extra* ration coupons.

"Oh yeah, some of the bigwigs hand 'em out like candy. Big spenders."

Mimi said nothing. She was sure her duties at the OPA didn't include policing Kitty's tips, or anything about Kitty. The Majestic Café was jammed and the waitress barely glanced up from her order pad, though she seemed to consider Kitty a regular. They ordered coffee, scrambled eggs, and toast, but there was no bacon today, not for any amount of money or coupons. Kitty even gave her a glimpse of her coupon stash.

Mimi told herself she'd be a good investigator for the OPA. *Sure,* she thought, *when pigs fly.*

"Do you mind if I ask you a question?" she said, digging into her eggs.

Kitty arched a delicate eyebrow. "Shoot. I reckon you can't ask anything I haven't heard before."

"I've heard there are actually boats on the Potomac that are, um, floating houses of—of ill repute." It sounded silly the moment she said it.

"Boats of ill repute? No! Not really?!" Kitty laughed.

Mimi laughed too. "You're funny, you know that?"

"We're both funny. But the boats? That's true. Might be a dozen or more. Some are pretty scummy, but Madam Cherry's Treasure, now that one is different."

Madam Cherry's Treasure, Kitty explained, was a crisp white houseboat with a pink roof and pink shutters. The key to the floating brothels' success was a quirk of geography. They moored on the Virginia side of the Potomac, but Virginia had no jurisdiction over the river, or the boats. The entire Potomac belonged to either the District of Columbia or the state of Maryland, right up to the Virginia waterline. And Maryland and D.C., miles away across the river, didn't care about the "ladies of the waters" on the Virginia side. As a result, the busy floating pleasure palaces were seldom hassled by police.

"You might not believe it, Mimi, but lots of folks think we're practically performing a civic duty, satisfying all these hordes of lusty men, heading for the war. Who knows how many innocent women they would prey upon? It's the old lock-up-your-daughters thing. But women like me, we're nobody's daughters." Mimi was silent. "Hey, sis, you asked."

"I did." Mimi sipped her weak coffee to keep from asking more stupid questions.

"I worked on Madam Cherry's Treasure for a time," Kitty said wistfully. "One job I wish I could have kept."

"Really? Why?"

"It was nice. The boat's real pretty, oriental carpets, pink sofas, a bar in the corner for the clientele. It's sort of like a big floating house, with steps down to the party room and steps up to the girls' rooms. Four of them, with windows. At least twice as big as the ones at the Chicken Shack. Sometimes you could just lay there and look at the water. It was peaceful. Sometimes."

Mimi tried not to look surprised. "Did you have problems with the—clientele?"

"Not on the Treasure. Mostly officers, not enlisted men. Older guys with money to spend."

"It was better than the pink palace over on West Street?"

"There are sewers nicer than that cat house. No carpets, no sofas, no bar, though I always try to keep some whiskey on hand. It calms the new recruits."

"Whiskey, really? Where do you get that?" It was among the items strictly rationed by the OPA, though Caribbean rum was still flowing freely.

"Don't you worry. I got a supplier."

A legal supplier? Or one who charged way over the regulated price? Mimi wondered. Liquor violations reports poured into OPA from all over the country. Or Kitty's whiskey might be homemade moonshine, though where someone would find enough sugar to make it these days, Mimi could only guess. She wasn't about to press Kitty; she wasn't one of OPA's black marketeering investigators, and besides, it was Sunday. Everybody deserved a day off.

"If it was so nice, why aren't you still there?"

"That darn river. I was always seasick on the water, even though I don't get sick when I'm in the water. I grew up in the hills and hollers, never even been on a boat before. Anyway, I wound up working in town. We call it the Chicken Shack, because we're all cooped up, like chickens." She laughed. "But there's plenty of roosters to go around."

ଔ

The tantalizing aroma of roasting chicken greeted Mimi before she opened the front door. She was glad she had taken a long walk after her late breakfast with Kitty.

Her landlady had embraced the idea of a chicken in every pot, and she tried to have chicken as often as possible on Sundays. It wasn't always easy to find, and the butcher was often out of meat. But Addie was resourceful and not adverse to bartering, and she counted a number of farmers among her friends. She had connections.

Sunday suppers at the Richardsons' house were always served at four in the afternoon in the dining room, with the good china. Richie played requests. Mimi wouldn't dream of missing it, and she didn't mind helping with the dishes afterward.

Addie Richardson endeavored to make Sundays special, to keep things as normal as possible. Today's dessert was peaches and a dollop of whipped cream. The peaches this summer were especially sweet and succulent. Despite the Bible saying Sunday was a day of rest, Addie hardly ever took a deep breath. She reserved rest for sitting in her favorite chair with a sweet tea after the sun went down. She rarely touched spirits, but on occasion she consented to a sherry, or even a brandy, with her husband Derry.

Addie was a pragmatic person. Bad times were something through which you battled and survived. In her childhood in Forgotten Creek, West Virginia, Addie's family never went hungry, and she always had clean clothes to wear. She counted her blessings. But when an earnest young lawyer from Alexandria, Virginia, came to town on business, Addie set her sights on him.

Mimi had heard Addie tell this tale many times.

Derry Richardson been sent by his law firm to oversee a contested will. The case kept him busy researching old documents in the town's offices, where Addie worked as a secretary. She was proud of her post and her secretarial certificate, earned over in Morgantown. At twenty-two, Addie had already refused the few eligible men in town, making her practically an "old maid." Like every other red-blooded American, she believed she was meant for better things. Like young Derry Richardson.

Derry was a good catch, but not an easy one. Addie was a little on the plain side, though she dressed well in bright colors, and a little on the plump side. But when he tasted her cooking at a church supper— Well, that was that. Plus, she was happily enthusiastic about his courting, and his lovemaking. Derry enjoyed buying things for Addie, like a new hat or a dress—her "fancy feathers," he called them—and a diamond wedding ring.

They counted themselves luckier than most in their big house on St. Asaph Street, the house Derry inherited from his father, who had inherited it from his father. The home dated from 1840, Addie pointed out to visitors, as witnessed by a well-worn 1840 silver dollar set in the top of the banister's newel post. A local custom, she explained, practiced in the finer Virginia homes.

Their daughter Julia was married and lived near Baltimore, where she worked at the Martin Company, building airplanes for the war effort.

"Imagine that, wearing slacks and working on the wiring on those big planes," Addie would say. "Such a little bitty thing! She never gave us a lick of trouble. Smart, too."

Mimi hadn't met the amazing Julia yet, but she looked forward to it.

Addie also lavished love on their son Richie, whose uniqueness just set another challenge for her. Even as a toddler he was beating rhythms on every surface. When he was five, she found him an old fiddle to play with, and soon their son started to play without instruction. Addie counted Richie as a gift from a God with a peculiar sense of humor. Derry accepted Richie in the way he accepted Addie, with bemusement.

Addie was one of the more formidable characters Mimi had ever met.

"You're back late," Addie said to Mimi.

"But still in time for supper."

"I had to help with the table setting," Richie told Mimi, before she'd had a chance to set her hat and purse down.

"I bet you did a good job," Mimi said.

"I did." He glowed with pride. "It was easy, but I do it 'just so.' The napkins are 'just so' and the silverware too. That's important. May I escort you in, Miss Mimi?"

They all sat down and joined hands in a nondenominational prayer, to a feast of perfectly roasted chicken, and from Addie's victory garden, fresh vegetables and a salad.

Mimi dutifully wrote letters home once a week, knowing that her chatty missives were not as important to them as the ones from her brother, in officer training in the Army Air Forces. She told herself she shouldn't feel closer to Addie and Derry and Richie than her own family (with the exception of Grandma Eileen, who wrote back faithfully), yet there were times she did.

The Richardson house was filled with music, not the aggressive debates her family enjoyed. Sometimes Richie would listen to the radio and then, with never a mistake, play the same songs on his violin or banjo. It was as if the music traveled into his ears and out through his fingers.

Mimi and Derry would sometimes talk about his work and the law. He wasn't used to seeing women in the courtroom, some even working as attorneys, but he admitted that in these troubled times, everyone needed to help out in any way they could. He was still amazed to see women pumping his gasoline and washing his Buick's windows.

After dinner, Mimi was free to use the dining room table to cut her pattern pieces. She would piece them together while listening to Richie's little concerts. Tonight, she continued to drape the violet gown on Addie's dress form, which Mimi had already adjusted to fit her own trim shape.

It kept her hands busy, but it couldn't stop her thinking about Kitty's stories and the women she worked with. Polly Brown's death was particularly troubling. What on earth would induce a woman to walk in front of a train? Mimi compared Tilly's melodramatic desire to throw herself in the Potomac with Polly Brown's completed suicide by train—both awful. Surely there were other ways to kill yourself, quicker and less painful. And she could have chosen to live. If she hated her profession and her life, couldn't she have done something else, run away, made a fresh start?

Or was it really suicide? Mimi jumped. She had accidentally stabbed herself with a pin.

ELEVEN

*K*ITTY HAWKINS LIVED in a world where women died on railroad tracks by choice, or possibly by someone else's hand. They slept with a new man every day, or maybe even every hour. They were manhandled and beaten by violent customers. They were whistled at and catcalled in public. They lived on the edge, and sometimes they died there.

Compared to Kitty's work, Mimi's job was tame. She had regular hours, most of the time, and the only danger was being bored to death. Not that she'd admit it. That would be unpatriotic.

She tried to keep her mind on her work Monday morning, but her thoughts kept tracking back to the woman Kitty called Polly Brown, who was killed by a train. Polly Brown, whose name wasn't even her own. Would anyone speak for her? And then there was all that whiskey Kitty seemed to be able to lay her hands on so easily. Surely it wasn't acquired through legal means. Mimi held on to Kitty's pronouncement that she intended to leave "the Life." Did she have an escape route? Would the people who controlled her life let her go?

Mimi told herself to keep her mind on her work.

Although Mimi worked at the OPA as a stenographer, she had hopes of moving up to a better position than just one of the "steno girls." Or the "word wizards," as they called themselves. Much of the populace only knew OPA as the agency that kept them from enjoying the goods they were used to consuming. And kept them from overcharging someone for their spare room.

In August 1941, with an eye toward the coming war, President Franklin Delano Roosevelt had issued an Executive

Order that established the Office of Price Administration to prevent war profiteering. The government would tell Americans what they could buy and how much it could cost. And Americans didn't like it.

Mimi often wished she'd chosen some agency more exciting than OPA, and less resented. For every housekeeper proud to sacrifice "for the boys," there were many others exasperated to give up small luxuries, to stand in line at the butcher's only to be told there was no meat this week. OPA would never be the Miss Popularity of government agencies. As if Mimi had had many choices—even in wartime Washington, good jobs were hard to find. At least she didn't have to wear overalls and tie up her hair.

But OPA was performing a real service. Mimi wondered if Eddie Falcone's parachute—the one that failed to open—was deliberately sabotaged. Did someone cheat the government by making shoddy parachutes out of substandard materials—and cause Eddie's death? Could the OPA's web of fabric regulations, despised though they were, help prevent another flier's death?

While rationing was grudgingly accepted by most, something tangible they could do for the war effort, as the weeks dragged on and the months seemed endless, their enthusiasm dimmed. *No more nylon stockings?!* The government needed *all* the nylon and silk to make parachutes? It seemed like a small thing, but women fought over the last available nylons. Women took all their money out of the bank and bought as many pairs as they could. They caused riots in department stores across the country.

Rayon was the new "wonder fabric," but it was a poor substitute for nylon and silk. Satin and silk were theoretically available for wedding gowns, but supplies were limited. It was a lucky bride who could find a decommissioned silk parachute for her wedding gown, a gown whose fabric might have sailed through French skies.

Gasoline, tires, and canned goods were also caught in the rationing scheme, as were fine woolens and leather. And now the government had announced shoes would only be manufactured in six colors: black, white, navy, and three shades of brown. And you could buy only two pairs of leather shoes per year. Fashion designers and manufacturers were quick to fill the void with substitutes, like canvas or other fabric shoes, with cork soles. What fashion-following female could survive on two pairs of shoes a year?

Being an ace stenographer and a champion shorthand-taker at OPA, Mimi didn't merely transcribe things, she learned things. And she rarely forgot a fact, especially an interesting fact. For instance, she was one of the few people in America who knew that nylon stockings were still being secretly manufactured at one factory—for the specific purpose of paying spies. Around the world, nylons were more valuable than gold, and they traveled better too; for example, concealed in the lining of a spy's clothing.

Gold was heavier—and noisier.

Sadly, Mimi had no one to tell this fact to. Being a spy would be a much more exciting job, she often thought, if you lived to tell the tale. But that tale might never be told, as those working for the Office of Strategic Services had to swear an oath of secrecy.

People might never know much about the OSS, but they knew where to find the OPA, in Washington, D.C., and around the country. They had the addresses. OPA had provoked legions of active complainers and indignant letter writers, such as a certain Mrs. Edna Devers, who regularly took it upon herself to address her florid letters directly to President Roosevelt, laying out her bitter complaints against OPA. Mrs. Devers ran a small apartment building in one of the Western regions. According to OPA investigators, she kept shoddy records to hide the fact she charged exorbitant rents, far above OPA's price ceilings.

"Your investigators Claire Burgundy and Della Thomas have nothing better to do than harass a poor widow in troubled times..." Mrs. Devers's letter, like many others, had been directed back from the White House to the Office of Price Administration for review.

If people were unhappy with making do with dinners of home-grown vegetables and one bite of meat, OPA officials were equally unhappy—with juries who failed to take their violations seriously, and judges who issued fines and jail sentences that were a mere slap on the wrist. Or as her boss, George Prescott, was fond of saying, "Another damn case down the drain. We nailed the bastard dead to rights, and for what?" Prescott would sigh a great sigh and reach for his pipe.

Mimi had her eye on something better than a stenographer's job, sitting on a hard metal chair, working at a small metal desk, surrounded by gray metal file cabinets. Her skills and intelligence quickly separated her from the pack, and she was assigned to Prescott, an attorney overseeing investigations. How long before she could move up into an assistant investigator slot, she wondered, or even to a full investigator?

She knew there would be bumps in the road. If she proved too competent as Prescott's Girl Friday, he wouldn't want to move her up. He was already becoming a little too dependent on her. And she couldn't look too eager, as if she'd claw her way over anyone in her path.

Yet among the many potential pitfalls in her path, Mimi's gender wasn't one of them.

Women weren't limited to the secretarial pool, not with the war on and so many men in the services. And in a brand-new government agency, there were fresh opportunities for women. OPA had many female supervisors, attorneys, investigators, and assistant investigators.

But when she approached George about moving up, he'd reply, "Why, you haven't been here any time at all, Mary Margaret. Less than a year. Best to learn the ropes first." Mimi knew all about the ropes. The ropes were holding her back. He took out his pipe, filled it and tamped it down, enjoying the ceremony of it. Mimi waited. "It's not that you're not talented.

I'm sure you could be an excellent assistant investigator. Someday."

George Prescott was a tall lanky man whose face grew sharper and his body leaner as the war dragged on. Caught between generations, he was too old to enlist, too young to retire. He wore his salt-and-pepper hair combed straight back, and his pencil-thin mustache punctuated his craggy face and hazel eyes.

Mimi assumed his style was inspired by movie stars, like Douglas Fairbanks Jr. and Errol Flynn, but George was not movie-star handsome. George was presentable enough in the morning, but by the end of the day, every hair was out of place, his tie was crooked, and his vest misbuttoned, like a badly dressed scarecrow. He was married to a tall and equally lean woman named Blanche, from a farm in Kansas. Instead of fattening up her husband, she too spent her days working for the war effort.

"There's always law school," Mimi told him. She would have to finish her bachelor's degree first, but she knew she was smart enough to be an attorney. If George Prescott can do it, she thought, I can do it too.

"Maybe now, but what happens when the boys come marching home? No one's going to want to hire a woman lawyer then."

She felt her blood pressure rise as she bit back her response. Besides, not all those men would be coming home. Too many would be traveling home in a flag-draped coffin.

"I need some coffee, George." He nodded and puffed away on his pipe.

Mimi marched down the hall to their break room. There was an old electric coffee pot which had seen better days, but there was no coffee to be had at OPA's offices. Some of her coworkers brought in their flavorless used tea bags. And because Britain had reportedly, and bizarrely, bought up the available world supply of tea, there would be no more of that black drink for the foreseeable future.

Mimi came prepared with a small tin of Postum from her desk. It was a supposedly healthy (and unrationed) concoction of powdered wheat bran and molasses to mix with boiling water. If she measured carefully, one tin would make about fifty cups.

"Drink something hot, Mimi, and ponder the wisdom of telling people what you really think. If you still feel it must be said, then you go right ahead." A little wisdom from Grandma Eileen. This might take more than one cup of Postum, Mimi decided.

She sat down at the metal table in the corner, so she could keep her eye on the door. Her time would come, she told herself. She could wait a little longer. Besides, George Prescott was by no means the worst boss at OPA, and she preferred his pipe smoke to some of the other men's godawful cigars.

Mimi called him Mr. Prescott in meetings, but he didn't generally require such formality. He wasn't a petty tyrant like so many bureaucrats, men who let a dash of power go to their heads like a double martini. He was a dedicated Democrat, with liberal ideas—except when it came to women's roles. George wasn't intentionally unkind. He was just a man. An old-fashioned man.

But you can't put the genie back in the bottle, Mimi knew. It was 1943. And she was headed for bigger things than a stenographer's pad. There were women, she was sure, who would be happy to scuttle back into the kitchen after the war, when the men came marching home. But how would they feel, she wondered, when they no longer had their independence, and their own money? With just her husband's "allowance" to run the household, feed the family, and clothe herself? Begging for crumbs, while he was buying himself new golf clubs?

Mimi's grandmother, from a long line of strong and determined Irish women, always counseled her to have her own money set aside, money no man could get his hands on. Even her mother had a secret stash of cash hidden away. Mimi started saving her pennies early, from babysitting jobs and working at a soda fountain. When her parents threatened to withhold funds over her plans to leave home, she had a tidy sum saved up for travel to Washington, D.C.

Mimi Smith longed to explore the world, and Washington was just a start. She was happy to have a job in the war effort, and a job that gave her a window into what was going on in the world. Yet her biggest single regret about her job at the Office of Price Administration: *the building*.

When she arrived for her first interview, she was horrified to find OPA was not housed in one of the Capital City's many beautiful older government buildings, replete with columns and cornices, statues and stately decorations. The OPA and the Census shared a bland, boxy, modern edifice at Second and D Streets, Southwest, known at first as the General Federal Office Building. It was immense and ugly, a six-story eyesore thrown up hastily in 1939 for desperately needed office space. Mimi hated it.

Her friend Franny often pointed out that *some* people appreciated her building. It was so *clean*. And *modern*.

"Modern? It's not even Art Deco," Mimi complained. "It's more like Art Bleccho. Even the Naval torpedo factory has bigger windows! And a view of the river!"

There were much more attractive buildings nearby. Mimi was always the first to volunteer to walk documents over to other agencies, and she spent many lunch hours strolling along the National Mall, taking in the majesty of the Capitol and the quirkiness of the Smithsonian Castle and the museums. The most valuable artworks had been moved away from D.C. for safekeeping, but the museums remained open, even adding hours. I may not be a Smithsonian anymore, she thought, but those are still my museums too.

Most weekdays, Mimi caught the bus from Alexandria into D.C. Sometimes she was even lucky enough to find a seat. Like everything else in Washington, the buses were full to bursting. There were only two bus stops before hers, but her bus was usually packed. Where did all these people came from, she

wondered, all those cities and towns? All joined together for
one goal: to win the war.

Mimi struggled to stay upright as the driver careened
around the city's streets with his heavy load. She held on to her
shoulder bag and lunch box, usually containing a sandwich
wrapped in reused wax paper and a piece of fruit, packed by
Addie.

Now she sipped her second cup of Postum in the break
room and wondered once again about Kitty. Where was she
living? Where was she getting her hootch to calm down her
customers? And would OPA care? Mimi had once ventured the
radical idea to George Prescott that a bit of minor flouting of
the rationing regulations wasn't all that bad.

"Don't kid yourself, sister," George growled. "Selling an
extra pound of sugar or overpricing a bottle of whiskey may
seem minor, but people commit much bigger crimes and cheat
every which way just to keep the black market going. Other
people suffer, because they can't get ahold of legal goods or
afford black market prices. It's simply unfair."

"It's not like it's murder," Mimi had answered.

"I wouldn't be too sure about that. People commit all kinds
of crimes, for all kinds of reasons. There's murder afoot
wherever money is involved."

"But you're always complaining that people just get slapped
on the wrist."

"And it's a damn shame. Too many of our violations are just
misdemeanors. But when we get big cases, sometimes they can
be tried under other laws as felonies. Just because something
ends up in a higher court doesn't mean OPA didn't uncover it
in the first place. Loads of big crime prosecutions have started
with our own investigators here at OPA."

"Like what? What crimes? You mean even murders?"

"OPA never gets the glory," George had rumbled on,
ignoring her questions. "We're the bad guys! Because we won't
give Mrs. Jones enough sugar to bake her green apple pie. Mr.
Jones can't have his morning coffee. Junior can't tear off to

lover's lane with his girlfriend, burning up gas and wearing out tires." He puffed grumpily on his pipe. Mimi sighed.

The sun pouring in through the break room windows fell on a discarded copy of *The Washington Star*. Nothing brought the war home like the daily news—dispatches from journalists like Ernie Pyle, writing about the Army Medical Corps in North Africa, or photos of bombing expeditions in LIFE magazine, or that troubling picture of a bullet-ridden B-24 Liberator bomber in *Esquire*. Mimi remembered closing the magazine and setting it face down, her hands trembling. She hated to think of her lost Eddie and his last moments in his plane, just before jumping into the vastness wearing a parachute that would not open.

It was a crazy world, Mimi thought. News came from overseas that seemed unbelievable, but the unbelievable was everywhere. People had their lives turned upside down. War did crazy things to people and made some brave, others crazy. Sometimes both.

Even quiet Mrs. Martin, who used to be Mrs. Millie Goldstein, one of Addie's honey harvest helpers. She lived down the street from the Richardsons. She had told Addie (and Addie had told Mimi) the heroic tale of how she made it out of Germany in the Thirties, after the Nazis came to power. The Goldsteins were Jewish, but they weren't religious. Millie's husband was a respected university professor in Berlin, and she was acceptably blond. They felt safer than most. Still, her husband took the precaution of arranging for passports in her maiden name, Martin, instead of the more identifiably Jewish Goldstein. They made plans to leave.

But they waited too long.

One night two men in Nazi uniforms came to the door and escorted her husband away in the dark. Millie Goldstein never saw him again. Rumors started circulating in the neighborhood that she would be among the next wave of Jews swept up by the Nazis. She was being called a dangerous radical. She was being watched. No one knew where the rounded-up people were being taken, but Millie knew she couldn't wait any longer. She had a six-month-old child.

One summer's day she put her infant son in his pram, setting him gently on top of a small mattress stuffed with all her money, valuables, and identification papers. She gathered a few other necessities: an extra pair of sturdy walking shoes, her winter coat, a hiker's rucksack, and a canteen.

Millie Martin Goldstein tried not to think about the danger on every side, she simply placed one foot in front of another, a young mother out walking with her baby. Step by step. Slowly she passed through cities, small towns, and farm country, sometimes paying for a room at a hostel, sometimes settling in for the night among the trees and haystacks, quieting her crying child with a song. Her calves grew hard as her body grew lean. She wore out her first pair of shoes, and her first pram. Sticking to the back roads, she tried not to think about anything except keeping her feet moving—until she crossed the border into the Netherlands. Eventually she made it to Britain, and finally to the United States and Alexandria, Virginia, where she had family.

Millie had walked halfway across Europe in three months, pushing her son in a pram.

"Worse than anything I ever heard of in Forgotten Creek," Addie said to Mimi, shaking her head. She welcomed Millie Martin into her crew of honey harvesters, and she was one of Addie's best workers. Millie's baby, the one in the pram, was nearly ten years old now. Millie lost track of the rest of her family when the Nazis crushed the Warsaw Ghetto. If Addie added a little extra honey to Millie's pay, no one seemed to mind.

Mimi finished her Postum and carried the newspaper back to her desk. Headlines highlighted riots in California. Soldiers and sailors and even civilians in Los Angeles were attacking Mexican and Black men over their distinctive "zoot suits," baggy suits in loud colors with long coats and voluminous trousers. The white servicemen's flimsy excuse was that all that excess material was "unpatriotic." The newspapers were calling these skirmishes the Zoot Suit Riots, with horrifying reports of men's clothes being torn off in the street fighting. L.A. had closed the city to all servicemen.

These zoot suits seemed to have lit the flames of racial hatred. They were a colorful flag of identity for minority groups. Now an L.A. city official was calling on the War Production Board to step in and investigate the zoot suiters' "fabric violations." George Prescott would not be happy about this turn of events. Even First Lady Eleanor Roosevelt weighed in on the Zoot Suit Riots, calling them out as sheer racism. She said the country hadn't done enough to address these problems.

Mimi showed the newspaper headline to her boss. He brushed it aside.

"Her! Don't bring that woman up in my office. That ugly, interfering female—"

Mimi stared him down. "Eleanor Roosevelt is the First Lady of the United States! And she can't help how she looks. She never had braces, you know, even if her family was rich enough."

George Prescott reached for his pipe again. "Almost time to go home, Mary Margaret."

Mimi stood her ground. "Sometimes I wonder if I'd be more valuable in the Navy."

George's pipe froze in midair. "You wouldn't be thinking of leaving us, would you?"

"I'm not sure," Mimi answered. "I don't know how much good I'm doing here."

"You're valuable here, Smith. I know it doesn't always feel like it. But remember, you're working for the United States government. It's a privilege."

Mimi stalked back to her own little metal desk in the office next door. One of the other stenographers, Sally Post, buttonholed her on the spot.

"Mimi! Guess the latest rumor!"

"I couldn't possibly. Rumors grow like grass around here."

Mimi liked Sally because Sally had even more freckles than she did and not just on her nose. Sally wore her long brown hair pulled back in a ponytail, with clips to hold the flyaways. Her lipstick had long since been chewed off and her blue cotton gingham dress was limp from the heat.

"Coffee! Roosevelt's going to stop rationing coffee! We'll be able to buy all the coffee we want. Sweet hot coffee!" She closed her eyes in anticipation and inhaled the aroma of an imaginary cup of java. "Let the Brits have their weak tea. We're gonna have coffee again." Sally started singing the "Java Jive."

"You're kidding me. How reliable is this rumor?" Mimi could smell it in anticipation.

Sally smiled and wiggled her index finger to come closer. She whispered, "I just so happened to overhear the head of OPA mention to his secretary that we have ration books already printed with coffee coupons—that *won't be needed.* Coffee! I can practically taste it. Now I might actually wake up before this war is over."

"If you can find any coffee on the shelves. Remember the nylons?"

"Let me enjoy this one moment, would you, Smith? I'll find me some real coffee if I have to steal a tank and hijack a grocery truck."

The war was doing funny things to people. Mimi lifted her cup to Sally in salute.

"And when I visit you in jail, Sally, we'll always have Postum."

TWELVE

"*L*OOKING MIGHTY ELEGANT, Mimi," Addie said. "Where are you planning on wearing such a gown?" "I have no idea. I have to finish it first." Mimi had been constructing the violet dress for a long time before she was able to drape it over Addie's dress form. Now she was lifting the material here and there, up and down, fitting it snugly to the form. "I hope I won't be too old to wear it by the time I finish it."

The dishes had been cleared away and the dining room transformed into Mimi's sewing studio. It was a bright and cheerful room, and the table was large enough to accommodate all the measuring, marking, and cutting. Mimi was especially grateful for the use of Addie's sewing machine, which normally was tucked away in a small sewing table, disguised by a lace tablecloth and a vase full of flowers from the garden.

Even if Mimi could have afforded a sewing machine, there were no new machines to be found. The Singer Manufacturing Company was producing such warlike machinery as M1 Carbine rifle receivers, Norden bomb sights, and Model 1911 pistols. Good for repelling Nazis, but not so good for creating clothes.

The gown would be stunning, if Mimi ever completed it, jersey in a vibrant shade of violet that reminded her of orchids. She had fought with the slippery material from day one. But dealing with stubborn fabric was the perfect antidote to a long trying Monday at the OPA.

Even with the inevitable pinpricks.

"Ouch! My fingers feel like they've been through a cheese grater," Mimi complained.

Addie laughed. Sewing simply wasn't one of her talents. She had happily given Mimi free reign over her sewing machine and dressmaker's form, gifts from her late mother-in-law. Addie considered sewing a delicate kind of torture. In the early days of her marriage, she had dutifully tried to stitch a few things together. The uneven yellow-and-green curtains in the kitchen were testimony to her efforts.

Derry came home one day to find his young wife sweating over her sewing machine, tearing her hair, and swearing. "Darling," he announced, "of all the laws in this country, there isn't a single one that states Adeline Richardson must master this iron monster."

Addie stopped mid-seam on that forgotten project and made love to her husband in the middle of the afternoon. She smiled at the memory.

"I'm glad you're getting some use out of these things, Mimi."

"I don't know what I'd do without them." After all, she couldn't go dancing every night, and working on this extravagant violet gown kept her mind off the world and all its troubles.

Mimi wiped her forehead and took a step back to admire her creation. The long slim skirt was attached to the bodice with a wide cummerbund waistband that dipped up under the bust. The set-in sleeves had presented a huge challenge, and Mimi had muttered many swear words under her breath. Now the gown draped gracefully on the dress form, as if to mock her earlier efforts.

"You're making real good progress," Addie remarked. "Such a nice violet color."

"I guess there will have to be an inaugural ball, or something like that." She took up a piece of sparkling sequined fabric to trim the cummerbund. Richie came in with his violin.

"That looks like a princess would wear it!"

He was right. It would suit royalty, or a Hollywood star. He played "The Sleeping Beauty Waltz" in its honor and bowed to the dress form as if dancing with it.

Mimi began to hand-stitch the trim on the gown while Richie played waltzes. Addie sipped her sweet tea and Derry nursed his bourbon on the rocks. He restricted himself to one drink most evenings. He was a connoisseur of fine bourbon, but the ever-present war made it difficult to find "the good stuff."

Mimi had labored on the gown many evenings after work. Now it was nearly finished, except for the hem and some bits of trim. They marked Mimi's progress, as "the Princess," as they started calling the gown, seemed to become another member of the family.

 C3

On Thursday after work, Mimi opened the door to the sound of vacuuming. Richie was nowhere to be found. The vacuum's sound hurt his heart, he always said, as well as his ears. It was more likely he was afraid of Evangeline Williams, the no-nonsense part-time housekeeper who piloted the family Hoover over the floors and oriental carpets. Evangeline was another intermittent member of the household, a local colored woman whose disdain could freeze anyone on the spot.

Before the war, Evangeline had worked full-time for the Richardsons, but she too marched off to a factory job to do her part for the war. The wages were higher. She and Addie hammered out an agreement: She would work three afternoons a week at their house after her factory shift. But in fact, Evangeline seemed to simply show up whenever she had the time.

She needed the extra money, of course, and the factory jobs might disappear once all the boys came home. But Mimi knew Evangeline was also reluctant to lose her conduit to Addie's honey. She was another regular honey harvest helper.

The first time Mimi met Evangeline she had not been prepared to find someone else cleaning the house. Addie hadn't said anything to her.

But the housekeeper was prepared for her. She shut off the vacuum.

"You're that gal from out West. I'm Evangeline."

"I'm Mimi Smith." She put out her hand to shake. "How do you do."

Evangeline stared at Mimi for a long moment. Mimi stared back. Evangeline cracked a smile as if this was a silly thing to do and took Mimi's offered hand.

"You're the boarder. You must've passed some kind of test. You're the first one Addie's taken on, and the city's been pressing her for months to do that."

"I feel very lucky." Music started up somewhere, as if to greet her.

"That boy don't never shut up," Evangeline opined. "If it's not his fiddle, it's his banjo, and if it's not his banjo, it's his mouth. Always yapping. But he's got a sweet soul. I give him that."

She tolerated his music, as long as he stayed out of her way, preferably in another room. Richie liked to play her happy swing tunes.

"This is a Duke Ellington tune, Evangeline," he would call out. "It's to keep you in the cleaning mood."

"Don't be a fool, boy," she would answer. "Money keeps me in the cleaning mood." She was saving her money for a purpose. Her daughter Molly Ann had already been accepted at Howard University in the District. She would be the first in their family to go to college, a source of boundless pride for her mother. In response, Richie would tease her with "We're in the Money." But today there was no music.

Although Evangeline was usually a woman of endless energy, she seemed drained today. She turned off the vacuum cleaner and inclined her head toward the violet gown gracing the dressmaker's dummy. The rhinestones and bugle beads around the waistband sparkled in the afternoon sun.

"You made this? Addie don't sew. You could put a gun to her head, wouldn't make no difference."

"Addie said I could leave it there until I finish the handwork."

"Pretty fancy." It was high praise coming from Evangeline. "Course I don't know where you're going to wear it. Maybe to London, to see the Queen?"

"I have no idea. I don't hear Richie, is he out?"

"He's in the back with that harlot."

"Harlot? You don't mean Kitty Hawkins?"

"That blond-haired troublemaker," Evangeline said. "Don't you be fooled by her. She may look like an angel, but there are fires burning underneath all that frosting."

"I feel sorry for her."

"And that's how it starts."

Evangeline turned her back and flipped the vacuum on. Mimi was dismissed. She wanted to know why Kitty was there, but her cotton dress was sticking to her skin with perspiration. She ran upstairs and changed into shorts and a navy sailor top.

On the staircase Mimi ran into Richie, his violin in his hands. The teenager seemed longer and lankier in the past few weeks. If she wasn't mistaken, there was a bit of new maturity about him.

"Kitty's got the quivers," Richie announced. "She wants to see you, Mimi. She's in the garden."

Addie was sitting at the kitchen table. Mimi looked to her for an explanation while Richie played something that sounded like horror movie music.

"Is that *quivers* music?" Mimi asked.

"Richie, stop that," his mother commanded. "Play something nice." He sighed dramatically and started in on a sad ballad.

"Quivers?" Mimi asked.

Addie sighed. "Says she's got a feeling something bad's gonna happen."

"Don't we all feel that all the time?" Mimi said.

"Yes, but this isn't about the war," Richie piped up. "It's different than regular bad feelings. Do you ever feel like that?"

"Sometimes," Mimi said, "but I've never heard it called the quivers."

"Kitty's outside in the victory garden. I'll fix us some tea."

Addie had a hundred ways of making her own "tea," mixing chicory with exotic extras from her garden, mint or basil or rosehips that had been collected in the fall. Today, she served up a pot of "sweet tea" with rosehips and honey.

Addie's victory garden was locally renowned, though every house in the neighborhood sported some kind of vegetable garden. No one tried to compete with Addie Richardson. She had beans, lettuce, corn, and multiple varieties of squashes, as well as cucumbers to make pickles. The aroma of ripening tomatoes added more sweet scents. The apple tree would provide a bounty later in the season, and a pumpkin vine crawled along the rear fence.

In the garden Mimi found Kitty Hawkins and sat down beside her.

"Richie said you wanted to see me," Mimi said.

Today Kitty looked like the young woman Mimi had met the year before, fresh from West Virginia. She wore old dungarees and a shirt tied at the waist. Most of her blond hair was concealed in a blue kerchief, a la Rosie the Riveter, and her face was clean of makeup. She had clearly dressed down to visit Addie. But she was trembling like a tuning fork.

"Kitty?" Mimi took her hand. Kitty shook her head. She seemed to be trying not to cry.

Unexpectedly, Mimi thought, they had become friends— perhaps not close friends, but friends who could share confidences. The kind of friendship that happened during a war. Mimi's parents would be horrified that she would even know "a woman like that." Her grandmother, on the other hand, would understand. Mimi hadn't mentioned her to Grandma Eileen, but now she knew she would. And the Richardsons always treated Kitty kindly.

Addie brought the tea and honey cookies to the pink-and-white rose-covered gazebo. She pulled Richie away, so the two young women could have some privacy, and Mimi and Kitty sat at the small table. Addie retreated to the kitchen and Richie sat by the back door playing Chopin, just loud enough for background music.

Mimi fished a hankie out of her pocket.

"Tell me what's wrong, Kitty."

THIRTEEN

"SOMEONE ELSE IS going to die," Kitty said without preface.

"People always die when there's a war," Mimi answered.

"This ain't about the war. This is close to home. One of our girls, Hattie, was found this morning, all beat up. Her neck was broken."

"She was killed? At the Chicken Shack?" *Hattie?* Where had she heard that name before? *At the dance at Chinquapin.*

"They found her on the bed, in the stall she used. I liked her in the beginning, 'cause she was friendly at first. Then she got less so. But I didn't want her dead. And somehow leaving her on the bed is so much worse than what happened to Polly. Like it's some kind of message."

"Her name was Hattie? That's unusual."

"She made that name up herself. For Hattie Carnegie, the dress designer?"

"Right, there was a Hattie Carnegie dress design in LIFE magazine this spring."

"I saw that too. Well, our gal called herself Hattie Carnegie Jones. I don't know what her real name was."

"Like Polly Brown?" Mimi asked. "What about you?"

"I don't have time to make up names. Maybe I should. Anyways, names don't mean that much to a lot of us. Most of us don't care to remember their names or their family."

"When did she die? I mean, when was she discovered?"

"I guess sometime this morning. Gretel found her when she arrived for her shift. You know we trade off beds."

"I heard that." Mimi wondered if they changed the sheets between shifts, but this wasn't the time to ask.

"Gretel screamed. You saw her. Short, stocky, and kind of mean? She's not much of a screamer. It sounded— Well, it made my blood run cold."

"You saw Hattie then?"

Kitty slowly sipped her iced tea. Her eyes glistened. "Hattie— It was hard to recognize her. I looked at her face and I—looked away."

Mimi didn't know what to say. "I'm sorry."

"We're all gonna miss having her there. Hattie'd take the real problem men. The bad ones, you know."

"Uncouth?"

"Uncouth is a walk in the park. I'm talking about guys who demand other things." Kitty made a face. "Guys who like it rough. You know."

Mimi didn't know, and it must have showed. "Do they hit you?"

"Among other things. You have a lot to learn, kid." She said *kid* like they weren't both twenty-one. Mimi let it pass. "There are guys that like to— Well, they want to do things no one likes. No woman, anyway. Hattie could handle them. For the money."

"How could she handle them?"

"Hattie was a big girl, like they say. Nearly six feet tall and strong. She wasn't real pretty, but that don't matter much to the men. Great shape though." Kitty took out a picture from her shoulder bag and handed it to Mimi. "They paid her more for, um, special services. Hattie liked money more than she hated what they did."

The picture showed four young women posing in front of Madam Cherry's Treasure, the floating brothel, among them Kitty and Gretel from the Shack. They looked ready for work, all wearing a bit too much makeup. Kitty pointed to a large brassy blonde with a hardened look. Her smile was ferocious, her hourglass figure a calling card.

"That's Hattie," Kitty said. "You know Gretel."

"What else was Hattie like?"

Kitty pursed her lips. "She seemed to think life was a game to be played, the way she played men. If she got enough money, she'd win."

"I guess she lost that game. This other woman?" Mimi indicated a petite unsmiling brunette, staring into the camera.

"Polly Brown."

Mimi took a longer look. Polly Brown had large eyes, lines in her face, and a tight mouth that hid secrets. "Was she older?"

"Twenty-five, though I know she looks like she's got some more years on her. That's what the Life does to you. There were days she had to drink her way through it. She was sick of the Shack, the men, all of it. Polly told me once, all she wanted was to be left alone. I started calling her Greta Garbo."

"Do you think she killed herself?"

"She had no call to be walking on those railroad tracks. She had a little extra money and she told me she was going to Baltimore for a party. I had a feeling she wouldn't come back, but I didn't think she was going to die. Doesn't make sense. But life doesn't make sense."

"Was she sad, depressed? I have a friend named Tilly. Since her fiancé was killed in the war, she just walks the river, trying to decide whether to drown herself."

"Polly was nothing like that. You have strange friends, Mimi Smith."

"Don't we all?" She paused, thinking. "Not all the servicemen are brutal, are they?"

Kitty crumbled a cookie and put a tiny bite in her mouth. She folded her legs under her like a child.

"Believe it or not, a lot of the soldiers, the sailors, the marines, the flyboys— They're sweet. Young, polite, and scared. It's the first time for a lot of them. Sure, they worry about getting killed out there. But they don't want to die virgins. I can't really blame them. Can you?"

"I guess not." So many people were jumping into ill-advised marriages after rushed romances. Imminent death might not be an aphrodisiac, but it certainly spurred action.

"I reckon they want to get it over with while they're still stateside," Kitty continued. "They don't want to mess with any foreign germs, not their first time anyway. The services make them see a lot of scary movies about the dangers of sex with foreign whores."

Mimi busied herself with her tea and stifled a laugh. "I'm sorry, Kitty. I just thought about what my mother would say about this conversation. She'd be speechless."

Kitty smiled. "Your mother should meet my mother."

God forbid. Mimi nodded. "It's a shame about Hattie Carnegie Jones, and Polly Brown."

"Two women I knew are dead and I don't even know their real names. It feels sad, you know?"

"Worse than sad. Forgotten."

Kitty set her teacup down. "Gretel saw more of Hattie than I did. Said she looked broken. *Broken.* Such a big, strong woman. It's a hard way to die."

"Sounds like a hard way to live." Mimi handed the photo back.

"We all plan to leave, head out someplace where no one knows us."

"Leaving is a good idea. The best idea." Mimi's throat was dry. She picked up her tea again. "Kitty, the sooner the better."

"With Hattie dead— I'm afraid, Mimi. What if the next one is me?"

"Why would it be you? It must have been something about Hattie," Mimi prompted. "A reason why. A motive. Why would someone kill *her?*"

Kitty rose to wander through the garden. She picked some mint and sniffed it before crumbling it, looking far more natural that when she was tarted up for work.

"Truth is, I can't tell you much about Hattie, because I don't know any details. But sometimes she tried to sell things, other than herself. Things that might not strictly have belonged to her."

"She was a thief?"

"Light-fingered Hattie, we called her, behind her back."

"What kinds of things did she finger?"

"Little things at first. A soldier comes in with nylons or a pint or two of whiskey, gin, what have you. He gets a little sleepy and wakes up not knowing what happened to his stuff. But he can't say nothing, because he'll get in trouble with his superior officers. They're not supposed to be frequenting cat houses."

"What did she do with the goods?"

"Sold them, according to Gretel. And things she heard about and didn't have in hand. Tried to sell those too. She got in trouble a few times. Come around with a black eye or swollen lip."

Sounded like Hattie Carnegie Jones was running her own private black market. "What kinds of things? Beyond nylons and booze?"

"Anything she could find out about. Sugar, coffee, tires."

"Tires? How did she accomplish that? She was hauling tires around?"

"Not Hattie, but she'd hear about things through the 'horizontal grapevine,' you know. She had friends. I don't know who they were. She'd finger things for someone and they would sell them to someone else. So Hattie's light fingers didn't always get soiled."

"Hattie was sort of a finder?" Mimi asked. "Was she running her own crime ring?"

"I wouldn't go that far," Kitty protested. "She wasn't sophisticated like that."

"Did you ever talk specifics with her?"

"No, and I didn't want to know." Kitty seemed alarmed. "If I'd heard something, it's not like I would rat her out. You didn't argue much with Hattie. Live and let live."

It occurred to her that Kitty didn't know what Mimi did for a living. Sure, she knew Mimi worked for the government in some boring office job, but not with the Office of Price Administration.

"She stole things to sell on the black market? Things that aren't available to everyone. Or she pointed them out, or had them plotted on a map? Or what?"

"You make it sound like she had a plan."

"Yeah, it does. Doesn't it?" Mimi leaned against the gazebo.

"Maybe. Maybe she did." Kitty picked at her fingernails. "Maybe when I get out of this business, there'll be things I have to say about that."

"When are you quitting?"

Kitty sat down and picked up her tea. "I'm just trying to salt some extra money away. My flyboy's coming home soon, and we—" The tea never made it to her lips. "But oh my God, what if the next one is me?"

"Why would you even think that?" Mimi squeezed Kitty's hand. The day was sweltering, but Kitty's hand was ice cold. "Could it be one of these soldier boys who killed Hattie?"

"Who else? But I don't know." Kitty looked young and scared and fragile. "Hattie could fight back. Fight dirty. And she died anyway."

"What do the police say?"

"Police! What do they care about a dead prostitute? They asked a few questions and then carted her off somewhere to a pauper's grave. Sure, she was a certain kind of woman, but she wasn't trash." Tears glistened in Kitty's eyes.

"Have some more tea. It's good." Mimi poured from the teapot.

Kitty wiped her eyes and smiled. "There may be a war on, but I'd know Addie's chicory tea anywhere. It's so peaceful here."

"Why don't you just stay for a while?" Mimi suggested. The Chopin played on.

Kitty glanced at her wristwatch. "Oh God, look at the time. I have to get back."

"To the crime scene?"

"They only taped off Hattie's room. For now. The rest of us, we're still working." She stood up and grabbed the rest of the cookies, wrapping them in a napkin. "I know Addie won't mind."

Mimi walked Kitty through the kitchen and dining room, past the nearly finished violet dress on the dummy. Kitty stopped and stared at it, mesmerized. Her face was luminous.

"That's the princess dress," Richie put in. "Our Mimi's been working on it real hard like."

The wide jeweled cummerbund sparkled in the afternoon light. Richie started playing another princess tune. "That's beautiful. What's it for?" Kitty said to Mimi.

"I don't know yet. It's been so difficult to make, it might be my very last creation."

"I've never seen anything like it."

Mimi lifted the draped skirt for Kitty to feel the fabric. "The material called out to me, but it's awful to work with. Jersey is so slippery."

"It's like something in the movies. Something you'd wear in ballrooms, with crystal chandeliers and cocktails. And men in those suits. Those tuxedos."

"Yes, it's a fantasy dress. Maybe you could make something like this. You could use Addie's sewing machine and I could help you—"

Kitty groaned at the thought, still caressing the material. "I've put together too many grain-sack dresses. Ruined sewing for me forever. Trying to find enough sacks with the same pattern, and then you see everyone in town wearing the same things. Everyone worrying about whether they got enough dang grain sacks. Though some folks would get their material at the Five and Dime. But this feels beautiful. It's like nothing I've ever seen."

"My friend Gloria created the pattern for me."

Kitty's eyes widened. "Your dress designer friend? I thought you were making her up! So where do you expect to wear this—this designer creation?"

"No idea. Gloria says when the material or the pattern calls to you, you have to make beautiful things, simply for the 'somedays' in our lives. Especially now, with the war on. Creating beauty is an act of faith."

"You think things will really get better? There really is a someday?" Kitty's eyes welled with tears.

"Sure, and someday I'll finish this thing. I'm nowhere near as good as Gloria, but she's taught me a lot."

"And someday she's going to be a famous designer?"

"I hope so. Being famous sounds crazy, but she's got talent. If anyone can make it, Gloria can. She set her sights on it. She's working in the New York garment district, and she wants to go to fashion design school."

"There's a school for it? I learn something new every day."

"The world is full of things we've never thought about before." *Like what the life of a magdalen might be like,* Mimi thought.

Kitty stroked the fabric with something like awe.

"This is a spring color. Prettiest violet I've ever seen. Like orchids in a corsage. Not that I ever got one. What did you call this fabric?"

"Jersey. It's called that because the original knits were made in Jersey in the Channel Islands. Great Britain. It's been made since the Middle Ages."

"You are a font of information, Mimi Smith, like a geography and history lesson all in one. Say, aren't you breaking some of those government fabric rules?"

"I'm toeing the line. The way it drapes makes it look like more material than it really is. Besides, those regulations don't apply to home tailors."

"I wonder what it would feel like to wear such a gorgeous thing." Kitty seemed to have forgotten her troubles for the moment. Mimi credited the dress.

"You can try it on when it's finished."

"You'd let me do that? Someone like me?" A pang of sadness went through Mimi's heart. "I'd like that."

"They say clothes make the man. That goes double for women." Mimi impulsively reached for a scrap of her leftover material, about thirty inches square. She offered it to Kitty. "Here, this is extra material, and it might make you a scarf."

Kitty gently took the fabric and held it up to her face, staring at herself in the front hall mirror. She smiled. "This is really my color." The clock struck six. "Oh darn. I'm late. Thanks for this, Mimi. It's glorious."

Kitty squeezed Mimi's hand for a moment and then ran out the front door, the beautiful material wrapped tightly around her fist.

FOURTEEN

*K*ITTY LEFT WITH prettier things on her mind than when she arrived that afternoon. But Mimi's brain wouldn't let her sleep that night.

Two women were dead, both of whom worked in the stalls at the Chicken Shack. Kitty was consumed with the quivers. Hattie Carnegie Jones had been murdered. Polly Brown's death was either murder, suicide, or an accident. Mimi dismissed the accident angle. She couldn't imagine anyone taking a stroll on the railroad tracks and not hearing the massive roar of the engine or the warning blast on the horn or feeling the rumble of the oncoming train beneath their feet.

Suicide or murder? Kitty said Polly didn't talk about killing herself, like Mimi's friend Tilly did. She was secretive, but not obviously depressed. Mimi thought it was more likely that someone pushed Polly Brown in front of an oncoming train.

The deaths of two women who worked in the Chicken Shack in the same month couldn't be a coincidence, could it? Kitty knew something, but she hadn't come to terms with the deaths yet. At least Mimi thought so. Hattie was a known thief. Polly was more of an enigma.

Kitty was right about one thing. Polly and Hattie may not have been their real names, but they were real human beings and deserved more than a forgotten burial in a pauper's grave.

Don't kid yourself, sister. They could all be murder.

George Prescott's words came back to her. The cases OPA investigated *could* involve murder. Perhaps not a lot, but a few. However, once those cases got to the felony level or suspected felony level, they were taken over by other agencies. Unless—

and it was a big unless. Unless the agency requested special jurisdiction, because it had an unusual angle on the case or some special access. Could this be one of those cases?

Mimi pondered how someone would go about investigating these women's deaths. As usual, she reminded herself she was not an OPA investigator. She decided not to share any of her suspicions with Prescott; not yet anyway. It wasn't her job, and like all bosses everywhere, he wouldn't understand. First, she needed more information.

Someone was killing magdalens. Someone strong enough to overpower a reputedly big-boned and dirty-fighting woman like Hattie. A strong woman unafraid to fight back. Hattie dabbled in the black market. Mimi made a note to ask Kitty about whether Polly was also involved with Hattie's dangerous sideline.

After fitful hours tossing and turning, Mimi dragged herself out of bed and wrote down everything she knew. She included Gretel, who found the broken body of light-fingered Hattie, the soldier named Lou whom Mimi had seen exiting Kitty's room, and the woman named Polly Brown, who died on the railroad tracks. It wasn't much, but at least she was able to sleep.

On Friday morning, over hot cups of Postum, Mimi chatted with a sleepy Sally Post, who rubbed her eyes and yawned. Their caffeine-free Postum wasn't waking anyone up. The highly anticipated coffee rationing announcement hadn't yet been made.

"Busy night?" Mimi inquired.

"You know it. Nothing fun though." It was obvious Sally had spent her time in the sun. Her nose was sunburned and her face sported a new crop of freckles. "We picked peaches, cleaned peaches, pitted peaches, and canned peaches."

Sally lived with her family in Arlington while waiting for her sweetheart to come home from the war and save her from a life of drudgery.

"Where did you find the peaches?"

"My uncle's got a farm, and on this farm, there was a pickup, and you know the drill. He's got gasoline stamps, so he came and got us. Free labor. Worked till midnight."

"Peaches sound delicious."

"I'll like them, once I stop hating them." Sally stirred her drink. "I can still smell peaches on my skin. It's a good crop. But my mother is a vicious taskmaster."

"Hey, Sally, theoretically, what would you do if you stumbled on some black-market activity?"

"Not a damn thing." Small in stature, Sally was large in opinions. "Not my job. My job is boring, but it's safe."

"What if what you found could hurt a lot of people?"

"I'd find a way to pass the buck. And it's not my buck. Why are you asking?"

"No particular reason."

"You're trying for an investigator's job, aren't you?" Sally gave her a skeptical eye.

"Haven't you thought about moving up?"

"Hey, I paid my money, I took the stenographer's course, I know shorthand, and I can type seventy-five words a minute. Why on earth would I want a tougher job, dealing with a bunch of jerks stealing such small stuff? I mean, all they get is a slap on the wrist, mostly."

"What about excitement?"

"Excitement, my eye! You want to tell Mr. Nobody he's been selling gin for two dollars more than is strictly legal? He'll take a pop at you. Pow. Right in the kisser. Who needs it?"

"I see you've thought this through, Sally."

"That's my hobby. Thinking."

"That's very practical." If Sally was content with her lot in the typing pool, so be it. Less competition, Mimi decided.

"Hey, have you seen *The More the Merrier*? That Jean Arthur's a real hoot. And topical. You know how jammed up things are here. Well, this movie's got these two guys and a gal having to share an apartment in Washington, D.C., sleeping in shifts. But it's not as racy as it sounds."

"I'll have to catch that one."

Mimi fixed herself another cup of Postum and pretended it was coffee.

Friday passed in a blur of typing up responses to citizen complaints. George was in a foul mood and Mimi was stumped about what, if anything, she should do about Polly Brown and Hattie Carnegie Jones. She'd have to check the newspapers at the Queen Street library on Saturday to see whether there was any more information on their deaths.

And poor Kitty. What could anyone do to help Kitty? Except encourage her to get out of the Life. But would Kitty actually take the first step?

FIFTEEN

*L*OCAL WOMAN DIES IN TRAIN ACCIDENT. *The Alexandria Gazette* gave Polly Brown's death a paragraph. It drew no conclusions as to why she was walking on or near the train tracks on an early June evening. However, it noted Miss Brown was a practitioner of the "unfortunate trade." Mimi had hoped for more from her trip to the Barrett Library on Queen Street.

She turned to the second death. Hattie Carnegie Jones's homicide two weeks later was magnanimously awarded two paragraphs in the *Gazette*. But the notice was placed on an inside page where it could easily be ignored. It also drew no conclusions but had a barely stated subtext that murder was the kind of thing a woman could expect if she dabbled in the trade of "a lady of the evening."

The librarian raised an eyebrow over her horn-rimmed spectacles when Mimi inquired if there were any other recent murders in town. "Why would a respectable young woman like you be interested in murder?"

Mimi looked around and whispered. "I'm writing a murder mystery. Like Agatha Christie."

She didn't know why she said it, except the librarian looked like a mystery reader. The woman wore her salt-and-pepper hair in a top knot, and her trim purple-and-blue rayon dress featured a whimsical novelty print of clocks. And it was the right thing to say.

The librarian warmed right up. She was sorry, there weren't many murders in Alexandria, but she suggested Mimi look at Washington, D.C., where more of that sort of thing happened. She could also recommend several personal favorites by Miss Christie.

Mimi left the library with scant facts, but a couple of Agatha Christies. She headed to the farmers' market on King Street, held continuously every Saturday in Alexandria since the 1750s, or so the locals said. Even George Washington had sent his produce to this market. The sounds of buyers and sellers and the aroma of fresh produce made it seem like more normal times. Mimi tried to inhale the moments and save them for later. She bought a few non-rationed items. After sipping a cold Coca-Cola, she picked up more violet thread at Murphy's dime store.

The morning was steamy, and she planned a quiet afternoon with a book. Or possibly a visit to the municipal swimming pool, where she could cool off and stop thinking about death. But back at the house, she found Kitty waiting for her in the dining room. As usual, Addie had supplied sweet iced tea and cookies.

"I have a couple of favors to ask you," Kitty said without preamble. "And just how do you know so much about clothes?"

"Favors? Clothes?" Clothes were the last subject Mimi had expected Kitty to come asking for advice about. "What are you talking about?"

"I need your help, Mimi Smith."

Kitty gestured down at her faded day dress, perhaps one of the famous flour-sack dresses she'd mentioned. It was decorated in violets and pansies, but Kitty had fashioned the violet material Mimi had given her into a flounce on the side of her skirt, twisted into a rosette at the top. She had finished the fabric's edge with a delicate stitch and attached the whole thing with a pin. Kitty was a better seamstress than she had let on. She had potential, Mimi thought.

"Oh, that. My friend Gloria."

"I really did think you were making her up. Until I saw that violet dress."

"I'll let you know when I'm making things up. Gloria has an eye for design and sewing, and I might have picked up a few tips. I like what you did with that material I gave you. It's clever."

"I saw something like it in a magazine." Kitty smiled and stroked the jersey fabric. "But I need to go shopping for a dress. Something nice, classy. Rich looking. Right away. My man is coming home soon. My Nathan."

"He is?" This was someone Mimi wanted to meet. "His name is Nathan?"

"Nathan Albemarle. Isn't that pretty? I just got his telegram. I want to look like a lady when he gets here. I got forty-five dollars. I have an emergency twenty, if that's not enough. Do you think that's enough?"

"It will do. Tell me more about this Nathan of yours."

"Well, Nathan is from one of those hoity-toity families."

"Hoity-toity?"

"High-hat. Nathan's not like that. But his people wouldn't like me, even if I wasn't a whore. His family lives on Mansion Drive."

"Mansion Drive in Alexandria? I guess that says it all," Mimi said. Mansion Drive meant money and high society.

"He wants me to meet his mother and brother when he comes home. It scares me to death, Mimi."

"That would terrorize anyone." Mimi tried to imagine the scene, the wealthy family and the magdalen from West Virginia. Even if she weren't a practitioner of the oldest profession, Kitty would be pretty exotic for Mansion Drive, full of huge, beautiful homes off Russell Road. "What are they like?"

"He doesn't talk about them much."

"They don't know about you?"

"Course not. They'd take one look at me and throw me out the door."

"That's why you need new clothes?" Mimi didn't know how much of this was fantasy and how much reality, but she was afraid Kitty might cry any second. "Does Nathan know about you? Everything?"

A tiny nod. "He understands that I had no choice, really. But I'm his choice."

This Nathan sounded a little too good to be true. "You said you had a couple of favors to ask?"

Kitty's shoulders slumped and a sudden gloom settled around her.

"I got plans, happy plans, future plans," she said. "I got a chance here, Mimi, and I'm trying to outrun the quivers." She grabbed her iced tea with both hands and took a deep breath. "But if I don't make it, if something happens to me, there's things I need you to do. I want you to take some things home to my family. There's some money. For a funeral for me, and some for my mama."

"A funeral? Stop talking like this. Don't even think that. Nothing will happen."

"You don't know that. People disappear, they die every day."

"Like Polly Brown and Hattie Carnegie Jones?"

Kitty nodded. "Now, if anything happens to me, give this to my mother."

From her purse, she dug out an old-fashioned cameo necklace, cream on brown, a pretty woman's face in profile. It looked quite old.

"Your mother? Listen, nothing's going to happen to you."

"Then you keep it for me until the quivers go away. My mother's back in Forgotten Creek, West Virginia." Kitty took out a small pad of paper and wrote it down.

"Is there a street address?"

"Not really. House don't have a number. It's on County Line Road. It'll get there. And there are other things I want her to have. Don't forget my ration books, they can use them, and there's some other things."

"This is crazy talk, Kitty—"

Kitty put up a hand to stop her.

"I'll write everything down. I been saving money for my first home with Nathan. Keep what you need to settle my affairs. If my family won't have me back there, I'd like to be buried here at St. Mary's, if they'll have me."

"I don't believe this for a second, Kitty Hawkins, but why wouldn't you want to go home to Forgotten Creek?"

Mimi had never thought about where she should be buried, but she realized she didn't want it to be in Denver. There was nothing for her there.

"I don't think they'd want me. The rest goes to my ma, along with some extra sugar and coffee. And make sure she gets the cameo necklace. I gave her a lot of trouble." She dangled the delicate cameo on its thin gold chain. "I took this with me when I left. It was my grandmother's, and then my ma's. Course she never wore it. Not once. It was too good to wear, that's what she would say. She was saving it for some special occasion. Some someday that never came."

"I know people like that. Doesn't make any sense to me."

"My ma, she always said I'd come to no good end. I'm that tarnished nickel. I took this out of spite." She handed the cameo to Mimi.

"Kitty, why are you asking me to do this?"

Kitty grinned. "You're the only sap I know dumb enough to do this."

"Oh yeah? What if I just stole everything from you?"

"Yeah, but you won't. I'd haunt you." Kitty wore a smug smile. "Besides, you're a born goody-goody."

"Ha. It's not as easy as you think, being a goody-goody."

"That's not all I need, Miss Goody-Goody." Kitty picked up another cookie. She eyed the violet dress in the dining room through the open kitchen door. "I need your help, so I don't look like a tramp when I meet Nathan's family. If I meet his family."

"Why me?"

"First, you got good taste. Second, you're bossy. You followed me right into that ladies' room and started combing my hair, making me wash my face. You made me look almost like a lady. Nobody else would have done that."

"I don't think I'm bossy."

"Yes, you are. A bossy goody-goody. Probably 'cause of your red hair."

"It's auburn, not red."

"See? Bossy."

"You don't look like a tramp."

"Not right now." Kitty looked at her with such hope and expectation, Mimi couldn't say no. "Think how good I'll look if I listen to you, Miss Bossy Pants."

"Oh, all right. Let's go shopping. First I have to change."

Mimi dashed upstairs to slip on a light blue skirt with deep pockets and collect her shoulder-strap pocketbook. Shopping with Kitty? This would be an adventure. And colors and fabrics and the way the lines of a dress fall were things Mimi enjoyed. Even with government restrictions on fabrics and skirt sizes and pockets and cuffs, she liked seeing how designers came up with clever and beautiful clothes in spite of the rules.

She and Kitty caught a crowded bus into D.C., heading for the big department stores, Garfinkel's and Woodward & Lothrop. There was nothing like a girlfriend shopping trip to make for easy conversation. They might start out talking about their favorite colors, and then eventually all their dreams would come tumbling out. At least that's what Mimi was hoping for.

"Kitty, tell me all about Nathan."

SIXTEEN

"THERE'S NOTHING WRONG with him. He's not disfigured or anything like that," Kitty said. As if a man would have to be defective in some way to love her. "He's cute as can be. And he was drowning when I met him."

"What did you say?"

"Drowning in the river. Last summer. Bunch of us went to cool off, over to Hunting Creek. Didn't want to show up at the city pool. Gretel went there once. They said they didn't want her kind and wouldn't let her in. So, we go to the river."

"I never thought about that."

"The pool in town is for whites only and no whores. The colored people got no pool, so they go to Hunting Creek. Those folks ain't snooty about us being there. Especially after I pulled some of their kids to shore. I feel real kindly toward them."

"And your fellow was having trouble in the water?"

"Nathan. He can fly, but he can't swim." Kitty grinned at the memory. "It was an awful hot day. I could see he was having trouble and panicking. Going down. You know, drowning don't always look like drowning."

"I didn't know you could swim."

"Like a duck. We had a town pool for a couple years before it closed. One of the few things there was to do in Forgotten Creek. I worked as a lifeguard."

"Women can be lifeguards?" Mimi hadn't encountered any.

"They can be when that's all you got. My big brother was a lifeguard before he left town. That left me. Us Hawkinses all swim. We lived near a creek and my ma insisted we learn. She didn't want any drowned babies."

"You saved Nathan?"

"Sure. Wasn't difficult. Kept him afloat, found a log he could grab hold of, and dragged him to shore. Couple of guys he was with hightailed it out of there. Guess they thought he was done for. One of them was his own brother. Can you imagine? Anyways, I stayed with Nathan until he calmed down and caught his breath. He called me his magical mermaid." Kitty's face glowed with emotion.

"I'm sure you looked like a mermaid, with all that blond hair." Mimi could picture it spreading across the water. "When did you tell him what you did for a living?"

"Right off. He was so nice. I didn't want him getting the wrong idea. We both felt something then and there and he paid for my time all weekend long. I may be his mermaid, but he's my prince."

ଔ

Kitty's request to go shopping was simple enough, but it proved more arduous than Mimi expected. Kitty was not comfortable in big, bright, shiny department stores, or with making so many decisions.

"I've never been anywhere like this before," she kept saying. "It's so enormous! And so fancy."

"Think of all the things you've seen that no one else has," Mimi suggested.

"Did you just make a joke?"

"Maybe."

Before they entered the stately Woodward & Lothrop department store in downtown D.C., Kitty took a ring box out of her pocketbook and opened it. She slipped the sparkling diamond ring on her finger. The stone, set in platinum, twinkled in the light.

"Oh, my goodness, Kitty. It's gorgeous."

"I told you he was serious. Three quarters of a carat, extra bright. I don't wear it much. Thieves, you know. I always put it back in the locker where I keep all my valuables." Kitty produced a key. "This is a copy for you. I checked and made sure it works. Locker's paid up through the end of the month. By special arrangement."

Mimi took the key. Such a small key for such big dreams. "A locker at the station?"

"Alexandria train station, not D.C. The number's on it. If you have any problems, ask for Stan, he's some kind of manager. One of my regulars. Nice guy."

It made sense to keep things locked up there. The station wasn't far from the Chicken Shack or Kitty's rooming house on Henry Street. But it was far enough away from the other magdalens, those who might have larceny in their hearts. Or their fingers.

ogogo

"You said you wanted to look like a lady," Mimi reminded her.

"I didn't say *old* lady."

Mimi gritted her teeth and explained that looking like a lady didn't involve snatching up every glittering thing that beckoned her. The saleslady may have raised an eyebrow over Kitty's faded dress, but she snapped to attention when she spied that diamond engagement ring.

After Kitty tried on and rejected a pile of dresses, they finally found a dressy polished cotton suit dress with a matching jacket in a rich royal blue. The shade deepened Kitty's eyes to dark azure. The fabric shone like satin and featured simple princess lines, with a scoop neckline trimmed in subtle re-embroidered white lace. The jacket had elbow-length sleeves trimmed in the same lace and featured a sewn-in self belt. Kitty might be mistaken for a sorority sister.

"This is something you can wear to meet his family. It's on sale and you have a lot of money left over."

"It's kind of plain," Kitty remarked. "But in a classy kind of way. I like that it's sort of shiny."

"That's why it's polished, like satin, not like rayon," Mimi said. "And you could dress it up with a jeweled pin. Or your pretty cameo necklace."

"The color suits me real well." The outfit also hugged her slim figure perfectly. Kitty stared at her reflection as if unsure if it was really her. "It doesn't really look like me."

"I thought that was the point."

"I'll take it." It was the perfect meeting-your-boyfriend's-family suit dress. Still, Kitty seemed to want something else. She spotted a rack of evening wear that had been marked down and sped toward it like a toddler spotting a beloved toy. Her hand traveled to a long crepe gown in a lovely light morning-glory blue.

It was a divine dress, and the slim silhouette would flatter Kitty's figure. The gown zipped on the side for a close fit. The azure gown featured a sweetheart neckline and a long peplum overskirt that dipped deeper in the back than the front. Both the sweetheart and peplum were trimmed with embroidery and silver and white bugle beads and pearls. The three-quarter sleeves were also trimmed at the cuffs. It was beautiful, tasteful, and offered more than enough sparkle for a magpie like Kitty.

Kitty stood there staring at it. Mimi picked up the sleeve with the sales tag. "It's on sale. It's in your budget. And it's a heavenly blue shade, perfect for you."

"It's so elegant. Do I dare?"

"You have enough for both dresses. Even if you don't have plans for it now, Gloria says when a dress really speaks to you, you must give it a chance."

Mimi gathered the dress from the sales rack and handed it to Kitty. She turned over the other dress to the saleslady to set aside.

"Your friend would be hard on my pocketbook," Kitty said.

"Try it on. What could I hurt?" Mimi knew exactly what would happen, and Kitty needed to feel she deserved it.

"But is it patriotic?"

"This dress is already made. Someone has to buy it, Kitty. Why not you? It might even be older stock, made before the latest fabric restrictions." Mimi shot a look to the saleslady, who nodded on cue and put a bright smile on her face.

"Yes, I'm sure that's true. Give it a shot, honey," the woman said.

Kitty emerged from the dressing room. Everyone in the department spun around to look at her as she approached the mirror.

"I look different," Kitty said.

"You look stunning," Mimi remarked. "Like an angel on a blue cloud."

"Like a movie star," the saleslady proclaimed. "I'm not kidding. Like Ginger Rogers."

Kitty laughed, looking at herself in the mirror. She'd never had this experience before. "I guess I better take it then." She paid her money and estimated how much she had left. She sighed. "I've never paid so much money in my life for anything." She collected her shopping bag with glassy eyes.

"Maybe we should take a break." Mimi's energy was flagging, and Kitty was looking slightly inebriated from all the shopping.

"We have some specials in our tearoom today," said the saleslady, ever helpful. "Seventh floor. They have lovely tea sandwiches." Mimi thought the tearoom sounded wonderful, but Kitty was on a spree.

"First I need shoes," Kitty exclaimed. She pulled out her ration book and found the right coupon for a new pair of leather shoes. Mimi fished around in her handbag for an aspirin. Her head was pounding, but in a good cause.

They proceeded up and down escalators and elevators until Kitty found a pair of pumps in a dark blue, with a small platform sole and a dignified heel that would go beautifully with the royal blue dress. She also found some high-heeled dancing shoes in cream-colored cloth which didn't require ration coupons.

"I'll never forget today, Mimi. I've never had such fine things in my life. I've never had so much fun with a friend."

From the shoe department they marched on toward millinery, where a dab of white and light blue caught Kitty's eye. It was barely more than a wide azure band that matched the dress. Topped with a froth of lace and a small white veil, it made the sweetest picture atop Kitty's blond hair, almost like a bride. And in the lingerie department Kitty stopped on a dime at a frilly pale pink nightgown.

"I don't usually wear these things. But when Nathan comes home—" She smiled at Mimi. "He calls me Katharine."

The nightgown, the matching robe, and other necessities were added to her shopping bags. Even Mimi had never shopped for so many things at one time. This was beginning to look more and more like a trousseau.

"Kitty, are you getting married?"

A laugh and a blush. "That's the plan," she replied with a grin.

Mimi sent a prayer heavenward that Nathan Albemarle's family from Mansion Drive would never find out the truth about Katharine Hawkins of Forgotten Creek, West Virginia. Or if they did, they would forgive and forget. And as happy as Kitty seemed with their buying expedition, from time to time she'd stop and stare at her new friend and say, "You promised. Remember?"

Despite the sick feeling she had every time Kitty said it, Mimi would say, "I promise. Didn't you have a boy back home?"

"Sure I did. Josiah Jordan wanted to marry me. Joe. He wasn't like everyone else. He went to college. He even got a degree at Morgantown."

"West Virginia University?" Mimi juggled her share of the bags, thinking Kitty must have made those salesladies' day.

"Then he goes and comes back to Forgotten Creek! There's a whole world outside that tiny dot on a map. I couldn't believe it. I couldn't see living my whole life in Forgotten Creek.

There's a reason they call it that, you know. He promised we'd leave one day, but I couldn't wait. Can you understand?"

"Obviously. I'm here and not back in Denver, where I was born."

"And Denver is way bigger than Forgotten Creek. So you and me, sis, we were both born in the wrong place."

"Must have been some kind of clerical error," Mimi said.

"For both of us. You're so far from your hometown, your people. Does it ever bother you?"

"I'm home now," Mimi grinned. "The wide-open spaces were not for me. They were too wide open. And too brown."

"Guess we have that in common too. Say, are you hungry, Mimi? I'm about ready to fall down."

"I was ready for that an hour ago. If they give out medals for shopping, you'll get a Medal of Honor."

Laden with Kitty's packages, they skipped Woodies' fancy tearoom and stopped in at a little diner on the next block, a sliver of a place between two tall buildings. The waitress wore a mint-green uniform and white apron that matched the rest of the décor. A small cap perched on her head. She caught Mimi's eye and gestured to a couple of stools at the end of the counter.

She and Kitty snagged a couple of swivel seats still spinning, vacated by two older businessmen. Mimi ordered a chicken salad sandwich and coffee. Kitty got the spaghetti plate and a Coke. Inhaling the steam from the heavy porcelain cup of something hot that resembled coffee, Mimi took a sip and felt her headache subside.

"About this boy back home you mentioned," she began.

"He's a farmer, but not a typical farmer. Joe's got new ideas about things. He went to the university and had big dreams, but when his pa died, he took over the farm. Last I heard he's waiting for his brothers to grow up so they can take over and he can join up for the war. Someday. Someday is too far away for me. So a year, year and half ago, I caught a ride out of town with some local boys joining the Army."

"Did you ever think about joining up? Like the WACs?"

"I'm not very good at following rules."

"Me neither. And you came to the wicked big city instead."

"I tried a few regular jobs, but they didn't work out."

"Like helping Addie with the honey?"

Kitty looked up. "That was more of a favor. Addie don't really pay much, except in honey. I tried factory work, but I hated it. I sort of fell into the Life."

"Fell into it?"

"You really don't want to know." Kitty sipped her Coke.

Mimi really did want to know. She took a bite of her sandwich. There was a lot more salad than chicken. "I don't want everything, Mimi, but I want something."

"And Nathan can give you those things?"

"Yes." She paused to reflect. "But more than that. He gives me respect. And love. And I do love him."

Mimi wondered whether this Nathan Albemarle was just a fantasy, her Prince Charming, not on a horse, but in a uniform. Just a way out of the life she'd fallen into. *And did he really exist?* He must, Mimi told herself. Kitty was no liar. And she had a ring. Perhaps he wasn't quite as dashing as Kitty implied? Was he really from Mansion Drive? One of those grand homes on the hill? Still, Kitty came alive when she talked about Nathan. Her eyes sparkled. There was a different energy about her. This was the Kitty Mimi had seen when she was wearing his ring.

"Are you going to be married in the church?"

"Courthouse. Nathan isn't Catholic, and who knows how much penance I'd have to make before they'd let me get married." She cracked a small smile. "Miles of prayers."

"You could work it out," Mimi insisted.

"Don't be too sure. Anyways, the wedding's got to be right away. And Mr. Albemarle will be here in a few days." She seemed to think of something. "I can wear my light blue gown to the courthouse, can't I?"

There was so little silk and satin available for wedding dresses, many brides were wearing their best suits or dresses.

"Yes, of course you can. But wouldn't you rather have a real wedding?"

"I would. But I'm trying to outrun the quivers, you see. I'll be safe from them when he comes home."

She still had the quivers. Mimi worried about the promise Kitty extracted from her.

"Let me know when you set the date. Addie will want to make you a wedding cake. And you'll need photos. Derry has a good camera."

"I'd like that. I'll let you know. Nathan says we don't have to live here. We can always go away."

"What about his family?"

"He says I matter more to him than they do. I've never mattered that much to anyone. Not even Joe. Nathan has a brother and a mother. His father's dead. I guess he's got that in common with Joe."

"He sounds wonderful. And he's getting more than a wife. He's getting a lifeguard too."

Kitty laughed. "I'm giving him swimming lessons, first thing."

They were interrupted by a deep, thick hick-accented voice from behind them. "Hello, Kitty girl! What're you doing in this neck of the woods?"

Kitty dropped her fork on her plate. She turned her face toward the speaker.

"Clem. What are you doing in this neck of the woods?"

Seventeen

"GOT ANY SUGAR for me today, Kitty girl?"

"I'm clean out of sugar coupons. You must be mistaking me for somebody else." Kitty didn't meet his eyes.

"We ain't back home, Kitty. You always got some sugar for good ol' Clem."

"You must be looking for Hattie. She's dead, you know."

"I hadn't heard."

He blinked, but he showed no sign of being affected by this news. This man wasn't a soldier, a sailor, or a flyboy. Despite his brown suit and hat and tan shirt, he had the look of a laborer. He didn't wear a tie and his nails were dirty. His hair was sun-streaked, his hatband sweat-stained. Clem's face was all raw angles, his skin stretched taut, dark from working under the sun.

"I don't know nothing about no sugar," Kitty repeated. "Can't you see I'm with my friend here?"

Clem spared a nod for Mimi. "How do, miss."

"She's quality, Clem. And she's my friend. Leave her alone."

Clem shrugged and turned back to Kitty. "You on vacation, girl?"

"I'm not working right now. Got it?"

"No sugar for poor ol' Clem," he lamented. "Any word on where Hattie stashed her goods?"

"Hattie kept herself to herself."

He snorted. "If you think of something, you let ol' Clem know."

"I don't know nothing." There was steel in Kitty's voice.

"Well then, catch you later, alligator." He tipped his battered hat. "Shame about Hattie. Real shame. I'll be seeing you around, Kitty girl."

Clem turned on his heel and shuffled out of the diner. Mimi watched him go. Kitty picked up her fork and twirled her spaghetti.

"What was that all about?" Mimi asked.

"Nothing."

"Didn't seem like nothing."

"Less than nothing," Kitty said.

"He knew Hattie?"

"Lots of men knew Hattie. She was a popular gal."

"He seemed interested in you and her belongings."

"He's a buzzard. Buzzards always gather to clean the bones. The buzzards wanted Hattie. She was broken, and now she is gone."

Is Clem a buzzard? Mimi shook off her dread. "Tell me about Clem."

"Clem's not interested in me, he's interested in—the business."

"You're familiar with him. Was he working with Hattie?"

"Maybe. He used to live near Forgotten Creek. He showed up here one day." Kitty set down her fork. "And Hattie— Truth is, Mimi, I'd tell you if I knew. We didn't share secrets, Hattie and me. The other gals and me, we aren't really girlfriends, like college coeds or something. Hattie kept to herself, and like I said she tried to sell other things, not just herself."

"What kinds of things?"

"I told you."

"Tell me again, Kitty. Why?"

"Hattie figured that the things she heard about but didn't really own, they had to belong to rich people. Richer than us, anyway. So what did it matter? They could always get more, because people with money got ways and means. They don't care about ration books. Gretel says Hattie got into trouble a few times for selling things she didn't own. Maybe they weren't even there. Didn't even exist. I don't know. Maybe that made somebody mad."

"If you knew what kind of trouble she got into, we might be able to understand what happened to her, and who might have killed her."

"That's the thing, Mimi. I don't want to know."

"I suppose not."

Mimi silently chided herself. Most people wouldn't want to know. And the answers might not quiet the quivers Kitty had. The quivers Mimi was beginning to feel.

"You make it sound like she had a plan." Kitty pouted. "I'm not sure she ever planned any of it. Most of us try to forget what our customers talk about. Hattie, she liked to remember."

"Such as?"

"Oh, you know," Kitty said. "A new set of tires waiting for someone at a gas station. A case of liquor. Things like that. I told you we called her 'light-fingered Hattie.' It's not like I know the details."

Human nature was a funny thing. Mimi was inclined to let small things go. If people wanted to pool together their ration coupons to bake a cake, it didn't bother her. However, when things weren't so small, and murder could be involved— That was different. Even for a stenographer.

"What do you know about the black market?" Mimi asked.

"Nothing. Besides, black market sounds like a really big thing. Hattie was just into penny ante stuff."

"The black market can be large, or it can be small. She was dabbling."

"Well, if she was, it's got nothing to do with me." She finished her Coke.

"What if stealing and playing around with bad guys like this Clem got Hattie killed?"

The other woman went silent for a moment. Kitty seemed to have a talent for compartmentalizing her feelings. Nathan Albemarle slipped into one of them, selling her body into another. Still another belonged to West Virginia and the family she left behind. Maybe all those compartments helped her survive.

"Why do you even talk to me, Mimi? Most people, most women, wouldn't come near someone like me. Aren't you afraid I'll contaminate you?"

"Aren't you afraid I'll bore you to death with my goody-goodyness?"

Kitty laughed out loud. "You got me. I just want your fashion advice, sis. But I'm serious."

"Contaminate me? No. We're responsible for our own actions. And where I'm from, out West, what they call fallen women, or prostitutes, were always part of our history. We can't just sweep them under the carpet."

"That's what we are, somebody's secret dirt."

"My grandmother was so full of stories, usually with some moral or some Bible story. She told stories to warn us and to entertain us. When it came to Mary Magdalene, she would point to Mary's modern sisters and the great love and understanding that the Lord had for them."

"My granny would have hit me over the head with that Bible."

"Mine even pointed out Mattie Silks to me when I was a little girl."

"Mattie Silks? Who's she? Don't sound like a real name."

"It was the one she was known by. She owned a famous house of ill repute in frontier Denver, called the House of Mirrors."

"Your whorehouses have names?"

"This one did. Mattie was ancient by the time I saw her, a tiny lady with a shriveled apple of a face."

"I don't believe it. Where did you see this famous madam?"

"At the racetrack."

"The racetrack?" Kitty started to laugh. "You hung out at the racetrack with your grandma?"

"The Irish love their horses, and my grandmother loved to bet her pin money on them. She won more than she lost, and Madam Mattie had a prize racehorse. Mattie and my grandmother were at the track so often, they always waved to each other. And back in the eighteen hundreds, Mattie supposedly fought a pistol duel with another madam over a man. During the duel, they shot him. Guy named Cortez Thomson."

"That's pretty funny. I reckon he deserved it. Probably the cause of the duel."

"Another time Mattie took all her girls on a vacation to Europe. Told people over there she ran a little boarding house for society ladies."

"Golly. We don't get vacations. I'd like to ask Madam Cherry for a trip to Europe, watch her face."

"When you're married, Kitty, life will be different. Anyway, I think out West people are a bit more accepting of the oldest profession."

"You got a lot of funny ways to describe that profession."

Mimi nodded. "There are even people like my grandmother who think that soiled doves—"

"Soiled doves? That's rich! That's what they called us?"

"Soiled doves were closer to saints than sinners, she said. The prostitutes followed the men, so they arrived out West before the other women came. They followed them to the mining camps and when smallpox broke out, everyone fled except the ladies of the night, who stayed behind and nursed them."

"That's because they had no place else to go, Mimi."

"They risked their lives and some of them emerged disfigured. One was known as Silver Heels."

"Your grandma sounds like a real pepper pot."

Mimi's turn to laugh. "She is the bane of my father's life. He never expected to be living with his mother-in-law, especially one who never shuts up. My mother turns a deaf ear."

Kitty thought for a moment. "Maybe Nathan and I should move out West after the war. I wouldn't have to worry about these snooty people here finding out about me."

"We all have things we'd like to keep quiet," Mimi said.

"Ain't that the truth." Kitty ordered a piece of the blueberry pie. "I'm going to have a baby, Mimi. I'm three months gone."

"Oh my God!" Mimi managed not to spill her weak coffee, but it was a near thing. "Is it Nathan's?"

"Course it is. I know you're wondering how I know. He's the only one I never used protection with. I have my own supply of rubbers. I knew right away. I just knew he put a baby inside of me. Like a little light. I could feel it. It don't make any sense, but sometimes your body tells you things."

"I guess you would know." Mimi really had no idea.

"Besides, all those GIs— Believe me, they don't want a disease from us as much as we don't want any babies from them. And we don't have any diseases. Madam Cherry makes sure of that."

Mimi put up her hand.

"Wait, let's get back to the baby. Have you been to a doctor?"

"Like I said, we get regular checkups and all. That's another reason I'm getting out. I won't be able to work much longer. I'll start showing."

"Oh, Kitty, please be safe." Mimi felt tears spring to her eyes. She brushed them away before Kitty could see them. "Does Nathan know?"

Kitty nodded. "That's why he pulled some strings and took on extra missions, so he can get home, so we can get married. I can get ready for the baby, and I'll be able to wear my ring all the time. That's if nothing happens."

"What could happen?" Mimi said, thinking of the hundreds of things that could happen.

Kitty finished her pie and opened her coin purse.

"Are you finished, sis? I gotta go." Their moment of intimate girlfriend talk was over. The waitress asked if they needed anything else. Kitty said no and fished out her money. "It's on me, Mimi. Thanks for helping me, the shopping and all. You're so sweet."

"You're welcome." Mimi realized they had just spent hours shopping and she hadn't bought anything for herself.

ca

Mimi reached the Barrett Library on Queen Street minutes before it closed. She wanted to comb through their newspapers for any information about the mysterious Nathan Albemarle and his family. Her friendly librarian was eager to help.

Bingo. He really existed. Nathan's mother appeared regularly in the society pages, with the Red Cross and other charity events. The articles helpfully mentioned that her son, Nathan Albemarle Jr., was a pilot in the Army Air Forces. Her other son, Jubal, two years older, was at home. Either he hadn't joined the service yet, or perhaps he wasn't suited to it. Perhaps he had some impairment that kept him from joining up. Like Richie Richardson, who was brilliant with the violin, but didn't fall in line with most people's expectations.

In the grainy news photographs Nathan's mother, Mrs. Charlotte Albemarle, appeared large and imposing, what everyone called "big-boned." She wore dark dresses with white collars and cuffs, and silly little hats perched on her head. In some photos she wore glasses. She might have been attractive in her youth, but those days were behind her. Mimi placed her age at mid-to-late fifties.

Charlotte Albemarle never really smiled for the newspaper cameras. She posed her mouth in a little line that barely turned up at the ends, as if being asked to smile was too much of an effort. Maybe she had bad teeth. Mimi tucked all this information away for later. Her librarian apologized, but the library was closing.

"You must be gathering information for your mystery. What do you expect to find in the society pages?"

"Characters. Interesting characters."

"Very good idea. Miss Christie would agree. She's always writing her murder mysteries about people with money.

Where there's money, there's a motive for murder, she would say."

"It seems that way, doesn't it?"

Mimi could have gone dancing with Roz and Franny that evening, but she was afraid of meeting someone equally as colorful as Kitty, who might extract further promises from her. She turned her friends down. She needed someplace quiet, someplace dark, where she could disappear. And above all, someplace cool on this hot summer night.

There was only one place that fit the bill. Mimi went to the pictures at the air-conditioned Richmond Theatre on King Street. It looked like she was seeing the movie Sally at the office had recommended, *The More the Merrier*. Sally said that Jean Arthur was "a real hoot."

EIGHTEEN

SUNDAYS IN ALEXANDRIA for Mimi were generally low key. This Sunday was not one of those.

Even though Derry would have preferred the services at Christ Church on Washington Street, with its pedigree of historic worshippers that included George Washington and Robert E. Lee, the Richardsons worshipped together at the neighborhood Baptist church, where Addie felt more comfortable. Derry, Addie, and Richie were back home well before Mimi returned from Mass at St. Mary's.

Mimi sensed something was wrong before she walked through the front door. All the usual enticing aromas were missing. She had grown to expect the scent of chicken or ham, or if meat was scarce, then a thick stew, with onions and herbs. But today, dinner had not been started. It wasn't the only thing that struck Mimi as odd. She'd hoped to see Kitty at church, but Kitty wasn't there.

Mimi opened the front door to find Addie in hysterics, a worried Derry by her side. Richie was running from one side of the room to the other, something he did when he was not supposed to be playing his violin, but he wanted to.

"Burglars! Thieves! My sugar!" These were the only words Mimi could make out amidst the weeping and wailing. She looked to Derry for an explanation.

"It seems a thief has stolen the bees' sugar from the cellar, all that was left over from last winter."

"How much sugar?"

"A thousand pounds, more or less."

"More or less? That's an awful lot of sugar." She knew it was stored in fifty-pound bags, but that was much more than Mimi expected. She supposed there was no regulation requiring

Addie to return the sugar, though the surplus would technically have to be used before more was issued. Could this be considered hoarding? Mimi shook her head to clear it.

I am not an OPA investigator! I am a stenographer!

"There are a lot of bees and many beehives, and Addie has always been able to make her supplies stretch," Derry said. "Strictly legal."

"You would be the person to know," Mimi said. "I just didn't know she had so much."

She hadn't paid much attention to what lay behind the locked door in the basement, but shouldn't she have had an idea? The scene at the diner the day before with the mysterious Clem replayed in her head. He said he wanted sugar, too. Mimi had assumed he meant sex.

Was that really just the double entendre she had taken it for?

"It's not for our use," Addie managed to say between sobs. "It's for my precious bees. For the honey. For our friends and neighbors." She wiped her eyes with an embroidered hankie.

"What happened?"

Derry, normally calm, rubbed his face in agitation. "Near as I can make out, we were at our respective churches when persons unknown broke into the cellar from the backyard. I would say most, if not all, of our neighbors on our street were also at church at the time."

A pair of slanted doors covered the stairs to the cellar from the outside, an entrance once used for coal deliveries. Who took the sugar? Mimi wondered. Who would even know there would be so much sugar?

"But those doors are always padlocked," she said.

"Hacksaw would be my guess." Derry patted his pockets to find his pipe and tobacco. He filled the pipe, tamped it down, and lit it, a comforting ritual he shared with Mimi's boss.

"It wasn't as if the sugar was lying out in the middle of the cellar," Mimi added. "It was locked away in the closet." The space had been specially built for Addie's precious supplies.

She was security conscious, apparently more so since the war began and goods had become scarcer.

"That lock was also cut through," Derry said. "Discarded on the floor. None of us has touched anything. Not even Richie."

"That's right, they didn't touch me, and I didn't touch anything," said Richie, interrupting his pacing.

Mimi walked through the kitchen door to the yard and peeked out. The cellar doors were flung wide open. "The police?"

"Just called them. I imagine they'll be here by and by."

"I wonder what my boss would say."

"You're thinking the sugar's going to wind up on the black market?" Derry asked.

"It crossed my mind."

Richie paced the room again and reached for his fiddle and bow. He looked to his father for permission. There were rules about when Richie could play music, and Sundays before five in the afternoon were quiet time.

"That thought occurred to me as well." Derry nodded to his son. "Go ahead, son, we'll bend the rule this once. But keep it soft and light for your mother. Nothing dramatic."

"Thank you, sir." Richie launched into a quiet tune suitable for a summer day.

"And Mimi, would you wait to call your boss until the police make their report?"

"The government?" Addie said, alarmed. She hiccupped through her tears. "You're not bringing the government into it?"

"I'm not sure the police would even alert OPA," Mimi said.

"I'm sure they would not." As a local lawyer, Derry had reason to know this for a fact. "However, it's always better to have all the information first."

Mimi replayed her conversation with Kitty in her head. The dead magdalen Hattie Jones and her petty thefts. Clem and his quest for "sugar." She decided it was too soon to suggest a connection to this sugar theft. George Prescott would think she was crazy. Or writing pulp fiction.

A knock at the front door interrupted them. Two Alexandria police officers, one tall and one short, waited on the front porch for all the neighbors to see. Addie wrung her hands while Derry let them in. The cops looked like Mutt and Jeff, but their names were Officer Gregson, the tall one, and Officer Warwick, the short one. They seemed to know Derry Richardson well.

Once inside and given a capsule description of the crime, Gregson and Warwick, followed by Derry, Addie, and Mimi, trooped down the cellar steps to inspect the broken locks. They agreed: It was a hacksaw.

"Who else knew about the sugar?" Officer Gregson asked.

"No one outside the family," Derry assured them. But this was the kind of town where everyone was considered family.

"What about you, Miss?" he asked Mimi, but Addie jumped in to answer.

"Mimi Smith is boarding with us and she's family too."

"She's like my sister Julia," Richie added, "only she likes my music better than my real actual sister."

The cop smiled. "Anyone else? You got help that comes in?"

"Evangeline Williams, she's our part-time housekeeper," Addie said. "Part-time since she decided to go work at the factory. She's been with me for years. She would never think of such a thing as stealing. Honest as the day is long."

Derry concurred. The thieves must be strangers, he said. Though there were friends, neighbors, customers, acquaintances, who knew of Addie's little Kingdom of Honey and might have guessed there was sugar to be had. Officer Gregson assured them that a detective, one Lt. Baker, would be coming soon to make further inquiries. Gregson and Derry shared a look.

"This is more than a misdemeanor, Mister Richardson," Officer Gregson said. "That was a ton of sugar."

"Actually, it was half a ton of sugar," Richie said.

"It could certainly encourage a thief. Someone with a very large sweet tooth," the officer continued.

"Like a bear," Officer Warwick agreed. "And there ain't no bears in Alexandria, Virginia."

"It's not much sugar when you consider how many beehives I have to feed over the winter," Addie said. "That's what I was saving it for. It would just be a start on this next winter."

Derry put a calming hand on Addie's shoulder. The officer assured them their report would go to Lt. Baker. These cops clearly didn't want to deal with a felony, or a potentially hysterical woman.

After they left, Mimi asked Addie who else knew about the sugar. "Kitty Hawkins, for example?"

"No, not her," Addie said quickly. But Mimi saw a shadow of doubt cross her face.

Lt. Samson Baker arrived a half hour later, stepping heavily through the front door in tan slacks and a rumpled tan jacket over a pale blue shirt. His tie was loose and he was sweating. It was midafternoon, but he had the air of a man who'd been up since midnight.

Addie apparently knew the lieutenant well. "Coffee for you, Sam?"

"Thanks, Addie."

"Appreciate your coming, Sam." Derry and the detective had met too.

"Sorry it's under these circumstances." Lt. Sam Baker was a middle-aged man with a thick head of wavy tan-colored hair, going gray. A map of lines circled his eyes. Like Mimi's boss and Derry, Baker was apparently too old for the draft and was needed on the home front. With a strong cup of Addie's real coffee, the coffee she only brought out on the Sabbath, and a generous slice of cake, he seemed to come back to life.

"So, you got yourself a little break-in," he said with a Southern accent. "That's a lot of sugar, Addie."

Addie's tears started once again and Derry rushed to her side. "What do you think, Sam?"

"I think you figure out where it's going to be sold or used, you figure out who stole it."

"Richie, dear, time to do your outside chores." Addie obviously wanted him out of earshot. His head dropped, but he put down his violin and went outside.

"Miss?" Lt. Baker turned to Mimi.

"Mimi Smith," she said. "I live here."

"Smith." He made a note in his notebook. "Thank goodness for simple spelling."

"Mimi is part of the family," Addie said again, to Mimi's surprise. No one mentioned that Mimi worked at the Office of Price Administration. A mere stenographer would be of no interest. She also realized that the large amount of stolen sugar would most likely take it out of OPA's jurisdiction. As the officer said, that much sugar was a felony, not a misdemeanor.

"This used to be a nice quiet little town," Baker sighed. "That's the way I liked it. Not much crime, let alone serious crimes. But this war— It's not just overseas, it's a war here at home too."

"Times have changed," Derry said.

"How is Rhonda Fay?" Addie leaned over to Mimi and whispered, "Rhonda Fay's his fiancée. They've been walking down that aisle for years."

"I heard that," Baker said. "I'm old, Addie, but I'm not deaf."

"Good to know," Addie said. A little laughter helped break the tension.

"I don't see Rhonda Fay much these days. She's working at the Navy's torpedo factory, you know. Gets off work smelling like a grease monkey, dirt on her face. Happy as a pig in— Well, you know."

"Dirty work must be hard on her."

"I don't know about that. She seems to enjoy it an awful lot."

"Women need a little pin money, I always say," said the queen of honey.

Mimi said nothing. What Addie called pin money was no doubt a hefty sum. She knew Addie kept her own account at the bank. Derry said it was just easier to keep the honey business separate, for accounting purposes.

After the polite preliminaries, Lt. Baker get down to business. He turned to a clean page in his notebook. "Now. Who knew you had sugar?"

"Anyone who knows anything about the bee business," Addie said. "We didn't talk about it. Most people just know I have honey to sell."

"This was more than petty theft," Baker said. "These thieves—"

"You think there were more than one?" Derry interrupted.

"More than likely. One man could make multiple trips, I suppose, lifting all those fifty-pound bags. But it's heavy work. Two or three men make more sense. They also might want a lookout while they're hacksawing off the locks."

"Professional thieves then," Derry said. "Most folks would know everyone would be out of the house on a Sunday morning, attending church."

"Would you say this is a church-going neighborhood?" Baker asked, knowing the answer.

"Yes, indeed," Addie said. "We Richardsons go to the Baptist Church, and Mimi here attends St. Mary's Catholic. Everyone goes to church, except Mrs. Martin, who goes to the Synagogue on Saturdays. And she lives so far down on St. Asaph, she couldn't have seen or heard anything."

Baker drained his cup and stared mournfully at his empty plate. Addie jumped up to resupply him with coffee and cake. "These thieves were prepared with a hacksaw, they knew the sugar was locked up, and they seemed to know their way around your cellar. They knew the precise location of the locked-up sugar stash. Did they take any honey?"

"If they did, it was just a jar or two," Addie said. "I'd have to check my inventory."

"Interesting." Baker scratched his day-old beard. "Grabbing a jar of honey because it was handy would be merely a theft of opportunity. Your sugar, though, that had a bigger purpose for them. Not only that, but they were also in and out quickly, in the time it took everyone to attend their respective churches."

"That's simply horrible." Addie teared up. "You can't be talking about our neighbors."

"Who else is familiar with your home? Your housekeeper?" He checked his notes. "Evangeline Williams?"

"Evangeline comes two, three times a week, when she's not working at the torpedo factory. But she's been with us ever since Richie was a baby."

"You trust her?"

"Absolutely." Derry was quick to jump in. "She keeps us all in line, and she is honest to a fault."

Richie must have abandoned his outside chores, because his violin was making itself heard. It reminded Baker that he was part of the family.

"What about your boy?" Baker held up his hands. "I'm not blaming him. I know he's a bit different from other boys. But you know what they say. Loose lips sink ships."

"He just plays his fiddle." Derry sounded offended. "He wouldn't say anything."

"Not intentionally," Baker agreed. "Of course not."

"More coffee?" Addie offered.

"No thanks, Addie." Baker didn't need to say much more. He'd planted a seed that Richie Richardson, who liked to talk when he wasn't playing music, could have inadvertently said something to someone. "I'll see what I can find out. You'll be hearing from me."

Lt. Baker put his notebook back into his pocket and shook out a Camel from a pack of cigarettes. He lit it as he waved goodbye and let himself out the front door.

No one had mentioned Kitty Hawkins. Was it because her life seemed hard enough as it was? Or because no one wanted to put her under a police microscope? Mimi didn't believe Kitty had anything to do with the break-in, not personally. She'd helped with the honey harvest, but that was far away, down the river, not at the house. But could she have let the information slip? To someone like the late "light-fingered Hattie"? Someone who spread the word that there was sugar to be stolen? Hattie was a wild card. And that sleazy Clem had been pressing Kitty for sugar the previous day.

"May I use the phone?" Mimi asked. "I'd like to call Kitty."

"You don't think she—" Addie started to say.

"I don't think anything, Addie, but she keeps some seedy company."

Mimi didn't know whether the Richardsons were aware of the other women who worked at the Chicken Shack, the women who had died. Polly and Hattie. Derry gestured his assent.

"Use the phone in my office, Mimi. There's more privacy."

She retrieved the number from her purse and slipped into Derry's inner sanctum. Once the home's second parlor, the first-floor room was now a library, with book-lined walls, thick oriental carpets, and Derry's big mahogany desk. She slid the double pocket doors closed. Taking a leather side chair, Mimi dialed the telephone. The residents of the rooming house shared a single wall phone in the hallway, Kitty had told her. Mimi let it ring. On the seventh or eighth ring, a female voice answered.

"Yeah? Hello?"

"Is Kitty Hawkins there?"

"Think she's sleeping."

"It's important."

There was a pause and a reluctant sigh. "I'll go see."

A few minutes passed. Kitty came to the phone, muffling a yawn. "What do you want?"

"It's Mimi, Kitty." Mimi was mindful of Kitty's quivers. She didn't want to make things worse for her.

"Mimi?" Kitty was instantly wide awake. "Is something wrong?"

NINETEEN

"I'LL MAKE THIS quick, Kitty. There was a break-in at the Richardsons' house. This morning, when everyone was at church."

"I didn't make it to church this morning. Late night. What'd you say? A break-in?"

"Someone made off with about a thousand pounds of sugar. They cut the lock on the cellar door. Someone knew it was there and locked up in a specially built closet. They cut the lock off the closet too. They hauled it out in fifty-pound bags."

There was a gasp on the other end of the line. "No. Not Addie's sugar. That's the sugar for the bees— Wait, Mimi, why are you telling me this, anyway?"

"You knew there was sugar to feed the bees. You know how much it takes to feed them."

"Anyone would know that. Anyone who knows bees. Lots of people keep bees these days."

"I'm not saying you had anything to do with it, Kitty. I'm just saying you might know something, even if you don't know you do." Mimi couldn't help thinking about Clem, the raw-boned man who was quiet but oddly menacing, with a hint of violence. "What if Hattie Jones knew?"

"Hattie?"

"She made a practice of finding things out, didn't she?"

"But she's dead. And how would she know?"

"Idle talk. A theft like this takes time to plan. And you were telling me Hattie liked to sell things she didn't own."

"I don't like blaming Hattie for everything. She can't stand up for herself anymore."

"And Kitty, what would they use all that sugar for? Are they breaking it down to sell in five-pound bags? That's penny ante, like you said Hattie was. But that's a lot of work for a few pies. What else would make sugar so valuable?"

"Shine," Kitty said reluctantly.

"Shine?"

"Moonshine. My guess. Hootch. Booze. Liquor. I don't know, Mimi, that's the only thing I can think of. Takes a lot of sugar to make it. The more sugar you got, the better the shine and the better the price."

Mimi was learning new things. "You're talking about illegal whiskey and stills? Really?"

"You got it. Moonshine. Near everyone I know back home in West Virginia makes a little shine, or buys it, or sells it. We call them still jockeys. It's not like Virginia, where the state revenuers are death on moonshiners."

"Huh. That's the first thing you think of?"

"I can't help the way I think. You can take the gal out of West Virginia, but you can't take West Virginia out of the gal. But I'm just talking through my hat, Mimi. I don't know nothing about this."

"How dangerous are these moonshiners?"

"Depends. They're just people. Country people. Some good, some bad. Mimi, I don't know who broke into Addie's cellar. I don't know who took the sugar."

"You may not know, but you have an idea."

There was a brief hesitation. "No, I don't. Really. And it could be dangerous to try and find out. Ask Addie, she would know."

Addie would know?

"You're not involved in it in any way?"

"Course not." She sounded hurt. "I'd never take anything from Addie. She's always been good to me."

"I'm sorry, Kitty. I know that."

"Gotta go. Mimi, you're the only one I trust. We'll talk later. If anything happens, remember, you *promised* me."

Kitty hung up. Mimi put the receiver back in the cradle and took a deep breath.

"Everything okay with Kitty?" Addie asked when Mimi returned to the kitchen.

"Far as I know." She took a paper bag filled with flour, salt, pepper, and Addie's special herbs. She tossed in pieces of chicken and shook the bag until everything was coated. Simple chores would help calm her mind, she hoped, and process what Kitty had said. Addie was already developing a plan to get more sugar for the next winter. She was putting the shock of the break-in behind her.

"I hope that nice Mr. Deacon is still on the ration board. When we talked last, he seemed downright reasonable."

Mimi handed over the floured chicken. Most likely they came from one of her farmer friends and not the grocery store, which was often out of meat even for shoppers with ration tickets. Addie readied the pieces for the large cast iron skillet. Mimi started assembling the ingredients for biscuits.

Soon, a delicious aroma filled the air. Mimi was grateful that even a daring daytime burglary couldn't keep Addie from her kitchen. The chicken was frying and carrots were roasting. The biscuits were ready to pop in the oven. Richie skipped into the kitchen, still playing his violin.

"Did you make that one up?" Mimi asked.

Richie smiled. "I reckon I heard it somewhere. Maybe on the radio. Maybe in my head." He was instructed to set the table. He reluctantly set down his instrument, but he kept humming his tunes.

Addie would know, Kitty said.

Really? Mimi's landlady knew all about moonshine and sugar and black markets in West Virginia? Addie was opinionated, kind, and Mimi's friend. And somehow because she was also from Forgotten Creek, she refrained from judging Kitty too harshly. Unlike Evangeline, for example, who clearly disliked her. Addie had welcomed Kitty to help at harvest time. She let her take fresh vegetables from her victory garden.

Kitty told Mimi she liked getting her hands in the dirt, because she grew up on a farm. And Addie's honey and fresh produce had to be welcome. Still, it was hard for Mimi to put the two pictures of Kitty together, the helper in overalls who was in love with a dashing flyboy—and the ill-dressed tart being mocked by military men at the dance.

But did Addie and Kitty have something else in common? Illegal liquor? Mimi tried to let that go. They were from the same hardscrabble place where making a drop of moonshine was just something people did. Knowing about it didn't mean you were involved in it. And Addie seldom took even a sip of Derry's bourbon.

After all, it wasn't like Addie had a still in her victory garden. Between the cornstalks and the apple tree, there wasn't any room for a still.

TWENTY

REMEMBER, YOU PROMISED.
Mimi wished Kitty had ended their recent conversation with anything but that. Those words kept ringing in her head for the rest of the day and night. They followed her to the office Monday morning. George Prescott was already at the office. Mimi was surprised; he generally wandered in later.

"May I talk to you, George?" Mimi entered his office, a warm cup of chicory in one hand and a small jar of amber liquid in the other. It had worked on Mr. Deacon.

"This better be good," he greeted her. "You know I like to start the week in a quiet frame of mind." Who didn't? She set the jar down on his desk. George picked it up, letting the sunshine flow through it, like liquid gold. "Honey? For me?"

"From my private stash. Honey from my landlady's bees. I earned it helping out with the harvest. No ration coupons required. I'm sure your wife would like it."

"I'm sure she would, if she ever found out about it. Something that will never happen. It will be just as good sweetening *my* coffee."

"Coffee?"

"We made a pot at home yesterday. Nearly as good today, warmed up." He pointed to a small red plaid Thermos.

She smiled brightly. "You might want to warm up your coffee."

"We're going to have a chat, are we?" George poured more hot coffee from his Thermos. He opened the honey slowly, as if it were a great treasure, and stirred a spoonful of gold into his cup. "All right, what's the story?"

Would that one jar of honey be enough? Mimi balanced her boss's potential bad mood against her possibly being found at fault if she held back information. You never knew what might be valuable in these troubled times.

"There was a burglary at the Richardsons' yesterday, while everyone was at church. Our respective churches."

"The Richardsons?"

"You know, I room with them."

"Ah, your rooming house." Calling it a rooming house may have been an exaggeration—Mimi was currently the only tenant outside the family—but it was technically true. "And I should care because? Well, I do care, but why particularly?"

"The thieves took a large amount of sugar."

"How much sugar?"

"About a thousand pounds," Mimi said.

"Mother of saints, why so much sugar in a private home?" George was alert now.

"It's to feed the bees, for the honey." She pointed to the jar he had just opened.

"That much for bees?"

"There are a lot of bees. Maybe a couple hundred hives. Or more. And that's just a start on what she'll need next winter, according to Addie. My landlady." She could tell George was just as incredulous as she had been. "Each hive might need a dozen pounds or more to get through the winter, she says. We're not farmers, or beekeepers, so I guess we wouldn't know, would we?"

"That's one hell of a lot of sugar," he said. "Outside our jurisdiction. Unless it all ends up in the black market."

"Where else would it end up?" Mimi asked.

He cleared his throat. "Even then, OPA would have to request oversight of the investigation. Let me get a pencil." He jotted down the details, the time, the address, and the name of the police officer in charge. "Seems like these people are getting more brazen."

"What people?"

"War profiteers, trying to squeeze a dirty profit out of this war."

"If you don't think OPA has jurisdiction, then why are you interested?"

"No telling when we might get involved with something outside the norm, when manpower is low. Local authorities could kick it back to us. And I like to know the depth and breadth of what the hell is happening out there. Don't get your hopes up for an emergency jurisdiction, Mary Margaret. That's pretty unlikely." George sipped his honey-sweetened coffee. "I'll give the Alexandria police a ring. See if we can get a copy of that lieutenant's report. You don't mind picking it up tomorrow on your way to work, do you?"

"Nope. Happy to." She tried to say it casually, without revealing her ulterior motive. The police department was in City Hall, only six blocks from the Richardsons' house. Although after picking up the report, Mimi would have very little chance of finding a seat on the bus to D.C., she would enjoy the early morning walk to City Hall, before the day grew hot. She loved to look at all the old historic homes along the way, wondering who lived in them. And she could read the lieutenant's report before turning it over to Prescott. "I talked with a Lieutenant Sam Baker," she told George. "He didn't ask me where I worked."

"And you didn't tell him?"

"I didn't think it was important. I'm only a stenographer."

George stared at her before answering. He didn't want to lose a good stenographer, and he knew Mimi was itching for bigger and better things. "Good. No sense in getting their backs up. I won't mention where I got my information either."

"Thanks."

"Mary Margaret, one more thing." George took his pipe out. A sure sign he had some thinking to do. "Do you think the folks you live with could be involved in some way? Maybe stage an elaborate break-in while you're away at church? Hide this sugar stash someplace, so they can get their hands on additional sugar?"

Mimi sipped her chicory while George puffed on his pipe. "Derry Richardson is a respected Alexandria attorney. I don't think he's the kind to run a criminal enterprise. And Addie, Adeline Richardson, knows every regulation in the book. She collects my ration coupons religiously and faithfully follows the letter of the law. She might tread delicately on the line, but she wouldn't fall on the wrong side."

"You're sure?"

Mimi smiled. "Addie'd be happy to tell you all about her business, her ways and means, the life cycle of the bee. And exactly how much sugar it takes to overwinter all those millions of bees."

"Millions, huh?" George shook his head. "I believe I can skip that particular pleasure. And I don't need any more unhappy housewives writing the White House with complaints about this agency."

At the grocers recently Mimi had overheard a woman who was receiving extra sugar coupons for canning fruit. "The government will never know I'm baking a green apple pie *for myself*." Mimi simply closed her eyes and moved on. People needed their small victories.

Mimi left George with his jar of honey, his warmed-over coffee and his pipe. Like her landlady, she decided the honey was simply a nice gesture on her part, and not some kind of bribe to gain information on a crime. She had made her report on the sugar theft, so no matter what happened, she couldn't be accused of hiding anything.

But nothing could eradicate the bad feeling she had. Dread settled on Mimi's shoulders like a fifty-pound bag of stolen sugar. Or like Kitty's "quivers."

Mimi tried to tell herself things were fine, her fears were nothing, they were normal. But she couldn't shake her own quivers. She had more questions for Kitty, and she hoped the answers would calm her fears. Mimi exited her usual afternoon bus several blocks before her normal stop and walked to Kitty's shabby rooming house, hoping to find her there, rather than at the Chicken Shack.

ognl

Mimi had never seen the place before. She knocked on the front door, but no one answered. She tried the door and found it unlocked, so she stepped inside. Individual mailboxes with handwritten room numbers lined the tiny front hall. Kitty shared a small second-floor room with two other women, number five. Kitty's name was there, which reassured Mimi she was in the right place.

There was a small living room to the left, where presumably the residents could greet visitors. The walls were a dingy yellow in the afternoon light, likely stained by nicotine from years of residents smoking. A shabby chintz-covered sofa and two mismatched side chairs surrounded a worn coffee table, scarred by carved initials and cigarette burns. The room smelled of cigarettes and desperation.

Mimi wanted to leave, but she kept moving forward. Beyond the parlor was a dining room with knockabout furniture, a large table and more unmatched chairs. A small buffet stacked with clean dishes leaned against a far wall. The kitchen lay beyond, but Mimi didn't venture there. She was certain she would smell boiled cabbage and burnt Postum. A tiny powder room was tucked under the stairwell, facing numbered doors for the residents' rooms on the first floor.

Up the creaky steps to the second floor Mimi found Kitty's room, number five, toward the back. There was no answer to Mimi's knock. She pushed the door open and walked in.

The light blue paint was old and chipped. The room was so crowded with furniture there was barely room to walk. Mimi maneuvered around bunk beds and a single cot, three small dressers and a tiny armoire. Hooks on the wall and the back of the door were heavy with garments. Next to the door hung a calendar marked up with work schedules. The occupants shared one small mirror, one small sink, and a small communal bathroom down the hall. The atmosphere of stale perfume and dust was suffocating. This place was worse than she had imagined.

"If you're looking for Kitty, she's not here," came a voice from behind her.

Mimi turned to see a striking dark-haired woman. "How did you know I was looking for Kitty?"

"The phone calls. Kitty told me she had a friend who might come by and ask about her. We don't have a lot of girlfriends visit here. She's lucky." The stranger leaned against the doorjamb with a languid grace. She wore a flowered wrapper that revealed more than it concealed.

"I'm Mimi. Mimi Smith."

"Seraphina. I work at the Chicken Shack."

"Do you all work there?"

"Pretty much. Members of the same sisterhood. Sometimes we trade off with Madame Cherry's floating pleasure palace."

Mimi smiled. "Kitty said she got seasick there."

"Those are the breaks."

"Do you know where Kitty is?"

"I imagine she's at work. Trying to stockpile some money. Your phone call last night got her moving."

"She's planning to move out."

"We're all planning to move out. All the time."

At the sound of the downstairs phone, Seraphina slipped out the door. Mimi took a long last look at the cramped room. Nothing of Kitty's spirit seemed to linger there, which saddened her more than she thought possible.

Exiting the dilapidated rooming house, Mimi placed one foot in front of another until she reached the Chicken Shack. It wasn't far, eight or ten blocks, yet it seemed like an epic journey. When she arrived, there was a commotion outside the bungalow. Police cars filled the alley next to the pastel concrete shed in back.

Mimi marched around the house to that four-doored concrete building. No one stopped her. Outside the doors, she counted three magdalens in hastily tossed-on clothes, a robe, a wrapper, a dress without undergarments. Kitty wasn't among them. Two GIs right behind Mimi spotted the police cars and turned around.

Between the sun, the humidity, and her growing dread, Mimi found it hard to breathe. There were two cops, the same Lt. Baker who had visited the Richardsons' home the day before, and someone who looked like a doctor.

Mimi was frozen in place as a sheet-covered body emerged on a stretcher from the room where Kitty worked. Mimi turned away and gagged. The woman named Gretel spotted her and headed her way. She seemed much younger than Mimi had remembered, and she was frightened.

"Is it—?" Mimi couldn't finish it.

"Kitty. It's her."

The police stopped the stretcher and called the residents over to make an identification. Mimi could see when he pulled back the sheet—it was Kitty Hawkins. Her white-blond hair spilled out around her face. No one else had hair like that, hair that seemed to be made of light. There were bruises on her face, but Mimi couldn't look any more. She sank to her knees and tried to breathe.

Gretel helped her to her feet. "She said you'd be here if the bastard got her. She said she could trust you." Gretel pointed toward the police. "Listen. You can't show them how you feel. No matter how scared you are."

Mimi's eyes overflowed with tears and her voice caught. "It can't be Kitty. I talked with her last night. I told her to get away."

"She didn't always listen. Did you notice? Kitty said you promised to 'take care of things' for her. It was pretty important to her." Gretel wiped a tear away with a grubby finger. "You know what she meant?"

Mimi nodded. "Yes." It hurt to get the words out. "She can't be dead."

"We say that every time it happens. Look, you can't do anything here now, while the cops are crawling all over the place. You should scram."

"May I talk with you later?"

"Won't do any good. But sure, why not?"

"Kitty knew something bad was coming. Did she tell you what it was?"

"Only that she was trying to outrun the quivers," Gretel said. "That's what she called her bad feelings. Now we're all saying it. All trying to outrun them."

"What about her guy? Her fiancé?"

"Nathan? He's not due till the end of the week. His leave got delayed and he had to fly one more mission. Leastways that's what Kitty said."

Mimi couldn't let herself faint or cry. Not right now. Another police car drove up.

"You got to get out of here. You'll just confuse the cops," Gretel said. "You want to talk, call me at the rooming house." Mimi glanced up at her. "We live at the same place."

You promised.

Kitty's words rang in Mimi's head. The extra key to Kitty's locker was in her purse. The key and the promise weighed heavily on her. Mimi wished Kitty had said more. She must have known more but was too afraid to say it. The killer who had murdered Hattie Carnegie Jones and possibly Polly Brown had now come for Kitty. Another horrible thought hit Mimi. Did her phone call last night drive Kitty to do something rash? Could Mimi be responsible?

Lt. Baker was deep in conversation with Officer Gregson. If possible, Sam Baker looked even more tired than the day before. Mimi didn't know whether he'd seen her, but she turned around and trudged back to the Richardsons' home.

You promised.

TWENTY-ONE

*M*IMI WASN'T SURE how she made it back to the house on St. Asaph Street that night, or how she'd avoided being hit by a car. She walked all the way in the heat and humidity. Her dress was soaked with sweat, but she barely remembered the journey. Her eyes were fogged with tears.

Breathing hard, she found herself on the front steps and opened the door. The music she heard when she entered the house threatened to shatter her. Richie was on his perch, playing the violin. The notes were so lovely, yet so sad. He didn't look up at Mimi as he played, but she knew he knew she was there.

"This is for Kitty. This is her song now."

"*Pavane for a Dead Princess.*" Mimi didn't bother to wipe the tears away.

"She was a princess to me." Richie's strings sounded as if they were weeping. "Don't you think she was pretty like a princess?"

"I do. She was."

Addie bustled out of the kitchen. "What's happened, Mimi?" Her landlady's face was ashen in the light, her curls askew, her lipstick inexpertly applied.

"Kitty is no more," Richie insisted.

"As Richie said, Kitty Hawkins is no more." Mimi's voice was shaky. "She's dead. But how did Richie know?"

Addie pointed the way. "Tell me in the kitchen." Mimi followed her and Addie grabbed two cups. She poured some of the Sunday coffee, cut with chicory to make it last.

"How did he know?" Mimi repeated.

"He just does. He's always had that gift. Presentiment, they call it. He knew when my mother died and when Derry's brother died. He announces it through his music. It's like the angels whisper to him. Do you think that's possible?"

"I think they must." Mimi wondered if it were an angel named Kitty. The *Pavane* played on. She tried to lift the cup, but her hand shook. "Kitty—"

Addie reached out and steadied her hand. "Take a breath, Mary Margaret."

Mimi nodded. "I had a bad feeling all day. It just got worse and worse, until I couldn't stand it. I went to her rooming house. It's a depressing place."

"You knew where she lived? Wasn't information she generally shared." Addie cut a couple of small pieces of coffee cake for her and Mimi. Neither had much of an appetite.

"I don't know why we turned out to be friends. I suppose at first, I was just fascinated by her. I never knew anyone like her. But she never seemed hard, like you'd think she would be. She went to church at St. Mary's, did you know that?"

"No. I knew her family was Catholic. Not many of them in Forgotten Creek. Didn't occur to me that she'd keep it up after moving here. And working in that—profession."

"I never had a sister," Mimi said. "I don't know why, it felt kind of like Kitty could be my sister. Like she needed my advice. Stupid, I suppose."

"It wasn't stupid."

"She was getting married."

"Are you sure she was getting married?" Addie waved her cup. "I mean, what with her line of work and all?"

"I was skeptical too, but she had a diamond ring. A beautiful ring. His name is Nathan. She was excited that her flyboy was coming back home, and she was leaving her old life behind. Reminded me of my flier, Eddie. I wanted Kitty to have a happy ending."

"We all did."

"You know, we went shopping on Saturday. I finally figured out she was buying her trousseau and a gown for her wedding. Not white. Light morning glory blue." Mimi choked back a sob. "She didn't come out and say it until I asked. As if she was afraid it might not happen. She looked so beautiful. And so happy."

"I'm sure she wanted to leave that sordid life behind. Any woman would."

"She had more reasons than most. Kitty was going to have a baby."

"A *baby*? Dear God. The poor girl! She got herself a pile of trouble. And whoever killed her, killed two."

Mimi fought the urge to make the sign of the cross. "It makes it a double murder."

"But she wasn't at her room? Where was she? What happened?"

"I went to the Chicken Shack."

Addie looked around to make sure Richie was not within earshot. She whispered, "The Chicken Shack? Is that what they call the—the whorehouse?"

"It's a terrible place. Small, cramped, concrete, like a bunker. Hidden behind a nice little bungalow over near Braddock Road. Near the train tracks."

"How would you even know that?" Mimi sucked in her breath. She didn't want to confess that she had seen Kitty and followed her to the Shack. "Wait. I don't want to know. I guess you're the kind of person that people just tell things to."

"Sometimes. I don't know why."

"I can't imagine what that poor girl went through. And I won't think about what she had to endure with all those men."

She had to endure so much more, Mimi thought. "I went to her rooming house first. Woman named Seraphina told me Kitty'd gone to work. I arrived to see police cars all around the place. The police were there, carrying her body out of that awful little room. Under a sheet."

"Are you sure it was Kitty? Richie could be wrong."

"The policeman pulled the sheet down. From where I stood, I could see it was Kitty. Her face. Her hair."

"No one else I ever knew had hair like Kitty Hawkins. None of her family."

You promised. Kitty's words echoed in her head. Mimi wished she'd never known Kitty Hawkins, wished Kitty hadn't died, wished she hadn't promised to tell Kitty's mother if something happened. She couldn't stand it anymore.

"I have to get out of here."

"I'll keep your supper warm," Addie said.

Mimi fled the kitchen and headed toward St. Mary's, where she knew the scent of candles and incense and the stained-glass windows would offer her some comfort, and she could light a candle for her friend. Mimi ran the several blocks to the 19th century church with the stone facade and the distinctive tower. She pulled the heavy middle door open and knelt at a pew halfway to the altar. Colored light from the stained glass played across the sanctuary.

She tried to pray, but she could only weep. She gradually became aware of Richie's violin, soaring as she had never heard it before. He had followed her into the church, a couple of pews back from where she knelt and cried.

Other than Richie, the church seemed to be empty. Until Mimi saw the black skirts of Father Forsythe's cassock and heard the uneven cadence of his steps. Everyone knew he had suffered a grievous injury in the early part of the war, and he had since resumed his duties as a parish priest. He often seemed to Mimi an angry and bitter man, but he was kind to his parishioners. Mimi assumed he was only angry with God.

Father Andrew Forsythe was not supposed to see battle, he was merely an Army chaplain, but nobody told the enemy that. And now everyone in the parish seemed to know his story, another humbling reality of his life. Mimi knew the story because he had shared it in a homily on pride and vanity.

He had been willing to give his life for the good of the church, for the faith, for God. But he hadn't considered the cost of losing his right leg, the leg he relied on to round the baseball diamond when he stole bases. The leg he barely thought about before. Father Forsythe had spent time recuperating at the Army Medical Center in Washington, D.C., but no matter how good his new artificial limb was, it wasn't as good as the real thing. And a Silver Star and a Purple Heart could not replace a leg. He knew now how other disabled soldiers felt. But that empathy was poor payment.

Children from St. Mary's School, who attended classes at the Lyceum on Duke Street, told wild tales about Father Forsythe. They swore he limped to St. Mary's Cemetery by the river every night to visit his buried leg. Mimi doubted that troop ships carried crates full of amputated body parts. It was enough that they managed to carry the wounded home. More likely, Father Forsythe craved a little peace on that bluff above the Potomac River, peace accompanied with the quietude of the dead.

He paused by the pew where Mimi knelt, his face composed. He still looked young, but his hair was turning gray.

"Mary Margaret?"

"Yes, Father. It's me." She turned around and put her finger to her lips to silence Richie. The boy set his violin down and gazed around the church. As far as Mimi knew, he had never been inside a Catholic church before. His mother would no doubt not approve.

"You have a heavy heart today?" the priest asked.

"Yes, Father."

She choked back a sob. He sighed, knowing the news was bad. St. Mary's had seen many tears and heard many sighs since the combat began. Father Forsythe recognized the tears of grief, of death. He spared a glance at the young violin player behind them.

"Was it a soldier?"

"No, she was a friend." She searched for a hankie to wipe her eyes.

"She was a princess!" Richie blurted out. "That's why I'm playing her my *Pavane*."

"For a dead princess. Of course," Father Forsythe said. "A beautiful piece. You may go on playing, young man. Softly."

Richie's violin wept more softly.

"Tell me about your friend," the priest said.

"She died today. She was murdered," Mimi said. "She warned me it could happen. I didn't, I couldn't, believe it."

Father Forsythe took a seat in the pew ahead of Mimi's. He turned around to face her, rubbing his leg. "She told you she'd be murdered?"

"Kitty had the quivers," Richie offered.

"She had a foreboding," Mimi said. "She called it the quivers."

"A foreboding? I see, her intuition told her."

"They, or he, killed a woman named Hattie first, and maybe a woman named Polly. Kitty told me she had a feeling it could happen to her too. She made me promise—"

"Who are 'they'?"

"I don't know who they are."

"Do you have any proof or evidence of this?"

"No."

"Have you told the police?"

"They were there. They don't care about women like Kitty."

"Women like Kitty? What do you mean? This friend of yours wound up here, working for the war effort?"

"Not exactly," she said. Though Kitty might have put it that way. Mimi pictured Kitty, defiantly wanting more out of life, convinced she had no skills, save for a few carnal gifts, and her beautiful face and body. And her hair. "She was a— I guess you could say she was a magdalen."

"Like Mary Magdalene, whom the Lord loved," Richie piped up.

"Richie!" Mimi glared at him. He shut his mouth and made a zipping motion.

"Seems like an unusual friend for you to have, Mary Margaret."

"These are unusual times," Mimi said. "She attended Mass here at St. Mary's. She was leaving that life behind."

"They all are. Every once in a while, someone makes it." The priest pinched his nose between his eyes, as if he had a headache. "You say you made a promise?"

"To tell her mother." Mimi's tears started again. "If something happened to her."

"Then you must do everything you can to fulfill that promise. Even if it's difficult. Where does she live?"

"Her family is in a tiny town in West Virginia. They don't even have a telephone."

"I see." The priest turned his attention to Richie. "Young man, you play a very fine violin."

"Thank you." Richie practically glowed.

"Would you have any interest in playing here at St. Mary's during Mass?"

"Mass?" Richie turned toward Mimi. "What's that?"

"That's our service," Mimi explained.

"They don't let me play at the Baptist church," Richie said. "My mother thinks people would stare at me. But I don't care if they stare. I love to play my violin. But I'd have to ask permission. The Baptist church is boring, you know."

"If you want to come to St. Mary's and play that fine instrument, I promise you no one will be bored. And no one will stare. Except perhaps with admiration." Father Forsythe pointed to the choir loft at the back of the church. "You would play up there, however, and you would have to strictly follow the choirmaster's rules and only play what he says and when he says to."

Richie was nodding his head wildly. "I can do that."

"The question is, do you know the music?"

"He only needs to hear it once," Mimi said.

"Once?" The priest stared at her, and then at Richie.

"Only once," Richie said. "It's a gift."

"I've heard of that gift. It's quite rare. Young man, you get permission from your folks, and we'll find a place for you. I believe Mary Margaret attends the ten o'clock High Mass."

"I can come with Mimi! All we have to do is ask my mother."

"We, Richie?" Mimi stared at him meaningfully.

"She'll listen to you, Mimi. And this is a very pretty church. Can't you hear how beautiful it sounds in here?"

TWENTY-TWO

L T. SAM BAKER was waiting for her in the living room, with Addie and Derry, when she and Richie arrived home. He had seen her leaving the Chicken Shack after all. The detective handed her an envelope with her name on it.

"Miss Smith, I don't know how someone like you would know the likes of her."

Addie had already prepared a slice of the coffeecake for Lt. Baker. He hadn't touched it. Mimi glared at him as she took the envelope.

"No, you wouldn't. We met at church." He looked skeptical. She glanced over the letter. It was one page, handwritten in a scrawl. "You already read this."

"I did at that. Legitimate police business." Baker folded his arms and waited for her to read it.

Dear Mimi,

I hope you never have to see this letter and I can rip it up laughing because I'm living my happy ever after with my husband Nathan and my child. If you do read it, it means the quivers got me. I know you want to know who did this to me. I don't know who he is. I won't know until he walks through the door.

Tell my mother I'm sorry for being a disappointment to her. She tried to tell me so many things and I wouldn't listen. I'm sorry for the people I hurt. I'm sorry for putting this on you. I have no one else to ask. Thank you for being my friend and for being such a goody-goody. I know you'll keep that promise.

Your friend,
Kitty

"What promise was that?" Baker demanded.

"To tell her family that she's gone. They live in West Virginia. Out in the country. Place called Forgotten Creek. They don't have a phone."

"You could write a letter," he suggested. "Send a telegram."

"Everyone in town would know before her family. They'd read that telegram first, just like you read her letter."

"That's a fact, Sam," Addie said.

Baker grunted. "If they have no phone— Well, we don't have the manpower to track down every victim's next of kin. If we contact the local sheriff, I'd say maybe you got a fifty-fifty chance they'd take the time to run it down."

"Kitty said the police wouldn't care about a woman like her," Mimi said.

"Can't say that's entirely untrue." Baker lifted his eyes to her. His expression said she could make his work that much more difficult.

"How did she die?" Mimi couldn't believe she asked him, but she had to know.

"Doc Henderson said she was beaten pretty badly. Her neck appeared to be broken."

Addie said nothing, but everyone heard her gasp and start to cry. Mimi bit the inside of her mouth to keep from tearing up.

"That's the same way Hattie Carnegie Jones died." Mimi said it softly, but Baker heard her.

"You're saying there's a connection between her and that other woman who worked at the Shack?"

"Kitty told me about Hattie's death. That's what started her quivers, and she couldn't shake the feeling something was after her."

You promised.

"What exactly were you doing there anyway?"

"I contracted a case of Kitty's quivers. Felt something was wrong."

"My officers were concerned about you being on the premises. I had to tell them you weren't that kind. It's pretty obvious, anyway. I told them you were some kind of social worker, poking your nose into places where it could get broken. They said they'd keep an eye on you."

"Gee, thanks."

Baker didn't seem to recognize the sarcasm. "And come to find out from Addie Richardson here, you work for the federal government, OPA. I guess you'd be pretty interested in that stolen sugar, taken from right under your nose."

"I'm a stenographer at OPA."

"So you say."

Let him think what he wants. "Besides, that amount of sugar makes the crime more than a misdemeanor," Mimi said. "That doesn't generally fall under OPA jurisdiction."

"Unless they ask to get involved." Baker fixed Mimi with a question. "Have they asked?" She said nothing, so he continued. "I understand the victim—"

"Her name is Kitty," Mimi said.

"Kitty was familiar with Addie's beekeeping business," Baker said.

"She had nothing to do with the sugar theft," Addie broke in.

"Where were you anyway?" Baker asked Mimi. "Just now?"

Richie spoke up. "At St. Mary's church. It's beautiful. I've never been in a place like that before. All the windows are colored glass with pictures in them. And there are candles that people light. Mimi lit one. It doesn't look like our Baptist church at all. No siree, not at all. And the preacher—"

"The priest," Mimi corrected him.

"The priest has a wooden leg, and it sounds like this." He thumped on the floor to demonstrate.

"Father Forsythe." Lt. Baker knew of him. "He gets around pretty good on that leg."

"He told me I can play my violin there. If I want to. If I get permission." Richie looked around to see if his parents were listening.

"And what were you doing there, young man, if you're a Baptist?"

"I went with Mimi." She gave him a look and he corrected himself. "I mean, I followed Mimi. She was sad. I've never seen her so sad. I was playing my violin for Kitty, and for Mimi too. She thinks I've been touched by angels. I heard her tell my mother that. Isn't that a nice thing to say?"

"Richie, that's probably enough," Derry said, proving he'd been listening too.

"And have you been touched by angels?" Baker asked.

"Maybe." Richie shrugged, half embarrassed, half proud.

Baker put away his notebook. "I reckon you have been touched. Miss Smith, I'm going to have to ask for that letter back. For the moment. And I'd advise you to be careful. If you hear anything that might help this investigation, you tell me." Mimi handed the letter back reluctantly.

"Are you going to tell the other officers I work for OPA?"

"Why complicate things? Social worker is bad enough." He paused. "One more thing. I gather you told your bosses at OPA about the sugar theft."

"Obviously. I want to keep my job."

"Just checking. Seems OPA has requested a copy of my report on that theft." Baker looked even more unhappy.

"My boss, George Prescott."

"What does he want with it, if the amount is over the OPA threshold?"

"He said he likes to know what goes on in the rest of the world," Mimi said.

"God help us all. Now it's the OPA. My job isn't difficult enough."

Mimi reflected that George Prescott would complain in exactly those terms.

"I'll be by the police station for that report in the morning, Lieutenant."

"Remember, Miss Smith, it's a report about stolen sugar, not a paper on a dead prostitute."

"I understand." Too well, she added silently.

"Those two things are just a sad coincidence, you got that?"

"I got that."

Addie placed a small jar of honey on the table next to Baker's untouched coffeecake. "That's not a bribe, is it, Miz Richardson?"

"Don't be ridiculous, Sam. That's just a free sample. Honey isn't rationed."

He pocketed it with a smile. Everyone in Alexandria and D.C. seemed to have an irresistible sweet tooth.

The sky was growing dark, and fireflies were dancing in Addie's garden. Mimi followed Baker out, but she detoured to the side yard. She sat down and watched the fireflies glow. The rest of the family made their way to the garden too. The house seemed to feel too closed in.

Richie touched Mimi's arm. "Kitty doesn't want you to be so sad."

"How do you know that, son?" Derry asked.

"She told me. And she's not scared anymore. Her quivers are all gone." Richie picked up his violin and began to play the *Pavane* again. The fireflies continued their dance.

℘

It was not to be a night for sleep. Addie and Mimi faced each other across the kitchen table. Neither had felt like eating supper, nor were they tempted by any of Addie's available sweets. Richie had long since been sent to bed. Derry was in his study, smoking his pipe and sipping a brandy.

"It's all connected," Mimi said.

"All of what?"

"Kitty Hawkins, Hattie Carnegie Jones, and Polly Brown, though I don't quite know how Polly fits in. Someone hates magdalens and believes their lives are worthless," Mimi said.

Addie shook her curls. "I feel so bad for the poor girl. Sweet sad Kitty."

"What if her death had something to do with the sugar theft?"

"That's ridiculous. And how could the other women be involved, if they were already dead before Kitty?" Addie protested. "And Kitty wasn't involved at all. She couldn't be. I don't think she was ever in my cellar."

Addie picked at the chocolate cookies she had baked that afternoon. She crumbled one onto her plate. The grocery store had a fresh supply of baker's chocolate, which was not rationed, and Addie had scored two whole boxes, early in the morning when the shelves were first stocked. But now, not even the prize of chocolate cheered her up.

"I don't know." Mimi tapped her fingers on the table. "Kitty told me Hattie liked to sell things she didn't have. She meant Hattie knew where valuable items could be found and she passed the information on for a fee. Things like liquor, tires, coffee, sugar."

"Sorry, Mimi. I only have room enough to worry about Kitty and my sugar and my bees. And I don't see how they could be tied together."

"Addie, that sugar isn't being broken down and sold in five-pound or two-pound bags. That's a whole lot of sugar. Yesterday, Kitty said the only use she could think of was in illegal alcohol. Moonshine. She called it shine."

"Not in Virginia." Addie lifted her eyes to Mimi's. "Virginia is death on moonshiners, except down in Franklin County, far as I know. And I've heard rumors that Franklin County is getting more dangerous too. I got cousins down that way."

"But you must know how it works in West Virginia."

"I left Forgotten Creek and all that years ago. I was never a moonshiner. Not personally. Nor my family."

"But you always had access to sugar, didn't you, Addie? I imagine it's hard to get sugar for the stills these days."

"With the war on, I've heard it's been tough, but why would I care? I wouldn't know firsthand. There are some pretty tough characters in that line of work. I wouldn't mess with them."

Mimi was trying to put things together in her mind, trying them on for size. "The black market isn't a place, or an address.

It's a network, stocked with ill-gotten goods to fill a need. Some of it is small, but other parts are huge and calculated and organized. People will do a lot of terrible things to get hold of scarce goods. They might even kill. People kill for the smallest reasons. That's what my boss says."

The agency files were filled with miles of reports. Some infractions seemed incredibly petty. Others were technically too large for the agency or involved the transport of goods across state lines. Still other files were simply unbelievable. Such as the recent hijacking of a supply truck filled with nylon fibers. The truck was headed to a parachute-making facility when it was stopped, hijacked, and diverted, and the fibers were used to make nylon stockings. When the government discovered the theft, OPA confiscated the stockings. They were sold to the public for five dollars a pair.

But why kill a magdalen like Kitty Hawkins? Simply because she got in someone's way? Could she have been trying to protect someone? Someone like Addie Richardson, one of the few who ever offered her friendship? Did she know too much about the thefts and how the racket worked?

Or was it something else, like simple envy? Someone jealous that Kitty was getting out of the Life? And who could that possibly be? One of her clients? Or one of the other women at the Chicken Shack?

TWENTY-THREE

"CAT DRAG YOU in this morning, Mary Margaret?"

"Thanks a lot, George."

George Prescott strolled into the office Tuesday, looking jaunty in his blue seersucker suit. But the day was young. It would be wrinkled and rumpled before it was over. He carried a cup of something hot in his hands and he seemed almost cheerful. Today, his battered metal Thermos contained "Roosevelt coffee," he told her, hot water poured over used coffee grounds. There was not much kick left. But the honey Mimi gave him yesterday would help.

Mimi knew she looked sleepy from her long night of mourning and questioning. Her face was puffy and her eyes swollen. Her smart black-and-white plaid cotton dress was an attempt to disguise how exhausted she looked and felt. It featured elbow-length sleeves with black cuffs, and standing black ruffles graced the V neckline.

The dress was always striking on Mimi, but her carefully pressed outfit had been crushed by the heat and humidity during her bus journey to D.C. this morning. She felt wrinkled and out of sorts, and the day hadn't even begun yet.

Mimi hated to ruin George's mood, but someone had to do it.

"And I may look bad, George, but I feel even worse. I have to talk with you."

His voice dropped. "Come into my office."

Mimi grabbed the police report on the Richardsons' sugar theft and rushed in. She waved the report aloft dramatically before setting it on Prescott's desk with emphasis. She'd read it while standing and swaying on the bus, having missed all the seats. It didn't tell her anything she didn't know. The report had abbreviated some of the details, particularly about feeding the bees and how much sugar that required, and it demonstrated that Lt. Baker was not much of a writer.

"First, here's the report. Second, I have to take a couple of days off. And before you point this out, I know there's a war on. But I've earned the time. The complaints and the black market will percolate along just fine without me."

George removed his jacket and placed it over the back of his chair before sitting down. He waved her into his visitor's chair.

"When? When do you need the time?"

"Immediately. Starting tomorrow."

"What in Heaven's name is going on? You act like there's been a death or something."

"There has been a death."

Mimi refused to cry in front of George, but it was hard for her to speak without crying. She finally managed to tell him about Kitty without choking up more than twice, and about the promise she had made to deliver the bad news to Kitty's mother. He was incredulous.

"How do you even know a woman in that profession?"

"My mother would tell you it's a special talent I have. Picking up strays. People, not pets."

"I'd like to have a chat with your mother someday."

"I doubt that." Mimi allowed herself a smile at the image. George would be running for cover before he even got a word in. "Anyway, it's a long story."

"I'm sure it is. You have spoken with the police?"

"Lieutenant Samson Baker. He also responded to the Richardsons' sugar theft. He wrote this report. It's a small city, homicide is uncommon. At least it used to be."

George rubbed his eyes. "Was Kitty Hawkins involved in the sugar theft?"

"No. She might have known who was. She denied it. She told me nothing."

"You're telling me she might have known something, without knowing it, and now she's dead." George sipped his cup of weak coffee. "This is an unattractive coincidence. I dislike coincidences. Where are you heading?"

"A place in West Virginia called Forgotten Creek."

"Nice name. Sounds like moonshine territory. I like this less and less, Mary Margaret."

"I promised her."

"You said a couple of days?"

"Maybe more. I have to take the train, and with soldiers crowding all the trains—"

He raised his coffee cup to ward off any more bad news. "Finish your work and take the afternoon off, Mimi. I'll give you two days, three if absolutely necessary. Stay out of trouble, if you can, and for God's sake, don't pick up any more strays."

಄

"Is there anything of Kitty's left?" Mimi asked Seraphina, the woman she'd met the day before. She was back in the cramped room Kitty had shared with two other women. A somber Seraphina followed her upstairs.

Mimi was trying to tie up any loose ends and collect what was left of Kitty's belongings. She was grateful that George had given her the rest of the day off. She had so many errands to attend to before her trek to West Virginia.

"Nope. Nothing. That's the way it is. You leave or you die, the stuff you leave behind is fair game." Seraphina's large, amber-colored eyes glittered in the light. Two tortoiseshell combs held back her long curly black hair from her delicately featured face. She wore a pink rayon day dress. "We don't mean anything bad by it."

"I understand." Another reason why Kitty took such care with her belongings that mattered. She locked them away at the train station. "Were you a friend of Kitty's?"

"We worked together." Seraphina turned around cautiously, satisfied that no one was listening. "We got along. She didn't look down on me or anything like that."

"Why would she? You shared the same profession."

"But not the same race. You can't tell, can you?" Seraphina looked amused. "I'm mixed. My father was white. My mother was black."

Mimi stared at the other woman, a beauty in any race. Mimi didn't know whether she would ever get used to all these categories and variations of people and classes and colors and why it mattered so much here. "I thought it was illegal for black and white couples to be married in Virginia."

Seraphina laughed softly. "I never said they were married. It's an old story here. Anyway, I go where I want. Most white folk think I'm Italian, or maybe Spanish." She paused. "Black folk, they can tell. They know my story without a word. They know I'm passing. Most of them don't have much to do with me."

"Oh." All that Mimi could think of to say. Seraphina waved at the room.

"Kitty didn't keep much here. None of us do."

"What about the Chicken Shack? Would she have left anything there?"

"Pretty obvious you never been inside the coop. You bring yourself in, you take yourself out. Besides, the cops closed it down. After Hattie and then Kitty."

"Really?" It made sense, but Mimi hadn't thought about it. She didn't think the police were expending much effort on Kitty's murder.

"Maybe just a few days, maybe more. They're talking to Madam Cherry."

"Because she owns the Chicken Shack?"

"She's telling them she had no idea what went on in there. She's just a businesswoman." Seraphina laughed again. "Everyone knows what goes on where. It's a little game Cherry plays with the cops."

"You think nothing will come of it?" It was depressing to think women were being murdered and yet the oldest profession soldiered on, collecting more young female victims.

"Bottom line, they think places like the Chicken Shack are preventing worse crimes. A way to protect their wives and daughters."

"Kitty said something like that."

"Anyway, a day or two off is not the worst thing in the world. I know where I can go if I'm low on cash, a place where it's mostly for colored men."

"You work there too?"

"I'm open minded when it comes to money. Why do you care about Kitty Hawkins anyway? She wasn't your kind, you know."

Mimi leaned wearily against the door jamb, as limp as her dress. The house was hotter and more humid inside than it was outside.

"Kitty was my friend, and now she's dead. I met her a year ago under different circumstances, and recently I got to know her better. There was a sweet side to her. Someone killed her and someone killed Polly Brown and Hattie Carnegie Jones. At any rate, I made a promise to Kitty, if something happened to her."

"A promise?"

"To tell her mother she's gone."

"So that's it." Seraphina's expression changed, from inquisitive to troubled. "Kitty said she'd never go back there."

"And she won't. Unless they want to bury her."

ɔ೩

The small key Mimi held in her hand fit an olive-green metal locker, one of the larger ones, at the Alexandria train station on King Street. She took a deep breath and inserted the key to the matching numbered locker.

Inside, Kitty's meager treasures came into view. Most of them were packed in a new green marbled Samsonite suitcase and a small matching traveling case. Her shopping bags from Woodie's were there too: her wedding gown, the suit dress, and the accompanying trousseau items.

"You must be Mimi Smith." A tall man with thinning hair startled her. He wore a white shirt and olive-green pants that matched the lockers.

"Are you Stan?" That name popped into her head. The man who had made "special arrangements" with Kitty to hold that locker for her.

"Yep. Kitty said you might be coming by for her things. In case she had to leave in a hurry. But I heard a real bad rumor."

"Not a rumor, Stan. Kitty was killed Sunday night, or early Monday morning."

He rubbed his head. "Sorry to hear that. Hell of a thing. She was a nice kid." Stan helped Mimi gather everything up. He made sure she had the right train ticket for West Virginia the next morning. "Be sure and get here early, and we'll try and get you a seat."

The small station was crowded with servicemen and women, friends and family, coming and going. There were tears all around her, happy tears for people coming home, sad tears for loved ones leaving. Their emotions and Mimi's left her feeling raw. With Stan's help, she maneuvered her way with Kitty's baggage through the crowd and out the station door to wait for a cab. She shared it with two other people off the last train.

The Richardsons' house wasn't far, but Mimi was the last to be dropped off after the cab cruised through Alexandria, dropping off the other passengers. She didn't think she could feel any more exhausted, and she tried to keep her mind blank as she went through the motions robotically. She had used most of her free hours after she left the office. It was supper time.

When Richie saw the cab stop at the house, he bolted out the front door and helped Mimi with the bags and Kitty's suitcases. She was happy to have him share the burden. Her arms ached, as did her heart. Though Addie had baked a savory chicken pot pie for supper, Mimi merely picked at her food. She had no appetite. She made her excuses and soon escaped to her third-floor room.

Once there, Mimi opened Kitty's cases and bags and spread her things out on her bed and her steamer trunk. First, she set aside clothes for Kitty's funeral, but she couldn't decide whether it should be the suit dress or the light blue wedding gown. She was unsure whether Kitty's family would even want the lovely peignoir or other items, or just assume they were the product of ill-gotten gains. Mimi realized she didn't know where or when Kitty's funeral would even happen.

It was almost too much. *Oh, Kitty.* Tears trickled down Mimi's cheeks as she mentally itemized things. There were two-pound paper bags of sugar and real coffee and a three-pound box of unopened Whitman's chocolates, perhaps gifts from her johns. Kitty's good leather purse, which she found tucked into the suitcase, contained her most valued things. The diamond engagement ring that she shyly, yet proudly, wore while shopping for wedding clothes. Mimi added the cameo necklace Kitty had taken from her mother and wanted returned.

Mimi found a couple of envelopes full of cash inside a zippered compartment. One was earmarked for Kitty's funeral expenses. The other was designated for her family. There were a couple of ration books. Some of the coupons were gone, but the rest would be useful for a large family without a lot of resources. It seemed Kitty had thought of everything. Inside another compartment were photos of Nathan Albemarle, smiling and handsome in his uniform. There were also photos of Nathan and Kitty, wearing the silly grins of people in love. Classic engagement photographs. The pictures made Mimi's heart ache. She set them aside.

Inside a small jewelry box with Kitty's name on it was a pretty pin of a red cardinal, Mimi's favorite bird. Kitty had included a note to Mimi: It was a thank-you gift. Just the kind of pin, she wrote, that a goody-goody like Mimi would wear.

Mimi wrote an inventory of everything and decided what she would bring with her to Forgotten Creek the next day. She would mail the heavier items after she got back. Other things and other thoughts she left for later. She wanted to be able to judge whether there was anything in Kitty's belongings that related somehow to her murder.

Mimi planned to return most of the photos to Nathan, as well as the diamond engagement ring. There was a military address for him, but because he was also expected in Alexandria at week's end, she hoped she could meet with him somehow. Perhaps she could find him through his family. She had their address on Mansion Drive. She shoved that thought aside.

First, she had to worry about Kitty Hawkins' family—and a trek by train to West Virginia.

TWENTY-FOUR

"ORD OF ADVICE," Addie said over Mimi's shoulder later that evening. "Don't go off to Forgotten Creek looking all Washington, D.C., like you're a big city society lady."

"Do I look like one?" Mimi smothered a smile. No one had ever accused her of looking like any kind of society.

"Maybe not to you. I see that snicker. But over in that part of West Virginia, you'd be surprised."

"You certainly look uptown yourself, Addie. Not like someone from the country."

Addie wore a sedate black dress with purple contrasting trim on the collar and cuffs. More somber than her usual attire, it was apparent she had donned it to mourn Kitty. Her earrings were jet, with a matching necklace. Addie's curls seemed limper tonight, less optimistic than usual.

"That's because I work at it. With you, Mimi, it's natural. You don't have to think about it."

"I like clothes, that's all." She pondered her wardrobe. "However, I seem to be at a loss right now."

Mimi was trying to decide what to take with her for her short, and hopefully just overnight, visit. There was no way she could make it in a shorter time frame. The train trip would take at least five hours. It arrived in Forgotten Creek in the early afternoon and returned only once a day. There was also a possibility she would get bumped to make way for military personnel. She prayed there would be a room where she could stay.

"There used to be a rooming house on Main Street," Addie said. "I haven't been back there in some time, you know. Could be crowded. You never know these days. Mrs. Simmons used to run the place. She'd always let you sleep on a sofa if she was full up. Tell her Addie Meadows sent you."

"I will." Mimi took a deep breath. "Sofa sounds mighty glamorous, but I'll take it."

"They won't cotton to you if they think you're some rich lady looking down your nose at 'em."

"I'm not rich." Mimi counted her pennies, put money into war bonds with every paycheck, and always felt strapped. "And my nose is too short and freckled to look down on anyone."

"They have different ideas down in Forgotten Creek. You're lucky to have a good job, but I wouldn't mention it's with the government," Addie said. "You have a nice place to live too, so to those folks, you're rich. And your clothes— Well."

Mimi glanced at the wrinkled dress she'd worn that day and hung on a hanger. It would have to be handwashed, starched, and ironed again. "Don't worry, Addie, I'll be thoroughly rumpled after that steamy train ride."

"It's a long ride, longer if the train has to stop for a cow, or hits one, and then there's the bus to Forgotten Creek. Guaranteed to hit every pothole in the road. That place should have stayed forgotten, if you ask me." Addie had said it before and she would say it again. "Poor Kitty never had a chance."

Mimi put aside a couple of dresses that Addie said were too "city-looking." They finally decided on a dark turquoise blouse and a full Mexican skirt, black with a multicolored floral pattern around the bottom border. Mimi loved it and always associated it with summer nights. She'd worn it so much it was faded, but it would be more comfortable for a long train ride than a slimmer skirt. These items were pre-war, and the full material of the skirt marked it as an older piece. She could pair it with any color in the floral border. Mimi especially appreciated the skirt's deep pockets. She added a wide purple cummerbund belt and a deep rose blouse to wear the following day. Muted colors, nothing solid black. She didn't want to look inappropriate for being the bearer of bad news, but resembling the Grim Reaper wouldn't do either.

"That will be fine," Addie said. "Wear comfortable shoes, you'll be walking a fair bit. Saddle shoes, I think."

Mimi added a black sweater and scarf. Even though the mountains of West Virginia weren't anything like the Rockies, Addie said it would cool down after dark. Mimi packed her necessities in a light canvas shoulder bag, her toothbrush and toothpaste, comb and brush, a small jar of cold cream, rolled-up fresh underwear, and a nightgown, in case she was lucky enough to find a room for the night. The items for Kitty's family filled the rest of the compact bag.

Her traveling purse with a shoulder strap contained Kitty's photographs, the cameo necklace, the ration coupons, and the money she had set aside for her family. It also had Mimi's always important 'war paint,' powder, foundation, lipstick, brow pencil, and her Maybelline cake mascara. For rouge she would simply add a couple dots of lipstick and rub them in. She included a couple of hair clips. Mimi could wear the pocketbook across her body and not worry about losing her valuables. She perched on her bed.

"What about Kitty's suitcase and those clothes?" Addie asked.

"After I get back, I'll send them whatever I think is appropriate. I don't want to make too many decisions until I know the lay of the land."

Addie picked up the royal blue dress and jacket. "This is mighty pretty. Mighty fancy."

"She was going to be married in that, until she found the blue gown. I encouraged her to buy it because it was a good outfit to meet his family. Now I suppose she might be buried in it."

Kitty's earthly remains had been collected by the police and they weren't going anywhere soon. Mimi could make a final decision on the outfit later when the police were through with the body.

Addie picked up the morning glory blue gown and gazed at it in awe. "Stunning. Kitty getting married? It's almost too sad to think about."

"It's beautiful, isn't it?" Mimi picked up Kitty's unworn hat and the cream-colored dancing shoes. The hat was very sophisticated, and yet with the small white veiling, it had a hint of bridal to it. "These really complete the outfit."

Addie stroked the trim on the gown. "I don't think I've ever seen anything so fine. Well, except for that violet dress you're making downstairs." She sighed deeply. "Kitty would have been the most beautiful bride. Notwithstanding her occupation. And the poor little baby."

"It might have worked. If only—a million if onlys."

"Don't take all this on yourself, Mimi. We can decide the rest when you get back."

Mimi's eyes threatened to overflow with tears. "Thank you, Addie. I'm going in circles."

"Stop. You're packed. You're finished for now. And don't wear any lipstick while you're there. Kitty's mama don't hold with that kind of thing."

"But wearing lipstick is patriotic! Telling me not to bring my war paint is like telling me not to breathe," Mimi said. Addie gave her a stern look. "Okay, I won't wear it, but I am bringing it along. Maybe a lighter shade."

Mimi stood and hefted her canvas shoulder bag. It was manageable, even with all the things she was bringing to Kitty's family, including the sugar, the real coffee, and the chocolates. It wasn't nearly as heavy as the burden of telling her family that their Kitty was gone.

TWENTY-FIVE

*T*HE TRAIN STATION was jammed again the next morning. With a little help from Stan, Mimi was lucky to get a seat on the C&O and West Virginia. Although people waited with tickets in hand, some of them would not be able to board. Instead, they would be first in line for the next train. She tried not to worry about them.

The sign "Whites Only" still jarred Mimi. The waiting area for "Colored" was further down the platform. She had never seen anything like that in Denver.

Addie and Richie insisted on seeing Mimi off, which felt ridiculous to her: The station was a mere dozen streets away from their house. It wasn't as if she was leaving from the beautiful beaux arts Union Station in Washington, D.C., full of imposing columns and important people. However, she had a much better shot at grabbing a seat at the humbler station in Alexandria.

Still, her landlady and son made it seem like a momentous event. As she boarded, Richie handed Mimi a brown paper bag with sandwiches, several large juicy peaches, and a generous slice of honey cake.

"So you won't get hungry," Richie said. "Who knows what they have on that dining car anyway? Everything might be gone." He was obviously repeating what he'd heard his mother fret about while fixing Mimi's provisions. He handed her a Thermos full of Addie's special tea, sweet with honey.

"Thank you, Richie. I wouldn't have thought of it." Mimi gave Richie a hug and Addie insisted on one too.

Stan, Kitty's special friend at the station, helpfully ushered Mimi into the last available seat, much to the outrage of another woman on the platform. The woman complained loudly that she would have to wait for another train now, one that might not even arrive today. There were no guarantees in wartime, and Mimi wouldn't have said anything, but Addie stepped up close to the woman.

"My friend is on federal government business," Addie said.

"Well," the woman sniffed. "She should have worn her uniform then."

"It's *secret* government business." Addie gave the woman her sternest look.

I'll have to keep that in mind, Mimi thought. *On secret government business* might be a handy phrase to remember, even if it wasn't precisely true. Stan told her to take care.

"Best of luck," he said. "I don't envy you this mission of mercy."

He departed as the train engines rumbled to life. It took her a few minutes to settle into her green upholstered seat near the window. It was still warm. It had recently been occupied by a sailor, who bounced up from his seat and jogged away when he realized this was his stop. A soldier helpfully slung her canvas bag on the rack above her seat. She wore her purse over her shoulder, patting it occasionally to reassure herself that it was still there, and she kept the paper sack with her sandwiches and Thermos next to her on her seat.

Mimi allowed herself to feel a little relief that the first leg of the trip had begun. She was grateful to be seated next to a window. She lifted it a few inches, spotting Addie and Richie waving to her from the platform. She waved back and laughed. This trip shouldn't be such a big deal. It wasn't really, was it?

The sharp smell of oil and the sound of metal against metal filled the air, and once the train pulled out of the station, the constant rhythm of the wheels provided a steady soundtrack. Mimi had an Agatha Christie to read, but she was too fidgety to concentrate. Kitty and the promise she had made to her were never far from her thoughts.

The train crossed the Potomac River to its first stop in the District. It was crowded with soldiers and sailors and marines, many of whom disembarked at Washington's grand Union Station, only to be replaced by more, pouring through the aisles, racing toward any available seat. The porters were busy directing people, sweat beading on their foreheads, mopping their faces with large white handkerchiefs. The train began to move again.

Once the train pulled away from the D.C. area, the green fields, forests, and farmhouses took over. The contrast of the quiet countryside, deep in summer green, was startling next to the endless khaki uniforms that clogged Washington and Alexandria.

The small towns and postage stamp train depots were reruns of her departure, people rushing on and off, travelers lucky enough to have a ticket, military men fortunate to have a few days of leave. There were tears of joy and tears of grief with each arrival and parting. Even in the tiny stops up the river in West Virginia, there were crowds waiting for trains, everyone in a hurry to get here and get there. It was exhausting to witness.

As the day wore on, the heat on the train rose until it was nearly insufferable, lulling Mimi into a foggy state. Feeling dazed, she left her seat after the GI next to her promised he would keep it safe for her.

She squeezed into the ladies' room and splashed water on her face and the back of her neck. Her face was glowing red from the heat. She dabbed on just a touch of Max Factor Pan-Cake makeup in Cream No. 2 and rubbed it into her skin, following that with powder. It improved her flushed face. She reached for her red lipstick, ready to dab a bit on her cheeks and rub it in for a little color, when she remembered her landlady's warning. She settled for pinching her cheeks and biting her lips. She brushed her hair and tied it back with a scarf.

Returning to her seat, she ate a Spam sandwich, one of the juicy peaches, and helped herself to a cup of Addie's sweet tea. Mimi was glad the soldier in the next seat was asleep and she didn't feel the need to share. She didn't know when she would be able to eat again, so she saved the rest for later.

Mimi began to wonder if they would ever arrive in Forgotten Creek, or if this was a kind of endless purgatory. She dozed for a while and awoke with a porter standing before her, the soldier next to her shaking her shoulder.

"This is your stop, miss."

The depot sat halfway between two small towns. Forgotten Creek was one. Mimi's journey had another leg to go.

She held on to her bags as she lurched down the stairs to a dirty train platform next to an old depot building, the color sucked out of it by the sun and wind. It hadn't seen a paintbrush in years. It was as if the days of the Depression lingered here.

Mimi had a moment of panic. Why was she here, why did she feel compelled to do this in person? Would it have been so bad to send a telegram to the family? No, no, she told herself, a telegram would just shock the whole town and feed the gossip mill. Everyone would know Kitty Hawkins was dead before her family knew. She had to do this.

You promised.

Mimi pushed open the creaky depot door and inquired about another ticket, one for the bus. The clerk eyed her suspiciously and said she had to wait at the station, and she could pay on the bus to Forgotten Creek. It came once a day and would be along soon. Maybe. Mimi had no idea how she would get back to the train after she completed her task. Was there even a taxi? Maybe she could hitchhike.

She used the restroom and filled her now-empty Thermos with cold water. There was no place to eat nearby, and she was grateful for Addie's provisions. She grabbed a bench and ate the second peach. A third peach, the sandwich, and a piece of cake were left.

God bless you, Addie.

The bus was waiting outside the depot door and Mimi had to run for it. Luckily, the driver waited a full thirty seconds for her to struggle up the steps and pay the fare. It was, as Addie predicted, a very bumpy ride.

After a bone-rattling journey, the bus dropped her off at Homer's General Store in the middle of town on Main Street. On first glance, Forgotten Creek looked as dusty and dirty as the train depot. Another one-horse town with a half dozen buildings and a two-block long "downtown." Nothing stood out except an ancient grain silo—probably a local landmark. Mimi thought it must be the closest thing to a high-rise building in this town.

The one-story general store featured an overhanging roof and a porch that needed paint. Men in well-worn overalls sat on makeshift benches playing checkers at small metal tables. They looked up from their games when Mimi showed up.

The weather felt pleasant, with a mild breeze, not as hot as Washington or as humid. She took a deep breath and told herself to keep going. Her task would eventually be over. She needed only to confirm directions to the Hawkins place, which shouldn't be too hard. Addie had forgotten the exact roads to take, but she said everybody in town would know where the Hawkins family lived.

Apparently, Mimi Smith was the most interesting thing that had happened there all day. Heads swiveled as she tramped into the general store with her canvas satchel. Addie had warned her that she might still look "too clean and fancy," even after that hot five-hour train ride. Maybe she did. But her cotton skirt and blouse were damp and wrinkled. Surely that should give her some points.

Inside the store, the wooden floor was wobbly, with rough, uneven planks. Shelves lined the walls, and two aisles were well-stocked with canned goods. A few shoppers were inside, and the checkers players crowded the front door to see what this exotic creature from Washington, D.C., was up to.

"You lost, little lady?" a heavyset man inquired. He wore a white work apron over his clothes. He didn't seem unkind, just curious. "We don't have many visitors in Forgotten Creek."

"Are you the manager?'

"Manager, owner, and proprietor of this establishment, at your service."

"I'm looking for the Hawkins place. Mrs. Netty Hawkins?"

Mimi didn't divulge any more information. She didn't know whether anyone knew Kitty was dead, or whether the police had even tried to contact the family.

"And what would your business be with the Hawkinses?"

"I know their house is about two miles from here," she continued, determined not to be bullied. "If you could just show me the way, I can walk. I couldn't call ahead, because they don't have a phone."

"No, they don't," he said. "The Hawkinses don't get many visitors."

"I have a message for Mrs. Hawkins." Mimi wanted to say it was none of his or anyone else's business, but she held her tongue.

"Where you from?"

"Alexandria, Virginia."

There was a swell of murmurs from the crowd behind her. *Should I have said I was from the Moon?* Mimi caught the eye of a careworn-looking woman near the meat section. The woman was probably younger than she looked. Two toddlers grabbed at her knees. She smoothed her faded calico dress.

"They're on up the road. Up the holler." The woman pointed. "That a-way."

"I was going to tell her, Muriel." The owner glared at Muriel, who shrugged wearily.

"Thank you, Muriel," Mimi said. "I appreciate it."

Mimi retrieved a dime from her purse and inserted it into the bright red-and-white Coca-Cola machine. The shiniest thing in the store, the Coke machine took pride of place by the counter. The bottle rattled noisily and emerged. She popped the cap on the bottle opener.

"That's two cents deposit for the bottle." The store owner extended his hand and she put two pennies in it.

Ellen Byerrum

"I'll take her over to the Hawkinses," a low rough voice said. "I got my pickup. Goin' that way." The crowd parted for an imposingly large man in grease-stained overalls. His face was dark from the sun. Unruly black curls dipped over his forehead, longer than was fashionable, but there was nothing fashionable about him. "You got my order ready?"

"Sure thing, Joe." The owner was quick to place two full paper bags on the counter.

As the man counted out his money for the bill, Mimi marked that his features were regular, his teeth white and straight, and his eyes were a blazing blue, in contrast to his complexion, tanned from the sun. He squinted at her and scowled. Mimi scowled back.

"I can walk, it's no trouble," she said.

"It's a long walk, two miles with that bag. You look like you'd blow away in the wind."

Mimi worked hard to maintain her figure, especially with all of Addie's good food. "I would not! Not with this heavy bag."

He laughed, then he turned sober. "Alexandria's where Kitty Hawkins went. This have something to do with her?" She stared at him and couldn't bring herself to say anything in front of this general store audience. "You need a ride, don't you?"

Mimi considered the man. He seemed more concerned than menacing. "Yes, but the gasoline— The rationing. Can you afford it?"

"I'm a farmer. Got all the gas I need."

"Thank you. My name is Mimi Smith."

She waited for him to introduce himself. She wasn't about to get into his pickup if she didn't even know his name. Muriel spoke up.

"This here old boy is Mr. Josiah Jordan. He don't have much in the way of manners, but he's only half as scary as he looks, miss. You'll be fine."

Mimi stared at him quizzically. Josiah? That name sounded familiar.

"Yeah, I'm Joe. Let's go, if we're goin'."

He gave Muriel an evil look and grabbed Mimi's canvas bag, slinging it over his shoulder, proving he had some manners. He picked up the heavy bags in his order as well, as if they weighed nothing.

He pointed the way out the back of the store and headed toward a rusted baby blue pickup that had seen more than its fair share of miles. He tossed all the bags in the bed of the truck, but he didn't bother opening her door for her. Mimi barely had time to shut her door before they roared off. The truck's windows were rolled down, blowing her hair, but the cab was full of the aromas of hard work, oil, and tobacco.

"Thank you, Mr. Jordan." She leaned her head against the seat and closed her eyes. It was turning out to be an epic journey, and the midday sun was hot. Mimi took a swig of the Coke, letting the cold liquid tickle her throat. Josiah Jordan took his time to speak.

"I take it the news is bad?"

TWENTY-SIX

"**Y**ES, IT'S BAD."

Mimi figured there was no sense in lying. The whole story would come out soon enough.

"Why else would a stranger come all this way?" Josiah said, almost to himself. He glanced at her. "You don't look like the kind of person who'd deliver bad news."

"I don't? How do I look?" Was there something wrong with her faded skirt and plain blouse? "What does someone who delivers bad news look like?"

"You look like the big city is all." Josiah flicked his eyes back to the bumpy road. He swerved to avoid a hole the size of a cow.

"I promised Kitty—something." Mimi didn't know what else to say.

"Even though she was up to no good? You don't have to deny it. I know what she was doing. Takes a while, but word usually winds its way back to Forgotten Creek. I knew the day she left, she wouldn't be back. Kitty was selling herself, like her mama said."

There was a mournfulness in his tone. How was Mimi supposed to answer that?

"That's what the police say."

"The police are involved?" He hit the steering wheel so hard it made the truck shake.

Mimi worried about the gas cans in the truck and prayed the sun or the rocky road wouldn't ignite them. She could see how Kitty wanted to get away from these rattletrap trucks and tarpaper shacks and outhouses. Away from men who wore tattered, patched overalls.

"Sorry," Josiah said sheepishly. "Won't happen again. Kitty is dead, isn't she?"

She took a big breath. "I'm sorry."

It was almost invisible, but he flinched. "Me too." He spared her a sideways glance. "Kitty Hawkins was always hellbent on getting out of here without knowing how to survive in the world."

Mimi thought she'd cried all her tears, but now a few escaped and trickled down her face. She wiped them away, thinking they were for more than Kitty, for all the women whose lives were torn apart, by this war, by poverty, by where they came from and where they ended up. If Kitty couldn't survive in this world, could Mimi? Could anyone? She fished a hankie out of her pocketbook.

"I didn't know her very long," she said. "But there was something sweet about her, despite everything."

"Don't feel bad, Mimi Smith. I couldn't do anything about her. Never could. Your visit to the Hawkinses is about Kitty, then?"

"I'm afraid so, Mr. Jordan."

"Call me Joe."

They lapsed into silence. Joe drove fast down the rutted dirt road, burning up precious gasoline and rubber. Another smell wafted in on the breeze. Mimi sniffed.

"Sour mash," he said. "Smell's like Zeke's still's up and running again."

Mimi raised her eyebrow. "Oh? Moonshine?"

"You don't shock easy."

"There's a war going on." Moonshine seemed minor in comparison to Kitty's murder. "Did you know her well?"

"Everybody knows everyone here. I knew Kitty. Where are you from? Don't tell me it's the South, 'cause you don't sound like anyone from around here, or south of here. Matter of fact, you don't sound like anyone from anywhere."

"Denver, Colorado."

Joe whistled. "That's a long way off. Way out West. What're you doing in Alexandria?"

"I came to work for the war effort."

"You got a job?"

"I have a government job, and I was warned not to tell anyone that."

He chuckled. "Good advice, unless you work for the Post Office. Folks round here give the Post Office a pass. How would they get their government checks without it?"

"It's not the Post Office."

"I ain't gonna pry. You ain't married?"

"No."

"So what's wrong with you?" Mimi stared at him to make sure he was making a joke.

"He died. Being a hero. Jumping out of a plane into combat with a parachute that didn't open. There's a war on, have you heard?"

That shut Joe up. The pickup slowed as he maneuvered up a narrow dirt road. Mimi held on as the truck veered around more bumps and jostled her spine. It finally came to a stop at a ramshackle pile of wooden shacks that seemed to add up to a house.

"We're here," he said.

Mimi blinked. She stared at the Hawkinses' domain. It reminded her of the abandoned homesteads that dotted the Colorado mountains and plains. However, this humble two-story house was in a lush hollow, surrounded by emerald-green woods, not a landscape of dried-out tumbleweeds and hungry coyotes.

But the beauty was all in the land. The house looked like it would fall down in a windstorm. The yard was crowded with old tools, an old car off its wheels, rusting auto parts, and a dozen or more chickens.

"Oh my," Mimi breathed softly.

"I'm not saying Kitty was wrong to get away from all this grandeur," Joe said. "She always wanted something she couldn't have, much good it did her. But she could have married me. We were childhood sweethearts, you might say. I work hard and I live a far sight better than her people do. And with times a-changing, who knows what the future might bring?"

Mimi looked at him and tried to remember what Kitty had told her about Josiah. "You were the boy she left behind."

"I was the boy. Now I am the man. Here comes her ma. Let me help you down."

Mimi turned to see a slight woman with dirt brown hair caught up in a messy bun and a leathery face full of wrinkles. Never in a million years would Mimi have picked this woman as Kitty's mother. She might have been her grandmother, and she had none of Kitty's delicate prettiness. The woman's faded homemade apple-print dress hung on her gaunt frame and reminded Mimi of the dress Kitty had worn, made of grain sacks. Joe opened Mimi's door and helped her down to the rough and uneven ground. The old woman narrowed her eyes at the two of them.

"Mrs. Hawkins?" Any traces of a rehearsed speech fled her thoughts. Instead, Mimi took Kitty's treasured cameo necklace out of her purse and put it in the woman's hand.

Netty Hawkins flinched. She stared at the necklace, then she raised her head to consider Mimi. Her eyes were full of pain.

"So my girl done got herself killed."

There was no easy way out. "She asked me to bring this to you, if anything happened to her. I'm so sorry." They were silent for a moment.

"You come a long way?"

"Alexandria, Virginia." Mimi would have said from Washington, D.C., but she'd been warned that a lot of country folk distrusted the nation's capital. "My name's Mimi Smith."

"Mimi?"

"Short for Mary Margaret."

Netty Hawkins's gaunt frame shook in a silent sob. "You might as well set a while. I got a pot of chicory coffee on the stove. We best go inside and you can tell me what you have to say. I swear the very trees have ears in this holler. You'd think the crows spread gossip as fast as they can fly." She lifted her fist to a group of the birds, a murder of crows. "Git now." The birds scattered.

The three of them marched up crooked wooden steps to a front porch. Joe grabbed Mimi's canvas bag and opened the door for the women. Netty waved Mimi to a chair at a scarred wooden table and slowly poured cups of chicory for them. Joe pulled up a chair as well. The home brew was bracing, black with no sugar.

"Thank you," Mimi said. "It's what I needed after a long trip."

"Much obliged, Miz Netty," Joe said.

Netty picked up a bag of knitting and her needles. Her hands kept a steady pace with the click-clack of the knitting needles, the soft blue yarn taking form as a sweater.

"My little Katharine is dead. I knew it would come to this when she left. She was my little blond baby, hair as white as cornsilk, till she was thirteen. Then it turned pure gold. I could always spot her, even in the tall grass, with that hair peeking out so bright. Like there was a light shining through her. Ain't that right, Joe?"

"That's right, Miz Netty," Joe replied.

"She should have stayed here and married you. That's what I wanted for her. But Katharine Hawkins was never one to listen to her mother. Or anyone else."

A shadow crossed Joe's face, but he wiped it away with one hand. "That wasn't her way. You can't cage some birds. And Kitty was a rare bird."

Netty turned her attention to Mimi, staring at her clothes and bag. "How did you know Kitty? You don't seem the type. Particularly knowing what kind of life she'd fallen into."

"I was her friend, but to be honest I didn't know that much about her. I used to see her at church, at St. Mary's. She was sweet and I liked her." The scene from the recreation center with the soldiers mocking Kitty played in her head. She decided her stories about Kitty would have to be carefully edited.

"Church? Kitty was sweet? Well, that does surprise me. Tell me one thing. Why do you care, Miss Mary Margaret Smith?" Netty's faded blue eyes were piercing.

"No one should die the way Kitty did."

Netty Hawkins sighed. "Somebody killed her. You ain't told me how it was, but I'm guessing it was bad." The older woman paused her needles to straighten out the ball of yarn. Mimi could have kicked herself for letting that slip.

"Kitty made me promise to tell you if something happened to her."

"Why would she make you promise such a thing?" Netty wound yarn around the needles and clicked away again.

"She knew if something happened, the police wouldn't make any effort to reach you. She didn't want you to hear it like it was just gossip, I suppose. And she knew she could count on me."

"Why'd she think something would happen?"

"Kitty said she had the *quivers*. She was convinced something bad would happen."

Netty stopped knitting for a moment and glanced up. "The quivers." She said it as if it explained everything. The needles began their click-clacking again.

"I met Kitty collecting honey. I room with Addie Richardson in Alexandria. Kitty helped out last September when Addie's honey harvest was in. Addie sends her sympathy."

"Addie Richardson! My goodness. I recollect Addie, all right. She was just Addie Meadows back in the day. Set her cap for that big city lawyer Derry Richardson the moment she set eyes on him. She always had a purpose, did Addie."

"She's very purposeful." Seems like everyone knew Addie and what she was like. This was a very small town.

"The honey harvest? That Addie loved her bees, and her crops. Bet she's making a pretty penny on it these days. Not that she needs the money, with her fancy lawyer husband."

"A lot of people wait all year for Addie's honey," Mimi said. "Neighbors leave their mason jars with her for harvest time. All labeled."

"Quite the businesswoman, Addie Meadows. I hear she's got a big old house there in that Alexandria town. Too bad she had that idiot boy." Netty's needles barely slowed down.

"Richie? He's a sweet boy, and he plays music like an angel." If no one here will stand up for Richie, I will.

"We all got our troubles, I guess. At least I got seven more. And grandbabies too. They treat their mama right." Netty looked at the half-finished sweater. It was child sized. "My daughter Lucy's near twenty and fixing to get married soon."

Netty tilted her head at a school photo on top of an ancient upright piano. Lucy was apple-cheeked and healthy looking. She had brown hair kissed by the sun and bright blue eyes, but any resemblance to Kitty was just a suggestion. The piano held a crowd of photos, none of which featured Kitty. Mimi tried to sort out the other Hawkins children. There were two older married sons and Lucy, and there were four others in the Hawkins tribe, ranging from about 16 on down to about six years old. A couple of the youngest ran in and out of the house, retreating after they spotted a stranger in their midst. Netty Hawkins shooed them away with a look.

It was warm and stuffy inside, and Mimi could see why Kitty wanted to flee this house. As she'd told Mimi, the Hawkinses were dirt poor. Everything was old and threadbare. A dusty crucifix hung on the faded floral wallpaper. The rest of the décor consisted of pictures torn out of magazines and old calendars, courtesy of Homer's General Store. The furniture was creaky, and the seat of Mimi's chair sagged.

The first floor contained the kitchen, dining room, and parlor. The wood burning stove and the fireplace seemed to be the only source of heat. Stairs led to bedrooms upstairs. Other doors led who knew where.

Mimi sipped Netty's hot chicory and thought about her own childhood. She too had felt restless and imprisoned growing up. She'd been desperately eager to leave Denver, but at least it was a city, though many locals still called it "Cow Town." Her family had sacrificed during the Depression, but they made it through, with hard work. It was a different world here in Forgotten Creek.

"Kitty was getting married," Mimi said to break the silence. "To a pilot in the Army Air Forces." Both Joe and Netty stared at her open-mouthed. The knitting needles stilled.

"I thought she was still living a life of sin."

"She was leaving that life behind. She was getting married. She had a lovely diamond engagement ring. I saw it myself. I helped her pick out her dress."

"Well, Jesus, Joseph and Mary! Maybe she did have honorable intentions at the end. You can tell me what happened to my daughter now, my poor little Katharine. I can bear it now."

Josiah grabbed the table with both hands, but he said nothing. Mimi stumbled through the sad story of Kitty Hawkins, as far as she knew it. "She was murdered, just like two other women before her."

"Were they whores too?" That word seemed awfully easy for Netty to say.

"I prefer to call them magdalens." Joe flashed Mimi a look, and he nodded.

Netty Hawkins snorted. "Magdalens. That word just pretties up a sordid business."

Mimi took a deep breath. "The police have her body. They'll probably release it soon. I need to know— Where do you want Kitty buried?"

"Buried? We are not going to bury her with her God-fearing kin," her mother shouted. "Good country people who did not stoop to a life of whoredom! That big city killed her. That big city can bury her."

"You want to condemn her to Potter's Field? You want Kitty to be forgotten?" Joe reached out for Mimi's hand and squeezed it in warning.

"Best thing that could happen to her. I know you were her friend, I don't know why, except maybe you got a bigger heart than most of us." Netty's voice dropped. "Besides my personal feelings on the matter, there ain't no money to bury her."

Netty's knitting needles went back to work and they didn't miss a beat. Mimi looked at Joe. He shook his head. Perhaps it was for the best, Mimi thought. Kitty had left money for her own burial. She must have known her family wouldn't want her back, even in death. But how could this hard old woman keep click-clacking away, in the face of her daughter's murder? Knitting away her daughter's memory, like Dickens's Madame Defarge?

Mimi remembered another story, courtesy of her Grandma Eileen. Madam Pearl de Vere, a famous "soiled dove" of Cripple Creek, Colorado, back in the last century, had died of a morphine overdose, broken-hearted over a failed romance. Her sister back East was duly notified and soon arrived in that mountain boom town to claim and bury Pearl. But when her sister saw the body, dressed for burial in her gaudiest finery, she realized Pearl was a prostitute, a madam who ran a brothel. Her sister walked away and left Pearl's body lying in the mortuary.

Families could be difficult, Grandma Eileen always said.

But unlike the madam's stuffy family, Cripple Creek appreciated Pearl. The townspeople were incensed that her family would refuse to forgive her, and they vowed to right this wrong. Madam Pearl de Vere was treated to the largest funeral Cripple Creek, Colorado, had ever seen.

Kitty Hawkins would have her funeral, Mimi decided. She would make sure Kitty was buried in Alexandria. If Madam Pearl de Vere deserved a proper funeral, so did she. She deserved to be remembered, by people who cared about her, not lost in faraway Forgotten Creek.

And besides, Mimi thought to herself, *I promised her.*

TWENTY-SEVEN

*I*F THESE PEOPLE refused to bury their own, would they turn down Kitty's money? Mimi wondered. Let's find out, she thought.

"There are other things Kitty wanted you to have. In addition to your necklace."

Mimi opened her canvas satchel. She pulled out two pounds each of white sugar and coffee and set them on the table. The three-pound box of fancy chocolates came next.

Josiah Jordan sat there stone-faced before pushing himself away from the table. He went to the kitchen to pour himself a fresh cup of chicory. Mimi watched him go. She pulled out an envelope with Kitty's ration book and an assortment of bills amounting to $350, which she placed in Netty's hand. The amount was written neatly on the envelope in Kitty's handwriting.

Netty looked mystified, but she opened the envelope. The ration book fell out on the table, but she grabbed the bills, counted them quickly, and tucked them in her pocket with the envelope. She glanced at the kitchen to make sure Joe hadn't seen the money. He was still standing with his back to them, drinking his chicory.

"You don't have to accept it," Mimi said softly.

"I'm sure this money ain't clean," Netty hissed too low for Joe to hear, "but I can't be bothered to stand on principle when my family has to eat." She didn't meet Mimi's eyes.

"I understand," Mimi said.

"I told her not to go," she repeated. Netty's hands reached for the packages.

"I might be able to send you a few other things," Mimi said. "They were too heavy for me to bring."

Joe returned with the pot of chicory. "Hope you don't mind, Netty."

"You're welcome to it." He filled her cup and Mimi's. "Look, Joe, Kitty's ration book, barely used. This is real coffee, and fine white sugar. Chocolates. I ain't had store-bought chocolates in, why, forever."

"She wanted you to have them," Mimi said.

Netty flipped through the ration book. "Kitty always wanted to live the high life, ever since she was little. Where she got her highfalutin ideas, I swear I don't know. I did my best to keep her away from the movies and all that sin. Did you know the Legion of Decency puts out a list of bad movies every month in the *Catholic Register?*"

"My mother used to post that list in our home every month," Mimi said.

"Mine too," Joe added with a small grimace.

"Kitty—she wanted so much," Netty continued. "Mama, why can't we have this, why can't we have that? Why can't we have an indoor toilet? I told her we were just lucky to have electric lights, from the rural electrification co-op. But that girl had a stack of wants high as a mountain." Mimi didn't answer. Netty Hawkins needed to talk. "We got us a bathroom in the house, cold running water and a tub and a chamber pot for the nighttime. Good enough for seven of my little ones, but the necessary is out back, and an outhouse wasn't good enough for Kitty, oh no, not good enough. I always had the feeling, that bad feeling, the quivers, she called it. Maybe you'd call it a premonition, about my golden girl. Near cut my heart in two."

"It must be hard." There were no words Mimi could say to comfort this woman. Netty returned to her knitting. She regarded Mimi with tired eyes.

"My tears are long cried out. I was always afraid she would come to a bad end. The day she walked out the door and got on that train to that wicked city, Washington, D.C., my Katharine's fate was sealed."

Like my fate, Mimi thought. And at least Kitty had a few moments of being Nathan Albemarle's magical mermaid.

"Kitty told me she worked as a lifeguard, and she graduated from high school."

"She was book learned, all right, enough to read them movie magazines, but she had no common sense."

Mimi noticed a Singer treadle sewing machine set up in one corner of the room. It was old, but well-polished, and it looked like it was in good repair. Cloth flour sacks and feed sacks were stacked in neat piles near it. There were sacks in small patterns and stripes and plain white. Mimi noticed that the younger children peeking through the doorways wore clothes in those familiar fabrics.

"You're very handy with a needle, and that sewing machine."

"The Lord provides us with talents, and the means to use them. I shudder to think what we would wear without them sacks. I make quilts with the scraps. We don't believe in waste here."

"I can see that," Mimi said. "I sew a little myself."

Mimi's mother despised sewing and bought her clothes ready-to-wear from department stores. She didn't know where her daughter's interest in unique clothes came from. Perhaps from the same glamorous movie magazines Kitty loved.

"I like sewing when I can get the patterns and the sacks in a good quantity. Then I can piece it together for dresses for the girls. With enough cloth, I can even piece together sheets and pillowcases." The larger feed sacks of rougher weave were handy for coverlets and curtains, Netty added. The plain white flour sacks were reserved for her husband's shirts.

Mimi glanced at her watch. "Time is getting on." She needed to that rooming house Addie had mentioned.

"There's no train back tonight," Netty said. "Looks like you're staying in Forgotten Creek."

"Addie said there's a rooming house near the general store." Mimi turned toward Joe. "If you could give me a lift back to Main Street, I'd appreciate it."

"Sure thing," he said. "I'll take you to the train tomorrow too."

"Thank you, Joe. Much appreciated."

"You forget about that danged rooming house," Netty said. "That woman will charge you two dollars a night and not bat an eyelash. You keep your money, Mimi Smith. You best stay here. That sofa ain't pretty, but it does the job."

"Thank you." Mimi was grateful for the offer, though she felt awkward imposing on Kitty's family. Still, the war had taught her she could sleep anywhere, even on a lumpy old sofa, and be grateful for small kindnesses. "I don't want to put you out."

"Least I could do, after you brought me my girl's things. That money will come in right handy, and coffee and sugar come a treat. And chocolates. 'Course I'll have to add some chicory to the coffee to stretch it out."

Netty's husband, Holden Hawkins, stomped into the house. Though he had a heavy step, he was a thin man in stained dungarees. His face reflected nothing. He seemed hollow, as if the wind had blown away whatever dreams and desires he may have had. He looked to his wife.

"I heard from one of the young 'uns." They shared a look, an understanding. He seemed to shrink before Mimi's eyes. "We knew this day was coming, Netty. How did it happen?"

"She met a bad end, Holden. Real bad," Netty said. "Same as a couple other women in that Alexandria city."

"Damn. Damn it all to Hell." He turned around and slammed the door. When he turned back, seeming calmer, his gaze traveled to Kitty's gifts on the table. His eyes widened at the sight of coffee and sugar, the ration book, and the chocolates. "What's all this here?"

"Things from Kitty," Netty said. "And there's a little cash too. Nigh on to one hundred dollars." This time Netty shared a look with Mimi. "This here is Miss Mimi Smith. She came all the way from Alexandria, Virginia, to tell us the sad news."

Mimi didn't blame Mrs. Hawkins for lying about the money. She probably was more in tune with their family's needs than her husband. And as Mimi's grandmother had often pointed out, a woman needed her own money, money a man couldn't get his hands on.

"Alexandria?" Holden glared at Mimi, but his wife stepped in.

"Miss Smith here had nothing to do with Kitty's—Kitty's work. They met at church."

"Church?" He looked skeptical.

"St. Mary's, in Alexandria," Mimi said. "She went every Sunday." Mimi wasn't certain of that, but it sounded good. "I have a regular job. With the government." This was no time to mention OPA.

"No offense meant, Miss—Miss Smith." Holden backed away. "You come a long way carrying bad news. We're beholden to you."

"You don't have a phone. And the police—" she began.

"Wouldn't expect no courtesy from them," he said. "We're much obliged, Miss Smith. But I don't understand. You could have sold these things, made some money for yourself."

Mimi shook her head. "I made a promise to Kitty."

He covered his eyes and shuffled to the sink to wash up. He limped from some old leg injury.

"He don't show much emotion, but he's hurting," Netty said softly. "He loves all his children."

ଔ

News of Kitty's death spread quickly through the "young 'uns," and as soon as the Hawkins finished their meager supper of potato and carrot stew flavored with pork belly, neighbors started showing up to express their sympathy. As Netty had predicted, the gossip spread as fast as crows could fly. The prodigal daughter had not come home, but word of her sad ending had.

The family headed out to the front porch to meet them. Mimi pulled on her black sweater against the cool evening air. She was the only one who seemed to feel it. Josiah Jordan had stayed for the family meal, already stretched thin on Mimi's account. Netty had insisted, and he didn't seem in any hurry to leave.

"As soon as you showed up from back East," he said to Mimi, "heading up the hollow to the Hawkins house, the rumors and speculation must have flown thick and fast. Everyone wants to show their grief over Kitty, sure, but they also want a peek at you and your pretty duds."

"Joe, these are my oldest clothes, and they're dusty and wrinkled. Addie told me what to wear. This skirt was from a little Mexican market in West Denver. It was dirt cheap."

Cheap, but vibrant and pretty, all the same. On Addie's advice, she'd left behind the gold hoop earrings she liked to wear with it.

Joe was amused. "Don't matter where you got it, it wasn't stitched out of a pile of flour sacks. Things are different here, Miss Mimi. I'm afraid you and Kitty Hawkins are going to be the topic of conversation here for some time to come."

Despite his fearsome appearance, she was finding Joe easy to talk to. He had a quietude about him that inspired confidence. Mimi appreciated the gentle way he treated Netty Hawkins, and how he seemed to watch over Mimi, just because she was a stranger.

"I don't mean to upset anybody, Joe."

"I know that. You did the Hawkins a good turn. Would have been a sight worse if they never found out about Kitty, or they found out later in some cruel way. Plenty of cruelty to go around these days."

"I didn't have to say a word. I gave Netty that necklace and she knew."

"Mamas are like that. Even one like Netty."

The neighbors brought food, which the Hawkinses graciously accepted—a loaf of bread, a dozen eggs, a slab of bacon. Old cars and trucks were parked all around the Hawkins home. Joe was right. All the farmers had plenty of gasoline to get around.

Holden Hawkins built a fire outside in a firepit. The visitors had come with their banjos, guitars, fiddles, washboards, and harmonicas, and they sat or stood around the fire and began to play in the twilight. Mostly hymns, but other tunes Mimi knew as well, like "Wayfaring Stranger," "Simple Gifts," and "Hard Times Come Again No More." Some sounded very old, like folk songs from deep in the hills, and Mimi had never heard them before.

Joe stayed close to Mimi, for which she was grateful. The bonfire and the music moved her more than she expected. Kitty's name was rarely spoken, but this was clearly a sort of wake for her, a memorial for one of their own. Everyone knew now that Katharine Hawkins was dead.

The neighbors didn't say much, but their songs conveyed their shared sorrow. Crickets and cicadas added their own rhythms, and the darkening air was thick with fireflies. Their flashing lights took Mimi's breath away. The fireflies in Alexandria were beautiful, but with no streetlights around, this show seemed even brighter. Netty Hawkins sat down next to her.

"Kitty was like a firefly too, all lit up one moment, dark the next. But her light was so bright you wanted to capture it, the way she caught those lightning bugs. That's how I'll always remember her, my white-blond child, running in a field, chasing fireflies."

"She was luminous."

"I reckon she was. I never thought about it that way."

"I think Kitty would like to be remembered that way," Mimi said. "They don't have fireflies where I come from out West. There's such a magic about them."

"The thing about fireflies is they don't last but one brief season." Netty spotted someone else to speak to and got to her feet, knees cracking.

Netty Hawkins wasn't about to cry in front of other people, Mimi realized. Not in front of strangers or company or her children, perhaps not even her husband. Her tears, if there were any, would come later, when she was alone. She was a woman whose own light had fled years ago.

Mimi, on the other hand, was moved to tears for Kitty, her unborn baby, and the flyboy she left behind. She wiped them away with her hand.

One of Kitty's sisters sat down close to Mimi as her mother left. Mimi looked for her resemblance to her sister. It was there, but it was faint.

"I hope I'm not disturbing you, Miss Mimi."

"Not at all. You're Lucy, right? You're Kitty's younger sister?"

Lucy nodded. She was slender with long curly dark brown hair and big bright blue eyes. Her shabby dress was pink and pretty but patched, with the look of a hand-me-down. This crowd was full of hand-me-downs, pretty and otherwise.

"I wanted to thank you for bringing us all them things from Kitty."

Joe rose from his seat on Mimi's other side.

"I heard tell there was lemonade. Would you ladies like some lemonade?"

They nodded. He exited to give them some privacy.

"You're welcome. But?" Mimi felt there was a "but" coming.

Lucy spun around to see if anyone was listening, then she took a deep breath. "You said there were some other things you might be sending us? I was wondering if there were any clothes of Kitty's? Her and me are pretty much the same size."

"That size being thin and pretty?" Lucy blushed and Mimi smiled. Although Lucy wasn't the beauty that Kitty was, she had a vitality about her. "There might be a few things."

"I'm not trying to be greedy. Honest. You see, I'm getting married soon, and it would be really something to have a dress that wasn't twice turned and thrice mended. It wouldn't even have to be new, just something different."

"How old are you?"

"Almost twenty." She said it as if her last chance might be passing her by.

"That's awfully young to sign up for babies and diaper duty."

Mimi thought it sounded positively medieval. And, she realized, *I sound like my grandmother.*

"Wade and me, we been waiting for times to get better. But they ain't getting better. Gals around here, we start getting married young. Sixteen, seventeen, eighteen. Why, Kitty was almost twenty-two. But you told Mama she was getting married soon?"

"Yes, she was planning on it. Very soon. She had a diamond engagement ring."

"Golly. Wade and me, we don't have much, and I sure would appreciate a store-bought dress for my wedding, if there was one, I mean. Wade would rather I have some good pots and pans over anything new to wear. He's practical minded." This Wade sounded like a real stiff to Mimi. But it wasn't her call. "Still, a gal has dreams, and I can't have a wedding gown. My ma never had one and it would be downright unpatriotic to wear one in these times, but it sure would be nice to have something new."

"Even if it's a hand-me-down?" Mimi asked.

"Story of my life. It would be new to me."

"What's your favorite color?"

"I've always favored blue, because my eyes are blue. But I like pink and yellow, well, anything would be nice. But not red, not red for a wedding. Kitty favored red. I don't think even Kitty would get married in red. And white would be out of the question. Because, you know why. You don't think Kitty would mind my asking, do you?"

Lucy seemed so hopeful, it broke Mimi's heart.

"Kitty's beyond caring now. Tell you what, Lucy, I'll see what I can find. I don't know what your family would want you to have. You know, things that belonged to her."

"They really appreciate the sugar and coffee." She lowered her voice. "And especially the money. Mama told me about the money. Even if it was ill-gotten."

"Kitty didn't leave that much behind." That was Mimi's opinion, but things were different here. Her few treasures might mean a whole lot more in Forgotten Creek.

"Anything at all would be a gift." Lucy was tearing up. "I'm sorry, I sound just like a beggar."

"What size shoes do you wear?"

Lucy stared at her feet. "Six, just like Kitty."

"There might be a new pair of shoes."

"Brand-new?" Lucy's eyes opened wide.

"Dark blue leather. Heels. Sunday go-to-church shoes, I'd say."

"Oh, Miss Mimi!" She couldn't get any more words out.

"What's your Wade do for a living?"

"He farms, with his daddy."

"He's not going to go to war and get sent overseas, is he?"

"Wade's got an exemption. He's the only son. Nobody else to work the farm."

"Haven't you ever wanted to leave Forgotten Creek?" Lucy's future life sounded awfully dreary.

Lucy's face registered shock. "Like Kitty? Of no! No, of course not."

"Not like Kitty. I mean, did you ever just want to get away from this place?"

"Never thought about that."

Was this the first time she'd ever contemplated it? Mimi looked around at the crowd. For the most part, they looked like solid, honest people. "Well, everyone has a different path. I left my home to work for the war effort."

"That sounds so sad."

"Not at all. I was ready to make my getaway."

"My path is with Wade, here in Forgotten Creek. Mostly I don't mind us being forgotten here. It's peaceful." Lucy gazed into the distance, thinking of something far away. "Thanks for letting us know about Kitty. It's tragic, but there's a kind of finality to it, you understand? We don't have to wonder no more. She didn't write us much, aside from a Christmas card, and that card just upset my ma."

Joe showed up with lemonades for Mimi and Lucy, accompanied by a tall slim young man, hardly more than a boy. Lucy introduced her fiancé, Wade. She and Wade left to give his condolences to Lucy's parents.

"Thanks for this, Joe. I'm parched." Mimi took a swig and made a face.

Joe laughed. "A little sour, I'm guessing." He had a bottle of beer in his hand.

Someone had forgotten to sweeten the lemonade. Or more likely, Mimi thought, any available sugar went to make moonshine. Her mouth puckered. She turned at the sound of another car arriving, a delivery van emblazoned with Frenchie's Hardware, in plain block lettering. Out of the driver's side door popped a familiar figure.

The man called Clem.

TWENTY-EIGHT

C LEM. THE MAN who had badgered Kitty about sugar after she and Mimi shopped for her wedding trousseau. What the heck was he doing here? Or in D.C., for that matter? He had known both Kitty and Hattie. He hadn't spotted Mimi yet, or maybe he didn't recognize her. She rose to take a closer look and Joe followed.

"Who's Frenchie?"

"He's the fat man in overalls and the red plaid shirt. Shoveling pie in his face. Why? What's going on, Mimi?"

Frenchie stood with a plate in one hand and a fork in the other. He was not merely fat, but big and imposing, despite the country-boy clothes. Clem, all skin and bones, shambled up to him, looking half the size of Frenchie. Clem wore olive workpants and shirt, appearing more comfortable in them than the ill-fitting suit he wore in D.C.

"I'm not sure." She pointed to the delivery van. "And that's his truck?"

"Got his name on it. Frenchie likes to put his stamp on things."

Soon Frenchie was deep in conversation with Clem. Mimi told herself it would be stupid to get involved in local business in this place where she didn't know how things worked. On the other hand, she could always ask questions.

"That man, Joe. The skinny one, Clem? He was in D.C. last week. I was having lunch with Kitty after our shopping trip, at a cheap diner. You know the kind. He strolled in and surprised Kitty. He probably saw her through the window. She acted like he didn't bother her, but I think he did. He also knew Hattie Carnegie Jones."

"Hattie?"

"One of the other magdalens who was killed."

"The same way Kitty was killed?"

"Yes."

"You know more than you're telling. How did Kitty die?"

Mimi took a deep breath before answering. It was harder than she expected. "Someone beat her and broke her neck. She fought back, but— She was so small."

"Damn, Kitty," he said to the dead woman who wasn't there. "Always getting yourself into situations you can't handle. Damn it to hell."

Mimi reached for his hand and squeezed it briefly. "I'm so sorry, Joe. It was the same with Hattie, but Hattie was a big gal. Seems like it would take a pretty sizeable person to do that."

"You didn't tell her folks anything about that."

"I've distressed them enough. It seemed unnecessarily cruel to tell them all that."

He focused on her, his expression softening. "That was considerate of you, Mimi. You were right, it's bad enough for them to know she's dead. To know what she'd fallen into. But you could be in danger too. What else do you know?"

"Not much. This Clem mentioned 'Frenchie' and complained he wasn't getting any sugar. That could be taken in many ways, considering Kitty's line of work, but I think he meant the actual white stuff, sugar. It was right before the robbery."

"What robbery?"

"At Addie Richardson's. Someone stole a thousand pounds of sugar."

He whistled. "That's a fair amount of the white stuff."

"For Addie's bees. She has a lot of bees. Certain people could have known about it, people who know about bees and honey. The robbers must have known." She broke off. "What's inside that truck, Joe?"

"Knowing Frenchie, could be anything."

"Says hardware. Tools? Things you could build a still with?"

"Could be."

Mimi inched nearer to the van, but she stopped before the men noticed her. "Would you mind acting like we're together, Joe?"

"Would I mind?" He slung an arm around her shoulder and grinned at her. "People will talk. This close enough?"

"Maybe a little too close," she said.

He readjusted his arm. "I don't want you getting hurt, that's all."

Frenchie opened the back door of the van and handed Clem a stoneware jug of something that could be liquor. She thought she saw something else in the back, large tan sacks.

"Is that moonshine?" Mimi whispered to Joe.

"Some of the best."

"Can we see?"

"Only if you want to buy some. Frenchie's kind of particular 'bout people getting too close to his van. He must have heard there was a gathering here tonight. His shine is good, not as good as my daddy used to make, but it won't kill you. He sells clear shine and the 'finer' homemade bourbon."

She reached deep into her pocket for the folded bills in her change purse. "I'd like a bottle of moonshine. For Kitty's sake, truly." She was suddenly terribly embarrassed. She could feel her face burning. "Believe me, Joe, I've never said anything like that before. I've never even bought alcohol. I don't know whether to get the shine or the bourbon."

"I believe you. Only difference is the bourbon's flavored with oak chips."

"Will five dollars do?" She assumed the price for a jug of illegal hootch would be well above the OPA mandated two dollars for a fifth of legal whiskey. She had also heard tales of people going blind drinking the stuff.

"Three will get you a jug. Extra buck'll get you a bottle or a jar with a fancy fake label." She rolled her eyes. He grinned again and took her three dollars. "Stay right here."

Joe waved at Frenchie, while Mimi retreated into the shadows. The flickering bonfire illuminated the fat man's truck. Joe Jordan was as tall as the big man, about half the width, yet twice the muscle. Beside them, Clem looked like a skinny rat. Frenchie greeted Joe with a grin. They exchanged a few words, and he opened the back of the truck. Mimi could see full and empty sacks of sugar. *Addie's sugar.* Her landlady marked her sacks with her initials in big black letters. In the light of the fire, Mimi could make out the letters A R in Addie's distinctive scrawl.

Clem turned and caught sight of Mimi. His eyes went wide and he ran his hands through his hair. *Did he remember meeting me with Kitty at the café?* Mimi immediately convicted him of the sugar theft. As soon as money and moonshine changed hands, Frenchie and Clem jumped back in the van and took off. Joe returned with Mimi's brown stoneware jug of clear shine.

"What about Frenchie, Joe? What's his story?"

"People don't mess with Frenchie. He likes living on the other side of the law. But he generally doesn't bother people who don't bother him."

"You don't bother him?"

"Frenchie don't mess with me. We all go pretty far back in this town. Here's your moonshine, lady." He showed her the jug but kept a grip on it. "Let me hold on to this for a while. You don't want to give people more to gossip about. I gotta say, Mimi Smith, you don't seem like the moonshine imbibing type."

"I'm not. But I'm pretty sure all that sugar in his truck was stolen from Addie Richardson."

Joe gave her a look. "You can tell one sack of sugar from another?"

"When they've got Addie's initials on them, I can. I've seen those sacks before, in Addie's cellar." Mimi figured the moonshine had to be some kind of evidence too. She wondered if George Prescott would reimburse her the three dollars. "Maybe I'll give Addie that jug as a consolation prize. She'd like to know where her sugar went."

"Son of a bitch, Frenchie," Joe said under his breath. Of all the people here, he seemed like the only one she could trust.

"Joe, I know I can't do anything about this, the sugar theft or Kitty's murder. Certainly not here and now. But I want to know what happened."

Joe lowered his voice. "You think Clem's involved in Kitty's death?"

"Maybe. He could be involved in the sugar theft. And I think he recognized me. Honestly, Joe, I don't want to talk here."

"That's good. Like Netty said, even the crows tell tales. I'll pick you up tomorrow morning round about eight. In the meantime, let me stash this jug in my truck." He headed toward his vehicle in the dark, jug in hand, and Mimi followed.

"What time does the train leave?"

"No train, Miss Smith. I'm going to drive you back to Alexandria tomorrow myself. I'm going to make sure you get back home safe."

"Oh, Joe. I don't want to take you out of your way."

"Ain't out of my way. I've been planning to join the Navy, do my duty. Hand the farm off to my brothers. I've got a chat scheduled with a recruiter in Annapolis this coming week. With my college, they say I can go right into Naval Officer Training."

"A ninety-day wonder, like they say?"

"You bet. An officer in three months. It's as good a deal as any you'll find in this man's war."

"Kitty told me you went to the university in Morgantown, but then you came home."

"My daddy died. I was needed at home, but now my brothers are old enough to take over the farming. Besides, they been waiting for me to leave. They're flipping coins over my room." He grinned again and his face lit up.

"You have a hankering to see the world?"

"Indeed, I do. Kitty used to tell me, 'There's a whole wide world out there, Joe.' Well, I'm planning to see it for myself."

"I'm glad you're not going to be a pilot."

Mimi stepped carefully to avoid ruts in the ground. Joe's truck was parked on a fairly level piece of land near the house. It was surrounded by twenty or thirty other trucks and cars, none of which were shiny and new.

"Navy's got pilots too, but we'll see." He opened the cab door, looked around to assess if anyone was watching, and shoved the jug under his seat. He slammed the door shut.

"What are you going to do with your truck?"

"Leave it with my sister in Arlington. She and her husband can use it while I'm away. They can drive me over to Annapolis. I want to join up there, after a few days on the town. And I want to talk to you about how Kitty wound up dead."

"At eight? I'll be ready." She doubted if she could sleep.

"Don't tell anyone anything about what we've been talking about, Mimi. You're a curiosity to these people. You keep it that way."

"You might want to go into Naval Intelligence."

"I might do that. I can keep a secret."

"Loose lips sink ships, right?"

"Something tells me you're no slouch at secret-keeping yourself, Mimi Smith."

☙

The neighbors were starting to pack away their musical instruments when Mimi and Joe returned to the house. The crowd was drifting away little by little, and the Hawkins family was letting the fire burn low and heading for their beds.

Mimi felt awkward about bunking down on the lumpy old sofa. She would rather have had a room for the night, even if she were overcharged. A room with a door that closed and locked would be reassuring. Not to mention indoor plumbing. She told herself the Hawkins home, full of noisy kids, was perfectly safe. Still, she had the tiniest worry that Clem and Fat Frenchie would show up to murder her in the night.

Mimi settled down into the sofa and pulled Netty's patched blanket and sheet up to her nose. She had decided to sleep in her clothes, even though she'd brought a nightgown. Her skirt and blouse were already wrinkled, and she could jump up quickly if need be. She sighed and rolled over. The sofa wasn't comfortable enough to really relax. Dreamtime was evading her.

When everyone was in bed, the girls in their bedroom, and the boys in their quarters in the cellar, the ramshackle house silent, Mimi heard her stomach growl. She found her purse and fished out the second Spam sandwich Addie had made for her. She ate it quietly in the dark and finally dozed off, dreaming of Spam and real coffee.

She awoke to the aroma of real coffee percolating, like a dream. It was a surprise. Netty was bustling in the kitchen making biscuits. Mimi sat up and threw off the thin blanket.

"You up, sleepy head? It's nigh on seven o'clock."

"My goodness." Mimi didn't mention she had lain awake half the night with her brain buzzing and her stomach rumbling. She made a trip to the outhouse, uttering prayers of grateful thanks that indoor toilets were integral to the rest of her life.

She completed her morning ablutions in the Hawkins's "bathroom" with cold running water, changed into her pink blouse and fresh underwear, and swapped her sturdy saddle shoes for sandals. She sprinkled water on her skirt to smooth out the wrinkles. She combed and pulled her unruly hair back with clips, letting her auburn curls tumble down her back. Returning to the kitchen for a cup of coffee, Mimi saw that Mrs. Hawkins had set her a place at the table.

"Help yourself to some breakfast," Netty said, setting down plates of food.

"Thank you." Mimi indulged in biscuits with butter and sizzling bacon. "Where's the rest of the family?"

"Eva and Emma are doing chores. Boys are in the field with their pa." Netty's hair was tied up in a kerchief for her housework. She wore a faded red blouse and old blue jeans that hung low on her hips and bagged out in the bottom. "We're much obliged to you, Miz Mary Margaret Smith, for telling us about our Kitty." And for bringing the sugar and coffee, ration coupons, and money, Mimi amended. She wondered whether Netty might have reconsidered bringing Kitty's body back home, but the subject didn't come up. "Neighbors were right generous last night, with their provisions, and their time, and their music. A real honest wake," Netty said. "Kitty would have liked that."

Netty Hawkins was a woman who had already given up her daughter for dead the day she walked out the door with her mother's purloined necklace. She had just been waiting for the death notice. Now that she'd determined she'd been right all along, it seemed to give her self-righteous strength. The same way she had tucked some of Kitty's money away so her husband wouldn't see it.

Mimi tried not to judge, and she could understand why Netty acted the way she did. Still, she did not like this small-minded woman. Kitty's parents had been so sure their daughter would turn out bad. Did their judgment and warnings send her straight to the life they feared?

The soon-to-married Lucy bounced in through the front door and poured herself a cup of coffee. She sat next to their guest from Alexandria and thanked her again.

"No need. It was something I had to do."

The wedding ensemble that Kitty bought would suit Lucy as well, Mimi knew. The beautiful blue crepe dress with its peplum was not merely fashionable, it was flattering, refined, and dressy. From hat to shoes, Kitty had shown great care in selecting each item. Mimi experienced a moment of pure sorrow that Kitty would never be able to enjoy her wedding ensemble. Would she want her sister to wear it? She didn't know.

On the other hand, she was sure Kitty wouldn't mind her wedding outfit making a big splash in Forgotten Creek. Would her mother hate it? It was clear Netty distrusted any of life's pleasures. Hard work and sorrow were all she ever knew. Why should it be different for her children?

"I'll send a few more things when I get back," Mimi said.

"I can't imagine there'd be more than what you brought already," Netty said.

"Her roommates took some things before I could sort through them. It's the way among those women. That's why Kitty kept her nicer things in a locker. That's where I found the sugar and coffee."

"It's right kind of you, Miss Mimi, to go to the trouble," Lucy said. "She must have appreciated your friendship."

Mimi laughed at that. "She called me a goody-goody."

"High praise, I'd say," Netty commented.

Joe's pickup truck roared to a stop on their dirt road.

"I better go." Mimi jumped up from her chair, ready to dash out the door.

"You set a spell. Joe'll want coffee first." As Netty predicted, Joe marched up the front porch, through the front door, and took the cup she offered.

"You ready to go?" he asked Mimi. She almost didn't recognize him.

"Joe, is that really you?"

"Why, Josiah Jordan," Netty said, "you look most ready to go to church."

"Josiah, you look like you're a-walking down the aisle," Lucy said with a wink.

Joe blushed and his smile was sheepish. He stuck his hands in his pockets. "Hey, I don't look that different. Same old Joe. Besides, I'm heading down to the big city. Gotta be presentable."

Joe had shaved off his black stubble and combed back his jet-black hair. He had a nice face, with a strong jaw. He'd exchanged his overalls for a clean blue shirt that made his eyes look bluer and a pair of respectable trousers. Mimi realized with something of a shock how handsome he was.

She followed him to the kitchen. "I want to tell you, Joe. I plan to send some of Kitty's clothes back here for Lucy. Suitable for any lady. They are beautiful, and they have never been worn."

"How do you know that?"

"I helped Kitty shop for them. I don't want there to be any problem with Lucy accepting them."

"Brand-new clothes? Are you kidding? That would be something, especially for her wedding day."

Netty brought her own dishes to the sink. "What's going on in here?"

"There are some clothes I can send for Lucy," Mimi said. "She'll be the most gorgeous bride Forgotten Creek will see, if you don't have any objections."

A strange look came over the old woman's face. "I believe Kitty was right smart to trust you, Miz Smith."

"Lucy knows I'm sending her a pair of new shoes, but I'd like the rest to be a surprise."

"Hope it don't just kill us all with the shock."

Netty smiled unexpectedly and patted Mimi on the back. Mimi collected her purse and her canvas satchel, grateful that Joe had showed up before she was put to work cleaning up after breakfast. Joe grabbed her satchel for her. It was lighter today.

"This all you got?"

"This is it."

As she and Joe settled into the truck, the members of the Hawkins family who weren't working in the field gathered on the porch to wave goodbye. Mimi laughed.

"What's so funny?" he asked.

"It's like I was their long-lost cousin or something."

"You were better than a cousin," he said, "you were Santy Claus coming with a sack full of gifts, and it ain't even Christmas."

A few miles down the road, or the "Hillbilly Highway," as Joe told her the locals called it, Joe stopped for a coal train crossing the railroad tracks. Mimi pulled out her makeup and

Ellen Byerrum

a small mirror from her purse. She applied some powder and lipstick, and she colored her cheeks by dabbing a little lipstick and blending it in. Joe flashed her an inquisitive look.

"I heard Netty Hawkins doesn't hold with makeup," she said.

"She don't, but I'd say you're just gilding the lily. You're pretty enough without all that stuff."

Mimi laughed. "You'll turn my head, Joe Jordan."

"You and Rita Hayworth. That's who you look like."

Mimi laughed again, but then she noticed his hands on the steering wheel. They were red and raw and scabbed.

"Joe, your hands are all bloody. What in the world happened?"

TWENTY-NINE

"MY FISTS MIGHT have met Clem's face." He glanced at his injured hands. "There might have been a slight altercation."

"And your face, Joe. I just noticed, you have a cut." Mimi reached for his face but didn't touch it.

"He got in a lucky punch."

"Oh, Joe. I didn't want you to get hurt."

"I'm not hurt, Mimi. You should see Clem." Joe kept his eyes on the road, but he sent her a smile. "Clem knew Kitty from Forgotten Creek. We had quite a chat about stolen sugar. He swore he had nothing to do with that, or her death."

"It's not like he would confess, would he?"

"When I got through with him, he would have. He also claimed neither he nor Frenchie had anything to do with the sugar theft. But I've got an empty bag of that sugar for you. It's in the back."

"Oh my God! You didn't! And I suppose they said it just fell out of the sky?"

"These boys didn't get to where they are by telling the truth."

They passed a small farm with cows standing in the field. There was a strong smell of manure. Mimi wrinkled her nose, thinking how much it reminded her of Colorado ranch country.

"What about Frenchie? You said he operates on the other side of the law."

"He does, but he don't get his hands dirty, not him personally. I don't see him going all the way to Alexandria to steal sugar, or kill Kitty. Besides, he's tight with her family. Why would he hurt her?"

At least that empty bag would be proof that Addie's sugar, stolen from Alexandria, Virginia, had somehow wound up in Forgotten Creek, West Virginia. Would her boss George Prescott be impressed? Mimi doubted it.

"Joe, you should probably know something. I work for the government, the Office of Price Administration, but I'm not here on behalf of the agency. This trip was just for Kitty."

He squinted at her and then cast his eyes back on the road. "OPA. *The* OPA? Black markets and ration books and price controls? You sure you're not here on business?"

"I am a mere stenographer."

"Mimi, you're not a mere anything."

"Thank you for that. But my job— It's not like I'm an investigator. Not even close."

There was no instruction manual to tell her how to go about becoming one. But there was no manual that told her not to try, either.

"I reckon you're the kind who's always got her eyes and ears open."

"Are you saying I'm nosy?"

"Not exactly. Are you?"

"Sometimes. Now that you know, if you want to stop and drop me off at the train, you still have time."

"OPA. That why you were so concerned that the sugar theft had something to do with Kitty's death?"

"It was a heck of a lot of sugar. A thousand pounds of the stuff, twenty fifty-pound bags. Kitty didn't know I worked for OPA. If she did, she wouldn't have told me about Hattie. She wouldn't have even talked to me."

"Hattie? You mentioned her last night."

"One of the other magdalens. According to Kitty, she was in the habit of selling things that weren't hers. She was killed the week before Kitty."

Joe turned toward the main road, away from the train station. "Seems to me you've been collecting a lot of information for a mere stenographer."

"You're not going to take me to the train?" She gazed at him in surprise. "You're really driving me all the way home?"

"When this is the most interesting conversation I've had in months? We got some talking to do, Mimi, and I think it's safer this way."

She hoped that was true. At the moment, Josiah Jordan was the only person in West Virginia she felt safe with. "Thank you. I don't think I could take another packed train ride."

"Does your agency investigate murders?"

"Not officially. My boss George, George Prescott, is routinely annoyed that although we have a mandate to investigate black marketeering, we have limited power. Most infractions under OPA jurisdiction are mere misdemeanors. When we uncover big thefts or stumble over other felonies, they generally get tossed to some other agency. Felonies go to police departments. OPA gets all of the hate and none of the credit. We usually handle the smaller stuff. But George says small things can lead to murder."

"Look on the bright side, Mimi. At least you're not with the IRS."

"That's looking on the bright side?" Mimi smirked. "Kitty was afraid of something, but she wouldn't tell me anything specific. All she would say is 'the quivers' told her something bad was going to happen. After Hattie and Polly died, she must have known she was in somebody's crosshairs."

"You're saying Kitty wasn't just a whore, you're saying she was mixed up in all this other stuff and it led to her being killed?"

"Don't call her that, Joe. A *magdalen*. And I don't know. Maybe she wouldn't play along. I don't know much about Polly Brown, but there might be a couple of people I can ask. She was the first to die, hit by a train. People say it was an accident or suicide, but these three deaths are too close together, too connected."

Joe was quiet for a moment. "If Frenchie and Clem had nothing to do with their killings, but the stolen sugar wound up here, then the link is somewhere in the middle. Between here and Alexandria."

"The link between the dead magdalens, the stolen sugar, and Forgotten Creek. Like what, a customer?" Mimi said. "And whose customer? The girls' customers, or the moonshiners'?"

"Or maybe a supplier? Whoever it is, this guy has killed three women."

"Perhaps a soldier," Mimi said.

"One who developed a taste for killing? But why kill women and not the enemy? This is something else." Joe fell silent again and kept his eyes on the road.

"Whoever killed Kitty must have decided she knew something valuable," Mimi said. "Or she knew too much. Kitty said anyone who knew bees could figure out where the sugar was kept."

"Kitty was my first love," Joe said quietly. "But she broke hearts all over town. And then she left. I forgot my anger long ago. Puppy love is like that. But Kitty chose to leave and she chose her life."

"If you don't mind my asking, why did you fall in love with Kitty?"

"Maybe because she was so different from everyone else? Like her mama said, Kitty shimmered in the sun. Not just her hair, but all of her. She was like a dream, I guess. A dream that disappears when you wake up. Maybe I just saw my dreams in her, and it wasn't really Kitty at all. I don't know."

They drove on in silence through the green fields and small towns, until Joe had another question.

"You said she was getting married. Did you say that just to make her family feel better?"

"No, she really was getting married."

"Was it one of her customers?"

"No. They met swimming in Hunting Creek, south of Alexandria. He was drowning and she pulled him out. Saved his life."

Joe whistled low. "I can believe that. She was a hell of a swimmer. I remember when she was a lifeguard, back when the town pool was still open. She was a sight in a red bathing suit." He paused. "Is he a nice guy?"

"She said he was. I haven't met him. He's a flier, a pilot, as far as I know. He's supposed to be back home in Alexandria this week. Oh God." Mimi leaned her head back against the window. "I need to find him and return his ring."

"That's tough. Do you know what you'll say?" He glanced over at her.

"Not at all. I'll play it by ear, I guess."

Mimi considered Kitty and Nathan Albemarle, the flier who was somewhere in the clouds of war. The boy who didn't know Kitty was dead. Why should Mimi have to be the one to tell him too?

Because I promised.

"How about you?" Joe broke in on her thoughts. "Do you have a beau, Mary Margaret Smith? Some soldier boy who's in love with those freckles of yours?"

"No. And leave my freckles out of this." Mimi closed her eyes to shut out memories of Eddie Falcone. The hot wind hit her face and she could taste the dust it left behind on her face and lips. The sunlight hit the trees, splashing stripes of light and shadow across the rough road. "I was sort of engaged for a while. I told you about him, remember?"

"What happened to him?"

"His parachute didn't open."

"Right. That's a bad break. Seems like neither one of us have been too lucky in love."

She smiled sadly. "Not so far. Anyway, that's why I'm staying away from love until the war is over."

"You willing to wait that long?"

"I'm willing to try."

"Doesn't seem right."

"Lots of things don't seem right. In the meantime, I do like to dance."

"That's all right then. Me too. Maybe we can take a turn on a dance floor before I commit my future to Uncle Sam."

"That sounds swell, Joe. I'd like to dance with you. It's good for forgetting."

"It's a date then."

There was a lull in the conversation as they slowed down through another small town. This Main Street had a movie theatre and a diner that looked popular. Mimi cleared her throat.

"Joe, do you think we could stop and get a Coke?"

"Throat dusty?"

"It's the Sahara."

"Mine too." He pulled over and parked the truck. Mimi wondered if shock absorbers were hard to get ahold of these days. Her spine was rattled from her head to her bottom. She took a deep breath and checked her hands for shaking.

Joe ushered her into the diner, and they ordered Coca-Colas.

"Joe," she began. "Did you ever think about Kitty?"

He sipped his soda before answering. "Every now and then. She never belonged in that family. It was like the stork dropped the wrong baby in the midst of all those Hawkinses. Oh, they're salt of the earth and all that, but you can see, a tad hard-bitten. Kitty wasn't like that. Least when I knew her."

"Funny how that happens," Mimi said. "Some of us have to leave home and make our own families."

"She asked you to tell them, if anything happened to her, didn't she?"

"She made me promise. I also insisted nothing was going to happen."

"And you kept that promise." He paused. "Not many people kept their promises to Kitty. Not even me. She wanted the easy life, I reckon."

"There was nothing easy about the life Kitty chose, especially the way she left it. She said she had no skills for office work, and she thought she wasn't strong enough for the factory," Mimi said.

"I guess she did what she thought she had to. But I'll never think it was right."

"Kitty knew where she wanted to go, someplace glamorous," Mimi said. "She didn't know how to get there. I guess Nathan was her shot."

They finished their Cokes. Joe tossed some money on the counter, and after a short trip to the restroom, where Mimi happily refreshed her acquaintance with indoor plumbing, he opened her door to the pickup, and they rumbled and jolted their way back onto the road that would take them to Washington.

"She knew someone was after her? Someone was going to kill her?" The truck swerved around a pothole. Joe's face was fierce as he wrestled the vehicle back on the road. "I mean, why else would she ask for a promise like that, the way she asked you?"

"She didn't tell me." Mimi would not want to be responsible for unleashing Josiah Jordan on Alexandria in a fit of vengeance. "But with the war going on, everybody seems to think about how quickly a life can end. And how nobody knows when it will. Quivers."

"Quivers." He sighed. "Well, all in all, you been real decent. More than decent. Her mama can use that money you gave her. I know it was hard for her to accept. Kitty couldn't have had much money, 'cept from selling herself like she did. You can make excuses, Mimi, and call it pretty names, but it's a dirty business."

"Some women fall into that life. They run around with the wrong man. They're in a strange city, no friends, no family, then the man up and disappears, or ships out and gets killed. The women fall victim to the wolves, and the wolves aren't always just men." She thought of Madam Cherry, the proprietress of the Chicken Shack and the riverboat. "Sometimes they're women too."

"Where are they going to bury her?" Joe asked.

"I thought they'd want to bury her in Forgotten Creek. Her mother was so harsh—"

"The Hawkinses couldn't afford a pine box. Or a box of matches. But they got land for her. A pauper's grave in the city ain't right."

"Once you're dead and buried, what does it matter?" Mimi felt the sadness descend and weigh her down. "Kitty left money for a funeral. She knew they didn't want her. I didn't believe it, but she was right. I'll talk to Father Forsythe at St. Mary's. Kitty was Catholic, and besides, I imagine they buried Mary Magdalene somewhere."

Joe stopped talking, keeping his attention on the road. Despite bouncing on the worn-out shocks, Mimi closed her eyes and slept.

She woke up when they hit Arlington. Joe took the Washington Memorial Parkway that stretched all the way from there to Mount Vernon. He was rubbernecking to see the monuments, but he missed hitting anything, much to Mimi's relief.

As they cruised into Alexandria and the Parkway turned into Washington Street, Joe said, "I hear Addie Richardson lives in a big old house. Are we close?"

"Not far. It's a lovely house, on a beautiful street. I was lucky to find lodgings there. Addie's been sweet to me."

"Folks in Forgotten Creek still talk about how she left town and married up. To a fancy lawyer."

"They need more to talk about in that town, I'd say. Isn't there a library?"

"Small one." He looked at her and snorted. "You're right. We're a bunch of squawking gossips, just like a flock of crows."

"Do you know Addie?"

"A bit. When I was a kid, she'd come back from time to time. Her folks were still alive. I was probably a teenager when I last saw her."

"Joe, do you mind if we take a detour?" All of a sudden Mimi felt she had to do something. She knew she wouldn't have any energy left over once she reached the Richardsons'.

He lifted an eyebrow. "What did you have in mind?"

"Kitty lived in a rooming house on Henry Street, just a couple blocks over. I might be able to catch one of the women she worked with. See what's happened in the last couple of days."

"As long as I can come with you. You don't mind my company?"

She smiled at him and brushed her hands through her hair. "I'd appreciate it."

Joe maneuvered the big pickup into a parking space in front of the dilapidated house that Mimi pointed out. He made sure his extra gas cans, which were full, were secure before they ambled up the walk.

"She wasn't exactly living the high life, was she?" Joe said.

"Not a bit. It makes me sad to think about it, but there are people crammed in like sardines in all these houses. They aren't all in Kitty's line of work."

Mimi knocked. To her surprise Gretel opened the door.

THIRTY

"MIMI! WHAT ARE you doing here?" Gretel's hair was pulled back into a ponytail, her face was clean of makeup, and her freckles made her seem younger and more innocent than she was. She wore a printed shirtwaist dress, brown with blue carnations. She threw an inquiring gaze toward Mimi's companion.

"Gretel, this is Joe. He was a friend of Kitty's. From her hometown," Mimi hastened to say. She didn't want Gretel to get the wrong idea about him. "You're not working today?"

"The Shack's been closed since they found Kitty." Gretel scanned the nearby street. "You want to talk, come inside." She opened the door wider and locked it behind them.

Mimi and Joe stepped into the sad little parlor. Joe had a calmness that seemed to have a similar effect on Gretel. He was going to be very impressive in a Navy uniform, Mimi decided.

"Hope you don't mind my being here, miss," he said.

"I don't mind." Gretel perched on the edge of the sofa, kicking one leg back and forth.

"Will you go back to work at the Chicken Shack?" Mimi settled on the chair across from her.

"I got no place else to go."

"Do you mind if we ask some questions?"

"Asking is free."

"Does anyone have any idea who hurt Kitty?"

"Could be the man in the moon, for all I know."

"I'm sorry, Gretel," Mimi said, "but three women are dead."

"You're counting Polly?" She stared at Mimi. "They said it was suicide."

"Did you think she was going to kill herself?"

"She didn't announce it."

"Was Polly a friend of yours?" Joe asked.

Gretel considered him. "Everyone's a friend. And no one's a friend."

"Was Polly selling things, like Hattie did?" Mimi asked.

"I don't know what you're talking about." She stopped swinging her leg.

"I think you do. Hattie sold information about things like tires, sugar, alcohol, maybe other things. She used what she overheard at work."

"Polly and Hattie were thick as thieves. Maybe they were thieves. It's possible, but I don't know. I keep to myself." She took a deep breath. "You think someone pushed Polly onto those tracks?"

"It's a possibility," Mimi said.

"That's horrible." Gretel jumped up and paced the room. "We're all jumpy as June bugs, what do you think? I'd leave if I could. But I got nothing. Nowhere to go. No way out."

Gretel hadn't been saving her money like Kitty had, Mimi thought. But that didn't save Kitty either.

"Don't you have family you can go to?" Joe asked.

"None who'd take me in. They kicked me out when I was sixteen. What was I supposed to do? Everyone knows me here. I couldn't even get a factory job."

"There are other jobs and other towns," Mimi suggested.

"If I could scratch up enough for a train ticket. Maybe I'd go to Baltimore." A slight impression of hope lit her face. But just as quickly it left. "But with the Shack closed—"

"Miss Gretel, I don't know you," Joe cut in. "But you gotta look up and around and not down. And be careful, because someone is killing whores. Mimi here likes to call you all magdalens, but this guy don't care what you're called, and I don't think he's going to stop."

"You a cop?" Gretel asked.

"No, ma'am."

"Not even the cops were talking like that. They haven't been back after collecting Kitty's body."

Gretel started to cry. Mimi reached for her.

"Do you know who killed her, Gretel?"

"I don't. I swear I don't."

"You might know something without realizing it, like who she was with last."

"I only know I left early that night. Before midnight. It was Sunday, not that much action. The last thing I saw was just a shadow with Kitty. Couldn't see his face. His shadow was big, but that time of night, everyone's shadow is big."

"What time was it?" Joe asked.

"Pitch dark. Maybe eleven o'clock. I opened my door for my—friend. Kitty opened her door. Shadows come from the streetlight on the alley side, where the men walk around. But what can you do?"

"Gretel," Mimi asked, "did you hear screams that night?"

"We hear screams every night," Gretel replied. "Some screams are like don't stop, I love it, and some screams are like stop, it hurts. Some guys, they want the sound effects."

"And that night? Kitty's last night?"

Gretel put her hands over her ears. "I don't know! What are you going to do if you find out anything?" Joe looked at Mimi.

"We don't know yet," Mimi said. "What about Kitty's room at the Shack?"

"What about it? She wasn't the only one who used it," Gretel pointed out. "Gal named Carmen was there earlier. But she told Madam Cherry, she's done there. She's not going back to that room."

"We'd like to see Kitty's room at the Chicken Shack," Mimi said. "Inside."

"Where she was killed?" Gretel looked shocked. "Cops put that room off limits."

"But the cops haven't been back, have they? Even though she shared that room with other women, no one's been there since the day Kitty was carried out. Right?"

Joe slightly increased the pressure on Mimi's arm. "Are you sure about this?" They shared a look. He turned to Gretel.

"Listen, Gretel, the cops are too busy to pay any attention to these killings."

"And you really think you can do something?" Tears leaked out of Gretel's eyes.

"If we figure out who did it, then you could steer clear of this guy, at the very least," Mimi said. "Kitty, Hattie, Polly. Who's next?"

Gretel wiped her tears away with the back of her hand. "I'll get my key. It fits all the doors. But you got five minutes. That's all. I'm not getting in trouble with Madam Cherry over this."

ɔ

The trio slipped through the alley-side gate, then around to the four doors of the pink concrete Chicken Shack. There were no sailors or soldiers about. Everything seemed quiet. Gretel unlocked the door.

The tiny room was stifling in the summer heat, and the concrete walls seemed to make it worse, even though they left the door open a crack for air. Gretel switched on a dim lamp by the bed. A small electric fan turned on with the light, both plugged into a cord that snaked out the window.

"Is anyone in the bungalow?" Mimi asked, peering out the window of Kitty's room at the little house that faced the street.

"Don't think so. Madam Cherry usually has someone watching over us, taking care of the rowdies and collecting money. Usually that mean old Ethel Jackson. But with the Shack closed, it's a holiday for everyone."

The small room was more depressing than Mimi thought possible. Not because it was squalid, but because it was so anonymous. There was nothing of Kitty left, except the dried brown bloodstains on the mattress. She blanched at the stains and Gretel turned her head away.

"We'll be out of here soon." Joe steadied Mimi. "You all right, Miss Gretel?"

"Sure. Just hurry."

The linens had been removed, though a thin pink chenille bedspread was carelessly tossed over the bottom of the bed. There was a chair, a small washbasin, and hooks on the wall for clothes. A tiny nightstand had a tiny drawer to collect money. It held no money now, just a few unopened condoms. Apparently, all the police left was the dust on the floor.

"They all look like this. Kind of depressing," Gretel said from the doorway. "We done here yet?"

Mimi got down on her hands and knees to look under the bed. Something caught her eye, smaller than a dime. She reached out for a white button with a hanging thread and a bit of torn blue material still attached. She stuck it in her skirt pocket and stood up. Sweat trickled down her back.

"We gotta go!" Gretel was rocking back and forth on her heels. "Please. Time's up. There's nothing here. Nothing of Kitty's, anyway."

They took one last look and left. To Mimi it felt like a mausoleum, a house of the dead. Joe opened the alley gate, while Gretel locked up and looked around nervously.

"Which room was Hattie's?" Mimi asked.

"She was on the end. Kitty and I were in the middle."

"And where did Polly work?"

"All the rooms, I guess, when they were vacant. Mostly she worked out of the same room as Hattie."

Polly seemed destined to remain a mystery. The trio scurried down the alley and back to Joe's pickup. Mimi and Joe dropped Gretel at the rooming house. Gretel seemed to have nothing left to say but goodbye. Then they turned toward downtown Alexandria.

"What'd you stick in your pocket back there?" Joe asked.

"Just a button. A shirt button, I'd guess." He stopped at a light and she pulled it out to show him.

"You think that's some kind of evidence?"

"Who knows?" Mimi said, turning it over in her hands. "It's not like it just came loose, it looks like it was torn off. There are still threads attached and a bit of material."

"You going to give that to the police?"

"Haven't decided yet. They won't care, will they? Besides, they already examined the crime scene."

"What are you thinking?

"It could be useful, even if it's not exactly evidence."

"Explain, please. I'm not good at women's thought processes, even if I do have sisters."

"If Kitty tore this button off the killer's shirt while she was fighting with the guy, he wouldn't realize it until later. His mind was on other things. He might throw the shirt away. Turn it into rags. Mention a torn button and most men wouldn't bat an eye. But if we find the murderer and let him know we've got the missing button she tore off, what's he going to do? He's going to look down at his shirt."

"That's quite a leap, Mimi."

"It's all I got right now."

"And this part about us finding the killer? You and me?" He cocked an eyebrow at her. "The two of us?"

"I'm not saying we will. But I'm hanging on to this button just in case."

"That's real advanced thinking for a mere stenographer." Joe flashed her a charming grin. "But I got to tell you, right now you look about twelve years old, with that dirt on your face, and those adorable freckles."

"That's good to know, Joe, because I feel about a hundred. And what did I tell you about my freckles?"

THIRTY-ONE

"WHY MIMI, YOU look all in." Addie greeted her at the door. "How did you get back here so fast?"

"I got a ride." Mimi felt like the truck she'd been riding in had run over her instead, her spine completely jostled out of place. It was a miracle that her jug of moonshine had made it through the trip. It was now hidden in her canvas bag.

"In what? A cattle car?"

Mimi gestured to the large man behind her on the front steps. "Joe Jordan was kind enough to bring me back. I promised him something to eat. I hope you don't mind."

Richie looked past his mother. "Who does that truck belong to?"

"That baby blue pickup belongs to me," Joe announced.

Addie was surprised, then recognition lit her eyes. "Why Josiah Jordan, come you on in. Thank you for bringing our Mimi back home." To her son she said, "Richie, this is Josiah. He's an old friend. From Forgotten Creek."

"I generally go by Joe." He held out his hand for Richie to shake.

"I'm Richie Richardson. Mimi is my friend."

"She's my friend too." Joe winked at Mimi.

Richie hugged Mimi. "I missed you!"

"How can you miss me," she teased him. "I was only gone one night."

"I missed you anyway."

"Thank you, Richie." Her eyes went to the mannequin in the dining room, wearing the lovely nearly finished violet dress. "I'm sorry, Addie. I meant to put that away before I left."

"Nonsense. We'll all miss her when you finish."

"I just have to finish some handwork on the trim and the hem."

"Didn't you get any rest?" Addie started bustling around, pulling plates for the table.

"I didn't get much sleep." Mimi laughed briefly. "I am a rumpled mess. Is my face still dirty?"

"It sure is." Richie lacked the ability to lie. "You got brown streaks all over it."

"Did you stay at the rooming house?" Addie again.

"No, Netty Hawkins insisted I stay with them. I slept on the sofa." Mimi rubbed her hip where a spring had poked her all night. "I was grateful for her, um, hospitality."

Addie lifted her eyebrows. "I figured you'd be hungry when you got back. We got us a treat. There's cold Virginia ham in the refrigerator. Got a farmer friend's been holding on to that ham for me. Smoked it good."

"Ham! I haven't had that in a long time. Sounds delicious," Mimi said. "Did you swap it for honey?"

"Honey and candles and some fine face cream. But that whole ham will last us a nice long time. Now, what else? We have some fresh bread and tomatoes. And a salad. Does that suit you, Joe?"

"I expect you know it does, Miss Addie," he said.

Derry came in from work, shed his pinstripe jacket, and loosened his tie. Because it was such a hot day, he had taken the liberty of rolling up his sleeves. He greeted Joe like an old friend.

Addie poured Joe some sweet tea and sliced a generous portion of pecan nut bread for him.

Mimi was amused that when you walked through the door, the first thing people in the South did was offer you food, even when they had little to offer, like the Hawkinses. She was hungry as well as grateful, but it wasn't that way in her family. Her family ate at seven in the morning, at noon, and six in the evening. If you dropped by in between times, you might get a cup of coffee, then you went away hungry. Snacking between meals was frowned upon, though they had been copious coffee drinkers before rationing.

Mimi excused herself to freshen up. She trudged up the steps to her room with her canvas bag, which held the empty sugar bag that Joe had gifted her and her jug of illegal moonshine. After her brief foray into West Virginia and the "comforts" of Forgotten Creek, Mimi could have kissed every familiar item in the room. Her trunk welcomed her, but Kitty Hawkins's suitcase reminded her she still had things to take care of. She retrieved the mystery button from her pocket and slipped it into an envelope in her top drawer.

Her bed called to her, but she washed the grime off and dropped her clothes in her laundry basket. She freshened her makeup, covering up those freckles Joe Jordan seemed to be so fond of, adding some Maybelline cake mascara and Victory Red lipstick. Her personal rebuke to Netty Hawkins. She brushed out her wind-tangled hair and changed into a fresh red gingham sundress.

"You look better," Richie announced when he saw her.

"Richie!" Addie said.

"It's fine, Addie," Mimi said. "Richie's right, I looked like something the cat dragged in."

Joe smiled at her. "You'd cause even more talk in Forgotten Creek looking like that."

Over a sumptuous meal of cold ham and bread and Addie's garden salad, accompanied by Richie's music, Joe explained he was going into Naval officers' training soon. He had a little time before they'd take him, and he wanted to see some sights in Washington.

Inevitably, the conversation soon turned to Kitty.

"How did your mission to West Virginia go?" Derry asked Mimi.

"I'm glad the Hawkinses know Kitty is gone," Mimi said. "They won't have to find out through gossip."

"True," Addie agreed. "They'll be collecting her to bury in the family plot?"

"No. They're against soiling their graveyard dirt with her," Mimi said bitterly.

Joe lifted his head toward Addie. "You know their ways."

"The Hawkinses are as hard as their lives," Addie said.

"Netty Hawkins told me there was no money for a funeral or for bringing Kitty back home," Mimi said. "She said to let the state take care of her."

"Not burying your own kin. That's beyond my comprehension." Addie gathered up the dinner plates.

"Kitty left money for a funeral, anyway," Mimi said. "She never thought she'd be going back to Forgotten Creek."

While Richie was in the kitchen helping Addie clean up, Derry reported what he knew. The police, along with the medical examiner, determined Kitty Hawkins's death was caused by a broken neck and fractured spine. It was ruled a homicide, perpetrated by persons unknown. If her coworkers at the Chicken Shack knew anything about the man who killed her, they weren't telling the police, he said.

Polly Brown and Hattie Carnegie Jones, two prostitutes who had hidden their real names and were far from home where their professions would not shame their families, were to be buried in nameless graves, he said. Mimi assumed the other magdalens would know and mark their graves with the odd bunch of flowers. Until even they forgot these women ever existed.

Kitty Hawkins would not suffer the indignity of an unknown pauper's grave, Mimi swore silently. Still, Kitty wasn't going anywhere just yet. The police had not released the body for burial, ostensibly because her murder was still unsolved. But it wouldn't be long, Derry said, even if the killer wasn't found.

For the time being, Kitty's body was at the Demaine Funeral Home on King Street. As a highly regarded local lawyer, Derry Richardson had friends and influence. Mimi guessed that some money had already changed hands to ensure that this fallen woman could remain undisturbed—in the short term.

"Our Kitty will not be shoved in a hole," Derry declared. "What do you think, Mimi? Where should we bring her?"

"I'll talk to Father Forsythe."

"Is he the one who said I could play my violin at church?" Richie poked his head through the kitchen door. His enthusiasm lit up like a firecracker. Mimi wondered if he had been eager all this time to be a part of a community.

"Yes, he is."

Addie rolled her eyes at the idea of Richie playing music at the Catholic Church. "I thought you'd forgotten about that, Richie."

"How could I forget?" He seemed stunned.

"Kitty was partial to St. Mary's." Mimi didn't really want to talk with the priest, but certain things had to be done. "And the cemetery is lovely and peaceful, with a view of the river." The fireflies danced there in the twilight.

"I'll pay for a headstone," Joe said suddenly, to everyone's surprise. "She won't be forgotten. And it'll read Katharine Lily Hawkins. Not Kitty."

"By the way, we found out what happened to your sugar, Addie." Mimi ran upstairs for the sugar bag. She placed it in her landlady's hands. For a moment, Addie was without words.

"It wound up in Forgotten Creek," Joe said.

Addie blinked. For a moment, Mimi was afraid she was having a heart attack. Derry poured his wife a drop of brandy.

"Where did you get that? How on earth did it—" Addie reached for the bag but didn't touch it.

"Mimi spotted it in Fat Frenchie's van," Joe said. "Handy you marked it with your initials."

"In Frenchie's van? And he just gave it to you?"

"I had a chat with Clem and Frenchie. I convinced them to hand it over. This is just one bag, they had more of them."

"A conversation?" Derry inquired.

Joe rubbed his bruised and scratched fist. "I was persuasive. Unfortunately, they didn't give me anything to go on regarding Kitty."

"You need some iodine on that hand," Addie said. Richie ran to the kitchen and returned with the small brown bottle. Joe flinched as Addie applied it. "You can't think this bag has something to do with Kitty. It's just not possible."

"We didn't get many answers back home," Joe said. "I think Clem would've told me, if he had anything other than a sugar bag. I certainly motivated him to talk. Now we have to think about the situation on this side of the mountains."

"The way we see it, there's a man no one knows." Mimi picked up the narrative. "A middleman who pops up with various commodities, most likely stolen. My guess is he leans on the magdalens who overhear loose talk and don't know it's valuable, until he pressures them into getting more and more involved."

"Is there a description of this man no one knows?" Derry asked.

"He's a big man. 'Bout the size of Frenchie, I gather," Joe said.

"Other than his size, there's nothing else we know about him." Mimi pondered how difficult it would be to defend yourself against a man that size. "I'm going to bring this bag to my boss tomorrow."

"I don't think it's wise to be involved in this," Derry said to Mimi.

"Wisdom is not my forte, Derry. Besides, if my boss thought I was holding back anything important, I could lose my job."

George Prescott would be annoyed either way, Mimi thought to herself.

⁂

Mimi carefully threaded her needle. She applied herself to stitching the beaded pieces to the wide cummerbund and cuffs of the glorious violet dress. After Joe had hit the road to his sister's house, she caught a second wind and brought her sewing supplies to the dining room and the dress form. She wanted to exhaust herself, so her thoughts wouldn't keep her awake. Richie played his violin softly. He liked to be around the action. Addie kept her company and brought her ice water.

"Surely there is no hurry with that gown. You don't have a big event for it."

"There might be a bit of a hurry," Mimi said. "I don't know when we're going to bury Katharine Hawkins, but she is going to wear this gown."

"Oh my. Are you sure, Mimi? To bury it and never see it again? It's so unique and beautiful."

"And so was she. You should have seen the way she looked at it, Addie. She was captivated. And there was always something about this dress, as gorgeous as it is. I suppose I knew it wasn't really a dress for me, but I had to make it anyway. I'm sorry I couldn't give it to her when she was alive." She wiped a tear away, which told her she must be very tired. "We'll take a picture of it."

"Kitty loves the princess dress," Richie broke off playing to say. "She wants to wear it. She says thank you."

Mimi and Addie fell silent.

It was unnerving to hear Richie's pronouncements, as if Kitty were whispering in his ear. Mimi was trying to get used to it. If it kept Richie cheerful and upbeat about Kitty's death, that was good enough for her.

"But what about the blue gown?" Addie asked. "It's lovely, and you thought it would suit her so well."

"It would, and we shopped for it together. But Kitty's sister Lucy is getting married in September. The Hawkins family make church mice look like Rockefellers. Netty seems downright proud of their poverty."

"Sounds like she hasn't changed."

"She was grateful for Kitty's money, but I saw her hide most of it so her husband wouldn't see it."

"Makes good sense to me. Holden Hawkins never was a financial genius. Money just falls through his fingers. It's common knowledge. Netty'll use it on necessities. Maybe some of it will go for the wedding."

"The blue gown will be very pretty on Lucy, and I don't think Kitty would mind."

Richie paused his playing. "She agrees. Lucy will be beautiful for her wedding. And don't forget the hat."

Mimi wondered if Richie really understood that Kitty was dead. And how did he know about the hat?

"Lucy was just a little girl when I saw her last," Addie said. "All skin and bones and big blue eyes."

"The dress matches her eyes," Mimi said. "I didn't tell her Kitty had bought her wedding trousseau. You should have seen how excited she was when I told her there might be a new pair of shoes. And, well, she can't get married in a flour sack, can she? I guarantee Lucy's pale blue wedding gown will be the talk of the town. The beaded embroidery is so unusual and that peplum is dramatic. Fit for a movie star."

Addie's eyebrows pressed together. "What about Netty?"

"I told her I was sending some things. She promised not to interfere. I don't want any talk about that dress being the wages of sin."

Addie couldn't suppress a chuckle. "I reckon she's feeling pretty darn conflicted right now. It'll do her a world of good."

Mimi finished the trim. She knotted the thread and neatly cut off the tail end, then stepped back to admire her work. The violet princess dress was as elegant as anything on a Hollywood screen. It was her finest work. She would finish the hem tomorrow.

"Addie, Joe will be coming by in the next few days, and we'll be stepping out. You don't mind, do you?"

Her landlady had a secret sort of smile on her face. "Not at all, dear. The Jordans are a fine family."

ত

She couldn't sleep. Mimi hadn't had time to explore the rest of Kitty's suitcase. Now at the midnight hour, and a little beyond, she opened it to see if it held more of Kitty's secrets.

Inside were Kitty's clothes, carefully packed within the cream lining. The new royal blue suit dress, the wedding gown, the pretty negligee. Almost more valuable, there were several pairs of nylon stockings, folded with precision, along with a lacey garter belt that would probably horrify Netty Hawkins.

The Samsonite suitcase was brand-new and had a green marbled finish. The matching carrying case would hold makeup and other vanity items, including an elegant comb, brush, and hand mirror. Together they presented the very picture of stylish honeymoon preparations.

In one of the suitcase's side pockets she found Nathan's letters, tied up with a blue satin bow. Mimi stared at them for a moment. "I don't mean to intrude on your privacy, Kitty, but I need to read these. I need to know if there's anything here that will give me some answers," she said to the empty room.

She untied the ribbon and opened the top letter. It was short, but heartfelt.

My Dearest Katharine.

You are with me always, but most of all when I am flying in the clouds. You are not merely my silver mermaid, you are my silver angel of the Heavens. Your wings are the color of your hair, as shiny and silver as the wings on my plane. You worry about my family. Never fear, if they disavow my love for you, I shall disavow them. As always, beware the Jubalation.

All my heart,
Nathan

What in the world is "the Jubalation," Mimi wondered, and why should she beware of it? And why did he spell it in that odd way? That word can't be spelled right, she thought. She opened the next letter.

Dearest Katharine.

I'm glad you can't see my plane today. It is shot full of enemy holes, but it still commands the air, so I can see you in the clouds.

We all have moments of fear. But I remember the day we met and how I thought I would drown, but there you were, saving me. You little bit of a thing. Smiling at me and chasing away those cowards who would love to see me swallowed by Hunting Creek. Your love saves me every day, Katharine. I want you to leave your working life, but do not go to my family. Stay away from false promises, and from the Jubalation.

   Yours forever,
   Nathan

Dearest Katharine,

   When I am most scared, and yes, dearest, we all get scared, no matter how big and strong we are, I think of you. Lately I've been imagining you with me, in the cockpit beside me, your small warm hand on my shoulder. I see you and your smile.

   It won't be long, my love, and I am so excited about our baby. So excited to be married to my silver angel.

   Your Nathan

All lovers had their own language, Mimi realized. The rest of us are outsiders. However, it was clear that Nathan was as crazy about Kitty as she was about him. Beyond that, these letters didn't reveal much, except that Nathan was fearful when he flew. It was disturbing that his plane was one of those Liberators, shot full of holes like the photos she'd seen in *Esquire* magazine. She didn't want to be the one to tell him about Kitty, his silver angel Katharine. Mimi didn't want to shoot holes through Nathan Albemarle's heart, or his future.

   She tucked the letters back in Kitty's suitcase. She couldn't bear to read the rest of them that night.

THIRTY-TWO

*A*DDIE RICHARDSON'S EMPTY sugar bag landed on George Prescott's desk with a soft thud. Mimi had hoped for a bigger thud, a little more drama, but this would have to do.

George had been happily preoccupied with his pipe and a pipe cleaner. Disturbed, he peered up at Mimi, and at the bag, and glowered.

"And what may I ask is this doing on my desk first thing Friday morning?"

"I'm back from Forgotten Creek, West Virginia."

"I can see that."

"Remember the sugar theft I mentioned? A thousand pounds of sugar? This was one of the fifty-pound bags that were stolen. It's empty now."

"I'm confused. I thought you went to West Virginia for a funeral. For that woman—"

"Kitty Hawkins. To inform Kitty's family of her death. I did that. The funeral hasn't happened yet."

"And you found the sugar? From the robbery of your landlady?" He looked confused.

"Found the bag. Has her initials on it. That sugar is most likely now distilled into a vat of moonshine, hootch, booze, illegal alcohol. John Barleycorn."

"John Barleycorn would be beer," George interrupted. "Are we talking about beer?"

Mimi snorted. "Bigger than beer. We are talking moonshine. This bag was last seen in the possession of a known moonshiner in Forgotten Creek, a character known as Fat Frenchie. I bought a bottle of his spirits. I'm told it's among the best clear shine available. I passed up his homemade bourbon, because it was two dollars more for the fancy bottle and the fake label. And I didn't buy it myself, I asked a local man to purchase it for me. In case it's evidence."

"Did you bring the moonshine here too?" George glanced around in alarm.

"Not to work. It's in a safe place. It seemed like the right thing to do. There are all kinds of OPA violations going on here, George."

George puffed furiously for a few moments. "Mary Margaret Smith, you seem to have gotten around. You were only gone two days. You didn't do anything harebrained, did you? Other than following a moonshiner around and buying illegal alcohol? And stealing an empty sack? Because those sound like pretty harebrained things to me."

"No. Other than buying outlaw hootch. And I kept my eyes and ears open." She didn't expect Prescott to jump up and down and congratulate her. Still, a little praise for her enterprise might be nice. Even if she wasn't officially involved on behalf of OPA.

"Alexandria cops are handling the sugar theft," George said.

"Almost as well as they're handling Kitty's murder."

"You're not saying this is all connected." He massaged his temples, where his headache was starting. "Tell me it's not connected."

"I can't. I'm not saying it's not. I think it is. But I can't say it is. Not yet."

"Let the cops do their job, Mary Margaret."

She allowed herself an elaborate eye roll while he puffed away.

"George. Do you want me to draft a letter for you to the Charleston, West Virginia, District Office?"

His glower grew darker. "A letter?"

"It's Region Three."

"I'm aware of that."

"People in the district might consider it a timely heads-up into local black-market activity."

He lit a match for his pipe again. "And it'll wind up nowhere." George Prescott was as sunny and optimistic as usual.

"But at least you couldn't be blamed for not informing them. In addition to moonshine, this Fat Frenchie character sells rationed commodities like tires out of his hardware truck. Who knows where he gets them?"

"You seem to have learned a lot, Mimi."

"Small town. Everybody knows everyone else's business."

"Okay. Say there's a scoundrel operating in Forgotten Creek and environs. Probably more than one. If he's that active, the district office probably already knows and has already handed the information off to the local authorities." It was clear George Prescott wanted to avoid the subject.

"You can't get justice in a small town where everybody knows everybody else, George. Where the local authorities, the deputies, and the cops are all someone's relatives."

"It's a sticky situation, I grant you, but they have authority over their own thieves and still jockeys." He set his pipe down in his oversized glass ashtray.

Still jockeys? That's what Kitty called them. "Unless OPA requests special jurisdiction over the case," Mimi pointed out. "In a tiny village people don't investigate their friends and family."

"I see you've been reading the OPA handbook."

"George, you told me anything we investigate could be dangerous. It could even be murder."

"Murder?" He set the pipe down. "Shut the door." Mimi shut the office door carefully and peeked out to see if anyone was paying attention. A closed door was the surest way to raise everyone's curiosity. "Are you telling me that this woman's death, this hooker's murder, is linked to black market thefts?"

"I didn't say that, exactly. I don't have that kind of information. Yet. If there is a connection, I haven't found it."

"And you're not going to find it. You're not an investigator, and if what you say is true, it could be dangerous."

"But wouldn't it be nice for OPA to take credit for something that serious?"

"Not at the risk of my people."

"Then I guess I should take back this piece of evidence." She reached for Addie's empty sugar bag.

George glared at her under furrowed brows. "You might as well leave it."

Mimi was fuming beneath her icy demeanor. "Do you want me to draft that letter or not?"

"What letter?"

"To the OPA district office to inform them of what may be going on in their own backyard."

"Go ahead. Draft a letter. I'll look over it carefully." He relit the pipe. "You're enterprising, Mimi, and that's good—to a point. But not to the point of murder."

"If someone is killing these women, he's getting away with it. I think he enjoys it, and he needs to be stopped. His black-market activities may hold a key." Mimi stopped at his office door. "Let me just say one thing."

"Just one? That will be the day."

"People out there don't think OPA applies to them. Even though they say they support our mission. Even though we got all those great articles in *Vogue* this month. The newspapers and magazines, they're still working with us, still trying to tell our story."

"Articles?"

"I gave them to you. They're on your desk, somewhere in this mess. But everyday folks think OPA is just the bully on the block, keeping them from buying steak. They don't see any harm in hoarding goods. They have no problem with buying from their local shady entrepreneur who magically comes up with goods they haven't been able to find in months. They pay a bit more than the price limits, but who cares."

"We're not popular. I get it." George was grumpy. And unpopular.

"But if they knew, if they realized that these criminals, who buy and sell illicit goods, might also be killing people? Murdering defenseless women over sugar and tires and meat and canned goods? Maybe they'll stop and consider. Maybe then they might realize the black market and the hoarding and the excessive pricing aren't something trivial. It might be sabotaging our troops. It might be killing them by diverting all but substandard materials." Mimi pictured Eddie Falcone and his failing parachute. "You were the one who said it, George. Anything can lead to murder."

She stomped away and left George Prescott sucking his pipe.

THIRTY-THREE

*T*HE PRIEST APPEARED in the dusk among the tombstones of St. Mary's cemetery. His black cassock flapped against his legs. Mimi could see the distinctive lurch of his artificial leg.

It wasn't quite dark, but fireflies began flickering and rising up from the wet grass around the graves. They weren't afraid of the dead.

Mimi was determined not to let him intimidate her, even if he had the authority of God behind him. The woman who answered the phone at the rectory said he wasn't in. Mimi had heard he liked to come here in the evenings, and she thought she might catch him. She approached, not knowing what to say. Father Forsythe spoke first.

"Storm's coming in. I can feel it in the limb I no longer have." She detected the vaguest hint of a smile. "Did you know, Miss Smith, that my missing leg is in fact buried right here in St. Mary's cemetery? I come here every night to mourn it. Or so they say. Our students have vivid imaginations."

"You've heard the rumors then," she said.

"Mary Margaret, some of us are smarter than we look."

"I didn't come to ask about your leg, Father."

"How refreshing." He leaned against the large standing angel near the front gate.

"I need to bury someone," she said. "I mean, someone needs to be buried. There is space available, isn't there?"

"Always room for one more sinner. Who needs to be buried?"

"Kitty Hawkins. Katharine."

He nodded. Mimi didn't need to explain. He knew. There had been a brief article in *The Alexandria Gazette.*

"The prostitute who was killed. The same as the woman you prayed for that day?"

"She has no family who will claim her."

"I recognized her picture in the paper. I sometimes saw her in church on Sundays. Usually the late Mass. Up late on Saturday nights, I suppose."

Mimi couldn't read his face in the dark. "Um, yes. I have money. It was hers. Kitty asked me to keep it for her funeral."

"You were friends with this woman?"

"I wasn't like her, if that's what you're asking. We were friends, and I felt sorry for her."

"A practicing member of the world's oldest profession?"

"In the footsteps of Mary Magdalene, you could say." He grunted. "Kitty was different. She wasn't hardened, she could be sweet, and funny, and she was so pretty. Kitty was luminous. She had a light inside of her."

"So did Lucifer."

"You can't refuse to bury her, Father." Mimi was surprised at her own boldness.

"Oh, I can't, can I?" He folded his arms.

"She was a Catholic. Maybe not a great one." Mimi didn't consider herself a terribly good Catholic either. She was on the verge of offering to do more penance, but she thought the last few days should count for something. "Kitty Hawkins attended Mass at St. Mary's and she deserves to be buried here at the church's cemetery."

"I've seen hundreds of men buried in mud in unsanctified ground. I suspect they found their way to Heaven."

"If we don't claim her, God only knows where she'll be buried."

"God will know, Mary Margaret. As a practical matter, how, may I ask, will you claim this poor woman without a family connection?"

"The mortuary took her because of Derry Richardson. If the church needs a reference, I could say I was a relative."

"A lie?"

"It isn't a lie if we're all brothers and sisters in Christ."

He smiled in the dark. "Point taken. But did Kitty Hawkins die in a state of grace?"

"She died in a horrible way and she was afraid of her fate. I'm sure she was in a state of grace." Mimi couldn't imagine that with death so near, Kitty wouldn't cry out for God's mercy. "At the end, she didn't have much time, but she was preparing to die. She told me so."

"And if that was a lie, I suppose you would confess it at a later date?"

"Your logic is unassailable, Father."

"You could say I've had practice." He gazed down at the river. The fireflies were dancing, thick in the evening air.

"She made me promise her so many things. This was one of them. I don't even know why we were friends. She seemed to need a friend, and I never had a sister. And Richie adored her."

"Richie. The young man with the amazing musical talent. His parents have consented to letting him play his violin at Mass, you know. I'm hoping he can drown out that one off-key singer in the choir. It's hard to fire a volunteer."

"I'll bring Richie with me."

He nodded. "It seems you were given a mission, Mary Margaret, and a difficult one at that. You've fulfilled your promises to Katharine Hawkins. Maybe she did have that light you talk about." He seemed older than his early thirties, but that was what war did to people. It settled burdens upon them.

"Please?"

Father Forsythe rubbed his eyes. "I will have to clear this with the monsignor. Never an easy task."

A disabled Army captain with a Silver Star and a Purple Heart might not impress the monsignor. But a parish priest could be dogged. Part of his job. Mimi's eyes filled with tears.

"You'll bury her then?"

"You've made your case. And I will make mine with the monsignor. Have faith. The rectory secretary will call you."

"Thank you."

"One more thing, Mary Margaret. You say that Katharine had a light inside her. Did you ever stop and think the light was inside you?"

"Me?" She stared at him in surprise. "No, not once."

"I'll see you in church."

timestamp CB

Later that evening after supper, Mimi finished hemming the violet dress, while Richie played the *Pavane for a Dead Princess* and other tunes. Joe Jordan swung by in time for a piece of peach cobbler and to see Mimi add the final stitches. Derry took several photos of 'the Princess.' Mimi wanted to send one to Gloria so she could see her design.

"That is mighty pretty," he said. "I can see a lot of work went into it. Are you sure about giving it to Kitty?"

"I'm sure," she said. "It's a gorgeous color, but it's better on her than me."

Joe and the entire Richardson family watched as she took the gown off the dummy and carefully folded it for the cardboard box she had ready. She started cleaning up all her supplies.

"Don't bother, Mimi. I'll put the dress form away," Addie said. "And I'll put all the threads and things in your sewing box."

"I appreciate that." Silently she marked it as one more item completed on her grim to-do list. "It's getting late. Do you think anyone will be there?"

Derry nodded slowly. "There's nearly always someone on the premises. I'll make a call and let them know you're coming."

"Shall we take a walk, Joe?" Mimi asked. "It isn't far and I need to stretch my legs."

Holding the dress box, Joe strolled with Mimi to Demaine's Mortuary. The mortician solemnly and with dignity took the box. He opened it to make sure it was acceptable.

"Well now, Miss Katharine will certainly look fine in this gown." He assured Mimi that she would receive all the loving care they could provide. "It appears the police will soon release her for burial."

"I hope so, even if they haven't caught the killer."

"And where will she be laid to rest?" he inquired politely.

Father Forsythe said to have faith. "St. Mary's Cemetery." Mimi was relieved to be able to say it to the mortician. This makes it official, she thought.

"Very good, Miss Smith. I'll arrange for the visitation and the Rosary with Father Forsythe."

"There might not be a lot of people attending. But I will be there."

"As will I," Joe added.

"Not to worry," the mortician said. "I know Father Forsythe. The good priest doesn't count the crowd."

THIRTY-FOUR

SOMEONE WAS FOLLOWING her. Mimi knew it without looking. A tickle of fear grew on the back of her neck and traveled down her spine.

It was Saturday afternoon. She was dressed casually in navy culottes and a red-and-white striped knit top, and she simply wanted to wander through downtown Alexandria, stare into the shop windows, and not think about Kitty and the other dead women and stolen goods and moonshine and the train tracks between them.

That was the moment she felt someone staring at her. She gazed in the dime store window, hoping to see their reflection. She spun around and no one was there.

Mimi stepped into the store. It was cooler inside. Stop it, you're fine, she told herself. No one is following you, you're tired and you're making things up.

Mimi marched to the fabric department, near the back of the store, where she felt safer. She pulled out the big Butterick pattern book and opened it on the slanted table. The saleslady recognized Mimi and left her to her own devices.

"Mimi?" someone said.

She jumped at the too-close voice. She spun around to see Seraphina, the pretty black-haired woman from Kitty's rooming house, at her elbow. Her heart was pounding.

"Do you always sneak up on people like that?"

"Not always. But it's good to know how to be quiet, whether you're coming or going."

"I knew someone was there, Seraphina. I didn't know it was you."

Seraphina leafed through another pattern book. "I didn't want anyone to think, well, that you know people like me."

"People like you? I hope you don't think I care about things like that." Mimi looked Seraphina over in her peach-colored cotton dress. "You look like any other woman, in a casual Saturday dress. Clean, pressed, charming. Thinking about a dance, or a date."

"All that? I'm impressed. I'm not thinking about a dance or a date. I'm sad, Mimi. And like everyone else at the Shack, I'm scared."

"You want to talk about Kitty?"

"About Kitty," Seraphina said. "It's a real bad way to die."

"That's what Kitty said about Hattie."

"It's not easy. We all think we're going to get out and leave the Life. Head out someplace where no one knows us."

"Kitty planned to get married."

"I know. We all tell ourselves stories. Most of our customers are in and out. So to speak. I mean, on the trains or the ships." Seraphina picked at her nails. "The troops come and go, the soldiers and the sailors, the flyboys, the marines. Mostly we never see them again. We know a lot of them are going to die, and that makes it seem less bad, what we do. Like we're not tramps. Like we're their sweethearts for a night. We can give them that. We let them go and we don't have the heartache of knowing for sure what happens to them."

"A lot of them are very young." Mimi could see the boys' faces in her mind.

She nodded. "Lots of smooth baby faces, not enough sense to come in out of the rain. Very polite though. How can these sweet little boys go fight the Jerries or the Japanese? Anyway, I don't think much about them afterwards, but there are the others."

"The others? What others do you worry about?"

"Repeat customers."

It had occurred to Mimi too. The killer was probably a repeat customer. As Seraphina said, the newly minted servicemen were in and out quickly, and they were grateful. They probably wouldn't be back.

"Let's get out of here and get a Coke," Mimi said. "On me."

"I'm guessing I've got more money than you."

"Then it's on you."

"The Majestic Café. They know me there and they don't ask any questions."

The café was just a few doors down King Street from G. C. Murphy's. Mimi and Seraphina entered under the pink-and-blue neon sign and took a Formica-topped table toward the back. Even though fans were blowing, it was warm inside and there wasn't much privacy, but no one was interested in their troubles. The woman behind the counter seemed to know Seraphina. She said nothing, but she brought over a couple of tall sodas without being asked.

"Thanks, hon," Seraphina said.

"You said to be wary of repeat customers."

"Like me, huh?" Seraphina smiled. "Yeah. You get to know their quirks. Some are creepy, a couple downright scary. They want weird stuff. Want to slap you around. Things like that. But that's the thing: You get used to them. They turn into regulars. You stop being scared of them. But maybe you should be."

"Seraphina, are you saying you think you know who killed Kitty, and Hattie? And Polly?"

The woman played with her paper straw. "I couldn't swear to it."

"But you have an idea. Why don't you go to the police?"

Seraphina laughed, showing off straight white teeth. "We don't talk to the police. Besides, I got a deal with Ethel."

"Ethel? Who's Ethel?"

"Ethel Jackson's the gatekeeper at the Shack. Lives in the bungalow, takes the money, gives us our cut."

"Is she Madam Cherry?"

Seraphina laughed again. "She works for Madam Cherry."

"What kind of deal do you have?"

"She keeps a lookout for the police, and the men I don't want to mess with. Signals me if she sees them. We got a buzzer system, she rings one way if it's the cops, another for a new customer, another way if it's a regular."

"Does she check them in, check them out?"

"I don't know her system for that part of it. It's like magic. The men, they just suddenly appear."

"Do you know a man named Clem?"

They were interrupted by a woman approaching their table. Seraphina leaned back, the new woman leaned forward. Seraphina took the moment to ask the waitress for a piece of chocolate pie. There was a freshly made pie in the tall glass case.

"You must be Mimi Smith," the woman said.

Mimi had never seen her before. She raised an eyebrow. "Yes."

She was a well-preserved woman in her forties or fifties. Mimi wasn't the best judge of age, yet she could tell the woman had money and took care of herself. Her hair was dark without any sign of gray, her makeup carefully applied, her tailored suit a conservative navy. Her impressively tall navy hat with elaborate flowers and velvet ribbons was worn on the side of her head, and it had a blue veil that fell just below her eyes and nose. You might have thought the Majestic Café was a fancy hotel in the District, Mimi thought.

"May I join you?" the woman asked and sat down before Mimi could answer.

Seraphina said nothing and watched the woman. They seemed to know each other.

"Do you know who I am?" the woman asked Mimi.

"Should I?" Mimi said.

"She's famous in certain parts around here." Seraphina smothered a laugh. It made Mimi uneasy. Was she being set up somehow?

"Are you Madam Cherry?" Mimi didn't quite know why she said it. Perhaps because there was a bravado about the woman that suggested power and ruthlessness.

"Some people call me that." She pulled a pack of Luckies from her trim purse and shook out a cigarette. "It's one of the names I go by."

"Do you want me to call you Madam Cherry?"

"If you like." The woman pulled out a silver lighter. "The original Madam Cherry is long gone. She reigned on the Potomac River in the early part of the century. I bought her houseboat when she retired." She flicked the lighter, lit the cigarette, and inhaled. "You may call me Madam Cherry. It's prettier than Nancy, don't you think?" She exhaled a thin ribbon of smoke over their heads.

Mimi had no idea what to think. She stared at the cigarette, afraid it might set fire to the veil. But the woman was a pro and the veil stayed intact. Was she really sitting with the notorious madam?

She was distracted by Gretel, who cast a shadow at the front door and slipped into the chair next to Seraphina. She nodded at Mimi but didn't say anything. Madam Cherry signaled to the waitress for a cup of coffee. She indicated coffee for Gretel too.

"Cream, if you have it, hon."

The waitress laughed in response. "That's a good one."

Madam Cherry turned her attention to Mimi. "You needn't worry, Miss Smith, most people don't know who I am. Most of those who do would never admit it."

"You wanted to speak with me?"

"Yes. About Kitty Hawkins."

"What can I tell you?"

"I knew she wouldn't be with us for long," the madam said. "You begin to be able to read people. Kitty had a year or so in this business. That's all. But I never suspected she would leave the way she did."

"Have the police found anything?" Mimi asked.

"I told you, Mimi," Seraphina said. "That'll be the day."

Madam Cherry sucked in more smoke and exhaled smoke rings. "You don't know how the police in Alexandria work. A whore's death means nothing to them. But it means something to me. And to you. That makes you different from most folks. You seemed to get close to Kitty."

"We were friends. And I'm so sad that she died. Maybe because that other life she wanted seemed so close. She makes three deaths in your business that I know of," Mimi said. "Kitty, Hattie, and Polly."

"And I can't afford to lose any more. Believe it or not, I care about my women. And death is bad for business."

Seraphina averted her eyes and played with her chocolate pie. Gretel touched her arm and they shared a look.

"Why tell me?"

"You've been asking questions. You work for OPA. Interesting. Is the government getting involved in this?"

Mimi wondered where this strange woman had vacuumed up her information. It wasn't a secret, but she hadn't broadcast it either. Besides, her job was a tiny cog in a big machine.

"I don't represent the government. I'm just a stenographer."

"The government? You work for the government?" Seraphina's golden eyes went wide.

"But you're asking questions and that's more than anyone else has," Madam Cherry said. "How did you meet Kitty?"

"I met Kitty last year when we were harvesting honey from Addie's hives."

"The Richardson woman."

"You know her."

"I know she sells honey and it makes her a very popular lady. It's a small town."

Mimi took a long sip of her Coke. "Then I went to a dance for the torpedo factory workers and friends. Kitty was there. A bunch of crude soldiers were harassing her. 'Here, Kitty, Kitty.' They were cruel and rude, and I didn't like it. I made a bit of a scene and dragged her away from them."

"That's why I tell our ladies not to mingle out there. It rarely ends well."

Seraphina spoke up. "Kitty didn't like following the rules."

"One reason I knew she wouldn't last." Madam Cherry blew out perfectly formed smoke rings. "If I'd known what would happen, I would never have taken her on."

"I don't know about that," Seraphina said. "The men liked Kitty and that white-blond hair of hers."

The madam fixed Seraphina with an eagle-eyed glare. "Men all have their types, Seraphina, that's why you're so popular."

"Because I'm *exotic*? And most can't tell I'm a mixed-blood gal? Those who can tell like me because of it."

"What about Hattie Carnegie Jones?" Mimi cut in.

"Hattie was solid, she could have worked her way into management," Madam Cherry said. "She had a way of handling the bad eggs. But I didn't find out until too late that she had a regrettable habit of selling things she didn't own. Hattie was playing a dangerous game, counting on her marks not to squawk."

"And Polly?"

"Polly was friends with Hattie and they were part of the same game."

"Swimming in the black market?"

"Couldn't prove it by me. Polly always seemed to have money though, more than she made at the Shack. Anyway, official word was suicide. I don't believe it, but nothing I could say would change that."

"Terrible way to die," Gretel said. "I heard she killed herself, but now I think she was pushed, especially after Kitty and Hattie were murdered."

Madam Cherry returned her attention to Mimi. "Did Kitty tell you anything?"

"She may have had suspicions, but she never said who she suspected. She said she wouldn't know until he walked through the door."

"Well, someone is killing my women and I have to do something about it. If the cops won't do anything, there are those who will."

"What do you mean?" Was this woman talking about vengeance? Paying someone to find the murderer and exact revenge? It was a good bet she knew someone capable of that.

"You only have to remember one thing. We both want justice," the woman said. "You can come to me with information. Any time. The police won't know, or care."

"Come to you? How am I supposed to contact you?" She didn't think Madam Cherry would hand her a business card. And she didn't.

"Tell Seraphina. She'll get a message to me."

"What makes you think I can find out anything?"

"I have a feeling." She stubbed out the remains of her cigarette. "And you've got the government behind you."

"I'm just a stenographer."

Madam Cherry laughed.

"I'm sure that's what y'all say. Well, if that's what you want to tell people, it's okay by me."

Where was she getting this? Did she think Mimi had some kind of important job with OPA? That might offer her some protection, but Mimi never liked to lie, least of all about herself.

"Kitty's sweetheart is supposed to be back in town soon." Gretel stared into her coffee.

"She told me. Can you let me know when he shows up?" Mimi said. "I have some things to give him."

The three women looked up expectantly. "Like what?" Seraphina asked.

"His love letters to her. Photographs. Things like that. I'm sure he'd want them back, and if he doesn't, he can dispose of them in his own way."

"I'll let Mimi know when he shows up," Gretel promised. Mimi wrote the Richardsons' phone number on a napkin.

"I'll make sure," Seraphina added.

"I'll leave it to you all then." Madam Cherry tossed a bill on the table. "Good luck, Miss Smith. Stenographer." She stood up and marched out of the café. Mimi and the others watched her go.

"She likes you," Seraphina said.

"How can you tell?" Mimi drew her eyebrows together.

"Don't worry. We can tell," Gretel said, tucking the phone number in her pocket.

Mimi was perplexed. Nancy Whoever, aka Madam Cherry, could be an ally. Or she could be lying. She said she cared about her women, but she never betrayed her emotions. She wanted information, but she didn't offer much. She was cool and detached. Were the three dead women really her 'valued employees'—or troublemakers?

Which side was Madam Cherry on? The murdered women, or their killer?

THIRTY-FIVE

JOE WHISTLED WHEN he saw her, a low appreciative warble. "I didn't expect to be escorting Miss Rita Hayworth to the ball this evening."

"Is it too much?" Mimi asked.

"No, I'd say it was just about perfect. Especially those freckles."

Mimi thought she had carefully hidden every trace of a freckle. She stuck her tongue out at him and he laughed. "Rita" was exactly the look Mimi had been going for, however, and she appreciated him for noticing. She didn't really care if it was too much, she was in a too-much kind of mood.

She was wearing a white dress with sheer three-quarter sleeves and a contrasting shimmery gold cummerbund. It showed off her figure and fit snugly through the waist. The dress material featured gold fans decorated with sparkling beads and the white and gold enhanced her coloring.

This frock was one of her dressiest outfits. It was Saturday night and Joe Jordan was taking her dancing at the Spanish Ballroom in Glen Echo, Maryland. It was the break they deserved in the midst of all this sadness, he said.

Mimi desperately needed a night away from thinking about murder and death. And though she felt guilty about that desire, even Addie and Derry encouraged her to take the night off. Richie picked up on that energy and played swing tunes while Mimi waited for Joe to pick her up and take her to the famous ballroom and amusement park on the leafy bluffs above the Potomac River.

The Spanish Ballroom had a dress code: dresses for woman, jackets and ties for men. This offered her a chance to wear one of her pretty ensembles without feeling unpatriotic. Mimi added a jeweled barrette to hold her hair back behind one ear and a glittery bracelet. She felt as glamorous as she could be, but she was knocked out by Joe Jordan.

"You clean up pretty well yourself," she said.

Joe was wearing a new-looking dark blue suit and a purple, blue and white patterned tie. "My college graduation duds. Don't get a chance to wear them much."

"You got a haircut too." She reached up and fluffed his newly cropped locks.

"My big sister took one look at me and said I looked like some kind of a wild man. I had to remind her that's how we all look back home. She said that's why she left. She brought out her shears and ordered me to close my eyes and this is what happened. That woman scares me."

"She's got a talent." Joe's hair was trimmed close on the sides, but still long enough on the top to comb back. "You look like a movie star yourself."

"We better hurry then, and not waste any of this stardust."

Richie was open-mouthed. "You look beautiful, Mimi. Kitty thinks so too."

"That is the perfect thing to say. Thank you, Richie, for the compliment."

Mimi couldn't quite believe he was in contact with a spectral Kitty, but it was sweet, nevertheless.

"This glamour certainly calls for a picture." Derry was eager to change the subject away from unseen spirits. He fancied himself an amateur photographer, and he produced his prized pre-war Leica camera. He soon had Joe and Mimi posing for photos like a proud father before the high school prom. Addie dabbed at her eyes and warned them not to be home too late.

"My truck isn't exactly a chariot, but it will have to do," Joe said. The blue pickup was as presentable as it could be. He'd washed it, scoured the dirt out of the upholstery, even applied some wax.

"It looks so shiny, Joe."

"And filled with gasoline. Luckily, it doesn't look like it, so gas thieves should steer clear. And if that doesn't work, I jerry-rigged a lock on the cap."

℃

The Spanish Ballroom was beautiful and imposing, and the band's music could be heard before Joe and Mimi reached the entryway. The evening air was perfumed with summer flowers and the sky speckled with bright stars and fireflies. Couples spilled out the doors of the Mediterranean art deco building whenever the dance floor filled up. Somehow, Joe was on a list and had a table reserved for him. The doorman asked if he was in the service.

"Navy. I report soon." The doorman gave him a prime table for viewing the action.

The tables were set up in the arched promenade around the stage, but those who had reserved them let other couples rest while they were pounding the floorboards. Joe escorted Mimi to the floor, where they tripped the light fantastic. At least, it seemed fantastic to Mimi.

"You're a wonderful dancer, Joe." She was a little surprised.

"I had to learn something in college."

They kept their conversation light and far away from Kitty Hawkins. Mimi felt unwanted weight slip from her shoulders with every swing dance, Lindy Hop, and fox trot. She was damp with perspiration when they finally took a break. Or glowing, as her friend Rosalyn would have it.

They reclaimed their chairs to sit out a number or two. She fanned herself and they ordered a couple of rum and Coca-Colas, like the song said.

"To the most beautiful woman in the room," Joe toasted her. "And it's a pretty crowded room."

He grinned, his eyes crinkled, and something in her heart lurched. She hadn't felt anything close to this since Eddie Falcone bid her goodbye. She told herself to be careful, yet she was also grateful to be alive and happy and in the moment for once. It was a euphoric feeling.

She was floating on clouds until someone familiar danced by. A soldier with a second lieutenant's butter bars on his shoulders. He walked past with a couple of drinks, then stopped, and retraced his steps. He leaned down and stared at Mimi. He placed his drinks on the table.

"Hey, Slugger. Looking good tonight."

She recognized him. "You!"

"Yeah, I'm the guy you slugged at that dance, a few weeks back."

Mimi was momentarily at a loss for words. Joe reached for her hand reassuringly.

"And you are?" she asked.

"Lieutenant Shaw. You remember. Lady, you really know how to make an impression." Joe stared at him. Butter Bar backed up a step, hands up, making a joke out of it. "I'm afraid I wasn't much of a gentleman and the little lady here punched me right in the gut. Rightfully so. Hey, are you in the service? No offense, but no uniform."

"I'll be reporting soon," Joe said. "I've enlisted."

"Army?"

"Navy."

"This guy is one of the GIs who was taunting Kitty," Mimi said to Joe. "The night I met her again at the dance."

Shaw kept his hands up. "I learned my lesson. Honest. Slugger here popped me a good one."

"Solar plexus," Mimi explained to Joe. "My grandmother taught me."

"Thing is, I never understood why you were standing up for the little—um, lady."

"She was a friend."

"That so?" Shaw clearly couldn't see how Mimi could be friends with a woman like Kitty Hawkins. "How is she?"

"She's dead."

"Oh, brother!" Shaw rubbed his chin. "That's too bad."

"She was murdered."

"That one? I didn't know about her." Something in his demeanor changed and he turned to go.

Joe stood up and stopped Shaw in his tracks. He wasn't unduly aggressive, but he was half a head taller and farm work had given him more muscles than the lieutenant. "Sit. Stay. Now, what do you know about Kitty Hawkins?"

Shaw sank slowly into a nearby chair. "Nothing. I was just surprised, that's all. I heard about that Hattie Jones, and that other one—"

"Polly?" Mimi cut in. "The woman from the Chicken Shack who died before Hattie was killed? What do you know about Polly Brown?"

Shaw was sweating. "Oh, you mean that dame who bought it on the tracks?"

"You had a little rhyme about her, didn't you? *Polly's the dolly who fell on the tracks, Polly's the dolly who's not coming back.* You knew her pretty well."

"Everybody knew Polly, if you know what I mean. Just another slut who was selling it cheap."

Joe loomed over Shaw menacingly. "A little respect here, Butter Bar."

Shaw gulped down one of his drinks. "You lay a hand on an officer, buddy, you'll wind up in the brig."

"I'm not in the service yet, but I'm going to be an officer. Ninety-day wonder," Joe said. "And until I am, I leave all my punching to Slugger here." He tossed Mimi a wry glance. "You can't arrest her."

"Hey, I'm sorry about Polly. No hard feelings."

"Tell us about Polly and Hattie," Mimi said. "I heard they used to sell things they didn't own. That's a clever game, isn't it?"

"Who are you people?" Shaw looked around nervously.

"You could call us—investigators." Mimi wondered where she got the courage to say that. Probably the movies. Heroines were always stretching the truth in the movies.

"Damn." Shaw was breathing hard. "I had nothing to do with Polly or Hattie's demise. Hattie was a good spotter. I'm basically a scrounger. You know what that is. I lay my hands on whatever my superiors want that they can't get through regular channels. But I'm not involved in civilian affairs, believe me. Hattie mostly spotted goods for the Hallelujah Man, not for me, but we did cross paths now and then."

Joe and Mimi exchanged a look. "Who is the Hallelujah Man?" Mimi asked.

"Just a guy," Shaw said. "A guy who has goods and supplies them to people."

"On the black market," Joe said.

"Some people might call it that. Others call it supply and demand."

"The Hallelujah Man steals and sells things?" Mimi asked. "Tires, sugar, household goods? Liquor?"

"I don't know if *steal* is the right word," Shaw said. "Maybe appropriates. He redistributes the wealth."

"He's a thief with a fancy name. Delusions of grandeur. And maybe a killer too," she said.

"You know this guy?" Joe leaned in on Shaw. "Be straight with us. Or be sorry."

"I know of him. I don't know his name. Truth, man. I've never met him. Hattie talked about him, he was just a connection and a client."

"Why Hallelujah?" Mimi asked.

"Hattie said it's because everyone is happy to see what he's brought to sell," Shaw said. "You know, he shows up and people say hallelujah. He's the man who's got the goods."

"Stolen goods at inflated prices," Mimi said. "Who gave him the name Hallelujah Man?"

"He did, I guess. He's not short on ego. So I hear." Joe's silence made Shaw squirm. "Listen, I got an important job. I work at the Pentagon. You know, the big one."

The Pentagon, that fabled brand-new building that had been Federal Office Building No. 1, had opened that January.

It sounded like a big deal. Working in a federal office building herself, Mimi was not impressed.

Just then a froth of red taffeta and a cloud of gardenia perfume passed by the table and stopped. The charm of the taffeta dress was in its rustling skirt, which flirted with the limits of the clothing regulations. The wearer looked lovely, and she had made sure her crimson lipstick matched her new dress.

"Lieutenant Shaw, I have been looking for you! Wherever have you been?"

Mimi would know that Southern accent anywhere. But she hadn't heard it in a couple of weeks. "Rosalyn, what are you doing here?"

The woman peered at Mimi for a moment before it clicked. "Mimi! Imagine seeing you here. Why, I'm dancing, of course." Roz had a hard time recognizing women when there was a man around. She was "glowing" in the humid night. Her dark curls had been wrestled under control with a matching red band wound through her hair.

Joe stood up. "You too ladies catch up. The lieutenant and I want to have a little chat outside." Joe marched Lt. Butter Bar toward the entry by his elbow.

Roz grabbed Shaw's drink before he could take it with him. "Thanks, sugar, I'm so thirsty. See you soon."

Mimi watched them go, then turned to Roz. "How can you go out with this guy after that night at Chinquapin Village?"

"I told you I thought he was cute. And what do I care about that tramp? Why, I just ran into Lieutenant Howard Shaw the other night. He remembered me and asked me out. And Mimi, he gave me a pair of nylons! Real nylon stockings. Can you believe it?" Roz was clearly impressed with the stockings and with any man who provided them, even though he was a Yankee with a New Jersey accent.

"You'd go out with this jerk for a pair of nylons?" Mimi blinked. "You saw how he treated Kitty, how he taunted her. He led the other soldiers. He was the ringleader."

She could still hear them calling, *Here, Kitty, Kitty.*

"Kitty? Was that her name? Mimi, she was just hillbilly trash. Like I told you, strictly Tobacco Road."

"She was a human being, Roz, and now she's dead."

"Dead?" Her large brown eyes widened in shock. It was an expression she had clearly worked hard on: Southern belle in distress. "No, why it couldn't be."

"She was murdered."

This time the expression looked more real. "But that's terrible, even if she was—"

"Yes, it is terrible."

"But what does that have to do with my lieutenant? My poor Howard?"

THIRTY-SIX

"*P*OOR HOWARD? WE'RE trying to find out what his connection was to three dead women, that's all."

"Dead women? He couldn't have anything to do with that. Not with a *death*."

"He is a soldier."

Rosalyn was one of those women who claimed she would never prefer *men* over her girlfriends. *I just hate women who abandon plans when a gentleman calls.* Yet she was the first to plead "patriotism" and jump through hoops when a man showed up. *My goodness, he's a GI, what can I do? He could be marching to his death!*

"You don't understand, Mimi. Lieutenant Shaw's an officer and a gentleman. He's stationed at the *Pentagon*. He's not going to be shot up or lose a limb or anything. And he gave me this pair of stockings. Real nylon. Look at these seams!" She lifted her skirt so Mimi could see.

Mimi groaned in disgust. It was the war, she thought. Despite Washington, D.C., having a constant influx of servicemen, men who were stable and single and in secure positions were not thick on the ground. And women were working everywhere they'd never been before, from factories to government agencies to taxi cabs. The world was turned upside down.

"And who is that handsome lad you're with?" Roz inquired, back in her best girlfriend mode.

"He's not a cowboy, you wouldn't be interested. Hold the fort, will you? I have to powder my nose."

"Can't promise I won't be dancing when you get back." Roz winked at Mimi—or possibly some man right behind her.

"I have no doubt."

Mimi couldn't stand another minute with Roz, and she didn't think it was wise to leave Joe alone with Shaw, or vice versa. She left the ballroom without powdering her petite freckled nose. She wasn't sure it would do any good in this steamy atmosphere anyway.

She was surprised to find it felt lighter and cooler outside in the moonlight, away from the thick of the crowd. The air was sweet. Was it honeysuckle or roses or both? She also detected a faint scent of chlorine, which drew her eyes to the Crystal Pool and its glorious neon sign. The giant entry doors were closed, and the swimmers all had departed for the day. Fireflies flickered in nearby trees.

She spotted Shaw and Joe conversing, thankfully without any punching. Shaw lit a Camel and inhaled deeply. She sauntered slowly over, knowing that Joe had seen her, and he could signal her if he wanted more time alone with Lt. Butter Bar.

"Mimi, come on over here." He waved and reached for her hand. "Apparently, the Hallelujah Man has friends in Forgotten Creek and thereabouts."

"Clem and Frenchie?" Mimi asked.

"I don't know any names," Shaw said. "It's better that way. I got no knowledge about no illegal activities."

"What about moonshine?"

"Don't know nothing about that neither. I'm supplied cases of whiskey in premium booze bottles, labels and all. Nothing to do with moonshine."

"From the Hallelujah Man?" Joe said quietly.

"Not directly," Shaw said. "It's premium bourbon too. And there's a war going on, in case you hadn't noticed."

"And they can't tell it's rotgut and not real Kentucky bourbon?" Mimi said.

"Now, don't be slamming high quality West Virginia white lightning, Mimi," Joe protested with a grin. "Course it does depend on whose still it comes out of. Lots of perfecting goes into that hootch. Ever since Prohibition. And I grant you, thirsty soldiers, very thirsty soldiers, might not be able to tell the difference between amber mountain dew and Kentucky's finest."

"I stand corrected." Mimi turned her glare on Shaw.

"Like the man says. That's all I know, lady. Swear to God."

"So you say. What if we need to talk to you again?"

"Not a good idea, Slugger," Shaw said. "Things will go quiet for a while, I guarantee. Nobody wants no trouble. Real sorry about the ladies. Truly."

"Did this guy kill them?" Joe asked. "This Hallelujah Man?"

"I wouldn't know. It's not like I'm asking around." He sucked nervously on his cigarette. "He's big, he's mean, and he's got a couple of screws loose. So I hear."

"What's his real name?" Mimi asked.

"I never asked." Shaw threw the butt down and ground his shoe on it.

"Is he Frenchie?"

"Only met Frenchie a time or two. Don't think so, but I wouldn't swear to it. Listen, I gotta go." Shaw made his break and double-timed it back to the ballroom and his lady in red.

"What do you think, Mimi?" Joe reached for her hand.

"We know more than we did before. But not enough."

He pulled her into his arms and they began to waltz. It was lovely out here. The music was fainter, but this dance floor was all theirs. They had the neon light and the fireflies all to themselves.

"Funny how things happen," she mused.

"Go on."

"If we hadn't come here tonight, we wouldn't have seen Second Lieutenant Howard Shaw."

"And I wouldn't know they call you Slugger."

"And somewhere out there is a monster who calls himself the Hallelujah Man. And he knows something about Polly, Hattie, and Kitty."

"More than something."

"What should we do, Joe?"

He held her close, moving in time to the distant music from the ballroom. "We should dance and hold each other tight as long as we can. Tomorrow will keep."

The band was playing Gershwin. Mimi would forever after think of Joe Jordan when she heard "Summertime." They clung to each other. It was the way people behaved during war time, and dances, and kisses, were a respite from their battles.

෫

Her dreams were interrupted too early by the church music right outside her bedroom door.

"Mimi, get up," Richie pleaded. "You don't want to be late to Mass." The Kyrie on violin was beautiful, if unexpected. "They said I can do it! I can play at St. Mary's today, if you take me there."

"Today?"

"Today!"

She growled into her pillow. She had been dreaming about dances and kisses with Joe Jordan and she wanted to cling to the memories. Hold on to them. She lifted her head. Her clock told her it wasn't as late as Richie feared. She had an hour to get ready.

"Hold your horses, I'm getting up." She'd planned on sleeping in and sneaking into the late Mass. But Richie and his violin were waiting, and they were very excited. She couldn't disappoint them. "Wait for me downstairs, okay?"

"I'll play you some getting up and hurrying music." He launched into "Boogie Woogie Bugle Boy" as he sped down the stairs.

Although she was grumpy and groggy, Mimi managed to make it to the church on time and wearing a smart ensemble, with Richie in tow. Once there, Richie turned shy and insisted that Mimi accompany him up to the choir loft, where she was allowed to sit by the choir director. With his violin's soaring first notes, the parishioners turned and gazed up to see who was playing that heavenly violin. Father Forsythe satisfied their curiosity during his sermon, and he introduced and welcomed Richie Richardson. At the end of Mass, the entire congregation applauded the young violinist.

As they exited the church, and Father Forsythe greeted the faithful, many waited to say hello to the young musician and praise his talent. Many had heard of Addie Richardson's musically inclined son, but few had laid eyes on him. Richie was all too happy to talk while Mimi stood by and yawned. Finally, a threatening dark sky encouraged them to leave. Richie couldn't risk getting his prize violin wet. He hadn't brought the case, because he had been playing it all the way to church.

Richie was on cloud nine. He practically sailed home next to Mimi. He couldn't stop talking about how wonderful it was, and when he couldn't find the words, he played his violin. In short, he was unbearable, but in a charming way. She realized he'd never had that kind of positive public attention before. His overly protective parents had always been afraid others would see him as some kind of freak.

They arrived back at the Richardsons' in time for the skies to open up and pour down rain. Richie replayed every note for Addie and Derry, with an accompanying story.

There was nothing for Mimi to do but nap and read an Agatha Christie mystery, recommended by her helpful local librarian. It struck her how little this novel had to do with real life, real nitty-gritty life.

And real nitty-gritty death.

THIRTY-SEVEN

MONDAY EVENING MIMI opened Kitty's green marbled suitcase in her room one last time, to fold all the wedding finery for her younger sister Lucy. She admired the lovely morning-glory blue crepe gown with its sweetheart neckline and deep peplum, trimmed in delicate beaded embroidery. The matching belt sparkled, and it would look perfect on Lucy's trim figure.

Mimi wrapped the petite veiled hat with tissue paper to keep it pristine. The delicate nightgown and robe still had their tags. Mimi left them on. Lucy and her mother could see that not only were they unworn, they came from a fine department store, and they were the highest quality. Perhaps Netty would faint at the prices. Mimi was fine with that.

There was also the respectable dark blue dress and jacket with white collar and cuffs, Kitty's first choice for her wedding, before they found the lighter blue gown. Mimi imagined this might have been the dress Kitty planned to wear to meet Nathan's family. She had even bought a pair of prim white gloves that matched the collar and cuffs. In a side pocket, Mimi found four additional brand-new pairs of nylon stockings. Quite a bounty and most likely gifts from one of the soldiers or sailors. Those nylons would be valuable on the black market, but Mimi would let Lucy decide what to do with them.

Mimi didn't begrudge Lucy a pretty wardrobe, especially because she'd grown up in such a deprived home. But she lamented that she would never see Kitty in her wedding gown. Mimi tucked Kitty's engagement ring away deep in her trunk, along with the packet of Nathan's letters. All that Nathan would have left from his magical mermaid.

"Don't be sad, Mimi."

Richie had slipped in and surprised her. Addie stood in the open doorway.

"I'm not sad. Come on in, you two."

She nestled the two pairs of shoes into the suitcase, the nearly new cream-colored dancing shoes, and the never-worn dark blue heels, being careful to stuff them with tissue paper.

"Should I play you some music?" Richie asked.

"I'd like that, Richie. Can you play me 'Summertime'?"

"Kitty is glad you're her friend, and she says don't worry, you'll figure it out."

"Figure what out?"

He lifted his violin in an elaborate shrug. "Beats me." The striking melancholy notes of "Summertime" began softly.

"Don't let Richie bother you," Addie said. "He's just always been that way."

"He couldn't bother me. Tell me, Addie. Do you think he can really see souls? Or hear them?"

"I try not to think about that. I take comfort where I can. Mimi, it's late. Can't you do that another time?"

"Joe's going to pick this up first thing in the morning. He has a few errands he needs to run back in Forgotten Creek. He offered to drop this off at the Hawkinses. It will spare me a trip to the post office. And all that postage."

Mimi would like to accompany him, but she wasn't sure how patient George Prescott would be if she asked for another day off work. She also had a few ideas she wanted to follow up. Questions to ask. She and Joe would compare notes later.

Mimi pulled out a piece of her special rose-colored stationery and wrote a note to Lucy. She suggested how she might wear the blue gown for her wedding, and she mentioned the cream-colored dancing shoes would be perfect for it, since there was sure to be dancing. She could save the good blue shoes for something else, like going to church. She also requested a photograph from the wedding and included a stamped envelope.

It was time to sort through the photos and set aside a few for Kitty's family. Some she would return to Nathan, along with his diamond ring. Mimi also wanted a couple of pictures of Kitty for herself, which she tucked into her trunk for safekeeping. Mimi had no control over what Netty Hawkins would think of these pictures, but Lucy might like them.

There was a picture from Kitty's first communion, all skinny knobby knees and a white veil. Her high school graduation photo, which had that shy hopeful smile most graduates flashed.

A more recent set of pictures had been taken at a professional photo studio and there were several copies of each. Kitty and Nathan, sitting side by side with his arm around her. Kitty alone, backlit and looking like a movie star. On the back of these Kitty had written "engagement photos." No doubt Nathan already had copies of these shots, so Mimi included one of each for the suitcase. She wanted Kitty's family to see that she hadn't been merely a "fallen woman," sunk into a life of sadness and sin. She was pulling herself out of it, planning a bright new future.

Mimi never told them about the baby Kitty was expecting.

⋄

"Don't borrow any trouble until I get back," Joe said. They were bumping along the George Washington Memorial Parkway toward Washington in his reliable pickup truck.

Mimi snickered at the thought. "I'll try and save it all for you, Joe. And you make it sound like I'm asking for trouble."

"You might not be asking for it, but it could find you."

She rolled down the passenger side window to take in the crisp morning air and enjoy the lush green of the Parkway's trees and grass, the blue of the Potomac River. It was going to be a beautiful day, clearer and drier than usual.

"Thanks for the lift. Normally, I'd be squashed on the bus, wondering why I'd bothered to iron my clothes."

"My pleasure. You're going my way. Easy detour to drop you off."

Joe was traveling back to Forgotten Creek for many reasons, including seeing whether he could get a line on the elusive Hallelujah Man.

"Do you think he's Frenchie?" Mimi asked. "Sounds like he's big enough."

"Frenchie's more fat than ferocious. But who knows? Frenchie and his buddy Clem don't strike me as the kind to beat up and kill women. Far as I know, Frenchie stays close to his home ground. Easier to keep tabs on the business of making hootch."

"But Clem travels. We know that. We don't know why, exactly."

"True. He was cagey about that. Not sure he wants to tangle with me again. Clem's pretty lazy, too. Those boys must have fallen in with some real bad company."

"Putting it mildly." She wanted to change the subject. "Thanks for taking this suitcase back to Lucy Hawkins."

She had insisted on keeping it in the cab by her feet, rather than letting him swing it into the back of the truck. It was too precious.

"I'll make sure she opens it in front of me, so I can tell you all about her reaction." He hadn't known Mimi long, but he seemed to understand how much that meant to her.

"I'd like that very much, Joe. Will your mother be okay without you?"

"She says she will. And she's got my brothers." This trip was another chance for Joe to say goodbye to his mother. "More waterworks, of course," Joe grimaced. "On the other hand, more home cooking. And I do love my mama's cooking."

Mimi dreaded telling Nathan Albemarle the news of Kitty's death. She wasn't even sure how to contact him. She would have to trust Seraphina and Gretel to send him to her when he showed up at the Chicken Shack.

Joe turned off the Parkway onto the Memorial Bridge. Mimi sighed. She'd be happy to step off the roller coaster ride that was his blue pickup truck, but she was sad to see Joe drive away.

"What if Nathan learns about Kitty from a newspaper?" So far, the papers had played down the murders, but that could change.

"You gotta let it go, Mimi," Joe counseled. "He may already know, but you can still give him back his letters and their photos. He'll want all that."

And Kitty's diamond ring, Mimi added silently. "You're right. I can't seem to stop worrying about it."

"There are so many things to worry about. Far as I can see, you got a range of troubles to pick from."

"I wish I could go with you, Joe." Mimi pictured all the work she had on her schedule, taking George Prescott's dictation, typing up endless correspondence. A long trip over bumpy roads in a jolting truck was suddenly more appealing than a day inside that stuffy, ugly OPA office.

"Me too. You're a good companion, Mimi Smith." They smiled at each other, and Mimi felt a jolt in her heart.

"Joe, what if we figure it out? Who it is? The killer. Just bring it to the police? Will they believe us? Believe it or not, I'm used to men not believing anything I say."

"I'd believe you, Mimi. But the cops? Who knows? I think we gotta give them something real, like a name, not just a bunch of suspicions. And we don't have much time. Or little Gretel might be the next on his list."

"We've got one name. The Hallelujah Man. We're close to finding our monster. I can feel it."

Joe pulled up to the dumpy building where Mimi worked. "What are you going to tell your boss?"

"Nothing yet. I annoy him. And he annoys me."

Joe squeezed her hand. "How is that possible?" He promised to call her when he returned, before shipping out with the Navy.

Keeping her head down and concentrating on her work kept Mimi busy through the day. She barely saw George, cranky from attending a full day of Monday meetings.

CR

After work, Mimi returned to the place where Kitty worked and died. But instead of going up the alley, she marched up the front steps and knocked on the door. Presently, the door was opened by Ethel Jackson, a black woman somewhere between middle and old age. Seraphina had told Mimi that Ethel had an arrangement with Madame Cherry over the goings-on in her backyard.

Mimi introduced herself as a friend of Kitty Hawkins, and the woman stepped out on her front porch. Ethel Jackson owned the trim little brick house in front of the Chicken Shack, she said, and she tended the roses that climbed up the walls.

Mimi asked her what went on in the building in back. Mrs. Jackson claimed it was a shed, that was all, and who did Mimi Smith think she was, asking her about her private business? It was just an old shed that she rented out, what with the war and all and people needing space to rent. She told Mimi she didn't bother with the people who came and went, though she admitted it was sad about the woman who died there, even though it was none of her business. Her dark eyes were lively yet wary.

Mrs. Jackson knew what went on in her shed, Mimi knew, and furthermore, she knew Mimi knew. Maybe she was enjoying bantering with this too-inquisitive young white woman on her stoop, a woman who clearly was not one of the magdalens. Gretel had warned Mimi not to underestimate Ethel Jackson. "She may look innocent," she'd said to Mimi, "but she handles every dollar that changes hands."

"If it's just an old shed," Mimi asked Ethel, "why are there four doors and four windows?"

"I like the way it looks." Nothing rattled Ethel Jackson. "I got no idea what goes on back in there. I'm a busy woman and I mind my own business and you should too." She turned to go back inside. Time to raise the stakes, Mimi thought.

"What does the Hallelujah Man mean to you?"

A pause. "The who?" Ethel showed the faintest reaction. She covered it up quickly.

"The Hallelujah Man."

"The only Hallelujah Man I know is Jesus Christ. Every Sunday at the Zion Baptist Church over there on South Lee Street."

"Be that as it may, I'm talking about some guy who calls himself the Hallelujah Man. He may have something to do with Kitty Hawkins' death."

"How should I know? Probably some man coming around them women with liquor and stockings like they do. I don't know nothing. I only rent my shed to Madam Cherry. That's it. Those problems are her problems."

"Let me get this straight, Mrs. Jackson. You take the men's money at the door, you buzz the girls, you send the men around back, you keep the accounts for Madam Cherry, but you disavow all knowledge of what goes on in the four tiny rooms in that concrete building of yours?"

"Wouldn't you?" Ethel inclined her head, ever so slightly impressed. "Besides, you seem to know it all already. You know more than you say."

"As do you. Look, I'm only interested in finding the man who killed Kitty and Hattie and Polly Brown. I don't want anyone else to die."

"What you gonna do if you find this Hallelujah Man?"

"I'll figure that out when I do. Tell me about the money. How does that work?"

Ethel sat down on a rocking chair on her petite porch. She didn't invite Mimi to take the other chair. Mimi leaned against the porch railing. It was late afternoon and a breeze picked up. The sun peeked through rustling leaves. Mimi was patient.

Mrs. Jackson finally cleared her throat.

"I takes the money up front, I press a buzzer, then I don't know what happens. The men might go around the block to the alley and through the gate to the back. Or they might just go away. None of my business."

"And the night Kitty Hawkins died. Who was the last person in her room?"

"I couldn't say. Them young white men all look alike, 'specially in uniform. 'Sides, who's to say one man don't pay for another man, so he's not seen. That happens, 'specially when there's officers partaking in—whatever they be partaking in. Sometimes they tips the ladies. Sometimes they gives 'em chocolates. Stockings. Liquor. Sometimes the ladies tip me. Other than that, it's none of my business."

"That's pretty convenient for you." For not knowing anything, Ethel Jackson knew a lot.

"It's convenient that I own this house and it suits a purpose and earns its keep. I pass no judgments. People rent my shed for their own purposes, and I have a bathroom off the kitchen the ladies can use if they need it."

"You're a regular angel of mercy, Mrs. Jackson."

Ethel Jackson cracked a wide smile for the first time. "That's the way I see it too."

"Did you like Kitty?"

"I like all of them the same. She stuck out because of that hair. She was popular with the menfolk."

"Could one of those men be the Hallelujah Man?"

"Like I told you, I don't know nothing about no Hallelujah Man, excepting Jesus, bless his holy name. That Kitty, she was different. She was neat, clean, never drunk. Going to get married, she said. One of them flyboys. Shame about that." Ethel rocked back and forth in her rocking chair, a troubled expression on her face. "You be careful, Mimi Smith. Don't be asking too many fool questions. I been patient with you, but sometimes not knowing things is safer than knowing them. And what're you going to do if you find this man? He sounds mighty dangerous. And that's all I got to say about that."

"Thanks for your time, Mrs. Jackson." You're not getting any more out of her, Mimi told herself. "If you think of anything important, or merely curious—or if you see the Hallelujah Man—you can get word to me through Gretel or Seraphina."

Ethel Jackson said nothing. She rocked her chair with a steady rhythm as she watched Mimi stride away.

THIRTY-EIGHT

MIMI SLIPPED THE blue satin bow from the letters Kitty had carefully saved. They were written in Nathan's clear handwriting, with evenly spaced lines. At first Mimi had thought they were a lot of romantic mush, but this time as she reread them, aside from his passionate feelings for Kitty, another thing stood out. Nathan's protective instinct for her, particularly when it came to his family.

He was willing to throw them over for Katharine Hawkins, his beautiful mermaid and lady of the evening.

The letters brought back Kitty's story about meeting Nathan. While swimming in Hunting Creek, his brother and friends had left him to drown and Kitty had saved him. At the time, it sounded like hyperbole, a convenient and dramatic way to explain how the couple had found each other. Nathan's brother couldn't actually have meant for him to *die*. Could he? Mimi's own brother was a pain in the neck, and they fought a lot, but he'd never actually tried to kill her.

Did Nathan Albemarle's brother Jubal want him to die?

"Mother praised him for the smallest things," Nathan wrote to Kitty. His mother, feeling sorry for her slower, older son, passed off his schoolboy episodes as boyish pranks, such as the times he would lock Nathan out of the house, or push him into traffic, or steal his bicycle. Or steal his friends' bicycles. It sounded to Mimi as if other boys were afraid of Jubal and did his bidding. Jubal would deliberately break things and blame his brother. He would lie repeatedly. At least according to the letters.

Older than Nathan by a couple years, Jubal still lived at home with his mother, Charlotte Albemarle. He was not in the military and would never be accepted because he had certain psychological issues, Nathan wrote. Nor could Jubal keep a girlfriend.

"He would be pea green with jealousy at my good fortune having a beautiful woman of my own."

There was more. As Nathan put it:

"I guess you could say Jubal helped make me the man I am, a flier in the Army Air Forces. The man my brother will never be. Perhaps he was hit in the head too many times. I don't want to blame him for his meanness, but it was always there. Good things came to me, and not to him. I don't know why I am telling you these things, when all I want to do is to tell you how much I love you, how much I miss you. But you asked about my family, Katharine darling.

"Remember this, sweetheart. Never approach my family without me by your side."

Mimi had questions. What was wrong with Nathan's family? How had Jubal Albemarle been hit in the head? Did he play sports? Did he get into fights?

"Beware the Jubalation," Nathan wrote in more than a few letters. Mimi had assumed it was a spelling error, but what did the Jubalation mean? Nathan and Kitty had their own private language. Perhaps the Jubalation was to be a big party when they met again. Or was it a mocking name for his brother Jubal—the Jubalation?

According to Nathan's letters, his brother had some kind of mental instability, though he didn't put a name to it. Second Lieutenant Shaw told her "the Hallelujah Man" had loads of ego and a few loose screws.

The Jubalation and the self-named Hallelujah Man—one and the same?

The little hairs on the back of her neck stood up and danced the tango. She tried to tell herself this theory must be wrong, this was a huge leap, but the more she tried, the more her heart told her she was onto something.

Jubal = Jubalation = Hallelujah Man = *trouble*.

Heart pounding, Mimi retrieved her notes from her trips to the library. They were sketchy, based on newspaper society articles. She'd seen a photograph of Nathan's mother, Charlotte Albemarle. Lurking in the background was her son Jubal. He was a bear of a man with a sullen expression.

Suddenly parched, Mimi ran downstairs in search of honey tea or lemonade. Addie was in the kitchen putting her Desert Rose dishes away. They matched her rose-patterned dress and her jaunty dangling rose earrings. Richie had already gone to bed, so there was no soothing musical accompaniment to Mimi's troubled thoughts.

Addie took one look at her and pulled two glasses from the cupboard. She retrieved the lemonade from the refrigerator.

"How did you know I was thirsty?"

"It's a warm night. Don't take a genius to see trouble in your face. What you got on your mind, Mimi?"

"Too many things." She sat down at the kitchen table and Addie joined her. "You know Kitty was engaged to a boy named Nathan."

"I seem to remember that. You told me, but you didn't give too many details."

"I didn't have many details. I know a bit more now. His name is Nathan Albemarle."

Addie sat up suddenly, her curls swinging. "Not Charlotte Albemarle's son?"

"Yes. Do you know her?"

"I know the family from way back."

"Forgotten Creek? That far back?" Bells were clanging in Mimi's head.

"Not Forgotten Creek, exactly, but the next town or two over. The Albemarles still have kin back there, but I expect they don't go back much."

"How do you know that?" Mimi lifted the cool glass to her forehead.

"Small town folk love gossip. I get letters from my cousin Sarabelle. Anyway, Charlotte's husband is long dead, she has no love for his family. She came from an even smaller town in West Virginia. Her husband was a banker from a family of bankers, next county over. Lots of folks from West Virginia came to the Washington area during the Great Depression. But those Albemarles, they are not nice people. He especially was not nice."

"How was he not nice?"

"You don't need a gun to kill people when you can just foreclose. Back in the Depression when so many folks lost their homes, the Albemarles made a lot of dirty money and brought it to the big city. And here they are, living in that big house on Mansion Drive." Addie refilled their glasses. "Now you take a good man like my husband, always taking cases from his heart and not his head. He makes a good living, but he gives his clients some leeway, lots of leeway. He treats people right." She sighed with contentment. "That's why Derry Richardson is beloved in this town."

"I've seen Charlotte's picture in the paper, hers and her son Jubal."

"Don't know a thing about her boys. But Charlotte, she likes to polish her image. All busy with her charities."

"I take it Kitty Hawkins would never be acceptable."

"Kitty wasn't the kind of charity she took on. The Albemarles would never marry a Hawkins."

"Are there still Albemarles in West Virginia?"

"Far as I know, the ones with money came to Alexandria. But the Albemarles are also kin to the Frenches. Forgotten Creek is full of Frenches."

"The Frenches?" Like Fat Frenchie? Why did everything circle back to Forgotten Creek? "Would you know if they're involved in moonshine?"

Addie paused to sip her lemonade.

"The Frenches own the hardware store. They're the ones who build the stills. Takes a lot of hardware. So many still jockeys back there. Kept the men working during Prohibition and the Depression. But my family was never any part of that.

Well, except for my Uncle Wilbur. But Wilbur's another story, for another time."

Mimi finished her lemonade and went to bed.

ભ

Early the next morning, a police car was parked outside the Richardsons' house. Lt. Samson Baker was behind the wheel. He honked at Mimi. She stopped and stared at him.

"Need a lift, Miss Smith?" he asked.

Her first instinct was to say no. But she opened the passenger door and got in. She was glad she looked prim and proper that morning, crisply turned out in her blue-and-white striped dress with white collar and cuffs. She had replaced the ribbon around her straw hat with one that matched the dress. Whatever Baker wanted, she thought, at least she looked perfectly innocent.

"You work for OPA?" he asked, without any small talk.

"I do."

"And you're a stenographer?" Baker squinted at her. "Really?"

"I am." What on earth is he getting at?

"Sure you are. Hell. I suppose you can't really tell me what's going on." He pushed his straw fedora back on his forehead. "But you can't fool me, Miss Smith, I know you've got more on the ball than that. You're investigating that hooker's murder."

"You can ask my boss, George Prescott."

"Yeah, and I'm sure he'll tell me the same thing. Stenographer." He snorted.

"That's correct." What was going on? You tell the truth and no one believes you. You tell a lie and everyone does.

"I gather you think the sugar theft and these other things are related to all these prostitute killings."

"Seems more and more obvious."

"You might be onto something at that. But just one thing, Miss Smith—if that's your real name—if you finger this killer, you'll need help bringing him in. And we need each other. I mean, how would it look to have this happening in my backyard and me caught twiddling my thumbs, while a little filly from OPA goes in and takes down the killer?"

"How would it look?" That wasn't exactly how Mimi had pictured it.

"Bad. It would look bad. I want to retire one day, Mimi Smith. And three murders—if Polly Brown was murdered and didn't jump in front of that damn train—three are a lot of murders for Alexandria, Virginia. More than a whole year's worth, back in the good old days."

"That's a lot of murders," she agreed. If he thought Smith was an alias, what would he think if she had kept the family name of *Smithsonian?*

Baker scratched his chin. "The way I see it, there's no reason we can't both share in the glory of bringing down a big bad black marketeer and murderer, is there?"

"Not at all, Lieutenant. I just want this guy off the streets." And I want a lot more than that, she admitted to herself.

"That's what we all want, Miss Smith. Alexandria is supposed to be a nice quiet little town. Like you, I want to nail this monster."

She stared at him and paused before speaking. "What if the monster is a big—and I mean potentially a really big—big shot, with a fancy name and an important local family?"

Baker considered the possibilities. "That what you think? Some Alexandria bigwig? That's a mite tricky. Better if he was some nameless scumbag. I've been here a long time and I know how things work. Is that why the feds sent you in? He's too hot to handle?"

"You know I can't answer that." Mimi wondered if her lack of sleep was making her invent this entire conversation.

"Course you can't. But I can't let the feds take all the credit. Matter of personal honor. We bring him down together—you and me—and the city will celebrate. Just tell me one thing, so I'm prepared. It's not the mayor, is it?"

The mayor? Mimi hid her surprise. "I'm still confirming a few things. I have to be very sure where I'm going. However, the mayor is not in my sights."

He exhaled in relief. "Whew. That's something." He drummed his fingers on the steering wheel, lost in thought.

"What about the Chicken Shack? Will you keep it shut down? All three women worked there."

"I'd like to say it was history. It's not really your high-class breed of cat house, is it? Just a pink eyesore on that alley." He took off his hat and ran his fingers though his hair. He started the car. "The way the powers-that-be look at things, the Shack's not going away, even if we close it down temporarily. We got too many randy, frustrated, and scared servicemen flooding this city."

"Do you believe it performs a public service," she asked, "like the ladies say?"

"The mayor certainly thinks so. I'm not debating the point. But it is, after all, the world's oldest profession."

"I have to catch my bus." Mimi opened her door. "One more thing, Lieutenant Baker. Is this a two-way street, information-sharing-wise?"

"Put it this way, kid. I got nothing, and it feels to me like you're closer to—something." She stepped out of the car and shut the door. He leaned his head out the window. "Stay safe, Mimi Smith. Stenographer." He chuckled.

"I'll try."

He hadn't actually answered her question. On the other hand, he clearly thought she was smarter and more important than she really was—and she had figured everything out. That was something, she thought.

If only it were true.

ભ

Mimi could tell before Seraphina even spoke. The news was bad. She didn't know if she could face more bad news.

The woman was waiting at Mimi's bus stop to meet her after work. She said she'd already waited through two buses. Seraphina's clothes were limp and wrinkled, and her face was damp. She mopped it with a hankie. Mimi had never seen the woman less than composed before. Mimi's own cotton dress had also lost its starch in the humidity.

"What is it?" she asked. "Just tell me."

"He's dead," Seraphina blurted out. She threw her arms around Mimi and sobbed.

"Who's dead?"

"Kitty's fellow."

"Oh my God. You're sure?"

Seraphina wiped her eyes and nodded. "You don't have to tell him about her now. I know that was heavy on your heart. But it still feels terrible. And I didn't even know him, except what I heard about him, from her. He sounded pretty swell. Had to be, to marry one of us."

"Nathan Albemarle? He's dead?" Mimi felt as if a sharp wind blew through her, spinning her thoughts around. It was a hot burning feeling. She wanted to sink to the ground and weep.

"It's him. We got word today. One of his buddies came round to the Chicken Shack asking for Kitty. He was miserable. He cried. I can't take it when soldiers cry."

"How? When did it happen?" There was too much death all around her, all around everyone.

"Same day Kitty died, I guess. Weird, huh? His plane was shot down."

Despite all that praise in *Esquire* magazine, Nathan's B-24 Liberator bomber hadn't come home safely. It could fly at 300 miles an hour, but it couldn't outrun its fate. His plane had already been shot full of holes once, according to his letters to Kitty.

"The same day? Does his family know yet?"

Seraphina shrugged. "I don't run in their circles. But the military lets you know pretty quick. They'll be getting their gold star for the front window."

"That may be true, but they may not be the kind to put their grief on display in the window."

"Maybe not. I guess that would make them seem too much like everybody else," she agreed. "Damn, I hate this war."

"Me too," Mimi said. "I hate it too."

THIRTY-NINE

*T*HE SMITH CORONA typewriter held pride of place in Derry Richardson's library, though he rarely used it. He was happy to let Mimi take over whenever she wanted. She was also welcome to his typing and carbon paper, after he had given her a short (and unnecessary) lesson on his treasured typing machine.

Supper was salad and scalloped potatoes and a bit of ham, but no one ate much. It had been a hot and tiring day. Outside in the garden, Richie was playing Schubert's "Ave Maria." Practicing for church, he said, though he really needed no extra practice. Addie announced she would join them in the library after cleaning up, if Derry and Mimi needed her company. Or even if they didn't.

Mimi clutched Kitty's stash of Nathan's letters. Having an exact record of all of them would be a good thing, she decided, to supplement her memories of her conversations with Kitty, and to support her suspicions of the Albemarle family.

"I won't take long. There are only about two dozen letters. And I'm a pretty fast typist."

"What letters?" Derry asked.

"Kitty's letters from Nathan Albemarle. I don't know who they belong to. Now that she's dead." She paused, feeling weighed down. "And so is he."

"Yes, it's sad and ironic that they're both gone so suddenly. The ownership of those letters could be debated," he said, "although you have possession of them with Kitty's implied permission. I rule in your favor. What's on your mind, Mimi? Surely you don't need a lawyer?"

She sat down in the chair next to Derry's desk.

"I hope not. Not in an official way. These letters may have clues. That's why I want to copy them, so I'll have a record."

"What kind of clues, Mimi?"

"What would you say if I found a suspect in the deaths of all three women?"

Derry stroked his chin. Mimi imagined that was his courtroom gesture, when he was summing up his argument. Addie bustled into the room, saw his chin-stroking, and sat down on the sofa.

"I see that, Derry Richardson. What are you thinking?"

He smiled at his wife and patted her on the shoulder. "Mimi says she has clues about the killer of the magdalens. And to Mimi, I say, are you sure?"

"There's one way to find out. First, the letters."

"Would we all care for some tea?" Addie asked. Mimi was about to say yes when Derry interrupted.

"This business may call for a spot of brandy, my dear."

"It's those wretched Albemarles, isn't it? I knew it." Addie retrieved the liquor and three crystal snifters. "Time for a postprandial brandy. Good for the digestion."

"And for carefully considering the facts," Derry said.

Mimi started to type. She let Derry read each letter as she finished typing a copy, and she answered his questions. He passed them to Addie to read them, but he cautioned her not to reveal their contents or any of Mimi's suspicions to anyone else outside their little circle. Except Joe Jordan.

"Heed the letters, Mimi," Derry cautioned after reading the last letter and handing them back to her. "Beware the Jubalation, he said. Young Nathan must have had good reason for that warning."

Richie's fiddle changed its tune, announcing a visitor at the front door. The violin and Richie escorted Joe to the library. Joe looked beat, but happy to see Mimi. Richie tried to sneak back outside, but Addie announced that it was his bedtime.

"I never have any fun," Richie complained.

"Sure you do." Mimi gave him a hug. "You have lots of fun."

"But I like Joe and I want to stay up."

"I like you too, kid, but we'll have other times," Joe said.

"Promise?"

"Absolutely."

Richie bowed to Mimi and his mother. He played himself off with his violin.

Joe had driven straight to the Richardsons' house from Forgotten Creek without stopping to eat. Luckily, Addie was ready for guests anytime. She made him a sandwich with generous slices of her prized Virginia ham.

Joe joined the party just as Mimi finished typing, and Derry and Addie finished reading. Mimi solemnly handed Joe the stack to read. She filled him in briefly on Seraphina's bad news: Nathan Albemarle was dead. Everyone waited in silence for Joe to finish reading. And eating.

"My sacred God. Course I've heard of the Albemarles," Joe said, putting the letters aside, "but I wasn't aware these folks were related to Frenchie and his people. That nails down the connection from here to there. As far as I can see, that multiplies the chances they are into every kind of crime. Hell. I hate thinking of Kitty getting caught up in their schemes."

"But how do you figure on finding out for sure?" Derry asked.

"By giving the letters back to his mother," Mimi replied. To their looks of shock, she added. "Not all of them, just a few. That's why I need the copies, to make my case."

"And why would you give them to Charlotte?" Addie was curious. "To taunt her?"

"To gauge her reaction. And Jubal's, if he's there. He knows what happened to the women. I'm sure he does."

"I'm going with you," Joe said.

"As am I," Derry said.

"It's good to have a team." Mimi smiled. A team that wouldn't have to depend on Madam Cherry and her underworld connections. Mimi knew she would never have called on that mysterious madam, whose loyalties and motives were so suspect. "Maybe you could wait in the wings, but I'll have to face this dragon alone."

Joe shook his head. "Not alone. I don't have a good feeling about this."

"I have to agree with Joe," Derry said. "I believe we should face the dragon in a united front."

"Include me in that assessment," Addie said. "There are too many broken families in the wake of the Albemarles. Too many victims. We don't want any more."

Mimi was outnumbered. Bless you all, she thought to herself.

"Okay. First I have to make a couple of phone calls. The Albemarles, for one. My *partner*, Lieutenant Baker, for another. He thinks I'm an OPA investigator. I may as well act like one."

"And so shall I make a call," Derry said. "I believe our good Evangeline is a friend of the Albemarles' housekeeper, Esmeralda."

ଔ

Later Joe and Mimi strolled outside, into the garden. Derry and Addie stayed discretely in the library.

"I don't know, Mimi, there were a lot of tears," Joe said. "Lucy and Netty both. They said they were happy tears, but those aren't the kind of tears I'm used to."

They sat under Addie's rose-covered arbor. The scent was intoxicating on this warm night. The sun had fallen in the West and the fireflies had begun their courting rituals.

"Joe, when a woman tells you she's crying happy tears, you should believe her."

"I figured you'd say that. I'm sorry I didn't have time to shave." He rubbed his jaw, covered in a dark shadow.

"You look fine to me, although you need a good night's sleep." She settled into the crook of his arm. It was an amazingly comfortable place. They sipped on one of Addie's celebrated chilled concoctions, with a touch of brandy and honey. "I take it Lucy liked the clothes?"

"Liked them? I thought she was going to faint. Or fly around the room like a bluebird."

Mimi didn't know why it was so important to her that Lucy approved. That the clothes that Kitty had so lovingly selected would be appreciated and cared for and not set aside for fear they were too good, too fancy, too sinful. Life was made for living and clothes were made for wearing. And for bringing the wearer joy.

"Tell me, Joe," Mimi said. "Paint me a picture."

He pulled her in closer. "She loved the clothes. I was thinking at first to just drop them off and run, but you saw how they are. It wouldn't do but I had to set a spell, have a cup of that coffee you brought them. I went and got the two suitcases out of the truck, and I let Lucy open them. She just gasped. Burst into tears. She couldn't even talk at first. I thought she was having some kind of fit. Even Netty was at a loss for words."

"That must have been something."

"Maybe you shouldn't have given her so much, what with the nightgown and nylons and all. All those pretty things came out of that little suitcase, the comb and the matching mirror and hairbrush. And all the clothes that just kept coming out of the big one. And the shoes! And the hat! The Hawkinses aren't used to all that. I'm not used to it."

"They may be the last nice things Lucy Hawkins gets for the next twenty years. I hope not. But at least she'll have that much."

"I was trapped there, drinking their coffee. And Netty was just as interested in that suitcase as Lucy. Everyone in the family had to gather round and watch, like it was some kind of magic trick."

"Did Netty make any snide comments about the wages of sin?"

"Not even one." He gestured with his glass. "Lucy ran off with the clothes and I thought I was home free. But then, don't you know, it was a Forgotten Creek fashion show. 'You got to see this, Joe, so you can tell Mimi. She'll want to know how much I love everything.' Then the tears started again. Good Lord."

"She's right. I do want to know." Mimi giggled at his embarrassment. "What did she look like in them?"

"That dark blue dress, suit, whatever it is, it's like nothing anyone in Forgotten Creek has ever seen. Lucy looked so grown up. Everything fit her real well."

"And the light blue?"

"The blue wedding gown? That's what they're calling it. Netty's already saying it will suit the younger ones when they're of an age, and Lucy allowed that her mother could wear the dark blue dress for the wedding, and I thought Netty would faint dead away. Netty, she says no, but then she takes the dress and puts it in front of her and looks in the mirror the way women do. So you know it's a done deal. Then Lucy runs out of the room and comes back in the wedding dress and that veiled hat thing, and the tall white shoes."

"Ah yes, the cream-colored dancing shoes," Mimi corrected him.

"I'd say she floated in, but Lucy, she was a bit tottery on those things. She promised to practice in them before she walks down the aisle."

"Was it *pretty*, Joe?"

He touched Mimi's face and gently kissed her on the forehead.

"Do you have to ask? It was like a movie. I never imagined Kitty's skinny kid sister would grow up to be a looker. Not like Kitty, and quieter like, but she'll hold her own. She was beautiful, Mimi." He paused. Another thought crossed his face.

"What is it? What do you want to say?" Mimi prodded. "Joe?"

He took a while before answering.

"Maybe it was a trick of the light, the way it streamed into the room, but for a moment, just a moment, I thought I saw

Kitty standing there, glowing in that light. Her pale hair, her face, her grin. Maybe it was just exhaustion, but I felt her there in that room. She was laughing, the way she used to when she pulled a prank on her mama. Like, isn't this a real good joke, Joe, that a Hawkins woman is going to walk down the aisle in the fanciest clothes ever seen in Forgotten Creek, West Virginia? Kitty knows her mama would never approve of that kind of extravagance—except for her daughters' sakes. I could almost hear Kitty saying, isn't this funny, Joe?"

"If Kitty chose to come back for a visit, I'm glad it was then and there."

"I must have been imagining things."

"I don't care. I'm glad you were there to see it. I was afraid maybe Kitty wouldn't want me to give her entire trousseau away."

"And this is the real crazy part. I felt a squeeze on my shoulder and then she was gone. And then it was just Lucy again, happier than I've ever seen her." He took another sip. "You did the right thing, Mimi. I'm sorry you couldn't have seen their reactions. You would have appreciated it more than me."

"No, this is lovely. I like hearing you tell it. You know how much I needed to hear that. How is Netty Hawkins doing?"

"She carries her grief in her heart. I don't think she understands why being so righteous and unbending hurts her so much. Hey, I almost forgot." He fished a small, folded piece of paper out of his pocket. "It's a little note, from Lucy to you. She didn't have an envelope."

Mimi opened the paper. The writing was large and round.

Dear Mimi,

There are not enough words, and I'm not good enough with them, to tell you how grateful I am for the amazing and beautiful and glorious blue wedding gown and the other clothes and shoes and things you sent me. Never in a million years could I imagine this bounty. That's what Ma calls it, a bounty. They make me so happy, and they make me so sad to know that Kitty won't be getting married

*and wearing them. I hope she knows what's in my heart because we
are all speechless. I hope she forgives me for accepting them.*
Thank you from the bottom of my soul,
Lucy Hawkins
P.S. I will send you a picture from the wedding. I promise.

"Well. She is her mother's daughter. And Kitty's sister."
Mimi sniffled. "Did you say goodbye to your family?"

"The waterworks! More tears. I was drenched in tears. I am
soaked in tears. I'm glad I'm heading to the Navy, where the
ocean will wash it all away. And my mother was highly put out
that she didn't get to meet the famous Mary Margaret Smith."

"I'm hardly famous."

"You are famous in Forgotten Creek. You gave these folks
gossip for months, Mimi. Years. I told her I'd send her a picture
of you. I can send one of us together, the one Derry took.
That'll keep the tale-telling crows going."

"Would you kiss me, Joe?"

"Thought you'd never ask."

He held her for a long time, and Mimi realized that this was
one of those small perfect moments that she needed to savor
for as long as possible. She couldn't decide what was more
intoxicating, the scent of the roses—or Joe.

ભ

"I need the day off tomorrow, George." It was early Thursday
morning.

"Friday? You want Friday off? You know how much work
we have on Fridays. And you've been taking a lot of time off."

"It's important, George."

"OPA important?"

"Yes. Important to OPA. And to me."

"If you think you got a line on investigating serious
violations, I need you to turn it over to someone else. An
investigator."

She thought Prescott might say something like this. She had rehearsed her responses before heading into his office.

"As it turns out, I am the only person who can do this. The only person who can connect the dots." Along with some help from a couple of other people, she thought.

George put on his fiercest courtroom scowl. "I am betting this has nothing to do with taking dictation and typing."

"Afterward there will be more than enough typing."

"You are on very thin ice, Mary Margaret Smith. Are you willing to stake your job on this request?"

Mimi was silent for a moment, weighing whether she could find another job at a government agency if she was fired. If she had a poor recommendation? If George Prescott called her a maverick or a troublemaker? Her skills were top notch, but her Achilles' heel was that she would never blindly follow orders, if she believed in her heart they were wrong.

She decided she could get another job. Somehow, some way. And "on thin ice" is just the way I skate, she told herself. She took a deep breath.

"I am willing to do that. I will bet my job on this."

George nearly dropped his pipe. "Well then. Take your day off. But keep me in the loop." He clamped his teeth down on his pipe and poked through his pockets for his matches. "And Monday morning, you bring me that illegal jug of hootch that you bought."

"The moonshine? I haven't even sampled it yet."

"And you're not going to! It's evidence, isn't it?" He spoke through gritted teeth, the pipe bouncing up and down. "I assume we'll be needing some kind of evidence."

"Yes, George, it is evidence." Under her breath, she muttered. "Spoilsport."

"I heard that."

Mimi fled his office.

FORTY

*T*HE ALBEMARLE HOME had been constructed not ten years before, but it looked as if it had been there for decades. Large and imposing, it was a handsome red brick mansion built in the Colonial Revival style with a black roof and shutters. The remaining trim was crisp and white. It had been built to impress, with its white two-story pillars flanking the front door and defining the semi-circular porch.

Mimi's Grandma Eileen would say these were the wages of sin.

Mimi trudged up the vast expanse of emerald lawn that separated the house from the road. The sky was bright and the humidity gone, as if in a perverse response to her mission. At the very least, she thought there should be claps of thunder and flashes of lightning, not this rare gloriously blue and verdant day.

There was no gold star in the window. Perhaps she had been right about this family not wanting to mourn in public. A housekeeper in a black-and-white uniform opened the front door, eyed Mimi with interest, and let her inside the polished entryway. The house was a standard center-hall colonial, the living room to one side, the dining room on the other, with the kitchen and butler's pantry behind it. Mimi looked around for possible escape routes.

"Esmeralda?"

"That'd be me, miss." She smiled and gestured into the house. "Just to your left in the living room. Miss Charlotte's waiting for you in there."

Mimi thought her look for the day was as demure as possible. The perfect goody-goody, Kitty might say. Her wavy auburn hair was pinned behind her ears with tortoise shell barrettes. Her deep copper-colored summer suit in a polished cotton was topped with a crisp white collar, and the copper blended with her hair.

For luck she wore the lovely cardinal broach that Kitty had left her. She even donned a pair of prim white cotton gloves. Her straw hat sported a shiny ribbon that matched her suit. Inside her straw purse she had tucked a small selection of Nathan's letters, retied with the blue satin ribbon.

As she stepped lightly across the immense blue-and-cream Aubusson rug, Mimi caught her first view of Charlotte Albemarle. The grieving mother sat like a queen on a sturdy Chippendale chair whose classic claw-and-ball feet peeked out behind Charlotte's polished black shoes.

Mrs. Albemarle was a heavy-set woman who sat at repose, yet her thick beringed hands clutched the chair's arms, ready to spring up quickly. Her black rayon dress with its ruffled white collar and cuffs was appropriate to a woman in mourning, but did nothing to soften her strong-featured face, with its jowly square jaw and small gray eyes. Her mouse-brown hair was flecked with silver and piled on top of her head, with a complicated mound of curls spilling over her forehead. She waved Mimi to a seat on the blue brocade davenport across from her.

She reminded Mimi of a bulldog ready to bite.

Charlotte sat behind a handsome leather inlaid coffee table, set with china cups and saucers and linen napkins. Esmeralda arrived carrying a silver tray with an ornate teapot, creamer, sugar bowl, and a plate of iced sugar cookies.

"That will be all, Esmeralda," she said to the housekeeper. "I'm Charlotte Albemarle," she boomed at Mimi. Her deep voice had broad southern strains.

"Mimi Smith. I regret we had to meet under such sad circumstances."

"Can't be helped, I suppose. Terrible times." She never took her eyes off Mimi, who gazed around the room seeking the absent Jubal Albemarle. What if he didn't show up? On the phone she'd told this woman she had Nathan's letters—wouldn't he want to be there?

"I am sorry for your loss, Mrs. Albemarle."

"Thank you. I find it hard to breathe at times, since I heard the news. Funny, I never thought I would lose my son Nathan. If his plane was shot down, I thought he would parachute to safety. He was my shining star."

Not the way I heard it, Mimi thought. "My—my fiancé died when his parachute failed to open." She didn't expect to reveal that, but it popped out.

"You understand then. War. Call me Charlotte."

Her hostess poured fragrant Earl Grey tea into two cups. Wondering where Charlotte Albemarle had gotten her hands on that hard-to-find brew, Mimi blew on hers and waited to take a sip. She wasn't really afraid of being poisoned or drugged, but better safe than sorry. *You've been reading too many Agatha Christies, Mimi.* Charlotte slurped her Earl Grey. Mimi took that as her cue to sip as well.

"This is delicious. I haven't had real tea in ever so long."

"Yes, times are hard. This tea was a gift. I've saved it for a long time. It was Nathan's favorite."

"I understand you have another son," Mimi said.

"Yes, my Jubal. He is such a comfort to me, especially now." She indicated one of the photos displayed on a baby grand piano. Mimi craned her neck to look at it.

"He takes after you."

Charlotte smiled in acknowledgment. "That's what people say. Poor Jubal is devastated by the loss of his brother."

There was a subtle change in the atmosphere, bringing with it an ill wind. Jubal Albemarle must have heard his name, because at that moment he stepped into the room.

Mimi stared up at him and couldn't look away. She knew he was big, but he was outsized, larger than she expected, at least six feet four. He shared the same bulldog features as his mother. Jubal was big and beefy with brown hair and dull brown eyes, but he didn't look athletic. His nose had been broken and sat crookedly on his face. There was none of the charm Mimi saw in the pictures of his brother. He wasn't smiling.

"Ah, Jubal, this is Mimi Smith. The woman with Nathan's letters."

"Nice to meet you." He said the polite phrase, but his eyes leered at her. "Aren't you a pretty one."

Moving slowly and deliberately, Nathan's older brother Jubal had the slow-witted affect of a football player kicked too many times in the head, or a fighter too long in the ring. He sat down near his mother in the matching Chippendale chair and cocked his head at Mimi, as if he were hard of hearing and trying to catch every word. He picked up one of the china cups. In his big hands it looked like a doll's teacup.

Mimi noted the position of the coffee table, between her and Jubal and his mother. The three formed a triangle around it, each close enough to touch the polished tea service. The hall was to her right, and to her left, a door to the side yard. She felt like bolting out the door, but she stayed put.

"It must be terribly difficult to lose a brother."

"Yeah. Difficult," Jubal agreed.

"Miss Smith, when you called you mentioned some letters from my son."

"Yes. Letters he wrote to Katharine Hawkins."

Charlotte Albemarle flinched ever so slightly at the name. "How did you know this Kitty Hawkins?"

She already knew about her, Mimi thought. She called her *Kitty.*

"We were friends from church. St. Mary's."

"Oh. Of course. Down on Royal Street. That Catholic church." Charlotte said it with a slight note of derision, as if it were obvious that the Catholics would let just anyone in. "I don't understand. How did you come by my son's letters?"

Mimi paused. "There is no easy way to say this. Katharine is dead. It was left to me to take care of her personal effects."

"I see." Charlotte didn't seem surprised that her son's fiancée was dead. She certainly wasn't upset by the news.

"Because of the nature of the letters, I thought you might want them back. Especially because Nathan and Kitty were engaged."

"Engaged!" There was a swift and sudden change in Charlotte's demeanor. "They were not engaged. I would know if they were. You must be misinformed."

"I'm sorry, I thought you knew." Mimi figured she'd press the point and see what happened. "The letters prove—"

"Kitty Hawkins was a cheap little hillbilly," Jubal rumbled. "Poor white trash. No one cares about a tramp like her." He shoved a cookie in his mouth whole.

"Jubal, control yourself," his mother cautioned, and he glared at their guest. She turned to Mimi. "I'm sorry, Miss Smith. You may not have known about her, seeing as how you met her in *church*. But Kitty was in an unfortunate profession. A lady of the evening, as they say. You must understand, my son Nathan would never marry a woman like that. He was an Albemarle. I can hardly account for her knowing him at all. In fact, I'm not at all sure that any letters you may have were actually written by my son. They must be forgeries."

"He and Kitty met in a near-drowning incident. She had been a lifeguard and she fished him out of Hunting Creek. She saved his life, after Jubal and his friends left him."

"I don't believe that at all."

"Jubal was fond of tormenting his brother, wasn't he?" Mimi caught Jubal smirking at the memory. "According to Nathan's letters."

Charlotte reached for her tea and sipped it as casually as if they were discussing a Sunday social. "I am heartbroken over my son Nathan's death, but I cannot waste any sympathy on this horrid creature who sold her body to strangers."

"Cheap whore." Jubal narrowed his dull eyes. "No whore was going to marry into our family. You gotta protect your family."

"You knew she was going to marry Nathan. You knew all about her." Mimi looked from one to the other.

"She deserved what she got. The whore."

"What she got?" Mimi repeated. She felt sick. "Then you know she was brutally murdered?"

Mimi heard a door open quietly.

"Please do not interrupt us, Esmeralda," Charlotte said, without turning to look. "We are having a private conversation in here. You have silver to polish in the kitchen." She focused back on Mimi. "A regrettable death, I'm sure."

Jubal continued staring at Mimi. "One little death."

"Not just one," Mimi said. Jubal laughed. "Someone is murdering ladies of the evening, as you put it. Katharine wasn't the first. And it seems to be involved with the black market here in Alexandria."

"I wouldn't know anything about the black market." Charlotte drummed her fingers on her teacup. "We are patriotic Americans here. I resent the implication. Where are those letters?"

"Here in my purse." Mimi thought she heard a slight movement in the front hall. She pulled out the letters and suddenly realized she didn't want these people to have them, not any of them. They belonged to Kitty and Nathan. Turning them over seemed like a sacrilege. Charlotte put out one large hand and snapped her fingers.

"Give them here." Mimi hesitated. The woman grabbed them out of her hands.

"Careful, you'll tear them!"

"Are these all of them?"

"All that I have here."

"Who else knows about these?" Charlotte demanded.

"I don't know if Kitty told anyone else. But you know how women are. We like to share our good news, especially now, when letters from loved ones are so precious."

"He was not her loved one."

"His letters say he was."

Charlotte Albemarle's face had gone pale beneath her ruddy complexion. "You read the letters? Nathan's personal letters? That's an invasion of our family's privacy." She shook the letters in Mimi's face.

"You just told me they were forgeries. Besides, both Kitty and Nathan were dead before I read a word of them. I had to know who to return them to. But maybe I made the wrong decision." Mimi tried to sound nonchalant. "Nathan mentions the many times you preferred Jubal to him, about all the terrible things Jubal did to him growing up, like leaving him to drown that hot summer day."

"Not so terrible," Jubal drawled. "He made it out alive."

"I don't believe a word you say," Charlotte jumped in. "And for the record, Jubal loved his brother."

"My brother," Jubal sneered. "Mr. Perfect. Now he's Mr. Dead."

"They aren't my words, they're Nathan's," Mimi said. "He didn't trust either of you. That's clear from his letters."

"Well, Missy, no one else is ever going to read these letters. I don't believe they even are from Nathan. I will deny they are his. No one will even know they ever existed."

She ripped the stack of letters in half.

"People will believe this."

Mimi pulled a five-by-seven photograph from her bag, one of the black-and-white engagement shots of Kitty and Nathan. There was nothing cheap-looking about Kitty, nothing that would give away her profession. Their arms were around each other. In love. Smiles so wide it hurt. Mimi held it up for Charlotte to see, just out of reach. Charlotte's eyes bulged as she grabbed for the photo. Mimi jumped out of her chair and raised the photo high.

"This is all lies," Charlotte cried. "How dare you disrupt my home with your filthy lies?"

"All lies?" Mimi asked. "Then what should I do with Kitty's diamond ring? Is Nathan's ring a lie too?"

"What ring?" Charlotte looked around wildly. "Jubal?"

"There was no ring, Mother," Jubal whined. "I didn't see no ring."

Mimi waved the photograph. "Nathan gave Katharine Hawkins a lovely diamond engagement ring."

"He did not give her any ring." Charlotte's eyes were slits of anger, her skin red and mottled with rage. "Another dirty lie."

Jubal rose from his chair. "We don't like liars, do we, Mother?"

"It's the truth, I've seen it, and the ring is in a safe place." It was locked in her steamer trunk. Mimi slipped the photo in her purse and backed away. "Nathan's letters tell Kitty to beware the Jubalation. That's you, isn't it, Jubal Albemarle?"

A low guttural sound emanated from the big man's throat, a growl that turned into a laugh. It made the hair on Mimi's neck do that tango-of-chills thing again.

"Nathan thought he was so smart," Jubal complained. "And then he goes and falls for that cheap little Kitty Hawkins, nothing but a low-down dirty whore."

"*You* are the Jubalation, aren't you, Jubal?" Mimi said. "You are the Hallelujah Man."

FORTY-ONE

JUBAL LAUGHED AGAIN, a guttural laugh like a growl. "That's me. They all say Hallelujah when they see me coming. I bring them what they want."

"Dirty goods for dirty money. Black market and murder." Mimi felt her blood rise. "Let me guess, you steal tires and sugar and anything you can get your greedy bloated fingers on. You take goods out of state to places like Forgotten Creek, West Virginia. That's where you pick up moonshine masquerading as fine bourbon, to bring it back to Alexandria. Is Fat Frenchie your shine connection?"

"Don't answer that, Jubal," Charlotte barked at him.

But Jubal seemed to be in the mood to take credit for his work.

"Fat Frenchie is my cousin. Kin take care of kin. Frenchie's shine is as good as any bourbon I ever had."

"No one would believe your ravings, Miss Smith," Charlotte said. "The Albemarle family is one of the most respected in Virginia."

"Among bootleggers and thieves," Mimi shouted. "That's why you made sure Kitty died. She knew what was going on. She was a threat."

"You're talking crazy, little Miss Mimi Smith. Someone should put you in the crazy house."

Charlotte gripped her chair with white knuckles.

"There's more." Mimi stared at Jubal. "The killer left something behind. He might not even know it. Katharine fought back with everything she had, and she tore a white button off his blue shirt. Her blood is probably on that shirt. The shirt with a missing button."

Jubal dropped his head and looked down at his bulk.

He even touched the buttons on the shirt he was wearing, looking for a missing button. *Bingo.*

"Don't worry, the button is safe too," Mimi said. "The police have it and they know all about it. Where's the bloody shirt, Jubal? Maybe you put it in the rag bag? Maybe you kept it, for sentimental reasons?"

"Shut up," Jubal pleaded, his growl turning into a whine. "Shut up. Shut up."

"Jubal? You left something behind?" Charlotte asked. "I warned you never to do that, son."

"It's not true." He lifted his head and sent a pleading look to his mother. He pulled a long piece of material from his pocket. "She's lying."

Now Mimi knew what Kitty must have seen the last night of her life. This lumbering wreck of a man twisting and turning a black silk scarf, as he was doing now. But Jubal hadn't made a move toward her. She realized he was waiting for his mother's command. How long could he wait? How much more did Charlotte want to know before she set loose her shambling killing machine?

"With Nathan gone, Charlotte, your vaunted name will go no further," Mimi said.

"My son Jubal will marry an honorable woman and carry on the family line," Charlotte bellowed. She tried to lever herself heavily to her feet.

"But he's not the best and the brightest, is he? What kind of feeble-minded monster could Jubal Albemarle possibly produce? The Army wouldn't even take him. Isn't that right?"

"I got me a deferment," the big man growled again, sending chills through her. "I ain't gonna die in a plane, like my fool brother."

"He's not a very bright killer, is he, Charlotte?"

"He can take care of a foul-mouthed hussy like you!"

Charlotte finally stood, looming nearly as huge as her son. Mimi backed away a step.

"Is that how you take care of business, Charlotte? You order your weak-minded son to murder your enemies with a silk scarf, or throw them on the train tracks?"

"I fix Mother's problems," Jubal said. "Kitty Hawkins was a problem. Pretty little problem. Too pretty for Nathan." He took a step forward.

"The police know where I am, you know."

"Another lie," Charlotte sneered. "Why would anyone pay any attention to a little nobody like you?"

"I work for the government, the Office of Price Administration. I investigate black market crimes."

Jubal's beady eyes rolled from his mother to Mimi. Charlotte nodded to him. "Do it, Jubal. This time, make sure no one knows. No mistakes. No torn buttons."

Nathan's big brother lumbered toward Mimi. She grabbed the heavy silver teapot and dumped the rest of the tea service onto the floor. Earl Grey spilled across the beautiful Aubusson.

"My rug! You've ruined my rug, my priceless rug," Charlotte screamed. Jubal advanced on Mimi slowly, still twisting the scarf.

"Can I do it now, Mother?"

"Yes, take care of her now, Jubal, like you did that greedy little whore, and the others, all of them, greedy whores!"

"Hattie was the most fun, Mama, she put up the most fight."

He lunged for Mimi, banging into the coffee table. She jumped out of the way, the silver teapot still in her hands. She lifted it high and pitched it at his head. Jubal staggered back, wiping at his eyes, blood and hot tea streaming down his face.

"Make her stop, Mama! That hurt," he roared. "You're going to die like the others. Polly, Hattie, Kitty. All them whores. Mother said to kill all the whores, and I did and I'll kill you too!"

"The police will be here any second."

And where the hell are they, anyway?

The big man reached for Mimi across the coffee table, grabbing her arm and dragging her toward him.

Where is Baker? Where's Joe? She kicked the table hard into Jubal's shins. He howled and dug his fingers into her flesh.

"Joe, I need you! Joe—"

Before Mimi could finish Joe Jordan was in the room, leaping on top of Jubal and tearing him away from her. Joe threw him down on the floor and pounded fist after fist into Jubal's face.

"Not so tough now, are you, big guy?" Joe landed another punch. "You're only a tough guy with women? That's the way it is?"

Charlotte bellowed for Esmeralda. She was surprised when the first person through the door was Lt. Sam Baker, gun drawn, followed by half a dozen police officers, including Officers Gregson and Warwick.

"Police? Why are there police here?" Charlotte shrieked. "What are you doing here? You can't be in here!"

"That's enough, Jordan," Baker ordered. "Leave enough of him for me to arrest."

Joe wasn't finished. The two men rolled on the floor, fists flying, mostly Joe's. Antique vases crashed against expensive furniture.

"You slimy toad!" Joe shouted. "You thing from Hell! Kitty Hawkins was my first girl, my first love, and no matter what she did in this life, no matter what she became, she didn't deserve to meet her end by a pathetic pig like you." He punched him again. "This is for Kitty." Another. "And this is for Mimi."

"Mama!" Jubal cried out. "Mama, make him stop! He's hurting me!"

Charlotte screamed, "Stop him, he's hurting my boy." She threw a slap at Baker. He ducked.

"Breaking my heart, Mrs. Albemarle," Baker said.

He nodded to Officer Gregson, who moved to restrain her.

"Get your filthy hands off me!" Charlotte Albemarle slapped the officer.

"Cuff her, Gregson," Baker ordered. "We'll add it to her charges. Assaulting a police officer. Going to be quite a long list."

The other uniformed officers broke Joe and Jubal apart. It took three of them to handcuff Jubal, while Joe dusted himself off. Mimi helped him to his feet. She touched his face. There was blood on his lip.

"You're bleeding." She pulled a hankie from her pocket. "Joe, Joe, are you all right?" Mimi's eyes threatened to overflow with tears.

He pulled Mimi to him. "Why, that's just what I was going to ask you."

The freshly handcuffed Charlotte Albemarle was quaking with rage. "I want these intruders arrested! What are you doing to my son? Arrest *her*, officer, not him! This Mimi Smith person broke into my home and tried to blackmail me with filthy letters, spreading lies, disgusting lies."

Baker took off his battered straw fedora and smoothed back his hair. "I don't think so, ma'am. Miss Mimi Smith here is working with us. We've been listening and taking notes."

"I will have your job," Charlotte thundered.

"You wouldn't want my job, lady."

Officer Warwick picked up the torn letters. He handed them to Lt. Baker.

"Those are private! You can't have those."

"Those are what we call evidence, ma'am. So yes, I can," he replied politely.

"You took your sweet time," Mimi complained to Baker.

"I wanted to dot every 'i' and cross every 't.' Like a *stenographer*." He winked at her and grinned. "But we got what we needed. Full confession and more. Holy cow, I didn't figure the mother was in on it. What a catch. And I'm guessing this bloated killer will sing like a fat canary on the rest of his bootlegging gang."

At that moment, attorney Derry Richardson strolled casually through the front door, rolling his hat in his hands.

He stared at the handcuffs on the formidable grande dame, now flanked by Officers Gregson and Warwick.

"Afternoon, Charlotte."

"Derry Richardson, where did you come from?" Her curls had come loose from the intricate hairdo.

"Why, I drove Lt. Baker and Josiah Jordan over here. We thought a police car would attract unwanted attention."

Derry had parked his 1941 Buick several houses down, after their little investigative group decided Joe's pickup would also be out of place on Mansion Drive. The Buick fit right in.

"You're part of this, this *conspiracy* against us?"

"Wouldn't call it that, Charlotte. Just keeping an eye on Mimi. She boards with us, part of the family. And I'd say the criminal conspiracy was entirely on your part."

Even handcuffed, Charlotte Albemarle tried to lunge for Mimi. "You would destroy me? My family? Why?"

Mimi's fingers were itching to slap her, but she refrained. Mimi backed away from the large angry woman and Joe stepped in between them.

"You destroyed yourself, Charlotte," she said. "You destroyed your own family. One thing you didn't know. You killed your only grandchild, the only one you would ever have."

"How dare you be familiar with me. I am Mrs. Albemarle to you." She turned toward Baker. "She's lying, make her stop."

"Kitty was pregnant," Mimi said.

The room went silent. Baker cocked an eyebrow at her. "How did you know that, Smith? We didn't release that information." She threw him a meaningful look. "I know, I know. You know things."

"That trollop could not have been carrying Nathan's child," Charlotte groaned.

"Autopsy showed she was pregnant," Baker said. "No one else knew."

"Kitty told me," Mimi said. "She knew it was Nathan's baby. She always used protection with her—her customers. But not with her fiancé. He was happy about the baby. It's all in the letters."

"Lies. More lies. I don't believe that. Kitty Hawkins was a whore. It wasn't his baby."

"You'll never know, will you?" Mimi said. "Just think, your only chance at a grandchild. Gone. It's a terrible thing to lose the mother, the father, and the baby all at once. And your family name as well."

Baker turned to his cops and the handcuffed Jubal Albemarle. "Call for a paddy wagon, boys. I'm taking no chances when we haul him in."

"What about her, Lieutenant?" Officer Warwick nodded at Charlotte Albemarle.

"Her too."

"How dare you! My husband was an important banker. My son was a war hero. Do you know who I am?"

"I know you're a killer," Baker said. "Conspiracy to commit murder, accessory to murder, attempted murder. Theft. Assault. Running a black-market operation and bootlegging. Course that's Miss Smith's territory. Oh, and assaulting an officer. And there's probably more. The DA and me, we'll tally it all up."

"Better duck, lady," Officer Gregson said. "Lieutenant Baker's throwing the book at you."

"That I am," Baker said. "The whole unabridged dictionary."

Derry patted Mimi's shoulder like a father. "I'm so proud of you, Mimi."

His praise was so unexpected, her eyes filled with tears. Her own parents never offered her any praise. At best they would accuse her of another harebrained scheme. For once, Mary Margaret Smith was unable to speak. She nodded at Derry.

Joe reached for her and wrapped her up in his arms.

FORTY-TWO

*T*HE *ALEXANDRIA GAZETTE* carried a front-page story on the arrest of Jubal Albemarle for the murders of three local women, including Katharine Hawkins. The story ran on Saturday, as there was no Sunday edition of the Gazette, and they included police mugshots of Jubal and his mother.

His mother Charlotte Albemarle was listed as an accomplice in his crimes, shocking the good citizens of Alexandria and Northern Virginia, and supplying scandalous tidbits for weeks to come. The news was rumored to have reached the newswire as far away as Richmond. And word had it that Forgotten Creek, West Virginia, was all abuzz with the tale as well.

Local attorney Derry Richardson, OPA "operative" Mimi Smith, and soon-to-be Naval officer Joe Jordan were mentioned prominently as having "assisted the police" in the investigation and the arrest of the suspects. Addie bought multiple copies of the paper.

Although the *Gazette* article made it clear the three dead women had worked in the "unfortunate profession," they clearly condemned the Albemarles for their deaths, not the victims. Other articles explored recent thefts of tires and sugar and other supplies and their possible links to the black market. They reported that OPA and the Alexandria police had obtained a search warrant for the Albemarle property and discovered an extensive cache of illegal alcohol and other black-market goods. A sidebar noted that Nathan Albemarle had been a war hero who was shot down in his plane and that he had been engaged to Katharine Hawkins. It included their smiling engagement photo.

Mimi was sorry this paper wasn't more like the ones she knew out West. *The Denver Post* would have splashed the story across the front page for days, with screaming three-inch headlines printed in red ink.

Jubal Albemarle would be branded a madman and a monster, as well as a murderer, and his mother as his unholy accomplice, a wicked betrayer of motherhood, womanhood, and human decency.

Aside from their mugshots, Charlotte was photographed covering her face. Jubal, who everyone agreed was headed for the electric chair, glared at the photographer, shaking his handcuffed fists. The judge denied bail for both mother and son.

Mimi had dodged most of the reporters' questions. Lt. Baker, on the other hand, enjoyed his moment in the sun, answering one and all. Mimi was quoted as saying that these women were fellow human beings and "deserved to live, like the rest of us."

Her mother would be shocked. Her grandmother would be proud. Mimi would soon have to write some very interesting letters home. But that would have to wait.

She stayed home on Sunday and wept. "I'm sorry about the tears, Joe."

"That's all right, Mimi, I've got a big shoulder to cry on."

ଓଷ

Monday morning had more surprises in store for Mimi. She didn't know whether she still had a job, or if she would be hitting the pavement looking for one. She wore her most meticulous war paint and she dressed carefully in her black-and-white windowpane print dress with the stiffly starched black ruffled neckline. Perched on the side of her head was a smart black straw hat, which showed off her face to advantage.

She decided she appeared more confident than she felt. It would have to do.

In her largest purse she carried the jug of moonshine Joe had bought for her from Fat Frenchie. She knocked on George Prescott's office door.

"Come in."

She straightened her shoulders and turned the knob. She strutted in and set the jug on his desk. She was sorry now she hadn't even taken a sip. Why was she such a goody-goody?

George waved his pipe. "That's the hot hootch? Good. I'll need your expense report too."

He had all the local newspapers spread out on his desk, including *The Washington Star* and *The Washington Post*. He waved her toward them with a flourish.

OPA AND LOCAL COPS BRING DOWN KILLER, BREAK INTERSTATE BLACK MARKET CONNECTION

Mimi was surprised to see she was mentioned in the story. *The Star* reported that the Albemarles were apprehended by the Alexandria Police Department's Lt. Samson Baker with the help of Mary Margaret "Mimi" Smith, an investigator for the Office of Price Administration.

"Investigator? I don't know where they got that information, George. I never told them anything like that. I never even spoke to the *Star* reporter." The paper shook in her hands.

"I know where they got that, Mary Margaret." George Prescott looked smug. "Me. I told them you're an OPA investigator. I couldn't very well have them saying the capture of these criminals was aided by an OPA *stenographer*, could I?"

She just stared at him. "I guess that would look silly."

"You got your big promotion, Mimi. Don't let it go to your head. I know I said everything OPA investigates could be murder. But gosh darn it, Mary Margaret, I never intended for you to put yourself in danger."

"You never wanted me to leave the stenographer's pool either. And George, I wasn't doing it for OPA."

"Understood. But you were dogged, you were determined, and you didn't let anyone stop you. Not even me, and you better not ever do that again. I guess we can chalk that up to your being from out West."

"I'm really an OPA investigator? I'm not fired?"

"Yes, you're an investigator. A full investigator. At twenty-one and a half, I think you might be our very youngest. Hey, I couldn't very well fire you after all this great publicity. And I didn't want to lie to *The Washington Star*. The newspaper of record for the Nation's Capital? Now they want me to write an op-ed for the paper. As if I have the time. It's a big deal, but it's also a big pain in the neck."

She realized she was still gripping the newspaper in both hands. George was complaining, as usual, but he looked pleased.

"And what's it about? Your op-ed?"

"About the black market. How it's not harmless or a cute game, it isn't just putting one over on the system, and sometimes it leads to murder." He pointed to an open notebook where he had roughed out some lines. "I expect you to help me with this thing. After all, you're the one who got yourself tangled up with a killer and his bloodthirsty mother."

"Do I get a raise?"

He groaned. "It's not untold riches, but yes, you get a raise. A small one." He picked up his pipe and jammed tobacco in it, then spent a few moments looking for his matches, which were on his desk. He finally got it lit. "You understand, most of what you'll do as an investigator will be drudgery."

Mimi suddenly felt lighthearted. "I'll have to get out of the office to do my new job, right?"

"Right," he grumbled. "Asking questions, following leads, interviewing witnesses and suspects, writing reports. But mark my words, Mary Margaret, it will never be this exciting or dangerous again."

"Understood, Mr. Prescott."

"Now get out of here. I'll have your first assignment for you in a day or two. Your first *official* assignment."

She danced out of his office and ran into Sally, who was holding up a copy of *The Washington Star* with its story on the arrests, the murders, and the black-market connection. She had circled Mimi's name.

"You've done it now, Mimi. I knew what you were up to all along. Investigator Mary Margaret Smith!"

"That's impressive, Sally, because I didn't have a clue. Well, maybe one or two."

β

"Investigator Mary Margaret Smith?" Joe teased. "You told me you were a stenographer."

He treated her to an ice cream sundae at the five-and-dime after work.

"My boss wanted OPA to take credit for our investigation, but he was too embarrassed to tell people my real job. So he promoted me in print. And then he promoted me for real this morning."

"If that don't beat all." Joe burst out laughing. "Had to save face, I suppose."

"I had to give up the moonshine, too. Never even got a taste."

"We all have to make sacrifices."

Mimi gazed at Josiah Jordan. He was handsome, stalwart, and he'd been by her side through the aftermath of Kitty's death, their investigation, and the arrest of Jubal Albemarle and his mother. She felt a sudden painful crush against her heart. This wasn't supposed to happen. She had promised herself this wouldn't happen.

"I'm going to miss you so much, Joe." She could hardly get the words out without tears.

"Same here, Mimi. I never expected to find someone like you. You don't lie, you keep your promises, you don't give up.

You're marvelous. I want— Well, I can't express it now. But maybe someday—"

"Someday." She was close enough to breathe in his clean spicy scent. She was close enough to kiss him. Mimi was never fond of the excessive description in romance novels, but the thought struck her that Joe Jordan was one toe-curling kisser.

ɷ

Katharine Hawkins' body was released for burial late the following week. The final preparations could go forward.

As it turned out, there were more people at the Rosary that Friday than Mimi expected. Many of the parishioners came to pray for the magdalen they had not known but had seen at services. Richie insisted on coming with Mimi and playing hymns on his violin, all pre-approved by Father Forsythe. Addie and Derry escorted their son.

The casket, covered with pink and white flowers, was open for the visitation before the Rosary. People who never knew her filed through to marvel at how such a beautiful young woman came to such a sad end. Despite her tragic end, Kitty's earthly remains were the picture of angelic repose. Billows of blond curls flowed to her shoulders. The violet gown Mimi had labored over made Kitty look like a princess, as Richie had predicted. A silver and white rosary was clasped in her hands. Mimi thought she detected the slightest hint of a mysterious smile on Kitty's face.

The funeral Mass for Katharine Hawkins was held Saturday, the next day, at St. Mary's Church. After the attention in the newspapers, the church was almost full of well-wishers, reporters, and curiosity seekers. George Prescott and his wife Blanche sat in the back. Lt. Baker and a few other officers were spotted in the pews. Even the mayor was there.

Joe came with his sister and brother-in-law and the sad news that his time stateside was at an end. The Navy was calling. He'd be shipping out in a day or two. Madam Cherry herself sat in the back of the front transom and wiped away an occasional tear. Seraphina and Gretel were by her side to say goodbye to Kitty.

Mimi's friend Franny Long arrived with Tilly and Dennis, the brother of Tilly's late fiancé who was killed in the war. When Mimi protested that there was no need for them to show up, Franny just wrapped her up in a hug. "That's what friends do, Mimi," Tilly said. There was no sign of their friend Roz, who must have decided a funeral for a magdalen was beneath her. That suited Mimi just fine.

Richie's violin soared through the "Ave Maria." Father Forsythe's homily was full of hope, not despair. He said Kitty's life, as short and tragic as it was, had brought a multitude together to contemplate her struggle and celebrate her next life. Judging her, which was so easy, should be left to God and not to idle gossip over the dinner table.

Following the church service, Lt. Baker appeared at Mimi's side and slipped her an envelope. She opened it: Kitty's last letter, the one she'd written to Mimi. Her breath caught.

"Don't you need this for evidence, Lieutenant?"

He shook his head. "I got all the evidence I need, Smith. You keep it."

I'll keep it in my trunk, she thought, with Kitty's ring.

ೞ

Joe caught up with Mimi and they stepped away from the small crowd that gathered at St. Mary's Lyceum for the reception with real coffee and cake, courtesy of Addie—and the parishioners, who had pooled their ration tickets, with a little encouragement from Father Forsythe.

Joe kept her company as they trekked the half mile to the cemetery for the final step in Kitty's journey, her burial. This time, few people were present. Again, prayers were said for the dead and Father Forsythe spared a blessing for Joe and for Mimi.

"I'll see you in church, Mary Margaret."

"Yes, Father."

"And at confession. You might want to make a list."

Joe couldn't keep from laughing. Mimi sighed. The priest chuckled and swayed away on his uneven legs. She and Joe stood sentinel at the grave. They stayed all afternoon and into the dusk, sometimes talking, sometimes silent. It was twilight when the gravedigger tossed the last shovelful of dirt over Kitty's earthly remains.

"Goodbye, Kitty," Joe said as Mimi squeezed his hand. "I hope it's a better world for you on the other side."

The first fireflies of the night began to flash, dancing among the white tombstones.

"They're welcoming her. It's like they know she's here," Mimi said.

"Maybe she is," Joe said. He held her a little tighter.

"Maybe they're taking her home."

Mimi imagined Katharine Hawkins and Nathan Albemarle together at last, somewhere up in the clouds. Or maybe they were right there with her and Joe, lighting up the night, just a couple of fireflies.

ACKNOWLEDGMENTS

EACH BOOK IS a journey that opens a door to ideas and subjects and personalities I never knew before. This book was both a delight and a challenge. Questions about life during WWII kept coming up and had to be researched. For instance, I had no idea that coffee was rationed and in very short supply during the early part of the war (until July 28, 1943), and like my characters in this book, I find it hard to imagine life without a daily cup of java. Many goods were hard to get during the war, reminding me of how difficult it was to find basic necessities during the early part of the COVID-19 pandemic.

As usual, I have people and places to thank for helping to enlighten me.

I appreciate the hours I spent at the Alexandria Library Barrett Branch in the Local History and Special Collections department, poring over war-era documents and photos. I am also grateful to the National Archives at Denver in Broomfield, Colorado, where I spent some delightful hours reading investigation files and letters of inadvertently humorous complaints to the Office of Price Administration. Some things never change.

Special thanks go to Peter B. Welch, CAPT, USNR (ret), who discussed with me issues around servicemen, military considerations, and joining the Navy during the war. Without Peter, I wouldn't know what "Butter Bars" are.

I'm likewise grateful to Jennifer Combs and Diane Morasco, with whom I consulted on issues surrounding the African American community during the 1940s.

To gain some insight into honey making during the war, Joe McGrail kindly showed me around his beehives and answered my many questions. It wasn't his fault I got stung on the nose by an irritated bee. I also attended a beekeeping workshop at Hudson Gardens in Littleton, Colorado, where my nose and I kept our distance from the bees.

The late Marge Muzillo was a U.S. Marine during WWII. She graciously allowed me to interview her for firsthand information about serving in the Marines during the war and why she joined up. Our two-part interview is available on my YouTube channel at https://tinyurl.com/ars6tfvu.

My thanks to Lila Steele, who gifted me with several marvelous 1943 issues of *Esquire* and *Vogue* magazines, which enhanced my stash of vintage *Mademoiselle* and *Glamour* magazines. These issues shed so much light on the World War II period. I also greatly appreciate members of my "street team," who read an early draft of my manuscript and offered their input.

Finally, there are not enough words to express my love and gratitude to Bob Williams, my most talented editor, proofreader, book designer, cover designer, and shoulder to lean on.

And as usual, despite my best efforts, any mistakes in the book are my own. However, some "mistakes" may actually be creative license, and please remember: This is a work of fiction.

AUTHOR'S NOTES

THIS BOOK IS a 1940s-era prequel to my Crime of Fashion Mysteries. I wanted to write about Mimi Smith, Lacey Smithsonian's famous great-aunt, as a vibrant and inquisitive young woman, at a time when she was alive and not merely a memory of times past.

In some of my books, particularly *Designer Knockoff*, I wrote enough about Mimi to provide some clues to her personality and life in Washington, D.C. I also gave myself unexpected problems, because Mimi worked for the long-defunct wartime government agency, the Office of Price Administration (OPA), which set prices, oversaw the ration programs, and investigated the black market. Who would do that? When the obvious agency to highlight in fiction about the 1940s would be the Office of Strategic Services, the glamorous precursor agency of the CIA? Apparently, I would. Although I admire the many people who have written about the spy side of things, there were many other jobs stateside that required investigation and detective work.

I was stuck with OPA, and I had to seek out records and archives to get a better picture of the agency. Some things that seemed obvious weren't. It took me a long time to find out where OPA was even headquartered. Mimi and I both hoped it would be in a fabulous building like so many others in our Nation's Capital. But no, it was located in what is now called the Ford Office Building, big, blocky, boring, and bland. I have also incorporated many Alexandria landmarks into the book, ones that were there during the 1940s.

And because so many people have loved Aunt Mimi's seemingly bottomless trunk of mysteries, clues, fabrics, and dreams, it also deserved its own origin story: where it came from and how it evolved. This book gave me an opportunity to explore certain traits that Mimi Smith and her niece Lacey Smithsonian share, including their love of fashion and how what we wear (and sew) tells a story, their willingness to plunge headlong into a mystery, and their insatiable curiosity to know how the story ends. I hope you enjoy it.

If you know Alexandria, Virginia, you may know that certain places named in this book have moved from their 1943 locations. For instance, the Demaine Mortuary, now on Washington Street, was then located on King Street. The Majestic Café, though still on King Street, was several blocks east, closer to the Potomac River. According to several essays by old timers, the term "Old Town Alexandria" is a fairly new appellation. During WWII the area we now think of as Old Town was simply "downtown" Alexandria. This is by no means an inclusive list of all the changes in the setting of this book.

There are also places in this book that do not exist anymore, including Chinquapin Village, which was built in haste to house families of workers at the U.S. Naval Torpedo Station (now the Torpedo Factory Art Center) and reportedly had 300 units. The village was situated near today's Chinquapin Recreation Center on upper King Street in Alexandria. All that remains on the site now are a few foundations, a doorstep or two, and an informational sign. The Chinquapin Village of the WWII era should not be confused with any real estate designations of present-day neighborhoods.

There was no St. Mary's School yet, so students attended classes at St. Mary's Lyceum on Duke Street. The Woodrow Wilson Bridge was years away from being built and St. Mary's Cemetery occupied most of that land, with a clear view to the Potomac River.

The Pentagon was brand-new in 1943 and originally called Federal Office Building No. 1, but it soon took on the name by which everyone now knows it, in celebration of its five sides.

The office building in the District where Mimi Smith works was the first General Federal Office Building, which was erected quickly in 1939. This huge bland building housed the

Office of Price Administration, the Census, and other agencies. It was later renamed the Ford House Office Building (for former president Gerald Ford) and still stands southwest of the Capitol, at 2nd and D Streets SW, Washington, D.C.

—*Ellen Byerrum*

ABOUT THE AUTHOR

MYSTERY AND THRILLER writer Ellen Byerrum is a former journalist in Washington, D.C., as well as a produced and published playwright. She tries not to repeat herself in her writing and in pursuit of research. She received her private investigator's registration in the Commonwealth of Virginia.

Her latest book, *The Brief Luminous Flight of the Firefly*, is the 1940s prequel to her Crime of Fashion Mysteries, and features a very young Mimi Smith, the "great-aunt Mimi" mentioned throughout the series. *Firefly* takes place during WWII in Washington, D.C.

Byerrum's screwball noir Crime of Fashion Mysteries feature D.C. fashion reporter Lacey Smithsonian, whose talent for solving crimes with fashion clues leads her to bodies dyed blue, haunted shawls, and the lost jewel-filled corset of a Romanov princess. Two of her books, *Killer Hair* and *Hostile Makeover*, were filmed for Lifetime television.

Stretching beyond the mystery form, Byerrum has written a stand-alone psychological thriller, *The Woman in the Dollhouse*, which *Best Thrillers* says, "bewitches on page one and continues to mesmerize until its shocking conclusion." She has also penned a middle grade mystery, *The Children Didn't See Anything*. More recently, she published a children's rhyming picture book, *Sherlocktopus Holmes: Eight Arms of the Law*.

In addition to her novels and stories, two of her plays (under the pen name "Eliot Byerrum") have been published by Samuel French, Inc., and are available through Concord Theatricals.

Her website is at www.ellenbyerrum.com. Readers can follow her online at www.facebook.com/EllenByerrum.

KILLER HAIR
The First Crime of Fashion Mystery

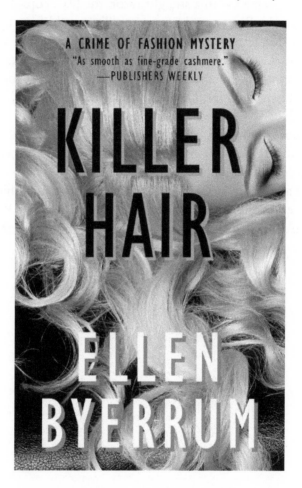

A CRIME OF FASHION MYSTERY
"As smooth as fine-grade cashmere."
—PUBLISHERS WEEKLY

KILLER
HAIR

ELLEN
BYERRUM

"And they say a bad haircut can't kill you."
Decades after THE BRIEF LUMINOUS FLIGHT OF THE FIREFLY, OPA investigator Mimi Smith's great-niece Lacey Smithsonian arrives in Washington, D.C., as a young reporter.

Lacey was a hard news journalist out West, but in Our Nation's Capital, "the City Fashion Forgot," she finds herself saddled with the fashion beat. She grumbles, but it's not a bad fit: She's the only one in the newsroom who knows how to dress with style—and what her clothes are really saying.

When a young hairstylist is found slashed to death and nearly scalped with a straight razor, the D.C. cops shrug it off as suicide. But Lacey knows no stylist would be caught dead with that terrible haircut! Plunging headlong into a (nearly) one-woman murder investigation, Lacey's only weapons are her nose for nuance, her sense of style, her talent for trouble, and her passion for pursuing a news story to the very end. And her friends. (And her fabulous vintage wardrobe.)

But meanwhile, an unknown slasher is looking for another beautiful head of hair. Can Lacey cut this killer's career short—before the killer cuts *her*?

Lacey's adventures in murder, romance, fashion, and comedy begin with KILLER HAIR, the first in Ellen Byerrum's bestselling Crime of Fashion Mysteries. Discover the entire series at your favorite bookseller.